Saint Illuminator's Daughter

A novel by
Michael Ippen

FriesenPress

Suite 300 - 990 Fort St
Victoria, BC, V8V 3K2
Canada

www.friesenpress.com

First Edition — 2019

This book is a work of fiction. Names, characters, places, and events either are the product of the author's imagination or are used fictitiously, and any resemblance to actual persons living or dead, events or locales is entirely coincidental.

ISBN
978-1-5255-5078-2 (Hardcover)
978-1-5255-5079-9(Paperback)
978-1-5255-5080-5 (eBook)

1. *FICTION, HISTORICAL*

Distributed to the trade by The Ingram Book Company

Acknowledgements

I would like to thank those whose advice, support and encouragement are the reason there is a finished manuscript. Beth Haysom, for her edits, suggestions, and thoughtful examination of character, plot, and story. Mike Frost for his thoroughness and encouragement. Herb Girard for his feedback, particularly regarding mining and tunneling. John Seeley and Ian Haysom, whose enthusiasm and commitment to the writing life sustained mine. Thomas Ippen, who, for all his tender years, is a better writer than I will ever be; Sarah Ippen, for her artistic inspiration; Daniel Ippen, you are my hero. And Stephanie, who has given so much to this book and to everything else for so many years.

Table of Contents

Chapter 1

The March sun was warm on everyone's face but hers. She watched the skinny kids playing stickball on the street between the puddles from yesterday's rain. Their shouts, so earnest, drifted above the honks of passing cars. She wondered how they had begged off church, or if their parents didn't care that they were missing the priest's carefully scripted wisdom. The dull, Sunday morning growls of the city reminded her that for most people, today was another day. Better than Monday, certainly, but otherwise indistinguishable from the previous Sunday or the one before that. As Spring approached, the street was filled with people who lingered on the sidewalk or, like her, sat on the dry islands of brick and stone in front of their apartment building, observing the comings and goings of others. Ernie Linklater, her downstairs neighbour, resplendent in his ratty bathrobe, black socks, and brown leather shoes, read the newspaper as smoke from his cigar circled a limp tangle of white hair. She scanned the article on Hawaii's successful bid for statehood. It did nothing to shake her resolve that life was merely a winding parade of unremarkable days that must be endured, until at last a notice appeared in the Obituary Section, to be read by one's friends, or, in her case, a few disinterested colleagues who wouldn't bother to attend the service.

Safir glanced at the telegram she'd received earlier this morning. She reread her sister's words: *The doctor says it was Father's heart. Stop.* She took a grateful pull on one of the last Turkish cigarettes Bey had sent at Christmas. It was dry, but still potent. The harsh smoke calmed her nerves as it chased away the competing stink from Ernie's cigar. She did the math in her head. Celik died six months to the day after their mother's sudden death. As she looked across Montague Street, tears welled, clouding her vision of the playing children and passing cars. She drew hard on the cigarette, felt the clench of her jaw spreading down her throat, into her chest.

"See you later, Mr. Linklater," she said to the back of her neighbour's head. He grunted, kept his face in the newspaper. Safir crushed the remains of the unfiltered cigarette beneath her shoe, brushed the dust off her cotton skirt and hurried indoors, out of the weak, Brooklyn sunshine.

Safir locked her desk at 6:30 PM precisely. The museum closed at six, but down in the basement the archivists' work went on, independent of visitor's hours. For the past two weeks she had been cataloguing a shipment of seventh century coins from Asia Minor, preparing identification cards and cross referencing them against coins in other collections. The Brooklyn Museum archives consisted of a maze of narrow corridors, rooms of floor-to-ceiling shelves overflowing with boxes, books, and filing folders awaiting permanent storage. The lighting on the lowest, windowless floor was poor, the ventilation worse. Half the staff were plagued with nagging coughs and red, scratchy eyes. Three and a half months and it felt like her first week. The habits and hobbies of her colleagues were un-visited countries, if only all of them could feel the same way.

She worked with Turkish antiquities, but in fact she merely did what she was told; there was little need for expertise of any kind. Except, perhaps, for patience and complete lack of ambition. She had abandoned her true calling, or, in truth, it had abandoned her. After her mother's death she found it impossible to sit at her piano—at any piano—so, like the last mourner at a funeral, she'd turned her back on what she loved most, unable to bear the music she created.

As she switched off her desk lamp and moved to the cloak room to retrieve her scarf and coat, her boss appeared, blocking her path.

"You're behind schedule. Again." Vincenzo D'Angelo leaned heavily against the door frame.

"It's detailed," Safir said, avoiding his glance.

"I asked for the catalogue last Friday." D'Angelo stuck a toothpick between his teeth and folded his long arms across his narrow chest. The Assistant Archives Director was all elbows and knees and reminded Safir of a poorly built hat rack. A hat rack that had grown up resenting better made hat racks. D'Angelo had the habit of squashing his glasses against a single black eyebrow that looked like an unkempt caterpillar had made a home on his forehead.

"It will be ready tomorrow," Safir said, slipping into her coat.

D'Angelo plucked the toothpick from his mouth and waved it in the air. "Not good enough, Miss Turan," he said. His tongue tripped hard over her name, as if it were a contemptible thing. "I will be reporting you to the Director."

Her chin dropped. "My father died two weeks ago," she said, immediately regretting her admission.

"Not my problem," D'Angelo said. "You'd think someone as desperate for a job as you wouldn't be making up excuses." His large, equine teeth unabashedly displayed when he smiled.

She summoned what it took to meet D'Angelo's eyes and caught the flicker of delight in them. She wanted to tell him off; to threaten him in return, but what would that do? The Director would never believe that D'Angelo had touched her, repeatedly, and that she had rebuffed him, first sliding beyond his reach, then, finally, pushing his groping hands away. Now he was making her pay. D'Angelo had said it to her face: *who would believe a crazy hermit spinster like you?*

"I'll work harder," she said, buttoning her coat. She shivered at the weight of his hand on her back as she fled through the door onto Washington Street, her hands fumbling to tie her scarf beneath her chin.

She walked quickly toward home, needing three matches to light a cigarette. On most days she rode the subway, wanting only to retreat to her apartment, but today the walk, though long and unseasonably cold, was vital. She pulled up her collar. The concrete sidewalk became a psychoanalyst's pillow: her rage diminished with every forceful step of her sensible shoes.

As she walked the street lamps washed the evening air with a clean, silvery glow, banishing the garbage and grime to shadow. The first pull on her cigarette settled her some, and when she exhaled the smoke carried a little more of her anger into the cool air. The weather had taken a half turn back toward winter, as if Spring was shirking her responsibilities. As Safir walked her thoughts found space for things and people not named D'Angelo. Memories of her father's hands filled her head: strong fingers stained nearly black from decades making the dyes used in carpets and prayer rugs. Celik was a master dyer and expert loom builder, and the colors he had created from the flowers and barks near Hereke lived in carpets hanging in palaces from Istanbul to Los Angeles. Those workman's fingers could also play piano. It was Celik who snuck her into the factory manager's office to play for the first time. She'd been seven, on her way home from school in Kemal Atatürk's new Turkish Republic, and after listening to Celik knock out a hasty *Für Elise* she'd squealed with delight when he lifted her onto the piano bench beside him and cupped her fingers in his own to make the keys sing. When the factory manager's wife interrupted them Celik had been embarrassed, bowing and apologizing, worrying his fez between those long fingers of his, but the woman gushed at Safir, and insisted that she come three times a week after school to learn how to play.

Safir wiped the dampness beneath her eyes onto her sleeve and lit another cigarette, her fourth since leaving the museum. If Celik had told her when and how he'd learned to play the piano she could not remember. Celik wasn't the sharing type. Nor affectionate. Familial, yes, but close? Never. Celik was seventy-eight. That fact had startled her. Piruz was only sixty when she died. Eighteen years between her parents and she'd never thought about it before? When she arrived at Montague Street her feet hurt, though her rage had subsided, replaced with all too familiar grief. She flicked her cigarette into the gutter and climbed the steps to the front door. She retrieved the mail from her letter box and hiked three floors up a creaky staircase. She would listen to Debussy on her phonograph and everything would be fine.

Safir toggled on the light switch, dropped her keys into a chipped, ceramic dish atop a battered wooden table in the narrow hallway. She set down the mail and untied her scarf, hung her coat on a hook behind the door and removed her scuffed, brown shoes. She placed them neatly side by each under the table and retrieved her slippers from their spot next to a pair of black patent leather shoes, the only other pair she owned. Mustafa appeared from the living room. She picked up the purring ball of black fur and rubbed her face in its neck, inhaling his smell. Mustafa smelled faintly of cardamom and cinnamon.

"Did you miss me?" She grabbed the mail from the table and walked the length of the hallway, passing the closed door of her bedroom, into the kitchen. Lights from the street below reflected off the peeling, once-white ceiling and reminded her of a Paris winter ten long years ago, when a heavy snow fell and turned Baron Haussmann's buildings to runny, vanilla ice cream. She opened a can of cat food, shook it into a bowl and refilled Mustafa's water dish. The cat watched her in silence, waiting for the bowl of food to be presented at his feet.

"Here you are, you fickle thing," Safir said, setting the bowl onto the floor. "You can't fool me with your cuddles." She scratched his neck as Mustafa settled into his meal.

She retreated to her bedroom, untying the bun that constrained her hair. Every work day she disguised her thick, black, grey-salted plaits. She scratched the itch out of her scalp and ran her fingers through her hair, delighting at the weight of it. She slipped out of her blouse and skirt and hose, washed her face and slipped into a flannel nightie and housecoat. She washed her underthings in the sink and hung them to dry. Years ago, she stopped feeling embarrassed for her hermetic ways. Mustafa, only four months into his residency, certainly did not give a fig how she looked, so long as he was fed on time.

With Debussy rising from her phonograph she reheated leftovers from her small fridge and the kitchen was filled with the aroma of places far removed. She sat at a small table opposite the stove and ate her rice with raisins and a bony chicken leg. She ate quickly, washed her plate and cutlery, then prepared coffee on the stove. She filled her copper *cezve* with two spoons of ground coffee beans from Bey and heated the long-handled pot, stirring as the mixture began to froth. She set her favorite cup and saucer—one of the few possessions that had been with her since leaving Istanbul—onto the counter and filled the cup half full. She returned the *cezve* to the burner and waited for the remaining mixture to boil, added a pinch of cardamom, then quickly filled her *kahve finjani* to the top. She stirred in a heaping spoonful of sugar, inhaling the aroma as she carried the delicately painted porcelain cup and saucer to the living room.

She sat on a threadbare sofa with her feet tucked beneath her, sipping the bitter-sweet drink, feeling the tension in her body release its grip. Then she indulged herself with another of Bey's cigarettes. As much as she needed to ration them, they were so much better than American-made. She exhaled deeply, staring at her favorite—and only—piece of art: a poster of Marcelle Meyer's 1938 concert in Paris. It was Meyer's last public performance of Ravel. She had been so excited when one of her fellow students had offered her a ticket, but Theo had refused to let her go without him. They'd had an enormous argument, their first as a couple and she had bowed to his judgement, after all, what did she, at twenty-one, know of the world compared to Theo Sauvé, concert pianist and professor? She rued that decision. Not the worst she'd made, but it still caused twinges of regret. Even Theo must have sensed his transgression, for he'd bought the poster from the concert hall and somehow got Meyer to autograph it. He'd presented it to her after supper: a scroll tied in a red ribbon with two carnations slipped inside. The love they'd made that night! How many miles she'd travelled—and what little distance she had come—since that night. Still, her years in Paris were the finest of her life.

She stubbed out her cigarette in the little ashtray at her elbow. She wanted to ask Beyham for another care package, but it was expensive and she was sure Bey's husband disapproved. Money better spent on their children, not on cigarettes for a crazy, unmarried sister half the world away. Her thoughts drifted back to home, memories tinged with sadness, always the sense of being out of place. The bleached, stuccoed walls and the green-painted front door were clear, but the interior, the places where the four inhabitants that were her family interacted; that had gone soft, made hazy by the intervening years. She saw her mother's silhouette at the small loom where she wove beautiful prayer rugs with wool dyed by Celik. Or at the oven, sifting, stirring, always over an iron pot or hand painted ceramic bowl. But her face, Piruz's face, was always in shadow.

In 1936 Safir left Hereke, a town on the fringes of Istanbul, for Paris. The family had ridden the bus with her to the station to put her on a train to Belgrade, Vienna and Paris. They'd said their goodbyes, dry-eyed and in a hurry to be off. As if her parents couldn't wait to be rid of her. It was a sense she'd had all her childhood, not in words, but in the silence that fell between Mother and Father when she entered the room. As if she were an interloper, an uninvited guest. Now, in the space of six months, they were dead. She was an orphan. Though in truth, she had felt like one for decades.

She uncurled her feet and stood by the piano. She brushed her hand across the tablecloth that covered the instrument. The desire to play as dead as her mother and father. She'd bought the Knabe upright as soon as she'd arrived in New York, still vaguely seasick from the crossing and stunned that she'd. It was a fine piano and a beautiful piece of furniture, built by the American Piano Corporation before the United States entered the war and the factory was converted to manufacturing aircraft parts. Despite its compact size it produced concert hall quality results. She had polished it religiously and dusted the keys and to this day still shooed Mustafa off with a firm clap of her hands. It was her prize possession, even if she never played it again. She'd spent all of the money Theo had pressed into her hands at their hasty farewell on a platform at the Gare Du Nord. He stammered trying to explain why he couldn't travel—yet—but that he'd follow her soon, within the month, he promised. The German invasion saw the end to that. She was glad that Theo had not told her of his true intention—to remain in Paris with his wife—else she would never have bought the piano. Over the years she had grown comfortable without Theo, and the Knabe and the music they made was the main reason.

She remembered how her Brooklyn neighbours used to complain to the Super. How he would knock, tentatively, at her door, scuffing his shoe tip and wringing his cap between his hammy fists. He liked her music, but the O'Reilly family across the hall didn't, and could she please keep the noise down? She was crushed. She'd stuffed a towel under the front door, closed her windows and drapes and stripped a blanket off the bed to cover the back of the piano but still the O'Reillys pestered the Super. Two weeks later Mr. O'Reilly died and his widow moved out. The Super knocked shyly on her door and told her that he was now getting complaints from the other tenants because they *wanted* to hear the music again, and they had written requests. He held out a fistful of crumpled slips of paper; *Beethoven's Pastoral Symphony, First Movement, Chopin's Revolutionary Etude, Grieg's Morning Suite from Peer Gynt.* Safir had hugged him, unwrapped the Knabe, thrown open the drapes and windows and unpacked her sheet music. Music filled the apartment.

Safir turned out the lights and carried Mustafa to the bedroom.

It was not until the next evening, as she sat on her sofa with Mustafa on her lap, that she went through the week's mail. Since her sister's package a week ago there was nothing she expected, so when she lifted the square envelope off the coffee table and felt its weight, she knew something was different. It took a moment to realize that she was looking at the franked seal of the Houses of Congress. She turned the envelope around in her hands. There had to be a mistake, yet there it was, her name: *Miss Safir Turan, Apartment 203, 109 Montague Street, Brooklyn.* Fear rippled through her body. She had done nothing wrong. She was an American citizen, paid her taxes on time, paid her rent on the first of every month, was kind to the beggar by the subway station when she had spare change, which was never but that didn't stop her from occasionally depositing a nickel in his palm.

She retreated to the kitchen for a knife, so as not to damage the envelope in case this *was* a mistake, in which case she would return the letter to its sender. A single page of matching square paper slipped from the envelope. Across the top of the page was an inscription: *From the desk of Weldon T. Henry Scott.*

Dear Miss Turan, the letter began, *I have been looking for you for a very long while. I apologize for the length of time it has taken. It is very important—for us both—that we meet. I am in New York the week of April 22nd. If you are available, and agreeable to meet, (which I desperately hope you are), please call my secretary at the number below. She will arrange for a car to collect you.*

Warmest Regards,

Weldon T. Scott.

That was it. Nothing more. Who was this Weldon T. Henry Scott—aside from being a senator from Pennsylvania—and why did he need to meet her? She reread the letter several times. *"It is very important—for us both..."* She smoked three more cigarettes, staring at the expensive stationery in her trembling fingers before switching off the light in the living room and retreating to her bedroom for a night of restless, interrupted sleep.

At work the next day—Saturdays until two o'clock—her mind kept reaching for the senator's letter. She vacillated between calling the number and throwing the letter in the trash. But neither satisfied. For a fleeting second Safir thought about asking D'Angelo if he knew of this Weldon Scott, but she quickly put that idea out of her head. D'Angelo would only twist things and make her the problem, increasing the doubt and fear already rooted in her mind.

She said nothing to anyone at the museum, which was easy as nobody had approached her and she'd liked it that way. On her lunch break she managed to check the phone directory. There was no listing for any Weldon T.H. Scott to be found. At two o'clock on the dot she put on her coat and tied her scarf tight against a slashing rain. She strode the block to the Central Branch of the New York Library and timidly approached a librarian on duty for information on the Senate.

The librarian smiled, seemingly impressed by her curiosity in the levers of American governance, and showed her to the records for both Houses of Congress. It did not take Safir long to find what she was looking for. Weldon Theodore Henry Scott. United States senator for the State of Pennsylvania. A Democrat. First elected in

1944. Born January 9th, 1894 in Bethlehem, Pennsylvania. Son of Ambrose Henry Scott, engineer and executive of Carnegie Steel, deceased 1940. The same year as her arrival in New York.

There was little more, other than a bill in 1948 that Scott sponsored, advocating more resources for the State Department's offices overseas. Safir pecked around in the journals a little, then left, avoiding the bigger rain puddles on her way to the subway. She passed St. Ann's Holy Trinity Church. Its red brick walls were slowly disappearing behind streaks of black mould and misshapen lumps of moss that grew in the crumbling mortar. The rain made the place more forlorn than usual. Even the stray cats that sat on the stoop had abandoned their posts. She shivered and hurried on. By the time she reached her apartment, her mind was made up: she would meet this Weldon Theodore Henry Scott and find out what he wanted. She shook the rain off her coat and scarf in the vestibule of her apartment building. There was a phone on the wall near the stairs and, to her amazement, no-one was using it. She wondered where the Primus daughter was; she virtually lived on the phone. She got the operator and asked her to call the number written at the bottom of the letter. A woman answered after the first ring.

"This is Safir Turan." A pause, which she rushed to fill. "I received a letter from Mr. Scott yesterday."

"Oh yes, Miss Turan," the woman said in a flat, formal voice, "I have been expecting your call."

"I would like to accept the senator's invitation," Safir said.

"Thank you. The senator will send a car for you."

Safir's heart skipped. "A car? No, I can take the subway."

"No trouble. The senator will see you Thursday next week."

Safir frowned. "I'm sorry, I work until 6:30 in the evening."

There was a faint rustling of papers in her ear. "The senator has kept next Saturday clear, does that work?"

"After two o'clock," Safir said, her voice getting smaller. "I don't want to be a bother."

"No trouble at all, Miss Turan. The senator's car will pick you up at two in the afternoon, next Saturday. What is your address?"

She told the woman, then asked, "Where will I be taken?"

"The senator now keeps a residence in Manhattan. He will be waiting for you. Good afternoon, Miss Turan."

"Thank you," Safir said to the sound of the line disconnecting. She set the receiver back in its cradle, her fingers shaking slightly as she reached for a cigarette.

It was the longest week of her life, waiting for Saturday to arrive. When the day came, she dressed in her nicest clothes—a navy blue wool skirt, white blouse, her nice black shoes—and took the subway to work. The short spell of good weather had been chased away by a persistent rain, so she took the subway, fighting back yawns thanks to another night of fitful sleep. D'Angelo noticed something was different and spent the morning hovering near her desk, peppering her with questions. When she refused to reply, he fell back to his customary mocking tone and insults. Safir ignored him as best as she could. At lunch she put on her coat and scarf and walked nearly a block to find a sheltered place to smoke. She was too nervous to eat. She stood beneath the awning of a Chinese laundry and watched customers come and go, hurrying with their packages through a curtain of rain drops.

When she returned to her desk D'Angelo was waiting, idly toying with a ninth century ceramic bowl found near Ankara. "You shouldn't be touching that," she summoned the courage to say, and waited until he set the bowl down.

"Who is he?" The Assistant Director leaned across her desk until his face was inches from her own.

"Leave me alone," Safir said.

D'Angelo sneered. "I think you're in love," he said. "That's why you've been acting all weird this week."

Safir took up the Turkish bowl and turned her back on him. He followed her, appearing next to the bank of narrow drawers along the wall. "So, who is he?"

She settled the bowl in its place, shut the drawer and walked back to her desk. D'Angelo was having none of it. Where she went, he followed. When she neared her desk, D'Angelo raced ahead and swung himself into her chair, stretching out his legs and crossing them at the ankles. "Some Kike or Polack from your neighbourhood, I bet."

Safir felt the colour rising in her cheeks. She closed her eyes, breathed deeply and turned to leave.

"Hey! Where you goin'?" D'Angelo jumped up to follow her. "You don't turn your back on me."

She marched to the Ladies Room and closed the door in his face.

"Get back to work! Break's over!" D'Angelo shouted through the door.

Safir waited five minutes, then peeked through a crack in the door. D'Angelo had given up. She hurried back to her desk, ignoring the glances of the other archivists.At two o'clock D'Angelo appeared. She didn't hear him approach. He grabbed her scarf off the coat rack and refused to return it. Instead he ran the scarf through his hands. He flipped the scarf over his head and tied it beneath his chin. He wrinkled his nose. "Smells like a whore's," he said, ripping it off his head and dropping it onto the floor. "Tell me where you're going," he said, his unruly eyebrow furrowed in anger.

Safir buttoned her coat, her voice shaking with rage. "Keep it," she said, kicking the scarf toward him. "I never want it back." She pulled a compact from her purse, powdered her nose with trembling fingers, snapped it shut and hurried for the exit.

A black, four door sedan idled at the curb, its uniformed driver standing patiently next to the car, his gloved hands folded comfortably at his belt buckle. Safir turned to see if D'Angelo could see what she saw. He was there, three paces behind, his long face awash with disbelief.

"If you must know," she said, her voice amplified with the satisfaction of the moment, "he's a senator and he lives in Manhattan!" She hopped over the puddles on the sidewalk toward the car.

The driver opened the rear door and closed it softly after her. She couldn't resist sticking out her tongue as the car pulled away from the curb.

They crossed the Brooklyn Bridge into Manhattan. Safir's excitement rose as the car headed north, toward Central Park. She inhaled the leather of the upholstery and settled into the comfort enveloping her. If nothing else came of this afternoon, it was worth the cost of a new scarf to see the look on D'Angelo's face. Maybe now he would leave her alone.

The car pulled up to a tall apartment building on Central Park West. The park the street was named for beckoned like a green invitation. Even in the rain Manhattan dripped with quiet luxury, a sense of nothing else to prove.

The driver turned off the engine and opened the car door. He held an umbrella over her head as she climbed out of the back seat. "My name is Jefferson, Miss. If you need anything, just ask. The senator's home is apartment eleven zero three. Let the doorman know you're expected. I will be here to take you home when you're finished."

"Thank you so much, Mr. Jefferson," Safir said. "My name is Safir Turan." She was breathless, feeling dizzy.

"I know, Miss," Jefferson said, walking beside her until they reached the awning over the front doors. He lowered the umbrella and tipped his cap. "It's a pleasure to meet you."

The doorman moved gracefully ahead of her and held one of the glass doors, then followed her in to summon the elevator. When the steel door slid open, he deftly reached around Safir to press the button for her floor. He tipped his burgundy cap and smiled, revealing two rows of bright, white teeth. "Good afternoon, Miss," he said, as if they had met many times before. His teeth were the last thing she saw as the door closed with a whisper on unseen gears.

The elevator door opened onto the eleventh floor. The hallway was lit by wall lamps that emitted a warm, gentle glow. Nothing like the bare bulb that hung from the hallway ceiling in her building. She stepped tentatively, her shoes sinking into a plush carpet. It silenced her footsteps and she felt she was walking on a cloud. She stopped at the right door, but before she could knock, it swung open with a vigorous rush of air.

"Good afternoon, Miss Turan." A tall, slender man with a head of glorious, white hair ushered her inside with a diplomatic wave and slight bow. "I am Weldon Scott. Please."

As she stepped across the threshold he added, "Call me Weldon. How do you do?" He extended his hand, which enveloped her small, cold hand completely like a warm, comfortable glove. He wore a crisp, white shirt, navy tie and fine, grey, woolen trousers.

"Fine, thank you," she stammered.

"May I take your coat? Is the rain wanting to let up at all?"

"It's not as bad as it was," Safir said, letting the senator lift her coat from her shoulders. He reminded her of an orchestra conductor, the way his hair swept off his forehead, thick and unruly, but in a cultivated way.

"Good, good," he said. He hung her coat in a closet as large as her kitchen. "Please," he gestured her ahead of him, toward brightness at the end of a short hall. "Let's make ourselves comfortable. I am thrilled that you accepted my invitation. Coffee or tea?" His smile revealed straight, white, teeth, like a movie star's.

"Coffee, please," she said. She stepped from the hall into a large room, bathing in the soft, afternoon light that spilled through windows overlooking Central Park. The room was chock full of furniture, antiques and fine things. Ornate, Middle Eastern lamps squatted on end tables carved from dark, deeply grained wood. There was a hint of furniture polish in the air. The lamps cast a warm, buttery light. Glass-fronted bookcases stood like sentinels against every wall, each filled to overflowing with books that looked like they came from a university library. Schubert was playing on an expensive phonograph. The notes lingered in the air around her head.

As she stepped into the living room she recoiled, her shoe in mid-air. The carpet, spreading before her in bright indigo and crimson, was one of Celik's. Made in the factory he had worked in for more than fifty years.

"Is anything wrong?" The senator stood beside her, following her glance. "Yes, all my carpets are from Hereke. They are some of the best made in Turkey."

"My father," she said.

Weldon Scott smiled. "I thought I might surprise you. I have met Celik Turan. He is one of the reasons I wrote you. I want to order another carpet and I thought you might help me."

"He died," Safir said.

Weldon stopped halfway to the kitchen. "What? When?"

"Three weeks ago. My sister says he had a heart attack."

Weldon hurried beside Safir and rested one hand tentatively on her shoulder. "I'm so sorry. Please, sit. And when you next write your mother, pass on my condolences to her."

Safir began to cry. "She's dead, too."

Weldon exhaled. "Jesus Christ, Scott," he said, staring at the ceiling. "Sit. Here." He guided Safir to a mohair sofa in the middle of the room. He handed her a handkerchief from his pocket. "It's clean," he said. "I'm such an ass, Safir." He backed away and almost sprinted to the kitchen. "I'll make the coffee," he said as he disappeared.

Safir dried her eyes and straightened her spine, taking deep breaths to calm herself. The sofa was so overstuffed she feared she would slide off the cushion onto the floor. Weldon scurried out of sight. She heard him banging cupboard doors and filling a kettle with water.

"I hope you don't mind your coffee on the strong side," he called. "After so many years abroad I'm afraid I can't stand our watered-down version. Not patriotic, I know, but there you are."

"I prefer my coffee strong," Safir said. Her gaze wandered from one piece of art to the next. She particularly liked a small tapestry that hung on the furthest wall. A brass label was attached to the wall beneath the piece. She rose from the sofa and moved closer, treading gingerly on Celik's carpet. The tapestry was Persian. She guessed the artist's origins, and was pleased to read *Ankara, Ottoman Turkey. Seventeenth Century.* The tapestry was rare, in immaculate condition. The weave looked as though it had been done last year. She was tempted to run her fingertips across its surface, but she resisted, with a pang of regret.

"The Ankara Tapestry," Weldon said, clearly relieved with a new subject of discussion. He carried a silver tray from the kitchen. He set the tray onto a low table and stood beside her, his hands clasped behind his back. "She's a thing of beauty, no? Such fine wool, and the colours! I purchased her from an antiques dealer in Istanbul—Constantinople as it was known as back then—and had her shipped home to Pennsylvania. That was in 1917. Bit of a struggle, what with the war on."

"It is beyond beautiful," Safir said.

Weldon raised an eyebrow and turned toward her. "Around the year you were born, I believe, if you'll forgive my forward manner."

Safir nodded.

Weldon averted his gaze. "I must confess, I forgot about her for a long time. When we—the United States—entered the war, I was summoned home, but returned to Europe after the Armistice. I remained overseas for twenty years and when I got back to the States, I was put to work for most of the *next* war, until I went for politics. This tapestry remained in storage for the duration. It was a lucky thing the seller packed her so well, the moths couldn't get in."

"This weaver must have been renowned in his day," Safir said. "The piece is extremely valuable."

"That's right," Weldon said, "you are now employed in this area."

Safir glanced at the senator. "It's only a recent job."

"I understand you are a pianist. And a talented one."

"No longer," Safir said, as she returned to the sofa.

Weldon clapped his hands, breaking the silence that fell between them. "Coffee, perhaps?"

"That would be nice," Safir said.

"How many sugars?"

"Three," Safir said, then blushed, embarrassed that he would think her greedy, but Scott's smile only widened.

"I take three as well," he said, dropping three cubes into her cup, hand-painted porcelain much like her own. Weldon's set boasted a gold leaf pattern that swirled across pale turquoise cups and saucers. "Milk?" When she shook her head, he set a tiny silver spoon onto the saucer and handed her the steaming coffee. "There you are," he said, "I hope you like it."

She stirred the sugar into the swirling coffee and lifted the cup to her lips. The first sip was heavenly.

"It's delicious," she said, setting the cup back on its saucer. "These cups are beautiful."

"Thank you," Weldon said. "I was given them by my staff when I left Geneva. They knew how much Turkey meant to me. Here," he said, "the cookies have pistachio in them."

She took one and balanced it on the saucer. She watched the senator take a bite from a cookie, chewing quickly. He reminded her of a deer she'd once spotted in Central Park: straight, stiff, even regal in posture. She nibbled her cookie, it was dry and stuck to her tongue, forcing her to drink too much of the coffee at once. It burned her mouth, but she inhaled deeply and blinked aside the tears forming in her eyes. If the senator noticed, he said nothing. She stared at the carpet beneath her feet as the heat on her tongue subsided.

"Before I explain why I invited you here," Weldon said, "do you mind if I ask you a question? You don't have to answer."

Safir shook her head quickly. "No, I don't mind."

"Your name. Safir. Do you know its meaning?"

"It means sapphire," she said. "My eyes were very blue, when I was born."

Weldon nodded. "Indeed, I believe you."

"They are not that blue," she said, looking down at the table. "I cannot remember if they ever were."

"Forgive my boldness, and I say this as a man who has traveled much of the world for most of my life, but your eyes are most beautiful. You're married?"

Safir flushed crimson. "I am not."

"I apologize. My age and station get the better of me at times. But honestly, you must have to fend them off with a bat."

She shook her head. "You have me confused with someone else." She kept her eyes locked on the *kahve finjani*. Her heart was beating hard. Fear grew in her chest, a heaviness that weighed on her lungs. Only D'Angelo knew she had climbed into the car that brought her here, but even he had no clue where she was. Would the newspaper care to write the story of her disappearance, when she failed to show at work on Monday?

"You have a beautiful name," Weldon said. "It matches you very well. You know most children in the United States are given dull names like Jane or Helen. Were you teased, when you first came to America?"

She nodded. "Some people are very cruel."

"We can be a very friendly people as a rule, but we're not a sensitive lot."

Safir tried to change the subject. "I read that you represent Pennsylvania. Why are you in New York?"

Weldon smiled, wiggled closer to perch at the edge of his chair. "To meet you," he said.

Her heart felt like it would burst out of her body. She set down her cup and rose, brushing her skirt with her hands. "Thank you, but I should really be going…"

"Your mother is—was—as beautiful as you."

Safir stiffened. "So, you knew *both* my parents?"

Weldon smiled behind his coffee cup. He took a loud sip and set the cup down on the table. He leaned back in his chair and folded his hands. "Please. Sit down. I don't mean to frighten you. Yes, I did know your mother as well as your father. In fact, I knew Piruz very well." He lowered his glance. "It is such a shock to hear she is dead. When?"

"Almost seven months. Last September. She was walking, she fell and was struck by a bus."

"How dreadful," Weldon said.

"Yes," Safir said. She settled back onto the sofa, her hands balled into fists in her lap. She felt the heat rise on her skin. "Tell me how you know them."

"Forgive me, I intended to start at the beginning. It's why I invited you here."

Safir glanced out the windows. A heavy, grey sky pressed against the glass. "I miss them," she said. She dabbed her eyes with Weldon's handkerchief.

"I am so sorry," Weldon said.

She met his gaze. "Why? Neither of them ever mentioned you."

"I'm not surprised." The senator leaned toward her. "They had every reason for doing what they did."

"What did they do?" Now a different fear gripped her.

"This is harder for me to say, now knowing what I know. But I am going to say it, Safir. I hope you understand."

"Understand what?"

"Celik Turan was a good man, Safir. He raised you and he certainly looked after you. But he was not your father."

Safir stared at the white-haired stranger who sat across from her in his sharply-pressed pants and spotless white shirt. "What are you talking about?" The urge to flee wrestled with a desire to choke the truth from the senator's body.

"I am your real father, Safir," Weldon said. "It is time I told you my story. *Our* story."

On Sunday Safir's restlessness got the better of her. Against her nature she took a trip to Coney Island. She'd been only once before, ten years ago, soon after her arrival in New York. Back then she was a performance-level pianist freshly arrived from France, weeks ahead of the German invasion. Back then she was grieving Theo, even as she suspected he would never follow her as he'd promised. And back then she'd known who her father was: a devout Muslim, good husband, a dyer of wool, a some-time piano player, a father to a pair of daughters.

This day the woman riding the bus under cold and threatening skies had no idea who she was. Her mother dead six months, her father gone less than a month. This day a stranger, an American senator no less, with Hereke carpets on his floors, said that while Celik was a good man, he wasn't her father.

She needed to feel the open air on her face; to inhale the salty tang of the ocean and simultaneously be far away from her suddenly cramped apartment oozing with rekindled memories, as thick and choking as wet cinders. Her swaddled piano cursed her. When she arrived, she found a bench and sat, her jacket wrapped tightly around her. She watched people, some tourists, but most fellow New Yorkers, going about their Sunday perambulations. She wondered what it felt like to be truly connected to a place. She imagined these strangers comfortable with each step, every gesture, every inane joke they told each other. Then, when her legs grew numb, she strolled the promenade, stopping at last to buy a hot, salted pretzel slathered with mustard. She ate it as she waited for the ferry as the light began to fade.

She slept through the night for the first time in weeks.

The next Saturday, at two-forty-five, the senator's car arrived in front of her apartment building. It was a cloudy afternoon as she waited on the step. She was nervous, her joints twitched with anticipation. She powdered her nose three times and checked her teeth in her compact's mirror. When the black sedan approached, Ernie Linklater set down his magazine and stared from his spot on the steps.

"That the ride you been waiting on?" he said as Jefferson moved briskly to open the door.

She tossed her neighbour a careless smile, then waved at Weldon's chauffeur like she was meeting an old friend. Did Jefferson know, she wondered, ducking into the car, that she was a senator's daughter?

At the apartment she was escorted to the elevator by the same doorman, who greeted her by name, but if he knew her new identity, he said nothing. Weldon Scott was waiting at the front door. He took her coat and hung it in the closet and led her into the living room. The smell of freshly boiled coffee was strong and pleasing. A piano concerto of Mozart's enlivened the air in the apartment.

"How are you, Safir? I expect Mozart will do?"

"It has been a strange week," she said.

"That I can believe," Weldon said, choosing an upholstered armchair for himself. As he sat, his back straight, his hands on his knees, he said, "This is not the kind of news one expects to hear out of the blue."

"It is almost too much to take in," she said. "Why did you wait so long?"

"I am guilty, Safir," he said, wringing his hands. "I have known you lived in Brooklyn for some time. I let my professional obligations dictate my actions for too many years. I want to make amends for that. Coffee?"

They drank from the same dainty cups, the senator taking sips without speaking. Safir listened to the music. Her doubts vanished, or at the least subsided in the swirling patterns of the carpet. It comforted her, knowing Celik's handmade colours were close.

"Safir," Weldon spoke, at last. "How you came to be is a long story. Will you allow me to tell it?"

She set down her cup and saucer. It took effort to pull her glance from the carpet. "Is Bey my real sister?"

"Yes, of course," Weldon said. "You have different fathers, is all."

"*Is all?*" Safir repeated. "Celik will always be my father." But even as she said it, she knew it was a lie.

"Perfectly understandable," Weldon said. He exhaled and tossed her a crooked smile. "I am relieved," he said, "more than you can imagine. Before I begin, can I get you anything? Are you hungry? Different music? I am sorry, I can't change the weather, it is another unexceptional day in Manhattan."

She shook her head and settled herself in a corner of the sofa. "No. Thank you," she said.

The senator refilled their *kahve finjani*, added sugar and milk to his own and pushed the sugar bowl toward her. He remained at attention in his armchair, one hand gripping the other tightly in his lap. His voice was gentle, just loud enough to be heard over the music, but there was something else: something reflected in his eyes other than his spoken remorse for years of ignorance he had imposed on her. For a moment she saw the two of them, sitting together in an apartment overlooking Central Park, and her heart was full to breaking for the miserable woman on the sofa. She heard the faint sounds of traffic on the street, imagined people hurrying along the sidewalk, Mr. Jefferson chatting with the doorman, their neatly pressed uniforms a stark contrast to the dull, grey, March sky.

Chapter 2

As a child I was a handful. My mother claims I was born stubborn and wilful. Common sense could find no way through my thick skull, she complained to my father on many occasions. I ignored my father's commands to *Use your head!* and *Look before you leap!* Such was the mainstay of my character through boarding school. In the Spring of 1914, it reached its zenith: I abandoned my studies at Yale, just twenty years of age. This was too much for my father to bear. He had put up with my obstinacy because he wanted very much that I should follow in his footsteps, but the steel business to which he had married his life held no appeal. It wasn't the noise or heat or grubbiness of the mill in Bethlehem, Pennsylvania, where I grew up, that repelled me. Nor was it the hard work required to become an engineer as he had done. Truly, his was a life of usefulness; of supplying America's growing cities with mammoth towers of steel. He fed the furnace of the American Dream. But to my inexperienced mind it was the sameness of my father's days that terrified me. He would come home to our comfortable house, halfway between Pittsburgh and Bethlehem, drained of vigour and zest, only to retire to his bedroom with a bottle of whiskey under his arm, to repeat the sequence the next day. Daily he grew older, less vital. Sundays were church services and picnics and family music recitations, but one day's respite could not repair the damage done by the previous six.

This was my father's life, and if this was how success was measured, I wanted no part of it.

Mine was a spoiled existence, I admit. It was thanks to my Swiss mother that I grew up with winter weekends in the Alleghenies where I hiked and learned to ski from an old Norwegian who taught me to distinguish October's early, heavy snow from February's dagger-sharp, crystalline offerings. We toured the Alps in summer and visited my mother's family in Geneva. It should have been no surprise to anyone when university turned out to be a bore for me. I looked for something fun to take its place. Better yet, it needed to be far from my father's crestfallen expression. So, I crossed the Atlantic. I did not return for good for twenty-four years.

My mother, bless her heart, came to my rescue in two ways. In truth, my love of mountains doubtless came from her Swiss blood, so she was partly to blame for my personal failures, as my father saw them. First, she deflected my father's critical gaze onto my younger brothers, suggesting in her quiet, practical manner that Deacon and Richard were better suited to the discipline of engineering, being more practical and less prone to absent-mindedness and self-centred pursuits. In this matter she was prescient, for both my brothers happily followed our father's career path. They became engineers and worked for Bethlehem Steel, married and generally flourished in the same neighbourhood.

Second, she provided me with the perfect escape: she convinced her family—a middle-class clan of dour burgher-meisters who had profited nicely from their Calvinist stoicism and dairy farming—to take me in. The Langenbrüners leased property high in the Alps. Through my mother's exhortations I was sent to work this property. I spent a marvelous June, July and August exploring the postcard-perfect landscape of the Bernese Oberland, oblivious to the darkening clouds spreading across Europe.

But this reprieve was not meant to last, and not because of the war. My maternal family's generosity extended only so far, and a distant, shiftless, American-born grandson who did little to earn his keep held no sway over their dour hearts. My delinquent nature stretched both their tolerance and their opinion of my mother's parenting, so by mid-August they focussed their efforts to casting me off their hands, under the guise of the burgeoning crisis arising from the Austrian Archduke's assassination in Sarajevo. By mid-August, as the rest of Europe was swallowed by the hysteria of a war that would certainly end by Christmas, they decided I must go. But where? I stubbornly refused to return to Pennsylvania. I would not give my father the satisfaction. And as much as they wanted me off their hands, they were decent enough to forbid me from rashly enlisting in the French army to fight the Hun. They did not want my death on their calloused hands.

The answer was found, without my knowledge or complicity, by distant relations whose existence I never knew. Two of my mother's cousins were Directors with the International Committee of the Red Cross. They came to my grandparents' aid by volunteering me for service in the field. Christian usefulness was always in demand, now more so amidst an escalating conflagration. To appease my mother's doting nature, they secured for me a commission to Ottoman Turkey. As Turkey was officially neutral (despite the efforts of both Germany and Britain), I would be reasonably safe, they concluded.

While shocked at the sudden turn in my fortunes, I accepted. My family's deft maneuverings therefore unknowingly laid the foundation for a career of international service, but of that I had no inkling when, on September fifth, 1914, I boarded the train to Constantinople with my two traveling companions, Doctor Frederick Solvein from Brussels, and nurse Angela Doebli from Zurich. Solvein was a tall, walking stick of a man in a constant state of outrage over the German invasion of his homeland, while Nurse Doebli was a quiet, birdlike woman who rarely lifted her pretty, upturned nose out of the book that was always perched in her hands.

The train from Geneva propelled us across Habsburg Austria to the fortified city of Trieste. The rail lines to the east had been blocked by the Serbs who—according to the Viennese papers—were to blame for starting the whole mess, first by assassinating the Austrian Crown Prince and second, by dragging Russia into the quarrel. The port was teeming with Imperial troops bound for Serbia. In this dusty chaos we boarded a Turkish steamer flying the flag of the Red Crescent, skirting the Italian navy and bypassing the brutal fighting inland. Our travel, though tense, passed uneventfully and two weeks after leaving Geneva we steamed between the steep, fortified cliffs of the Dardanelles to Constantinople, home of the Sublime Porte, where I was to begin my unlikely career with the Red Cross.

Constantinople was like no city I had seen before. The smells! The sounds! The colours! The crowds! People bustling in every direction, by every and any means possible. I watched a fisherman carrying a tuna on his back, secured with ropes across his chest. The fish was as large as a small piano. He disappeared off the dock into a maze of narrow lanes. As I sidestepped overloaded bicycles and dodged laden carts pulled by crazed fools, I knew I had left the ordered neatness of Switzerland far behind. I was lost in the whirlpool of my competing senses as I made my way to the American Embassy, a stone building fronted by Grecian pillars on high ground overlooking the Golden Horn and the Ottoman naval arsenal. While the International Committee of the Red Cross had no official business with the American government, the ambassador, Henry Morgenthau, was a close friend of my father's despite the latter's Republican affiliations. Their friendship preceded Morgenthau's political life, back to the days when the Ambassador had done work for the Bethlehem Steel Company. My father therefore insisted that, if I was to agree to the lunatic notions of my mother's relations, I must pay my respects to the Ambassador the moment I arrived. I suspected he was trying to place some bonds of safe-keeping around his lost son, and as stubborn as I was, I was not a complete fool. It did no harm to register with one's embassy in a land so utterly foreign as Ottoman Turkey, that mythical place of harems and hookahs.

Bidding a temporary good-bye to Solvein and Doebli, who nervously carried on by trolley bus to the headquarters of the Red Cross to secure our accommodations, I marched to the doors of the embassy and introduced myself. I was dressed in casual attire, hence receiving doubting glances from the two drowsy dough boys whose game of dice I had interrupted. They passed my card between each other, neither wanting to actually read it and thereby appoint himself responsible for sorting out my unexpected appearance. After a lengthy shuffling of boots, the younger of the pair led me to an antechamber with the highest ceiling I had ever seen. I had to squint to make out the pattern of inlaid tiles set into the stucco far above my head. On the furthest wall hung a limp, American flag above a faded photograph of President Wilson. The guard disappeared after pointing to a Byzantine mosaic set into the centre of the tile floor and ordered me to wait exactly there. I wondered for a moment if there were a trap door hidden in the design, and that he was on his way to the lever that would dump me down a dark sewer and vomit me into the smelly waters of the harbour.

But that did not happen. I was alone only a short while when a fez-wearing secretary in a rumpled, Western suit with a high collar entered from a side door and bowed deeply in front of me, his palms pressed together as if in prayer.

"Please come with me, Sir," he said to the floor. "His Excellency will see you right away." He gestured to take my straw hat, dangling from my hands, but I refused, probably rudely in his eyes.

He led me through the heavy door through which he had just emerged, and scurried down a dingy corridor faster than I expected from one so aged. Each of the many doors we passed was closed. I could have been inside any neglected office in any American city in the summer. Small, louvered windows above each door let in a dim light, but no draft that I could feel. I trailed behind, perspiring in the closeness of the corridor, breathing in the smoke that wafted off my escort's baggy clothes. It was a harsh scent, tinged with spices that brought to mind the curries eaten by Indians, though I could not identify any particular fragrance.

Inside a narrow, equally close room, Ambassador Morgenthau sat behind his desk under another faded portrait of Woodrow Wilson. He rose to greet me, removing his spectacles with his left hand.

"Mr. Scott," he said as we shook hands. He was smiling genuinely, or so I thought. "Good to meet you. I trust your father is well? I think the last time he and I spoke was in 1912, before the Democratic convention in Baltimore. He was still trying to convince me to switch horses." The ambassador chuckled. "Those were quite dramatic times."

"He is well," I replied. I knew very little of my father's political involvements, apart from how much he disliked Democrats. "And very busy, as ever. He sends his greetings and well wishes."

"Excellent. Yes, though it pains me to say it, our industries—especially Carnegie's steel works—will profit greatly should this war last the year. Please. Sit down. Tell me about yourself. I understand you have taken up with the Red Cross?"

"More the other way around, Sir," I said. I told the ambassador of my situation, briefly sketching the circumstances that led me to his offices. I left out my own culpability. He sat across from me and listened; his manicured fingers laced together in front of him on the desk blotter. He was stern of appearance, sporting a sharp, neat beard and mustache flecked with grey. This did not marry with the warmth of his voice. I knew he was a Jew, which had surprised me at first, however after musing on this fact as the ambassador spoke, I came to the conclusion that Morgenthau's appointment to a region where Muslim, Christian and Jew only superficially co-existed could not have been accidental. I marveled at how clean his desk was: I could see no hints of the work he must have to do, now that war had begun between the Great Powers. When it was my turn to speak, he hooked his spectacles over his ears and looked at me from beneath arched eyebrows.

"You strike me as a sensible young man," he said. "But then, you are a Scott, and in my experience common sense goes hand in hand with your ancestry." I did not contradict him, but could hear my father's voice, were he here in my place: "*You are half right, Morgenthau, where the boy is concerned. It's that damned Swiss blood of his mother's in his veins.*"

"These are bad times," Morgenthau said. "America will not be dragged into European arguments; I am confident of that. The Turks are officially neutral but the reality is very different. The Germans are building a wireless tower on the heights and bragging about it to everyone. Their officers command Ottoman forces. The Turks are mobilizing, and doing a horrendous job of it. There will be starvation across the Empire; the army robs its own people in order to supply itself. The railroad the Turks are building will link Baghdad to Berlin, if it is ever finished. German banks are financing the rail line. If they manage to connect through the Taurus Mountains, an engineering feat many think impossible, by the way, the Kaiser will have free access to the East, to its rubber and oil and its markets and trade routes." He paused a moment, to let the weight of his words land upon me. He sighed, disappointed, it seemed, at having to spell it out. "All completely unencumbered and beyond the reach of the Royal Navy."

I did not know what to say. This was well above my pay rate. Suddenly I was very tired and eager to be out of this overheated room. I needed to find my lodgings and some food and drink and a soft bed.

"The Russians will not stop them," Morgenthau said. "They have their hands full in Prussia. They can barely keep the Austrians at bay. Even the Turks can do better, most days. But it gets worse. The Ottomans think themselves westernized, at least this Committee of Union and Progress lot do. To become completely modern, they feel they must do away with some of the old ways. They embrace technology, Western style armies, banking and industry. They are Turkish nationalists, and as they scrub away the old, they take harsh measures against the groups they fear: Jews, Greeks, Assyrians, and Armenians. They regard them all as threats to their Turkish ideal."

The Ambassador rose from his chair and began to pace behind his desk, his hands clasped behind his back. "While the world watches the war in Europe, I am afraid there is a humanitarian disaster unfolding here. I have written home, asking for funds to be raised in relief. The Armenian population has been under siege for many decades, and it is getting worse. Much worse. Armenian scholars and priests, writers and professors are imprisoned. Armenian newspapers have been censored. We Americans cannot tolerate this. Bad enough the Turk robs his own to feed his army. It is the logical conclusion of ancient hatreds unleashed in a modern-day setting. The world must be made aware of this before it worsens, which is my great fear. You, Mr. Scott, can help in this endeavor."

It took me several minutes, as Morgenthau spoke, to realize that he was offering me a commission, even as I completed my work with the Red Cross. I was dumbfounded. I was being asked to provide information to the highest diplomat representing American interests in the region. Directly, though with great discretion and subtlety. I was being asked to be a spy! Morgenthau was still talking when the secretary returned to light the lamps that hung from the walls. I did not escape until the middle of the evening, so I was grateful that a carriage was waiting to take me to the Red Cross headquarters, many twisting streets away. I was too weary to do more than find my room, which I shared with the good doctor from Belgium, and fall into a confused, overheated sleep.

We remained in Constantinople for a nearly a month, gathering supplies for our relief mission to the south and east of the Empire. The Red Cross was besieged with requests for aid, to alleviate starvation in the south due to the mobilization, and to assist scattered

Armenian villages in the east where reports were being received almost daily that fathers and sons were being taken as conscripts into the Ottoman army. These actions left the remaining population alone to face the cruelty of the coming winter. Worse still, the reports claimed the women and children, now bereft of protection, were targets of rogue squads of thieves and brigands who stole, pillaged and committed atrocities too horrific to believe. There was urgent need for us in the hinterlands.

During this period, I was invited twice to the American Embassy as a guest of the Ambassador. The first meeting, a week after my arrival, was an afternoon tea where I was introduced to the British and French Ambassadors, as well as to the Austrian and German Envoys. If I worried that I was under-dressed before the reception I underestimated the degree of formality and glamour of the company. The guest of honor was the Ottoman Minister of War, Enver Pasha, one of the senior leaders of the Committee of Union and Progress who had formed the civil government of the Ottomans after deposing the last Sultan. Enver Pasha was a small man of quick movements, who clearly had no time for the likes of me. I was glad to be done with it all and escaped, perspiring heavily as I said my farewells. The sluggish ceiling fans and water-soaked reed-mats agitated by tired servants were grossly inadequate. I left pining for the deep snows of the Alps.

My last meeting with the Ambassador was arranged on short notice and involved a dinner invitation that I was pleased to accept, for my weeks in close proximity to Doctor Solvein and Nurse Doebli had done little to endear us to each other. I found both utterly boring, and I could tell they found me scatter-brained and lazy. It was as though I was confronted with the very characteristics my father wished *I* possessed and they went out of their way to remind me of this fact. I was therefore delighted to accept the Ambassador's dinner invitation, though there was much to do before our departure the next day.

I was delivered to the Embassy by the same tired carriage and driver as had escorted me previously. I was clean shaven, my hair well combed and oiled to make myself presentable to high placed diplomatic guests. I wore my best clothes; my only proper collar and I was surprised to discover there were no other guests. With the war in full force it did not seem possible that the American Ambassador would waste a precious evening alone with me. We ate in Morgenthau's private quarters. Chilled salmon in jelly. At first there was general conversation, though I admit I did most of the talking. The Ambassador seemed content to let me rattle on about nothing. I complained that everyone would be better served with Doctor Solvein in Belgium. I relayed the latest news from home, namely that my father had recently been promoted to a Director's position on the American Steel Commission. It meant little to me, but Morgenthau seemed impressed. He nodded appreciatively and made a note on a square pad of paper at his right hand. I noticed he appeared weary: crescent moons of shadow lay deep under his eyes and his skin, in the yellow lamp light, looked somewhat sickly. After our meal, we shared brandy and cigars in his study, a very neat, orderly room lined with books.

"Did I tell you how I came to this post?" Morgenthau asked, stretching his legs and folding his long arms across his chest. The brandy and cigar seemed to invigorate him. Smoke curled into the ceiling fan above his head and was sliced into thin filaments to vanish in the darkness.

I shook my head, studying the burning end of my cigar.

"Your father no doubt told you of my aspirations to Cabinet," he said, watching me closely.

If I betrayed nothing, it was because there was nothing to betray. My father rarely, if ever, spoke to me of events in his personal orbit; his vocabulary around me centred on the eternal disappointment of my pronounced lack of ambition.

"The President did not wish to upset his supporters, given how difficult the nomination campaign had been. The fight against Roosevelt took the starch out of him. He needed steel men like Carnegie to support him, and that was not to be with a Jew in Cabinet. So, he offered me this post. I don't mind telling you, I was not happy. Do you know what the President said? He said, 'Henry, I need a Jew in Constantinople. You can best appeal to the Arabs and Semites of the region. Give them a reason to think favourably of the United States.'"

"I was insulted at first, but told him I would think about it. Eventually I agreed. And, I must say, he was right. Because of the war the Middle East is a critical post, for here all the Powers come together to protect their interests. I have the confidences of many. I can go where they cannot. On top of that I am become a resource to hundreds of Constantinople's bright lights. The clerics, the church leaders, the civic leaders. And though I disagree with the Committee on Union and Progress on their goals, and particularly their methods, they are coming to realize they need America. They think of America as the place where anything is possible, a fresh start free from the arguments and confinements that plague Europe. America to them is a bastion of innovation and science. And you know something? They're mostly right about that."

The Ambassador refilled his brandy snifter and handed me a single, heavy envelope. He did not offer me more brandy. "In there you will find the names of agents, contacts in the cities to which you will be traveling. Talk to the missionaries, too, they have many friends who can help you. Don't forget, you are the logistical chap on this Red Cross mission, you won't draw the attention of German or British agents. Find out what they know."

"I cannot speak Turk or Armenian, though my German and French are passable. Is there anything in particular I should be asking?"

Morgenthau paused and stared into the darkness above his head. In the dimness he looked much older than his fifty-nine years. "If what I am hearing from the far reaches of the Empire is only half true, you will not have to ask a single question, in any language. Use your eyes and your ears, Weldon, and update me as often as you can. I pray these reports we are hearing are false, but my heart tells me otherwise." He sighed heavily as he crushed the glowing ember of his cigar into an exquisite porcelain ashtray.

Afternoon turned to evening, grey to black, but the senator showed no signs of slowing down. Safir excused herself and stepped cautiously along the hallway to the bathroom. It, too, was bright, glowing with an electric light amplified through crystal wall sconces. The polished chrome of the faucet and taps nearly blinded her. She washed her face and savored the feel of the hand towel, softer than her pillow. She adjusted her hair pins, powdered her nose and checked her lipstick. Somewhat refreshed, she returned to her spot on the sofa.

"Do you want to hear more?" Weldon asked.

"Certainly," she said. "Is it okay if I smoke?"

The senator retrieved a crystal lighter from the sideboard and held the flame beneath her cigarette.

"Thank you," she said, exhaling a train of smoke toward the ceiling.

In the year that passed I became a hardened veteran of Ottoman affairs, though I was barely twenty-one. Our tiny caravan crisscrossed Anatolia as the war in Belgium and France settled into a meat-grinder of a stalemate. Newspapers and dispatches from Geneva informed us that entire graduating classes of the École Militaire and Sandhurst

College had been killed in the first three months of war. In the Balkans, the Austrians had recovered from early setbacks to defeat a well-trained Serbian army. Of more concern to us, we learned that the Russian army was staggering in Prussia and Galicia, but they had proven the better force against a hasty Turkish offensive in the Caucasus. Enver Pasha himself had led the Third Army to disaster at Sarakamis in the high mountain passes. His army, unaccustomed to Alpine warfare, had been wiped out in the snow. Enver had retreated back to Constantinople, leaving the remnants of his army to fend for themselves. This humiliation meant hard times for all the internal enemies of the state, of which there were many. Greeks, Kurds, Assyrians, Jews, and Armenians felt the wrath of the Turk in every province our ragtag caravan visited. Everywhere we went, we were viewed with suspicion and given grudging, if any, support. Soldiers searched our baggage for any reason to detain us. Sometimes they confiscated our stocks, but our papers, my American status and the sanctity of the Red Cross protected us and mostly we were able to keep our precious supplies. I lived in daily terror that my secret correspondence with Ambassador Morgenthau would expose us. I carefully hid my onion skin letters inside the lining of my greatcoat. Even the good doctor and Nurse Doebli knew nothing of my surveillance activities, which, to my eye, were having little consequence on the lives of the unfortunate.

As we traveled, we heard stories of terrible mistreatment of villagers by local *Vilayet*—governors—and their garrisons. When we set up camp, whether in large towns or ramshackle villages, we saw proof of brutality and torture. Food shortages made an intolerable situation hopeless. Turks, as well as Armenians, were starving, but they, at least, had their homes. In Konia, we witnessed Armenians driven from their property, their possessions looted by their neighbours. Our tiny surgery, established in the courtyard of a deserted Armenian church, treated survivors with bayonet wounds and broken bones. It was all we could do to staunch the rising tide of disease. Typhus outbreaks were commonplace, and I was terrified of contracting the dread illness.

One day—a day before the Turkish governor demanded we leave town—Nurse Doebli came to find me. I was at the market negotiating with unwilling sellers for fresh milk. She was pale, shaking. "Come with me. Now." She pulled my arm, her fingernails biting into the flesh. She could barely speak.

I followed her back to the surgery. She led me inside—I was rarely afforded this right for the pair guarded their domain jealously—to where Solvein was hunched over the figure of a small, Armenian boy. It took me a moment for my eyes to adjust from the bright sun outside, at first, I could see nothing amiss. I was expecting a broken arm, or a torn scalp. The Doctor waved me closer. The boy's bare feet protruded out the bottom of the sheet that covered his body. I brushed past the doctor. A pair of horseshoes had been nailed to the boy's bloody heels. Solvein was holding pliers, about to remove the nails. I staggered from the surgery and vomited outside the door.

The terror went unchecked by the *Vilayet* and the *Mullahs*. Worse, we discovered that these officials were often behind the atrocities. The local fathers and sons were gone, taken at the end of a rifle to serve in the Ottoman army, or else shot on the spot. The remaining wives, mothers and grandfathers were unable to defend themselves. We found farms razed, animals butchered; starving children were forced to take to the roads in search of food and shelter. These luckless caravans soon became prey to thugs and roving bands of horsemen who earned more by looting than they ever could from farming or other gainful employment.

In the eastern city of Van—it was Summer, 1915—we came with supplies to the tiny Red Cross hospital situated high up on the ridge overlooking the lake. It was rugged country, and had seen much of the fighting for the Russians were not far from Erzurum near the eastern border. It had been a miracle, of sorts, getting through to the town with our supplies intact, for the Ottoman command was in disarray since the defeat the previous December, and desperate soldiers often looted passing trains. There was an American mission within the besieged town. They were amazed to see us and accepted our help with gratitude. There we witnessed the results of what could only be described as organized, deliberate brutality. The Armenian population, what was left, had taken up arms to prevent more killing and looting and mass deportation. We remained for two weeks, two hellish weeks, treating more wounded than our station could handle. We only left for Trabizond, on the Black Sea, at the insistence of the Armenian fighters, who demanded we escape and broadcast their situation to the outside world. They escorted us north, toward Trabizond, at their own peril, only leaving us when they were sure our Red Cross banners could be seen by the Ottoman artillery. When we arrived at port two days later, we were told that the rebellion had been broken with terrible consequences for the locals. I started suffering from nightmares, imagining the men and women who had sheltered us being tortured and executed.

Instead of taking ship at Trabizond, we restocked and turned southwest. I had contacted Americans at the port, traders who secured for us sulpha, bandages, food, and water, and who took my letters for Ambassador Morgenthau, but there was no good news for us. It seemed as if every corner of the globe was on fire. Worse, the Ottoman navy had laid siege to the port, so there was no safe passage to Constantinople, even had we desired to leave. We carried on by land.

The longer we were on the road, the worse the conditions we found. Villages had been emptied of their inhabitants, houses looted and abandoned by their persecuted owners. I found myself hardened against the violence, for I no longer wept at the sight of starving women and children wandering the highways. We offered what we could with grim determination. With the eyes of the world elsewhere, the suffering of Armenians counted for little.

On Christmas Eve, 1915, we came to Adana, a once pretty town south of the Taurus Mountains, situated on the rail line to Aleppo. I was not at full strength, having fought off stomach sickness since leaving that much larger city. I was angry, too, with Doctor Solvein, for had it been up to me, we would have remained in Aleppo assisting the swarms of suffering refugees, or we would have traveled to Deir Es Zor. We had heard it described as the very Gates of Hell. Surrounded by desert, it was the end of the road for thousands of Armenian refugees. All roads led to Deir Es Zor. After that, only oblivion. Reports had reached us that soldiers were forcing refugees into the barrens, forbidding them to return. There was no food, no shelter, no water, yet box cars full of Armenians continued to arrive. Typhus, dysentery and cholera were rampant. It was said that corpses lay everywhere. I was now utterly convinced that what was happening to the Armenians was not the product of local grudges or greedy governors. My letters to the Ambassador insisted that this was an organized program of deportation, banishment and murder.

The doctor and I had argued about our course of action. We were a small party, insignificant against the scale of misery that surrounded us. A drop of relief in an ocean of despair. Solvein agreed, but felt we could do more away from Aleppo, upstream of the endless procession of rail cars.

"In Deir Es Zor we will become like the Armenians. We will become victims too," he said.

"But Deir Es Zor is where the most misery lies," I said.

"Even the Archangel does not go into Hell to rescue the unfortunate," Solvein countered. "He intervenes where there is a chance of salvation."

It was a logic Doebli also supported, so I relented. We decided to leave Aleppo and head back to Adana. There, it was hoped, our tiny mission might provide succor to a few needy souls.

Adana had a ragged, dreary feel to it, with an air of desperation and hopelessness like so many other towns we had visited. Situated on the plateau south of the Taurus Mountains, Adana boasted a fine, German-built railway station and was a vital link between north and south, east and west. Tents and other forms of rough shelter had sprung up around the train station, filling the marketplace and fields at the town's perimeter. One glance and I realized that most of the squatters were displaced Armenians, their lean-to's purposely modest in an attempt to discourage further maltreatment by the Ottoman authorities. Huddled families were packed cheek-to-jowl, sharing a single blanket or tattered shawl for warmth. If they were forcibly displaced from here, only Aleppo and the inhospitable desert remained.

Once in the city I was quick to find the American Consulate- a decrepit building next to a foul-smelling garbage pit dug into the hard ground. I was able to rouse a servant and deposit there my encrypted letters to Ambassador Morgenthau. They were as urgent as ever. I was promised most effusively that they would go out the day after Christmas. I was glad the Americans in Trabizond had shown me how to disguise my letters by adding the true content one word per paragraph. The Embassy staff in Constantinople had a master cipher to decode the letter. I did not know the inclinations of the servant: for all I knew he was a participant in the atrocities that doubtless were occurring here. I was uncomfortable even to linger in his presence. The *fatwa* that had been issued against all Christians who were not German or Austrian meant he could cut me down where I stood without retribution and that would be the end of Weldon Scott.

Inside the small compound there were few Westerners left to share Christmas with us. The German-sponsored *Hilfsbund* were doing their best to clothe and feed the Armenian refugees. Understandably, Solvein was reluctant to remain near any German, but when he saw the genuine relief work the missionaries were attempting, he relented. Our lodgings had once been a primary school, now converted to provide rudimentary medical and relief services. The whitewashed walls were dingy from neglect and the ceilings soot-stained from the oil lamps and thick candles that were our only source of light after sunset. Doctor Solvein installed his inadequate surgery in what was once a cloakroom. According to the senior missionary, Sister Birgit, there had been no outbreak of Typhus since October. A trickle of medicine and food came via American steamer from Mersin, then by train through Tarsus. It wasn't much when more refugees arrived daily.

Being Christmas Eve, Solvein and Doebli were eager to attend services at the old church, not far from our bivouac. Many years before, the church had been home to a small order of Benedictine monks, but now it was being used by missionaries from Holland. When the good doctor discovered this he was eager to attend, and he escorted Doebli through the camps of the displaced with a noticeable spring in his stride. Though I did not consider myself a religious man, the months of rigorous travel and suffering I had witnessed put me in need of some spiritual renewal, so I accompanied them.

It was cold, but the air was still and the sky above us awash with stars. I was weary but content as we made our way to the narrow, stone building. The silhouette of a crumbling bell tower was visible against the sky. The cobbled square was empty, a stark contrast to the teeming camp surrounding our compound. The service had begun, for we heard singing from behind shuttered windows. Strong voices, clear and firm and steady. They were singing in a variety of tongues, Latin, Greek, and other dialects I did not recognize. But the sound was pleasing nonetheless. Pushing open the door I was surprised at the number of worshippers squeezed into the closely set pews. They were dust-streaked, shabbily clothed, and smelled. There were few men among the gathered. A silver-bearded priest in heavy boots thumped across a creaking, loosely-planked nave. He wore a broad white cap, ornately decorated. As he paced the wings of the cap flapped above his ears, like a gluttonous seabird unable to take flight. His voice was deep. And loud, for when the singing ceased, it filled the room.

We slid onto a bench at the back of the church. Several turned to stare at the three obvious foreigners. I will never forget those faces. Worn, deeply etched, their skin sunburned to parchment. Thirty-year-old mothers made old before their time by deprivation and fear. It was their eyes that moved me the most. Eyes that had seen intense suffering. Suddenly ashamed, I looked away, embarrassed to intrude in their moment of relief. One of the women, her brow covered in a thin, lace headscarf, smiled in welcome and gestured for us to stay.

The service did not last long. I did not take communion, I was too shy to leave my perch on the bench, however Solvein joined the line of worshippers, as did Doebli. They returned to their places, their eyes shining. Minutes later the priest, chanting and carrying a candle, led the procession from the church. Row by row the gathered stood and followed him into the night. We were at the back of the assembly. We emerged into the square and I began to shiver as the closeness of the church surrendered to a piercing wind.

The screams began before my eyes could adjust to the darkness. The crowd ahead shifted like a flock of startled birds, veering aside and stumbling backwards, pushing us toward the church. A group of Ottoman soldiers charged into the leading ranks. A fez-wearing officer struck the minister in the face with the butt of his rifle. Those nearest reached to slow his fall, and they were next to be attacked. Everyone scattered. Mothers tugged at the ragged sleeves of their children; I watched one elderly man stumble and fall. He did not get back up.

Doctor Solvein and Doebli moved to intervene. The doctor placed himself between the soldiers and the stricken minister. "Arretez!" he shouted, pushing an Ottoman soldier backwards. His gaudy epaulets did a crazed dance as he fell. Doebli huddled over the minister, her hands cradling his bleeding head, her back hunched to protect against the next blows sure to come.

The Ottoman soldiers did not take kindly to Solvein's intervention. His shouting in French did not help matters. Three Ottomans surrounded him, forcing him at bayonet point away from Nurse Doebli and the minister. They steered him toward a small group of injured Armenian men who flailed helplessly against the blows from Ottoman rifles. A heavy object struck me across the shoulders. I stumbled forward, toward Solvein and the Armenian men. I tasted Adana dust. Doctor Solvein, not yet realizing that the sound of his voice only increased the soldiers' anger, continued with a stream of insults. I prayed they did not understand, though I was proud of his misplaced courage. Moonlight reflected off a serrated bayonet. This was surely the end of us.

A new voice echoed sharply off the stones. I could not make out its source, for, still on my knees, my view was obscured by a scuffle of soldiers' boots. The Turkish words were harsh, but the voice was clear, decisive. There was unswerving authority behind it, and the soldiers had no choice but to obey, despite their anger. They stepped away from us, as one, and turned to face the voice.

When the Ottomans separated, their bayonets now pointed away from us, I saw four men in uniforms very different from the Ottomans. They wore the Habsburg insignia of the double eagle on their jackets, with a thin yellow stripe down the side of their trousers. The one who had spoken was not wearing Habsburg colours, but was dressed in civilian attire and he wore a red fez. His thick, dark mustache sat neatly above his upper lip. He carried a pistol in his right hand.

Faced with this new circumstance, the soldiers lost their fight. The Ottoman officer saluted and bowed his head, reluctantly. He spoke quickly, the word *Effendi* peppered through the ingratiating tone of his speech.

The leader of the Habsburgs spoke in a scolding voice and gestured angrily at the soldiers to leave. They did not argue, nor waste any time departing. They disappeared from whence they had come, and we were alone in the square with the man and his Austrian escort. We must have been a sorry sight to them, bloodied and bowed and knocked around, but relief poured through us like a river. Solvein shot me a glance that said, without words, that he knew full well we had escaped death. Nurse Doebli rushed to his side, weeping, and after a brief embrace she turned to tend the fallen men around us. I stood, wincing at the pain between my shoulder blades. The man in the fez faced me and asked, in perfect French, if I was unhurt.

"Ja. Danke," I replied, wanting to show him that I understood both French and German.

He smiled, but only just. He stood slightly shorter than I, but he was more solidly built. "I recognize the Belgian and the Swiss," he said, nodding toward my companions, "you are neither," he said, answering me in German.

"American," I replied, and extended my right hand. "Weldon Scott. From Pennsylvania. I am with the Red Cross."

He holstered his pistol and shook my hand firmly. "Neutral America," he said, switching to a heavily accented English. "You are scattered across this empire like autumn leaves," he said. He was not smiling.

"Is that a good thing?" I asked.

"Neither good, nor bad," he said. His blue eyes, bluer than any I had seen, held my gaze. "Only Swiss citizens may serve with the Red Cross, I think?"

"My mother's family are Swiss. They thought they were doing me a favour, though lately I wonder." I laughed weakly.

He ignored my jest and released my hand. "How long have you been in Adana?"

"We arrived today. I am not certain how long we will remain."

"We are stationed in Belemedik Dagh, less than one hundred kilometres from here. It lies beyond the Cilician Gates," he said, switching back to perfect French. He looked me over, then turned to take in the doctor and nurse. "If you wish to do some real good, come there soon. We have civilians, mostly Armenians. They are in great need."

"I will tell the others," I said.

"Good." He nodded. As he spoke, he tilted his head back, allowing his chin to point directly toward me. "Where are you lodged?"

"Our compound is just beyond the square. We are with the *Hilfsbund*."

"Good," he said again. "We will escort you there." He motioned his troop forward and gestured at me to walk beside him.

I was glad to be leaving the square. I was shivering, the shock subsiding. Solvein and Doebli and the soldiers fell into step behind us. Most of the Armenians had already fled.

"Why are you here?" I asked.

The Austrian spoke without looking at me. He kept his blue eyes fixed on the way ahead.

"We came for provisions, and to discover the whereabouts of our superior. He left us weeks ago, for Aleppo, and we have not heard word since."

"Do you imagine him captured?"

The Austrian now turned to face me. "I do not imagine anything," he said. "I deal with only the facts. Viktor Pietschmann is more than capable. His extended absence can be attributed to several reasons. He may have taken ill. He may have had an accident. He may have been detained. He may have been recalled to Vienna. We are seeking to determine the truth."

"We saw no such man in Aleppo," I offered, weakly.

He stared at me, then nodded curtly. "Thank you for that information. We will discuss its implications."

Our sorry procession left the square. We walked on an unpaved road between dilapidated buildings, all dark against the night.

"A bit of friendly advice," the Austrian said. "Try not to speak French. It is the language of the infidel. There is a *fatwa* against the French."

"Nurse Doebli speaks German," I replied, "but Solvein gets so angry when he hears it."

"You are American. Speak English. Especially to the soldiers. They may not understand your words, but to them America is a distant wonder. They possess no ill will toward it, as they do to France, or especially Russia. It is better than a bayonet in your belly."

As we approached our compound, we found the Armenian encampments in a state of extreme agitation. The fleeing crowd had raised the alarm. We were swarmed by women, some dragging or carrying small children. They were desperate for protection. The Austrian soldiers pushed through the jostling women and children, firmly but as gently as they could, toward the compound wall. The iron gates were closed. I felt a desperate tugging at my sleeves, slowing my progress. I stumbled into the crowd. My head was aching and my breath was laboured. Stern shouts from the Austrian soldiers and the children and women fell back, giving us a clear path to the gate.

A wailing rose behind us. The Ottoman soldiers had returned, in greater numbers, and were making their way toward us. Two were on horseback. Refugees scattered, avoiding the wild swings of batons and rifle butts. As if on queue, the gates swung inward, dragged apart by two *Hilfsbund* workers who had come, with lanterns, from inside the building. The light from the lanterns threw grotesque shadows across our faces.

"Come with us, inside," Solvein said, pushing through.

The Austrians made no move to follow, but remained facing away from us, their eyes on the approaching Ottomans.

"We are not in danger from this lot," the Austrian said. "Stay inside until the afternoon. It is the Christian holy days that make them most angry."

"Thank you," I said, reverting to English.

He flashed his first smile, revealing straight white teeth. "Come to Belemedik Dagh," he said. "See for yourself that there are other ways to fight this evil." He gestured to his company to move through the scrum of terrified refugees, toward the advancing Turks.

Solvein grabbed my arm and half dragged me through the gates. I stumbled after the circle of retreating lantern light, through heavy, timber doors as they slammed shut behind me, their iron bolts rattling home against the cold night air.

Weldon asked Safir if she was hungry. She did not want him to stop, but she had not eaten since breakfast. "A little," she said.

"You must accompany me to dinner, seeing as I am not a very good host. I have nothing to prepare for you here."

Jefferson and the car waited at the curb, and fifteen minutes later deposited them in front of the Carlyle Regency Hotel on Madison Avenue. A valet resplendent in his scarlet uniform held open her door as the sedan came to a stop.

"Senator Scott," he said with a smile, "so good to see you again."

"Thank you, George," Weldon said, pressing a coin into the valet's palm. "I want you to meet Miss Turan. Miss Safir Turan. She is a very special guest of mine. Safir, this is George, the best in New York at his job. Whenever I'm in town—which I hope will be more often, now—I always make it a point to visit."

The valet smiled, bowed and escorted them into the restaurant.

Inside was dark and smelled of cigars, French perfume and furniture polish. Painted murals covered every wall. Safir had read about them during her time in Paris.

"Yes, the *Madeleine* murals," Weldon said, smiling. "You know the story?" He nodded to the Maitre'd who met them at the threshold and led them to a booth in the corner. "Ludwig Bemelmans stayed at this hotel a few years back. He painted in exchange for room and board for his family. These murals are the result."

"I know the stories well," Safir said, craning her neck to survey the paintings above her head. At her elbow a nearly life-sized rabbit, dressed jauntily in a sky-blue suit, leaned against a tree, near a neat, whitewashed, garden gate.

"People are now calling this place *Bemelmans* for the art," Weldon said, "but I still think of it as the Carlyle. The food is good, the place is discreet but it can be boisterous enough, celebrities are always dropping by. But here we can carry without being interrupted."

Safir glanced shyly around her. Each table was crowded with well dressed guests who appeared to be enjoying themselves. Her notion of a meal out was the lunch counter up the block from the museum. Nobody there resembled these perfectly coifed, dressed-to-the-nines patrons. At the lunch counter they ate their chopped liver or tuna fish on rye with grim determination, their eyes staring unseeing into the street, locked in their thoughts, as distant as the moon. She followed suit, eating in a hurry and washing down her sandwich with a glass of water before sliding off her stool and scurrying back to the archives.

Weldon ordered each of them "T" bone cuts, rare, with fresh vegetables and new potatoes. "They do steak as well as anyone," he said, handing the menu back to the waiter. Over her protests he suggested a bottle of French wine, and she blushed in the shadows.

"Not for me," she said.

"Something else? A martini, perhaps?"

"I don't drink alcohol," she said, blushing.

"Ah," Weldon nodded, "Forgive me. I forgot you are Muslim."

"My father was Muslim and he drank. In Atatürk's Turkey we could be Muslim and Western at the same time. Many Turks drink. My father, especially after my mother died. So my sister says." She raised a cigarette to her lips. Before she could find her matches the waiter reappeared with a cut glass lighter the size of Mustafa's head and stood at silent attention as she touched the end of the cigarette to the flame.

Weldon nodded. "I understand perfectly. But if you have no objections, I will have the waiter bring two glasses. I don't want him to think I am a complete lush. I have to keep up some appearances, even if the election isn't until November."

Safir nodded and the waiter disappeared. He returned moments later with bottle cradled in his gloved hands. He showed the label to the senator, who smiled. The waiter poured just enough to cover the bottom of Weldon's glass and stood patiently at his shoulder as Weldon swirled the wine, sniffed it, sipped it loudly and pronounced it fit to drink.

"Delicious," he sighed. "Sure you won't have a taste?" When Safir shook her head, he shrugged. "So that, My Dear, was my first meeting with Paul Bahr. Engineer. Alpinist. Artist. Philosopher. Pianist. Friend. It was he who led me to Piruz."

"The man who saved you from the Turks in Adana," Safir said. She watched Weldon drink his wine, quickly, and the waiter who appeared out of nowhere to refill his glass.

"The same," Weldon said.

"Why wasn't he wearing a uniform the night you met?"

"He rarely did. Paul was a civilian engineer, enlisted by his government to assist the Turks. With the *fatwa* issued he said he could move around more freely dressed like one of them. He really did come to look the part," Weldon chuckled. "He kept the moustache well after the war."

"You stayed friends?"

Weldon set down his wine glass without taking a drink. "For many years. I had a lot of respect for him as well."

"Had? Is he dead?"

"I am not sure," Weldon said, wiping his mouth with his napkin. "We haven't spoken for years. A bit of a falling out, let's say."

"To do with my mother?"

Weldon frowned, reached out a hand to cover one of Safir's. "No. Nothing like that. And if you're patient I will tell you everything."

She wasn't sure how it happened, how the wine glass in front of her emptied- not once, but twice. How easily the wine passed between her lips, caressing her tongue and warming her insides! Memories of Theo at the *Café de la Paix*, the smell of cigarettes, the table stained with rings of red wine from their overfilled glasses, stumbling back to his apartment to make love, heat and sweat and hair oil as they wrestled on his lumpy mattress. Her cheeks burned; her eyelids were heavy. She forced down the memories and willed herself to listen to Weldon's voice.

It was early January and I found myself in a snow storm as our caravan navigated the steep and treacherous Cilician Gates. I have never been so cold. The wind whipped us cruelly and the pack animals we had paid dearly for in Adana brayed pitifully against the stinging sleet. We were a miserable, unorganized convoy making little progress along a stony path as ancient as Babylon itself. The cliffs to either side of us offered no reprieve. I laughed bitterly at the joke: we were the relief mission, but if we did not find shelter soon, we would be swallowed by the snows and lie frozen and undiscovered until late Spring.

Not far above the gates snow utterly blocked our progress. We had no choice but to turn back, and we knew our supplies would not last the return trip to Adana. We made our sorry camp under an uncertain overhang of rock and tried to get warm. I managed to start a fire—to this day I don't remember how in the teeth of that blizzard—and we huddled together, with the animals, behind a torn canvas sheet. It was lucky for us that the wind blew it away, exposing us, otherwise Paul's scouts would have missed us. This was after two long days stranded in place, our fire reduced to embers. But the snows ceased and the skies cleared and the sunlight scattered diamonds across the snow drifts, blinding us. It was the sixth of January. Epiphany. We were starving and frostbitten. The Austrians appeared on skis, silent apparitions gliding atop the fresh drifts.

A young, dashing mountaineer named Koelrasch poured brandy between my teeth. It burned my throat but brought heat back to my frozen limbs and lifted the fog in my brain. Koelrasch and Bildstein bore our packs and made a skid from their ski poles to carry Nurse Doebli. Without them we would have certainly died in those uncaring mountains.

We arrived just as darkness fell at the construction camp of Belemedik Dagh, named after the jagged mountain that rose nearly ten thousand feet above the Anatolian Plateau. Paul's first greeting was a scathing rebuke, in French, for risking our lives and those of his team. Though I had sent a cable from Adana telling him of our expected arrival he was certain no one could be so foolish as to attempt the ascent through the Gates until the weather turned. We did not receive his return telegram. We were fortunate that though he hardly knew me, he held my American common sense in such low regard that he ordered daily patrols, both to search for Ottoman soldiers, and in case we attempted the climb. In time I learned that Paul held everyone's common sense in similar poor esteem.

I was taken to a small house built from scrap wood and placed on a thin mat of straw. I remember a fire pit, for the smoke from the charcoal was bitter and strong in my nose. I lay there for days, my hypothermia and frostbite attended to by a young woman who fed me broth and who rubbed a thick, foul smelling paste on my feet. Her hair was as black as a moonless winter's night, and as long, though in the time that followed I rarely saw it liberated from the scarf she wore. Her eyes were bright, like stars. And her voice! Though I could not understand her words, they were an oasis in the desert my life had been until then. She came everyday to change my dressings and to feed me a weak broth with a heel of stale, black bread tough enough to break a tooth. She soaked the bread in the broth and fed me piece by piece, refusing to leave until I'd eaten every morsel. I remember a silver medallion that dangled from her neck, just below the hollow of her throat. It caught the light from the candles near my bed. The smiling faces of the Madonna and Christ Child, their golden halos faded with age, or smoothed by years of handling. Though I was in pain, lost, and far from home, suddenly I was content.

The storms passed and the sun was a welcome, though brief, companion, offering meagre warmth before it slipped behind the sheer mountain wall. The numbness in my limbs passed, only to be followed by intense pain and an infuriating itch, but the blood returned to my toes and fingers and I was spared amputation. Nurse Doebli was not as fortunate, for the frostbite had gone too deep. She lost two toes on her left foot. She limped thereafter yet exclaimed that most mornings she was certain the toes were still attached.

Once back on my feet I was eager to find the woman who nursed me to health. As soon as I was able to stand on my own, she disappeared. Desperate to find her, I asked Paul if he would take me on an inspection tour of the camp. He agreed, but did not specify when. "Regain your strength," he said. He nodded at my boots, set at the foot of my pallet. "Their quality saved your toes." I sent another silent prayer of thanks to my mother, who had sent them to me while I was in Switzerland.

Weldon paused. "You seem upset. Shall we call it a night?"

"My mother was Christian? Why else would she be wearing such a medallion?"

"She was Armenian, Safir. Your mother was a good Christian woman."

"I am tired," Safir said, after a long pause. "It must be the wine. This is too much to remember, too much to comprehend." She stubbed out her third cigarette. The restaurant had filled and emptied while the senator spoke.

Weldon signed for the meal. The waiter brought their coats to the table. The car was waiting at the curb. She told Jefferson her home address as the car pulled smoothly into the evening traffic.

The senator stared out the car window. The yellow light from the street lights cast his face in a waxy glow. He looked older, careworn. "I have something for you," he said, barely loud enough to hear over the engine, "but I don't want you to take it the wrong way."

Safir gripped the armrest of the car door. "What do you mean?"

"My apartment," the senator said. "It's for you. I want you to live there."

"With you?" Her voice faltered as the muscles in her throat tightened.

"No," he said, "Nothing of that sort." He seemed to shrink as he stumbled over his words. "I am in Washington most days, and when I'm not I will stay at the Carlyle. No, when I found out where you were, I rented the apartment for you. My assistant thinks I am crazy, but I insisted." He patted Safir's hand. "You deserve to be comfortable."

"Why are you doing this?"

"You are my daughter, Safir," Weldon said. His eyes brimmed with sadness. "I have avoided my responsibilities for too long. It is the least an absent father can do."

Safir looked out the window as the car sped across the Brooklyn Bridge. When she squinted, the electric lights on the bridge superstructure looked like a gigantic necklace. They rode in silence until the car reached Montague Street. Jefferson parked and came around to the curb and opened her door.

"Will you think about it? Please?" the senator asked, again taking her hand in his.

She stared down at his hands, the veins raised beneath the pale skin like blue, knotted strings. "I don't know what to do."

"I am sorry, Safir," he said. "It is a lot to take in."

"You're taking my past. My family," she said. "I feel them crumbling to dust."

A light rain began to fall. The droplets that clung to the car windows filled with the molten silver of the street lamp.

"You have your true identity," Weldon said. "And a new life. Think of it that way."

A bitter laugh escaped her lips. "What if my old self doesn't want to let go?" She hopped out of the car, past Jefferson, who waited silently beside the door.

"I'm sorry. You're too generous," she said, turning to the senator. "I don't deserve any of it." She fled before Weldon could reply, her shoes scuffing loudly against the wet sidewalk.

She woke Sunday morning with a headache, her mouth as dry as an ashtray and tasting twice as bad. She boiled water for tea, waiting at her kitchen table with her head in her arms. Mustafa circled her legs, meowing loudly.

"Stop, for God's sake!" she said, pushing him away. She instantly regretted her anger. "I'm sorry," she cried, lifting the kitten into her arms and nuzzling his face.

Mustafa let her apologize, then jumped down and circled his food dish, his tail in the air.

She fed the cat, made tea and lit a cigarette. She sat at the table, her bathrobe loose around her knees, and stared out the window. Rain pummeled the buildings, the asphalt, the sidewalk, turning Montague Street into something hard, flinty and cold. In the murky reflection she glimpsed a woman beneath a witch's tangle of long, black hair. Deep smudges lay in the hollows under her eyes. She sipped her tea and breathed through the queasiness in her stomach. It worked only as long as there was tea in her cup. She raced to the bathroom and vomited into the toilet. Her arms shook, her legs went weak and sweat bloomed on her skin, but the nausea passed. Her body, at least, felt better.

She drew a bath, washed her hair, nibbled on a piece of dry toast. She listened to a record of Shostakovich. The music lifted her spirits, a brief reprieve from the implications of the senator's story, a fragile state of grace. She went to the kitchen table, sufficiently restored to write her sister.

Dearest Bey,

I am desperate to know your memories of Mother. I am losing her face, her voice, her smile. Though I will say that her smile was meant more for you than for me. I remember a sad, distant woman, spare with her words and affection. Please, tell me your stories, so that I might have others to call upon. I miss you, Dearest, more than ever. Love and kisses,

Safir.

A loud knock at the door startled her as she folded the letter into an envelope. She froze. It was that time on Sunday when her neighbors were either at church or at a park with their families. The phonograph's volume was down. The knock repeated, and Safir jumped out of her chair.

She hurried, feeling exposed in her bathrobe, her hair swathed in a towel. She opened the door, expecting the Super, rumpled and looking sheepish for having to be the bearer of bad news. Perhaps a pipe had broken again.

Vincenzo D'Angelo stood in her doorway, his face swollen and red. She began to close the door, but he held up his hands, as if in prayer.

"Wait! Please don't send me away!" he said.

Safir hesitated. "What do you want?" she said through the sliver of space.

"I need to talk to you."

"It can wait until tomorrow," she said.

"No, it can't," he said, "I can't talk about it there."

"About what?"

"About you," D'Angelo said. His long face twisted by suffering. "I'm crazy about you, Safir. You been acting all strange, going off in fancy cars, meeting God-Knows-Who. You're killing me."

"You have been terrible to me," Safir wailed, opening the door wider.

D'Angelo stepped closer. "Hear me out, you gotta hear me out."

She smelled garlic on his breath, saw the sweat beading on his brow. Safir turned sideways and her boss shot past her, kicking the door shut. "What are you up to? I gotta know."

Safir's legs were weak. She leaned against the door, her hand on the knob. "What I do after work is my business," she said.

"Mebbe," D'Angelo said. He glimpsed Mustafa, sitting in the middle of the hall, his tail twitching. "Nice kitty." He approached the cat, but as he squatted near Mustafa, the cat dashed away. "Takes after his mistress." He rubbed is hands together as he disappeared into the living room. "That was you playing music? A piano, nice." A thin, unsure version of Chopsticks filled the room.

"Don't," Safir rushed to cover the piano.

D'Angelo slid off the bench, his hands in the air. "Okay, relax, I didn't mean nuthin'."

Safir resettled the cloth across the Knabe. "I don't play anymore."

"Suit yourself. I got all day. We can play something else," he said, smiling as he fell onto the sofa. He patted the cushion next to him. "Better yet, come over here. And take off that towel, I wanna see how long your hair really is."

"You need to go," Safir said, her knuckles whitening where she gripped her bathrobe.

"Nah," D'Angelo said. He planted his feet on the coffee table. "I like it here, can't you tell? You and me, we got some figuring out to do."

"I'll call the police if you don't go!" Safir said.

"No, you won't," D'Angelo said. "Not if you want to keep your job." He rose off the sofa like a mechanical toy, one limb extended at a time, then tiptoed toward her. "C'mon, Safir. Just one kiss and I'll go. Cross my heart and hope to die."

Safir picked up Mustafa, who had sidled up to her feet. She rushed out of the room, snatching her purse from the table in the hall. At the bottom of the stairs she passed Ernie Linklater. He was dressed in his familiar white cotton undershirt and ragged bathrobe, an unlit cigar in one meaty hand.

"You ok?" he asked as she brushed past him.

"There's a bad man in my apartment," she said.

Ernie frowned, glancing up the stairs. He shrugged, turned and followed her.

Safir stopped at the phone in the foyer. "Here," she said, pushing Mustafa into Ernie's arms, "hold him for me." With trembling fingers, she dialed Weldon's number.

"You're in so much trouble!" D'Angelo's shouted from the top of the stairs.

"Weldon Scott." The senator's voice was warm, confident.

"It's me. Safir," she said, her mouth dry. "I need help."

"I'll come at once," Weldon said.

Safir hung up the phone, grabbed Mustafa out of Ernie Linklater's grip and with a breathless *thank you* ran onto Montague Street. The rain pelted her face, every drop turning to steam as they touched her skin. Mustafa struggled in her arms, but she gripped him tightly, afraid he would leap into the road and be lost forever. She ran up the street to St. Ann's church, dark and shuttered. She stopped under the arch and leaned heavily against locked doors. Her legs gave out and she slid onto the concrete landing, unable to stand. She squinted through the rain to her apartment, watched as D'Angelo appeared on the stoop, Ernie Linklater right behind him. Her neighbour planted his hands on his hips, the unlit cigar still clenched between his teeth. The two men faced each other,

D'Angelo's arms waving wildly. She could not hear the words they exchanged, but she saw Linklater push D'Angelo toward the steps, his bulk preventing the taller, skinnier man from re-entering the apartment. It seemed like forever before D'Angelo threw up his hands and stormed up Montague Street, away from her. She closed her eyes and wept, her breathing deep, ragged and painful.

She jumped at the touch on her arm. It took a moment to recognize the men staring at her.

"Come along, Safir," Weldon said. When he removed his hat a lock of white hair fell over his forehead. He pushed it away with a gloved hand, straightened and turned to Ernie Linklater, his hand extended. "Thank you, Mr. Linklater, you've been extremely kind."

Ernie shook the senator's hand. "No problem," he said.

"Thomas," Weldon said, and Jefferson stepped toward Linklater, his own white-gloved hand outstretched. Ernie looked down at the folded bill in his palm, and with a smile and a nod toward Jefferson he turned back to the apartment, the end of his cigar glowing red.

"Let's get you into some dry clothes," Weldon said, offering Safir his hand.

"No," Safir said, "I'm not going back there."

Weldon glanced at Jefferson. "All right, Safir. We'll go to my apartment. I have some extra clothes there."

Jefferson nodded, retrieved the car from down the block and returned, holding the door open for Safir, who refused to let go of Mustafa. Weldon slid into the back seat next to Safir.

"Take us home, Thomas," he said, and smiled hopefully at Safir.

Chapter 3

The senator led Safir to the spare bedroom and retrieved a pair of pants, socks, and a shirt from his closet. "You can hang your wet clothes in the bathroom. I'm sorry, I've no idea what else you need."

"This is marvelous, thank you," Safir said, closing the door in Weldon's wake.

The spare room was larger than her own bedroom, furnished with a narrow bed beneath a carved, wooden headboard and an imposing wardrobe of polished wood so dark it looked black in the light that bled through closed curtains. The furniture would have suited a bedroom in an Alpine chalet. She ran her hands over the wardrobe doors and turned the knob in the door. It was locked. She stood on her tiptoes to peer through the dowels that ran across the front, above the doors, but she was too short to see inside. Inhaling the clean smell of furniture polish, she began the hard work of drying her hair with the towel Weldon had given her. Tying the long, still-damp plaits with the sash from her bathrobe, she dressed, tucking the crisp, white men's shirt into the waistband of the trousers. With a last glance at the wardrobe she slipped out of the room and returned to the living room.

The senator sat in the upholstered chair and pointed to a small snifter on the table. It held two fingers of brandy. "It will warm your insides," he said, hovering over her as she seated herself the dining room table.

"I will contact the police," he said, starting toward the telephone in the living room, but Safir put a hand on his arm and begged him not to.

"It will just make things worse," she said. She told him a little of her history with D'Angelo, which made Weldon angrier.

"This cannot stand," he said, his fingers curling into fists. "He's a bad apple."

"He is jealous, is all," Safir said.

"Jealous? Of who?"

"Of you," Safir said. "He saw me get into your car."

"That is no way for a gentleman to behave, Safir, though I am not surprised, given his ancestry. Sicilian, most likely."

She hung her head. "It's not all his fault," she said. "I rubbed it in, my meeting with you."

"And your cat," Weldon said, bending over with an outstretched hand in invitation. "What is its name?"

"Mustafa," Safir said. The cat, exploring the far reaches of the living room, turned at the mention of his name.

"Mustafa!" Weldon exclaimed. "After the great Atatürk, I am sure," he said. "I remember meeting him, once, in Ankara, the new capital city."

"When?"

"It was 1923, I believe, when the Republic was new. Full of promise. Atatürk was determined to send the Ottomans to the dustbin of history. Now as for your cat, his is a well-chosen name. He seems to possess a good sense of his own importance."

Safir smiled. "He is young and incorrigible," she said. "But I love him anyway."

"Good," Weldon said. "We can discuss the right thing to do about this D'Angelo fellow later. If you're settled, we should get you home," Weldon said.

When the car arrived at the apartment, Weldon insisted that he and Jefferson accompany her. Thomas carried a satchel filled with

Safir's dried clothes. She still wore the senator's navy-blue slacks and white dress shirt. She held Mustafa in her arms. The front door was closed, but unlocked. Weldon entered first. She waited in the hall."Nobody home," Weldon called.

Safir walked inside. She inspected every room. D'Angelo was gone, and nothing seemed to be missing. Her records stood in a neat row, undisturbed. Weldon nodded to Jefferson, who set the satchel on the floor and left with a reassuring smile.

"Thank you!" Safir called.

Thomas touched his cap in the usual way, and closed the door behind him.

"Everything in order?" Weldon asked. He moved to the piano. He stood beside it and folded his hands in front of his body, like a mourner at a funeral. "You no longer play? It looks like a nice piece," he said.

"Since my mother died."

He sighed. "Doesn't playing make you happy?"

"Not anymore."

Weldon patted the top of the Knabe. "Shame," he said.

"Thank you for bringing me home," Safir said.

"I can have my car bring you to work tomorrow."

"No, please, that's not necessary," she said. "I am fine now."

Weldon relented, but only halfway. "Jefferson will be there to pick you up after work."

"I don't want to impose," Safir said.

"You are not imposing," Weldon said. "I want to do things for you. And I feel strongly you should move into the apartment. Nobody will bother you there."

She stared at the shrouded piano. "This is my home."

As if reading her thoughts, Weldon patted the top of the piano. "You can bring this with you, if you want. Your records, I have a phonograph. And of course, Mustafa."

"You are so kind, there is so much to think about," Safir said. "Forgive my bad manners. Let me make you supper," she said. "I have enough for a stew, I think. You can tell me more about Turkey while I cook."

Weldon smiled, a faraway smile that made him look older than his fifty-six years. "That would be very nice."

"Let me change my clothes, make yourself at home," Safir said. As she hurried toward her bedroom she called out. "Please choose some music, anything you like."

"I will tell Jefferson to pick me up at six," Weldon said, hurrying down the hall.

After a meal of cooked turnips and rice, and strong coffee, Weldon chose a Mozart violin concerto from Safir's record collection. He settled himself into a hard-backed chair across from Safir, who sat on the sofa with her feet tucked beneath her, smoking a cigarette.

A week after my recovery, I had not found my nurse again, but Paul sought me out where I stayed with Solvein and Doebli. Paul led a pair of small horses and offered one to me. "We have a lot of ground to cover, and these animals know where to place their feet, even in the snow."

Paul looked as he had on Christmas Eve, dressed in a long, grey coat, but today he sported a grey, Habsburg cap in place of the red fez. His glacier-blue eyes sparkled in the weak sunshine. He rarely smiled. His mustache was thick, no wider than his nostrils, and neatly trimmed. He wore fine leather gloves and high boots brightly polished.

From the flimsy, hastily constructed timber house where Solvein, Doebli and I were billeted, we rode uphill to the tunnel. The pack horses wove between many small, windowless huts, similar in construction to mine. Smoke from cooking fires wafted from stubby chimneys made from unused metal pipe. I heard voices, men shouting, women calling to children, whose shrill responses suggested mischief afoot. All in a language I could not comprehend. I glanced at Paul. As if reading my mind, he said, "Armenians. Their husbands and fathers work for me."

Knowing who occupied these rude huts changed my sense of what they were saying. Rather than lamenting their condition they gave thanks for their situation: they were out of reach, at least momentarily, of those who looted, raped and murdered their kin. I craned my neck as we left the huts behind us, but there was no sign of the woman now haunting my dreams.

The entire camp comprised an elongated crescent that clung to the mountain nearly a thousand feet above the only road that linked the coast with the Anatolian Plateau. In summer it was sharp, bare rock, but now snow covered every surface save the steepest slopes. Near the tunnel mouth Paul led me to the very edge of the abyss, as close as the horses would go. The wind kicked up ice pellets in our faces. I had to shield my eyes to see where Paul pointed.

"There. Until this tunnel is complete that is the way north. You can see our main supply camp, near the turn. There's nothing of value left. We have moved up here, out of reach of the Turks."

"Is it that bad?"

Paul stared at me as if I was completely stupid. Even in the watery, grey light his eyes dazzled like sapphires. "You saw a little of it in Adana, and more elsewhere on your travels. Besides, camps are an invitation for epidemics. There are larger work camps on both sides of these mountains. They are overrun with Typhus. Here we maintain strict sanitary methods, drink clean water from mountain springs and keep waste away from our supplies."

"What about food?"

Paul hesitated. "That is a concern," he said, his shoulders sagging only a little. "It will become worse the longer we are here."

"What do the Turks have to say about relocating the camp?"

"I am expecting their official response any day."

"And then?"

"Dear Mr. Scott," Paul said. He turned his horse away from the precipice. "Turks are hunting Armenians to extinction. It is a sport for them. They will not spare the elderly, the infirm. And when they are done with Armenians, they will hunt Greeks and Jews, anyone not Turk. Surely you have seen proof of this? It doesn't matter that it cripples their government. But think on this: without these workers the tunnels will never be completed."

"Won't they just get their own people to do the work?"

"Turks are mostly uneducated farmers, fishermen and shepherds. They need training to work with equipment, to read blueprints and to understand calculations. The Turkish leaders know that if they replace all the workers the railroad will never be finished. Certainly not before the war is over, even if it lasts ten years."

"And you think they are safe here?" I shouted over the wind. I looked around me, absorbing both the beauty and desolation of the high mountain pass. It was hard to imagine there could be any safety here for half-starved refugees clinging to stones like cormorants on the cliffs of the Dardenelles.

"From the Turks, yes, but the mountains do not tolerate foolishness." Paul glanced over his shoulder. "Your rescue was a one in a million thing."

"I am forever in your debt," I said.

Paul grunted, kicked his horse ahead. "Once we have broken through, the time it takes to travel to Konia will be reduced by more than two days. Then the next tunnel must be built. Until then, the Armenians are safer up here, off the supply road. The same applies to you. The Turks are not happy that your fellow Americans have reported these outrages to the wider world."

He had to shout over the whine of a motor that was set on a rough scaffold. The motor turned great wheels that pumped air through pipes into the tunnel. A crew of workers tended the engine and works, carrying wrenches larger than my arm over their shoulders. Paul led me to the tunnel entrance, beneath the pipe suspended from the ceiling. He dismounted, tied the horses to a rail set into the stone wall and gestured for me to follow him into the mountain.

"We build their tunnels, but refuse to hand over the Armenians they want," he shouted into my ear.

As soon as I crossed the threshold of the tunnel, I was instantly warmer. The air was close, and water droplets fell in curtains from the chiseled rock a dozen feet above. I was soon sweating inside my heavy coat. Paul walked alongside a narrow-gauge track, passing an empty ore car. His breath escaped in heavy plumes that hung above his head. We walked toward the sound of a drill deep inside the mountain. I was soon out of breath, even the slightest uphill climb was strenuous for the air was thick and difficult to pull into my lungs.

Paul explained, in short, loud bursts, that since the war's start two tunnels had been completed, but this work was the longest and most dangerous they had encountered. Several workers had died in rock falls. Another had been killed in an accidental explosion. Everyday it seemed one worker or another was injured by rock or by the machinery hauled into place to split the rock. It was tough work, but work that the Turks and Germans desperately wanted completed, whatever the cost. An unbroken rail line from Berlin to Baghdad was the goal, a railway unencumbered by the British or the French, out of range of their naval guns. Its completion guaranteed resources for the German war effort. It meant wealth for the Turks, who could trade with whomever they wished, evading British, French and Russian interference.

After a quarter hour's walk, by my best guess, we began to see signs of activity. Teams of men were filling ore cars or cleaning drill bits or using hammers that I could not have wielded. Water used to cool the drill, and to suppress the rock dust, drained past our feet in a gutter cut into the floor. It ran as a stream out of the tunnel mouth, into a culvert, rimmed with ice, sending a plume of warmed water into the valley. At the rock face a dozen men worked, stripped to the waist, perspiration covering their skin. In the uneven, sputtering light from kerosene lamps they appeared wraith-like. A scene from Dante's Inferno. We were in one of the outer circles of Hell. Paul spoke with one or two, nodded, pointed into the dark. It all seemed vague and disconnected to me. I was sure my father would be able to make sense of it all. I only wanted to begin the walk back. I was claustrophobic, out of breath and nervous of the countless tons of living rock quivering above my head. And still I wanted to find the woman who had nursed me back to health. Perhaps Paul would lead me there next.

"The Turks send inspectors every ten days," Paul said, shouting over the concussion of the drill. "The last inspection was difficult," Paul said, "and that was *before* we moved camp. They threatened to replace me with a German engineer. It seems the Germans are more likely to turn a blind eye to what is happening, if it means completing the rail line. I told the Governor that the Austrian Empire is made up of many people who have lived together for centuries without resorting to this level of barbarism. He laughed."

The drill fell silent, and suddenly every droplet of water off the roof seemed to crash like cymbals into puddles at my feet. The men at the face filed past us, toward the entrance.

"They have set a blast," Paul said. He gestured for me to follow him out. "The *Vilayet*—the Governor—has promised to return with a strong contingent of soldiers."

"How long can you hold out?" I asked.

"Long enough."

"For what?" I asked, tramping heavily behind him.

"You'll see," he said. "Some of these men, and their families, have been with me for nearly a year," Paul said, watching the men walk past. He nodded, spoke, shook the hands of some of them. "They come from the east, most of them."

We arrived at the mouth of tunnel and were greeted by a fierce gust of wind that froze the sweat to my face. I shivered. The stream of wash water running past us in its shallow channel was already forming an icy crust. Paul stopped. I waited next to him.

"I was returned to health by the same woman," Paul said.

I glanced at him, tried to read the expression on his face. It revealed nothing, not even a hint of discomfort due to the elements. The intensity of his glance unsettled me.

"It was a slaughter," he said. He resumed his walk. We reached our horses, and they stamped their hooves, happy to see us, hopeful of imminent shelter. As we untied our horses Paul described the battle of Sarakamis.

"A hundred thousand Turks died in the snows of the Caucasus Mountains fighting the Russians," he said, shouting over the wind. "But you know that, Mr. American Philanthropist."

"That I am not," I said, laughing uncertainly.

"Then you must be a spy," Paul said. "Never mind, I won't tell the Turks."

"I am a very small fish in a large pond," I said.

"As am I," Paul smiled grimly. "I came to Turkey with Pietschmann and the men who rescued you. Our first mission was a rout. In the mountains near Sarakamis I was wounded and separated from my battalion. Shot by the damn Turks in their confusion and terror. Sabik Oshagian rescued me, though he was also injured. He has been with me since. Now that Pietschmann is missing, I have made it my job to protect as many of these people as I can."

"You're saying Pietschmann wouldn't?"

Paul held my gaze. "I'm saying that while we are protected by the mountains, the outside world, the British, the French, and the Americans—especially the Americans—will intervene. That is really why I asked you to come here when we met on Christmas Eve. You have resources at your disposal, I am sure of it. Tell the Americans what is happening. I have a working telegraph station here. Send word now. And we will do our best to hold out until help comes."

There it was. Paul had built a fortress to keep out the Turks. And I was trapped inside it with him. He knew that I was communicating with the State Department, and wanted me to help him. We rode back between the huts, silent, listening to faint strains of music leaking between the spaces between the ramshackle walls.

"That is a *duduk* you hear; their most beautiful music is played on it."

The notes sounded like an oboe, a mournful melody, perhaps more so riding the ragged wind as it chewed its way between the mountains. We did not speak again that day.

"The work here defies belief," I said to Doctor Solvein later that evening. We were billeted in the same house. Nurse Doebli and the good doctor had done away with any pretense of propriety and were sharing a bedroom. I slept in the main room, near the fire pit. Ever suspicious of stray embers, I pushed my mat against the farther wall, preferring flea bites to a premature cremation.

"That is stating the obvious," Solvein said. He had been working to near exhaustion caring for half-starved children and old men crippled by the cruel miles they had covered. He extinguished his lantern and retreated to the bedroom where Nurse Doebli waited for the warmth of his narrow frame against her spine. "The Turks will come," he called through the tattered curtain, "let's hope this Austrian has done enough to keep us alive."

"I sent Ambassador Morgenthau a telegram," I said. "He knows we were planning to come here. Paul wants me to send more cables. Morgenthau will recommend to President Wilson that we help the Armenians."

Solvein laughed. "Not before they help Belgium! But in any case, I believe we are on our own. And the CUP are not a patient lot. Not when there are Armenians to kill."

Safir was nervous when she arrived at work Monday morning. The subway ride was uneventful, though the crowded car smelled like wet dog thanks to a rain that showed no sign of stopping. She hung up her wet coat and hat in the cloakroom and tiptoed to her desk. It was always quiet in Archives, but this morning more so. D'Angelo was nowhere to be seen. She pulled on her gloves, turned on the lighted magnifying glass that sat atop her desk like a giant's monocle, and began to work. Every few minutes her eyes swept the floor, expecting D'Angelo staring at her from a corner, but he did not show himself all day. She had the urge to ask one of the other archivists, but she resisted. She did not want anybody to think she cared a fig about the man.

At six o'clock she found Jefferson waiting with the car outside the museum, just as Weldon had promised.

"Good evening, Miss Turan," he said, holding open the rear door.

Safir was aware that some of her co-workers watched as she slid onto the rear seat. "Good evening, Thomas," she said. "Thank you so much for coming to collect me."

"I am happy to do it," he said, gently pushing shut her door and hopping behind the steering wheel. "In fact, I'd do it even if the senator told me not to."

"You're very kind," she said, touching her cheek to conceal the flush that bloomed on her skin.

"The senator is leaving for Washington, soon," Jefferson said. "He has invited you to his apartment for a dinner that he has prepared himself. He told me not to take no for an answer."

Safir frowned. "I would like to," she said, "but I am so tired and Mustafa needs his dinner."

"I remember Mustafa. Has he recovered from yesterday's ordeal?" Jefferson glanced at her through the rear-view mirror as the car negotiated the traffic on Flatbush Avenue.

"He's fine, absolutely," Safir said. "But he's a creature of habit."

"How about I drop you at the senator's, then you give me your key and I go and feed Mustafa?"

Safir met Jefferson's glance. "You would do that?"

"Delighted," the driver replied. "The senator has been good to me and my family," he said. "I would do anything for his."

She looked out the window at rain-stained buildings as they passed by. She was the daughter of an American senator. What would that woman do? She rummaged through her purse and produced her apartment key. "All right, then, Thomas. We have a deal." She held it up where he could see it.

"Deal," Jefferson said, and shot her a wide grin.

The aroma of roasting chicken wafted into the corridor. Weldon answered the door wearing an apron and holding a large spoon.

"Safir!" he said, leaning in to peck her cheek. "I'm so glad you came, else I'd have enough food for days!" He swept her inside and shut the door.

"Mr. Jefferson has gone back to feed Mustafa," she said, shrugging off her coat and hanging it in the closet as if she'd done it a thousand times. "I hope he's not in trouble."

"Brilliant idea," the senator called back from the kitchen. "He's a clear thinker, a problem solver, that man. And Mustafa is a regal sort, he deserves his supper on time."

Safir ate a glorious meal of roast chicken, boiled potatoes and steamed peppers stuffed with beans and rice. Her stomach groaned under the weight of the food she had forked into her mouth.

"I learned to cook out of necessity," the senator said, when they were seated in the living room with cups of strong coffee. "Bless the Romans, they invented a clay pot to cook their food, and I have used mine since returning to America. It's my most valuable possession—next to the tapestry," he said with a laugh.

"It reminded me of home," Safir said. "My mother was a very good cook."

"I know," Weldon said as he sipped his coffee. "She taught me a little, in the short time we were together." He leaned back in his chair. "That was so long ago," he said, staring into her eyes.

Safir spoke to fill the silence. "Mr. Jefferson said you have to go back to Washington."

Weldon straightened, met her gaze. "I'm sorry, Safir, but I have been away too long. Duty calls."

"Will you tell me more of your story?"

Weldon nodded. "But really, it's your story, Safir."

Solvein was right. The Turks came four days later, thanks to a break in the weather. But Paul had not wasted time. By then his workers had transported all essential materials, food, equipment, horses, goats, and tools from the main camp to the head works. Shelters had been built inside the tunnel itself, beside the ore track. Rock walls were erected at the tunnel entrance, and part way down the winding path. I gave what assistance I could, but mostly I was in the telegraph shack, sending message after message to Morgenthau. No response came. Perhaps the wires had been cut, or they had been intercepted. I was not going anywhere soon, so when I was not composing messages, I assisted Solvein and Doebli moving their surgery into the tunnel, or worked with Sabik Oshagian and his crew reinforcing a reservoir to capture the water that fell through a fissure in the rock a hundred yards inside the tunnel. It must have originated in a hot spring deep underground, for it did not freeze. While we worked, Oshagian told me, in broken German, how Paul had saved his wife and son, along with two dozen other Armenian families, by insisting that they be brought to the tunnels to assist with the drilling and blasting works.

Oshagian was a stocky man, shorter than I by half a head, but strong as a bull. His face had been slashed by a Turk's bayonet when he was a boy, when the soldiers stationed in Erzerum got drunk and came through town, looking to cause trouble. He'd been playing in the street with two friends, had thrown rocks at the soldiers and nearly died for his boldness.

"They have persecuted us for centuries," Oshagian said. "This war is their chance to kill us off for good."

He explained, as we set rock into the wall of the reservoir and chinked it with waxed rope, that after their caravan had been forced from Erzerum, their homes had been ransacked, their possessions stolen. Neighbours, once friendly, took everything that the soldiers left behind. No matter how the war ended there was nothing to go back to.

"But no matter," Oshagian said, tears forming in his eyes. "We thank God for the Effendi's coming."

"It makes no sense," I said.

"Armenia was once a great kingdom, the oldest Christian Empire. But Ottomans destroyed it. There is a saying amongst the Turks: *One Armenian is worse than two devils*. They killed our leaders, our teachers, our priests. Turkey only for the Turks." His face was grim as he spoke. "Our God is not their God," he said.

On the days I spent with Oshagian I learned more about Paul, though my real purpose, I am not proud to admit, was to meet Oshagian's wife. But she remained aloof, segregated from the men and on the few occasions we came together, her eyes remained lowered and she answered my hesitant questions with a quick nod or a shake of her head before hurrying away with her son. She always wore a head scarf that covered most of her face. Even so I was amazed by her beauty. Her eyes were dark, but full of fire. I badly wanted to see in them the same desire I felt for her."

"I have a brother?" Safir felt she was clawing her way out of a deep sleep.

"Had," Weldon said. "Toomas died before you were born."

"Sabik was my mother's husband. What happened to him?"

Weldon sighed. "I will get to that, I promise."

Safir chewed her lower lip to hold back her tears.

"The Turks came, in a long file of mules and horses. As Paul had warned, the local governor led a squadron of soldiers and a baggage train of empty carts pulled by mules. It was a gloriously sunny day, bitterly cold, though the winds had dropped as the morning progressed and I watched their approach with Paul and Oshagian and the Austrian soldiers from behind the stone wall the Armenians had fashioned as a defense. The snow lay in deep drifts on the road below our camp. Above our heads Belemedik Dagh watched the caravan like a brooding giant. The women and children were sent into the tunnel with Solvein and Doebli. No drilling work had been done for three days as Paul put every effort into defending the high pass. The main supply camp had been stripped and abandoned.

"They will be here soon," Paul said. If he was afraid, it was impossible to tell. His gloved hand rested on the butt of his pistol, a familiar pose.

"They think they are bringing us away with them," Sabik Oshagian said, pointing at the empty carts. The anger in his voice was palpable. He crossed his thick arms across his chest and planted his booted feet firmly in the fresh snow. "They are mistaken."

Paul turned his gaze upon his foreman. In the sun his eyes were a glacial blue, and just as cold. "Don't worry, Sabik," he said. "We are ready if they try."

I did not share Paul's confidence. As the Turk caravan approached, I saw the machine gun mounted on sleds, pulled by a pair of horses. A dozen soldiers marched alongside, protecting the weapon. What could four soldiers and an engineer do to stop them?

"Shall we meet them at our front door?" Paul spoke in German and waved at the Austrians to follow.

I joined the procession, but mostly I wanted to be in the tunnel, with Piruz. If the Turks were really here to take the Armenians, I wanted to be close to her one last time. We hiked to the advance wall. The Armenians had cleared the path of snow, and had set stones near the precipice to protect us from soldiers climbing up from the valley. I hurried to catch up with Paul. "Do you think they are in a talking mood?"

"They will say they are inspecting the progress of the tunnel, which is probably true. Then they will ask to see my manifests and book of accounts. That is when they will demand I turn over the Armenians. They will say that they need the men for the army. They will demand the Armenians return to the camps in Konia or Adana."

"So why are you talking? You risk capture or worse."

Paul flashed a rare smile in my direction and switched to English. "It is all politics, Weldon, and most of politics is showmanship. The Turks expect a parlay, but they are not fools. They know that by abandoning the main camp we have no intention of obeying. They will be readying the machine gun while the governor is speaking. If I were them, I'd have a cannon hidden in one of those carts."

The stone wall jutted from the mountain's bony flank, six feet high with footholds on our side for men to stand upon and remain mostly protected. The Turks stopped forty yards from the wall. As Paul had predicted, two men advanced on horseback while the soldiers dismounted and began unpacking the machine gun.

The parlay, if one could call it that, did not last long. The lead Turk, a short man with a flowing mustache and sporting a red fez like Paul's, only with a thick gold tassel, angrily demanded that the wall be removed to allow his troop through. Paul climbed to the top of the wall and greeted the governor in fluent Turkish. I could make out only occasional words. *Greetings something, something Excellency. Most inconvenient will come down. At once.* Paul's words infuriated the *Vilayet*. I didn't need a translator to understand his outrage. He jabbed his finger toward the soldiers standing behind them. Paul held up his arms in a gesture of helplessness, as if he would love to help, but it was beyond his ability. *Two weeks*, I heard him say.

The governor swore, stamped his feet and waved the soldiers to advance. Paul jumped down from the wall into a snowbank, brushed himself off and nodded to Oshagian and his soldiers. An explosion deafened me. The soldiers were caught in an avalanche of rock and ice that swept them, machine gun, horses and all, off the narrow path beyond the arch. Only the governor remained on the road, for his short legs could not carry him fast enough from our defence. Where the Turks had been, rubble now lay a dozen feet thick. Oshagian climbed over the wall. He grabbed the governor roughly by his expensive collar. In French he shouted, "You should have stayed in your office! No more torturing children for you!" In a single, graceful motion he tossed the governor into the abyss.

Screams echoed across the valley. A ponderous silence followed. Oshagian peered over the cliff. He spat into the void, brushed off his sleeves and climbed back over the wall to join us.

Paul slapped Oshagian on the back. He turned to hike back to the camp. "I feel badly for the animals; they did nothing to deserve this."

That evening, the Armenians celebrated. Notes from the *duduk* filled the camp, along with the aroma of stew the women cooked over open fires. The men smoked pipes and passed around jars filled with a sharp liquor that knocked me off my feet. During the festivities I was able, for just a moment, to catch Piruz's eye. She sat near a fire, between Oshagian and Toomas. She shared the victory, though in a restrained, quiet way. I was emboldened by the liquor, and when I passed by, I smiled directly at her, and the look she gave me in return was enough to send me to heaven.

The next morning, I rose early and dressed. My head was sore but I could not lie in bed. I hiked to the tunnel. There I found Paul sitting on a stool. It was just after dawn, the air biting cold, the sky the colour of the pink roses my mother grew in Bethlehem. He had stuck an easel into the snow-covered rock near the edge of the precipice. Perched on an upturned crate, Paul sketched the mountain peaks at sunrise. His bare right hand was red with cold as he held a splinter of charcoal and drew it across the paper with a lightness immune to the elements.

"You seem completely at home," I said, speaking through chapped lips and doing my best to ignore the itching cold in my fingers and toes.

He did not look up. "I wish to preserve a piece of this place."

"Mountains look the same to me," I said.

He let his hand fall into his lap. "If I showed you a dozen such drawings, would you be able to tell me the scenes that are Austrian and those that are Turkish?"

"I'm afraid not," I replied.

Paul swiveled to face me. "Mountains are unique. As well, they are immune to the superficial variations of the season. The ice that lies thick on the saddles between peaks does not succumb in summer. See?" He pointed his bare hand to the most prominent peak looming four thousand feet above us.

"That is Belemedik Dagh. The highest of the mountains we cross. We are perched on his shoulder, boring our way like ants through his body to reach the northern way. Back in Austria, miners in every village from Ötz to Wollan pray to the spirit of their mountain to protect them, even as they wrench gold, garnets and coal from the depths. Every stray rock fall they attribute to its displeasure; every nugget brought to the surface is an omen of good fortune. Through it all the mountain sits and waits, ignoring our efforts."

"The ocean," I said. "The ocean is greater than a mountain."

Paul's shoulders shook with laughter. "I suppose you're right, my friend. An ocean is greater than a mountain."

"Sailors pray to the ocean spirits to keep them safe," I said.

"King Neptune, eh? It says much about us, that we look for benevolent gods wherever we are in danger."

"Don't you?"

Paul cocked an eyebrow. "I do not pray," he said, "to any god, but I do honor beauty, and these mountains—look how the morning sun colours the snow a delicate rose quartz. It is all the cathedral I require," he said.

"It is beautiful," I said, "though in present circumstances beauty is secondary. I am like the miner who prays for salvation."

"You take your superstition with a dose of pragmatism. Probably for the best."

A cadre of men appeared, pushing an empty rail car into the tunnel. Each man saluted as they passed. Paul watched them closely. "The locals we have hired on are no different than the miners back home. They are just as superstitious and easily frightened. Every crack in the rock is a sign, every loose stone that falls a warning."

"And what do they say about the tunnel? Will the mountain spirit grant safe passage?"

"Science and superstition coexist, but while the former guarantees an outcome, the latter relies on luck. I am a man of science. The drill we use has a specified capacity, designed for the particular rock it must pierce. There are no ghosts or mountain spirits to dull the bit, no matter what these men believe."

"But you must humour them, to get them to work?"

Paul squinted into the distance, then touched his charcoal to the paper, adding a detail to his sketch. "They work to avoid death. They have seen the evidence, first hand, of what awaits if the Turks retake them. As devout as they are, they do not expect God to pluck them up and carry them to America. It is to engineers and their machines and their own toil they look. They endure the underground because they must. It is better than waiting. We drill upwards and to the east, where there is a road, a path fit only for goats and shepherds. When their hammer blows smash through and we take that path out of the mountains to find sanctuary they will thank God. But they will know, too, there was nothing divine in their rescue. Science and strength will win the day, not superstition and religion."

Paul caught my glance. "Remember, young Weldon Scott, that when difficulties mount by whatever means at your disposal, you must climb higher. Above the fog, above the clouds. Above the noise. Always higher. That is all we are doing here."

The Turks had no idea that the drills had delved so deeply into the mountain. Under Paul's direction the drillers and blasters had veered from the designed track, to delve an escape. By making the tunnel eighty percent smaller the men made great progress. As the drillers worked the last rock face Paul rallied the Armenians, the local shepherds and labourers, to increase their efforts. Oshagian exhorted his comrades, reminding them where they, their wives, and their children would be if not for the blue-eyed *Effendi*. Even the children helped as they could. The camp was swarming with action as it prepared for the evacuation.

Paul invited me to the shack he used as an office and laid a map of the Taurus Mountains across a makeshift table. He traced his finger north and east. It rested on a village named Yelatan.

"Here is our best chance to protect the Armenians," he said.

"How far is it?"

"One hundred kilometres, perhaps one hundred and ten."

"Sixty miles?" I asked. "But there are no roads. How can we travel so far? There are children, old women. We've only five horses."

Paul looked at me. I was getting used to the feeling of being talked to as if I were an ignorant child. "There are roads, they are just not on the maps. The locals have used them for centuries."

"By locals you mean mountain goats," I said.

"There are several men among us who know these mountains better than any Turk. They will lead us, once the drill has broken through."

I was doubtful. "But the snow is too deep. Perhaps in the Spring?"

"The Turks will not wait for Spring. Besides, there are one hundred and thirty-four mouths to feed, including yours. Our food will not last."

"We nearly died coming here," I grumbled, dreading the idea of forging through waist deep snow.

Paul winked. "But you were not on skis!"

He led me to Oshagian's hut near the tunnel entrance. Row after row of wooden skis leaned against the wall. He knocked on the door and entered. Three Armenian women were seated around a long, rough table. Their sleeves were rolled up to their elbows while they worked to fix leather straps through holes augured in the sides of wooden skis. Another woman hammered iron cleats to the flat face of each ski.

"These bindings are simple and crude, but they will hold," Paul said, inspecting a ski. "We have repurposed our mining equipment, even the crates they came in."

He gestured to one of the women. She set down her work and approached us shyly, her eyes lowered. It was Piruz, and when she looked at me directly my legs turned to jelly.

"Good day, Frau Oshagian," Paul spoke in halting Armenian. "You of course remember Mr. Scott? The American?"

She smiled at me while Paul spoke.

"I am so very grateful," I said, and reached out my hand in greeting. Piruz hesitated, glanced at Paul before grasping my hand and quickly withdrawing it. The touch of her warm skin was like an electric current. She returned to her place at the table and took up the ski she was working on.

"She is as capable a foreman as Sabik," Paul said with a proud smile. "Piruz and her women form the skis over steam to curve their tips. We have made the bindings loose, to accept such boots and shoes as we possess. We are also fashioning poles. Two poles per person for greater balance. In the Norwegian style. Speed is critical. Axle grease will serve to waterproof the skis. Every man, woman, and child will ski through these mountains on paths known only to the villagers who mined the Belemedik Dagh."

Piruz must have understood Paul's speech was a compliment, for she blushed deeply. Her eyes, in the flickering light of the shack, were a luminous shade of green, set off by her sun-browned skin. While so many Armenian women wore their hardships and sorrow in deep lines and bent backs, Piruz appeared untouched by her travails, save for thin lines etched into the corners of her eyes.

Paul thanked Piruz and apologized for interrupting her work. She bowed her head in silent courtesy. The small boy I had seen before rushed to her, proudly brandishing a set of leather bindings he had tied. She bent closer to see his offering, and kissed the top of his head.

"Toomas. Sabik's son," Paul said as he led me from the shack.

"She is a beautiful woman," I said, shivering in the cold, damp air of the tunnel.

Paul shot me a look. "Sabik's wife is a gem among women. And she loves Oshagian completely."

"It is noble, what you are doing."

Paul stopped in his tracks. "You are ten thousand kilometres from home. How is that less noble?"

I blushed. "It is not the same thing at all," I said.

Paul chuckled. "No, maybe not. You have seen Piruz, and are besotted. You would rather cut off your arm than leave her."

Weldon turned to Safir and sighed. "He was right, of course."

It was late when Jefferson drove her home. As she put on her coat the senator made one more plea for Safir to move into the apartment.

"I would feel much better knowing you are here, when I am mired in Washington."

"I will think about it," she said. "It's so much all at once."

"Jefferson could stay in New York. I can spare him most days, my apartment in DC is close to my office in the Senate."

She passed a night in restless sleep, and returned to work to no D'Angelo. But instead of improving things, an uncomfortable feeling gripped her. Not only did she expect him to appear at any moment, she was now the subject of gossip in the archives. At the luncheonette she overheard two colleagues whispering that D'Angelo was having some sort of marriage trouble, and they looked at her sideways. Safir asked the waitress to wrap her sandwich and she found a bench across from the museum. The sky was dark and threatened rain, but she unwrapped her sandwich and placed the wax paper across the wooden seat and ate before the rain started. The afternoon was no better. She felt smothered by unwanted attention, which she had done nothing to deserve. It was agony watching the hour hand on the clock drag itself toward six.

At the end of her shift she fled the museum into the rain. Traffic on Washington Street was heavy, the tires of passing cars sizzled across the wet pavement. She was afraid to ride the subway and feel the accusing eyes of strangers upon her. A bone-deep weariness glued her feet to the sidewalk. She was close to tears. She bit her lower lip and forced herself to move, slowly, each step heavier than the last. Her mother's face appeared, her dark, brooding eyes as distant and guarded as always. The senator's confession had changed everything and nothing. She returned to the New York Library, Central Branch. She climbed the stairs and pushed through the heavy doors.

It was mouse quiet inside, despite the many people passing through her field of vision. The air carried a whiff of furniture polish and old books. The heaviness lifted off her bones. She approached the reception desk and leaned against the smooth granite counter, her palms pressed against its cool surface.

"May I help you?" A bespectacled woman in a blue dress glanced up at her from a large desk covered in books and newspapers. Her short, curly hair was neatly pinned flat with a silver barrette. She wore a necklace of small stones, perhaps they were pearls.

"I don't know if you remember me, I was here recently, asking about a senator."

The librarian removed her glasses, letting them hang from their cord. "I do. How can I help you today?"

"Do you have books about Armenia? My mother was Armenian," Safir said.

The woman smiled. "Then that makes you Armenian, as well." The tone of her voice made the statement a question. "We have many," she added, patting Safir's hand. "Come with me."

The librarian led Safir to a card file that filled a wall behind the reception desk. "Here," the woman said, riffling through the A's. "Do you know your way around the stacks?"

"Not really," Safir said.

"New to Brooklyn?" the librarian said. Her dark-rimmed glasses pinched upwards at the corners. She reminded Safir of a well-fed Siamese cat.

Safir shook her head, embarrassed.

"Never mind, we're all busy. My name is Harriet Dickinson. I am one of the senior librarians here. I'll show you around."

Harriet pulled a dozen books from the shelves on Armenia. She gave half to Safir and together they carried them like gold bricks to a table near a window. Harriet set her stack down and disappeared, returning two minutes later with a small *Reserved* sign that she set on the stack.

"There. If you want to take some home, see me and we'll sign you up for a library card. If you don't want to check any out, you can come back anytime and they will be here for you. Just put them in one of the carts when you are done, or bring them to me and we will re-shelve them. Happy reading."

"Thank you," Safir said, grateful for the librarian's kindness.

She took off her coat and hung it on the back of a chair and settled herself in front of the stack. These books contained answers. To use against the fear that suffocated her. She picked up the first book, a dusty memoir written by a German officer stationed in Ottoman Turkey during the First World War. He described caravans of women and children driven from their homes to die in the desert. He had taken photographs. She pored over grainy photos of naked bodies lying in gutters. Her fingers trembled as she turned the pages, each image capturing unimaginable misery. Her flesh crawled and her bones ached. Her mother could be one of those haunted, wretched souls that stared into the camera lens with resignation and despair.

Each day after work Safir returned to the library, to her stack of books. She brought a pencil and paper to make notes. She found, in one pamphlet, an address and telephone number for an Armenian Cultural Association in Queens. At work the next day, during her lunch break, she dialed the number, but there was no answer. She was not sure what she would have said, had anybody picked up, but she wanted somebody to confirm to her that the horrific things she had seen and read were true.

When she was home, after studying, she wrote to Bey.

I am in a terrible state, Sister. I believe it must be the after affects of Celik's death.

I have made the acquaintance of an American senator. It is hard to explain, I know, but he sought me out. He knew our mother long ago, before I was born. He has told me things I scarcely believe. Things I haven't the courage to tell you—yet. What do you know of Mother's childhood? Did they tell stories after I left? Please, if you know any, send them to me. Our parents' early years are darkness and mystery to me and I am desperate for answers. Perhaps it is too many years of living alone that makes me so in need. Write soon.

Love, Safir.

She rummaged through a box set high on a shelf in her closet. Photographs and letters, scraps that had followed her around. She found the photo she was looking for: taken by a street photographer at the train station in Istanbul in the late summer of 1936. She was on her way to Paris; the four Turan family members together on the platform. The train had just pulled in. Piruz stood behind Bey, her arms resting on Bey's slender shoulders. Piruz was looking beyond the camera, to where the train was going. Bey's grin showed the missing tooth from when she'd fallen and knocked it out. The gap was old enough to be part of who she was. Safir stared at the camera with a rigid, worried look that was as much hers as Bey's missing tooth. Celik stood behind her, his arms full of luggage. At the moment the picture was taken he must have been adjusting a strap, for his right arm was bent at the elbow, a blur of motion. The man looked poised to strike the daughter frozen in front of him. His expression was one of impatience, frustration, or fatigue. When her mother had sent her the photograph, she'd looked at it once and put it aside. She'd been with Theo then, and her family were a long way from her. Now it was just Bey and her. She smoothed the bent corners of the photograph and set it on her dresser, leaning against the wall.

After work on Saturday, Safir went to the library, signed up for a library card, checked out three books from the pile and carried them in a string grocery bag back to her apartment. She spent Saturday night reading at her table in the kitchen, her notepad filling with scribbled facts and dates as the ashtray filled with ash and cigarette butts. Mustafa circled against her bare shins, complaining loudly that she was ignoring him. She devoured Armenian history, returning always to the terrible years of 1915 and 1916. She paused only for the photographs, wondering if the long-dead eyes that looked into the camera were distant aunts or cousins who might have known her mother, or Sabik or Toomas.

When she met the senator on Sunday for lunch, she greeted him with an envelope. "I have written some questions for you. For when you are back in Washington. I thought perhaps you could write to me with the answers?"

Weldon removed a single sheet of neatly folded paper and scanned the page. "You didn't have to do this. I told you that you can ask me anything."

"I have been reading," she said. "I have so many questions I didn't want to forget them. They come to me when I cannot sleep."

"You do look tired," Weldon said. "How was your week? I have missed you."

"There are days when this seems like a dream." She frowned. "But my boss, Vincenzo D'Angelo, was not at work this week. That was better, in some ways."

"Interesting," Weldon said, avoiding her glance.

"It is," she said. "Though the gossip is terrible."

Weldon cleared his throat, ducking to read from the page Safir had given him. *"Do I have any other brothers or sisters?"*" He read out. He lowered the letter and shook his head. "No, you do not," he said. "Toomas was your mother's only son. She was changed, after he died."

"In what way?"

Weldon frowned. "In the ways you would expect a mother who has lost her child to change. She withdrew, became colder, more severe. Even after your birth—especially after your birth—Piruz was always serious, rarely joyful. I trust you witnessed that side of her?"

"It was the only side of her," Safir said, avoiding Weldon's gaze.

"She was terrified of losing you, as well," Weldon said.

"That's not how it felt," she said. "I went to the library," Safir said, changing the subject. "The pictures in the books show terrible things."

Weldon sighed. "I don't know how such things happen, Safir, but I know why. Ignorance." The early afternoon light streaming through the windows illuminated deep lines on his face and revealed the anguish in his eyes. "Ignorance fuels the fires of hate. Knowledge and empathy are anathema to them."

Safir met his glance and smiled. "I accept."

Weldon's face brightened. "Safir!" He jumped from his chair and hugged her tightly. "Thank you, thank you, thank you!"

She hugged him back, inhaling the astringent scent of his after shave.

"You are a good daughter to this foolish old man," he whispered into her ear.

"I estimate four days to reach Yelatan, if the weather holds," Paul said.

We stood at the furthest reach of the tunnel. I stood halfway up a pile of rubble, for in the interest of speed they had not laid rail track to carry away rock. Beyond the rubble the tunnel diameter shrank until it was barely large enough for two men to stand side by side. The horses stamped and needed to be cajoled into the narrowing space. Every member of the camp was present to witness the breakthrough. The air in the tunnel was tropical, sticky and humid. A cascade of water droplets like a summer shower fell roof. I was perspiring heavily in the funk. I smelled terrible and the closeness only served to remind me how long it had been since I had bathed. Excitement rippled through the onlookers. The drills were close.

Paul lay on the ground behind the miners, directing the men to the spot to set the drill point. Satisfied, he retreated as they started to drill. Our ears were shocked at the percussion of the drill as the bit penetrated the rock face. For a moment I imagined that Belemedik Dagh itself had cried out, pierced one final time by the sweating ants burrowing through it. Paul wore a thin cotton shirt, open at the collar, the sleeves rolled up to the elbow to reveal the ropy muscles of his forearms. Years of climbing and skiing were proof Paul was not the kind of engineer content to remain behind a desk. He wiped the sweat from his brow with a handkerchief as he approached. Even in the dim of the cavern his blue eyes sparkled like gems.

"This rock is very hard," he said. "Harder than much of the rock in the Alps. It is old rock, and gives way grudgingly. It is a good thing we are at the end, for our drill is almost beyond repair."

The excitement in his voice was contagious. I grinned and gave him a thumb's up sign as he hurried back to the drill crew. I saw Piruz and Toomas at the front of the gathered men, women, and children. Piruz was pressing her hands over Toomas's ears to block out the roar of the drill. If she saw me wave, she gave no sign. Solvein and Doebli waved at me, caught up in the fervour. Though we had not spoken much of late we knew enough to celebrate joyful news.

A shaft of light suddenly entered the tunnel, dancing off thousands of minerals set in the walls. Sunlight's first caress revealed colours unimaginable by torchlight. I gasped at veins of rose, purple, gentian, and gold, glittering like stars. Joyous shouts filled the air, and everyone shouldered closer to the smoking drill.

I stood in a gallery of sparkling gems. My thoughts were a swinging pendulum between victory and humility for what we had done. We had disemboweled Belemedik Dagh like worms in topsoil, and now celebrated like school children freed for summer holidays. Paul ordered the crew to pull the drill away. Split and broken rock tumbled around his booted feet. Daylight shouldered through the growing opening, turning every drop of condensation into a glittering diamond, a dazzling, tumbling curtain surrounding us in divine light.

Paul gestured to Sabik and his crew to follow him. The opening was still so small he had to crawl through the last shelf of broken rock. His boots vanished into the ragged circle of daylight. Sabik and the drill crew disappeared after Paul. A waiting silence filled the main tunnel. Sabik's head soon reappeared, silhouetted in the mountain's wound. "All good!" he shouted.

Men and women pushed past me to clamber through the narrow cleft in the rock. One after the next they wriggled through. I watched Piruz hurry past me to join Sabik. She gripped Toomas's hand tightly. She smiled shyly but I could think of nothing to do but smile back like a stunned fool. She waved at me to follow. I needed no further invitation. I crawled on my knees and elbows, my eyes on the soles of Toomas's felt shoes, and wriggled through the still-warm rock onto a flat plateau the size of a small courtyard. Sabik's crews were pushing aside snow and broken rock, widening the gap to allow our animals through. The Armenians danced in a circle, kicking up snow, tossing snowballs at each other and laughing and embracing. A capricious breeze whipped past the mountain's shoulders, stinging our bare faces. The mountain tops had vanished in cloud. I found Paul standing at the edge of the ledge with Sabik. Piruz and Toomas flanked Sabik, their arms around his waist.

"Tomorrow we say goodbye to you," Paul said, staring up at Belemedik Dagh's shrouded peak.

Sabik laughed, translated for his family, who cheered.

Paul slapped Sabik's shoulder and pointed north. "Pozanti lies over there," he turned and faced east, "but tomorrow we go there," he said. "We will ski out of this vale into one that bends toward Yelatan and the plateau. The Turks will not know our whereabouts for weeks."

"You are sure there is a path?" I asked. When I gazed over the edge, I saw only steep, snow-covered faces with no purchase, no means of traverse.

"There is a path," Paul said. "The local men know it well. There is a stone bridge that crosses the river. Once across our disappearance will be complete."

"Can the children hold up for three days?" I asked.

Piruz somehow understood my question, for she pushed Toomas ahead of her and spoke quickly, firmly, to Sabik.

"My wife says the children are lions, strong and courageous. They will not give up."

I shivered in the cold, swirling wind. Paul reached into a pocket of his woolen pants and retrieved a small, silver flask. He uncorked the top and took a short sip from it.

"Brandy," he said, offering me the flask. "I have saved it for today. Take some and pass it to Sabik."

I touched the flask to my lips and the brandy instantly burned my throat, warming my insides. I handed Sabik the flask. He stared at the pewter vessel, then drank and returned it to Paul. I watched Piruz's eyes, so wide, so beautiful in the sunlight, as they followed Sabik. Something other than brandy heated my heart.

"Why are you doing this?" I asked Paul, tearing my glance from Piruz as she embraced Sabik.

Paul's smile vanished. "When I was a boy, my uncle and I climbed many mountains. When this war is over, I will climb with him again. In the Zillertal he feels closer to God." He clapped his hands together against the cold and jammed them into his pockets. "You know I don't share his faith. Since coming here, I have met good men like Sabik, and bad men like the Turkish governor Sabik introduced to the abyss. I refuse to build another tunnel using people who know their only future is death. We will escape to Yelatan, where I hope to find sanctuary with the Red Cross. If we do, it will not be God's doing, but yours, my American friend."

"The world is praying for an end to this war, so that Sabik and his family will not be persecuted."

"The battlefields are overflowing with good Christians, Jews, and Moslems who blow each other to pieces while their wives and mothers pray for their safety. Prayer convinces men to live on their knees. Sabik, tell the others to make ready. Weldon, make sure that Doctor Solvein is packed. We leave before first light tomorrow."

Safir filled one box with kitchen supplies, her spices and hand towels, both of her cups and saucers, her copper *cezve* for making coffee, and one decorative spoon from the Eiffel Tower. There was not much in the ice box to take: one egg, half a stick of butter, a small bottle of milk and a near empty tin of cat food. She put these supplies in a string bag and set it by the door, next to a heavy box of record albums. The photograph from the train station stuck out between two records. She rolled up the Meyer poster and stuck it in the string bag. She had one battered suitcase of clothes. When the senator's car came for her Thomas insisted on carrying everything. She stood on the curb, smoking a cigarette, gripping Mustafa tightly under one arm. She stared up at her apartment windows; the years spent behind those glass panels already seemed blurry. Jefferson made three quick trips, each time to place her belongings in the trunk. When he slammed the lid shut it made a hollow sound that reverberated in her chest.

She slid into the back seat. Mustafa struggled to be free of her grasp. "You are homesick so soon," she said as Mustafa hopped onto the ledge in front of the rear windshield. At once he sprawled full length to bask in the sun. "Maybe you're just lazy," Safir said, turning her back on him.

The senator met them in the lobby and insisted on carrying a box into the elevator. He was buoyant, giddy, unable to contain his excitement. "Look," he said, when they were inside the apartment, "I have made room for your belongings!" He pointed to a bare space on the book case.

He handed her a key with a flourish, and took her on a tour. "I've moved my things out of the big bedroom," he said. "I've stored them in wardrobe and closet in the spare room. I promise to clear it all out as soon as I can. I hope that's not a problem."

Safir shook her head. "It's a beautiful piece of furniture."

"Yes, I had it shipped from Austria, but it's too large for my apartment in Washington, so I had it brought here."

"Please don't go to any more trouble," Safir said.

Jefferson set the records on the shelf. Weldon pulled one cardboard sleeve and squinted at the text. "*Beethoven's Concerti for Pianoforte and Orchestra,*" he read aloud. "Wilhelm Kempff. You have impeccable taste," he said, glancing at her. "But then, you are my daughter. May I play it? Piano Concerto Number Five is one of my favorites."

"Mine also," she said, retreating to the kitchen to empty her box of supplies. She closed her eyes; the music brimming from the phonograph gave her goosebumps. Each cupboard she opened was filled with everything she could want, including a new electric toaster, new pots and pans. The icebox held fresh vegetables, milk, butter, eggs, and cheese. "You didn't need to shop for me," she called.

When she returned to the living room, she found Mustafa curled on the sofa, sound asleep. She moved to shoo him away.

"No, no," the senator said over the music, "this is as much his apartment as yours. He can claim any spot he wishes." Weldon suggested they go to dinner to celebrate her arrival in Manhattan. Jefferson drove them to *Bemelmans* at the Carlyle.

Weldon introduced her to the smiling maître d'. "My daughter has had a long and difficult life, but I have successfully rescued her from the darkest depths of Brooklyn."

They all laughed. The maître d' walked like there were springs in his shoes and Safir felt the colour rising in her cheeks as they were escorted to their table. They ordered wine with their dinner, and Safir was glad to consent to a glass of her own. They settled into their booth with their wine and breadsticks. The sounds of people enthralled with drink, food, and each other settled on Safir's skin like cashmere. Half a glass of wine and she was feeling drowsy. Their food had just arrived when a man, dressed as immaculately as Weldon, approached from across the restaurant.

"Senator Scott?" he said, his hands in the pockets of his grey slacks. He wore a narrow, plaid bow tie matched by a crisply folded pocket handkerchief sharp enough to draw blood. He looked no older than Safir.

Weldon looked up from his steak. "Ahh, Doctor Young, is it? Forgive me, I'm getting forgetful as I get older."

The man cocked one thin eyebrow as his glance shifted from Weldon to Safir. "Yes. Yes. That's right. Doctor Young. How are you, Senator? Will you be in New York long?"

"Actually, I'm here tonight with my daughter." Weldon set down his fork and gestured to Safir.

"Daughter? Congratulations, Senator. Good evening, Miss…"

"Safir Turan," Safir said.

"Pleasure to meet you, Miss Turan. Call me Walter. All my friends do," he said, glancing at Weldon.

"Will you join us?" Weldon said, starting to shift over on the bench.

"No, I don't mean to interrupt," Walter said, stepping away from their booth. "I thought I saw you come in and wanted to double check. Next time, perhaps."

"Nice to meet you," Safir said.

Weldon stood to shake hands. "I'll call you?" Walter nodded crisply and vanished into the dimness of the restaurant.

Weldon sat down with a sigh. "He's a brilliant physician. His family are quite well situated in Bethlehem. They generously donated to my last campaign."

"You must have to remember so many people, being in politics," Safir said.

"That's a fact," Weldon said. "Now, where were we? Yes, the story. And we'd better not let these steaks get cold."

We left before sunrise. Paul transformed the confusion of shivering men, women, children, and horses who scrambled through the tunnel's exit into a column fit to travel. Watched over by an expanse of stars and the first ribbons of daylight, we helped each other put on the skis the women had fashioned. They were heavier and shorter than regular skis, but wider, better for deep snow. Shrieks of laughter echoed off the mountains at the first, awkward attempts on the plateau of Belemedik Dagh. Even Paul shared the fun. "See, Weldon, what I have done with my easel?" he called as he skied past me with remarkable ease. He had converted the easel's frame into his skis, and the rear support was now his pole. He carved graceful turns in the snow. He had discarded his red fez for a wool cap like the Armenian men wore.

Eventually the children's enthusiasm was directed to the tasks ahead. Our caravan formed a single, discernable line that spiraled like a giant snail's shell, filling the shelf outside the tunnel. I was placed near the front, close to Oshagian and Piruz and Toomas. I spoke sparingly to Sabik, and never to Piruz with her husband so close, but I was sure she knew how I felt about her, from the myriad, lovesick glances I sent her way. If Sabik suspected my true feelings he gave no indication. The Armenian miners and their families came next, with the loaded horses. Koelrasch, Bildstein, Huebner, and Makiymowicz held the rear. Solvein and Doebli were somewhere in the middle, helping the infirm and two injured miners who could not use skis. I skied behind Paul and two wiry shepherds from Yelatan who knew every goat trail between the Cilician Gates and Yelatan. The winds had dropped, meaning our progress was tested by fallen snow and daggers of ice that clung to the rock.

Paul did not hesitate. He pushed the caravan to ski hard, as quickly as possible. Once all were on the trail, he slipped to the side, allowing the line to pass. His movements were spare, crisp as he glided weightlessly atop the snow. He made sure we kept moving with words of encouragement to each skier. I was used to being on skis thanks to the many holidays my family had enjoyed, so I, too, slid aside and helped where I could, steadying the unsure, adjusting their crude bindings, encouraging with shouts of appreciation. Few of the Armenians had seen skis before, let alone tried to use them. They were heavy, which made travel harder. But most were quick to learn how to place their feet, using their poles for balance. Progress was much faster than trying to plow through snowdrifts on foot.

The men from Yelatan led our caravan north and east, piloting a way between the tall peaks that loomed above us. The way was very steep in places, and the Armenians fell often, struggling to right themselves in the fresh snow. More than once I came to Piruz's aid, where she floundered in drifts, sending up billows of powder in her frustration. I took her arm and lifted her sideways, so that her skis could rise above the snow and support her weight. Once, I brushed ice crystals from her cheek. Her smile, from behind a red scarf she had wound across her face, was as bright as the sun on the snow and I was more lost than before. I blamed the scarlet flush across my face on the cold. I think I made her laugh.

Despite the cold and snow there was a celebratory spirit throughout the caravan. We had outsmarted the Turks, if we survived. Still, progress was slow, and dangerous. It was soon clear that without the men from Yelatan to guide us, we would have been lost. The way back was no longer possible, uphill in deep snow. It was gravity and the certainty of the guides that kept our caravan going.

Paul halted an hour before dark, for there was much to do and the Armenians were chilled through and exhausted. He stopped where a heavy curtain of snow hung low across our path, and directed Sabik and me to dig out a space where we could camp. This was harder work than a day's skiing. We used the sleds to load out snow and pile it as a windbreak. As we worked, we saw that our roof was exposed rock, so at least if the snow came loose it might block our exit, but wouldn't bury us where we slept.

Doctor Solvein and Doebli helped the women build cooking fires, and began to heat water for soup and tea. It was the best tea I had ever tasted. The skin on my face was raw, my fingers frozen and my legs were stiff. I could only imagine what the Armenians were experiencing, but save for an infant's occasional wail, I heard no complaints.

After tending to the horses, Paul led Sabik, the Austrian soldiers and me to a place he had scouted with the guides. The sun had nearly dropped behind the mountains. A frigid wind now blasted its way through the pass, whipping up a froth of snow and hurling it into our eyes. Paul's mustache was caked with ice, and his sunburned face only served to deepen the blue of his eyes.

"This is the start of the stone bridge I told you about. It will take us over the river and into the next valley," he said in German.

"Is it passable in the wind?" Sabik asked.

Paul spoke Turk to the men from Yelatan. They had lived all their lives in these mountains, but had never been on skis before. They had learned quickly, and were proud of their new skill.

"Yes," Paul translated. The most dangerous section was only a dozen metres long, where there were no walls for us to use. "We must rope each other together well before this," Paul said. "We will anchor the rope into the rock ahead. Tomorrow," he said, looking at me, "I will need you up front with me, to help the guides. Sabik and Koelrasch, you will take the rear."

On the return to camp I spoke in English to Paul. "This is beyond the children and elderly. I have doubts for myself, and I have skied many times."

Paul did not meet my glance. "We will go slowly. But we cannot stay here and wait for the snow to get deeper. Once we are past the throat, the way will get easier."

I slipped through a wall of piled snow into the cavern that was my part of camp. I found Solvein and Doebli at a makeshift kitchen, serving soup. They were weary, but I had never seen them more content. They worked together as if rehearsing a dance, one never interfering with the other's movements. Doebli smiled at Solvein each time their eyes met. She had lost two toes on this adventure, but her spirits were high and she worked harder than any to ease the suffering of the Armenians.

As darkness filled the cavern and the meal fires were banked to embers, I struggled to sleep, despite my exhaustion. Restless, I rose from my bed of skis and blankets and sought the nearest fire, now only a winking, red eye in the dark. I squatted by the fire, extending my hands toward warmth. As my eyes grew accustomed to the dimness, I noticed I was not alone. A woman sat near the fire, her hands hovering over the embers for warmth. The bare skin of her lower arms glowed like bronze. Piruz smiled at me and my knees turned to jelly.

"You ski fine," she said in halting German.

Her low voice thrilled me, like the deepest notes of a bass after the bow has been drawn slowly across the strings. I did not reply until the last trace of her voice had dissolved into the darkness.

"Thank you," I replied, in terrible Armenian. I badly wanted to tell her she was the most beautiful woman in the world, but instead I said, "You did well today." I used German to fill the gaps in my vocabulary.

Piruz's smile widened. "Thanks to you," she said. "You were kind with Toomas."

"Where have you learned German?"

"The Effendi," she said.

"Sabik saved him," I said, gripping my leg to illustrate my words.

Piruz nodded slowly. "Bad," she said. "But now Effendi saves us."

"In Yelatan we will be safe," I said, trying to sound convincing. "Americans waiting." I hoped I wasn't lying.

She stared into the banked coals, her lips pressed tightly together. I will never forget her eyes, in the embers of that dying fire they reflected something darker than night.

Outside the Carlyle Hotel the senator stood next to Safir as the car idled at the curb.

"The Concierge says my room is ready, so good night, Safir. I must tell you, this is the happiest day of my life, save perhaps the day I fell in love with your mother." Weldon held Safir's hands in his own. "After so many years, to have you in my life is a gift from Heaven."

"I'm not used to you telling people I am your daughter."

"Does that bother you?" The senator's smile dimmed.

"No. I'm not sure," she said.

"But now you are home. Take as much time as you need."

She nodded. "I am very grateful."

"Good," he said, his smile returning. "I will come by tomorrow to check on you. Sleep well." He moved close to give her a hug. The faint, astringent scent of aftershave lay on his collar.

"Thank you," she said, retreating to the car. She waved after Jefferson closed her door. She watched out the window until Weldon turned and slipped into the hotel.

Safir sat in silence in the back seat of the limousine. Once, the tires hit a bad pothole and jolted her out of her reverie.

"Sorry," Jefferson said.

"Don't be silly, Thomas," she said. "You are a very good driver. It is the roads that are to blame."

"They're not what they used to be," he replied.

"Where are you from, Thomas? If you don't mind me asking."

"Baltimore," he said.

"Is it a good place?"

He tilted his head to look at her in the rear-view mirror. "Okay," he said. "It was better during the war. Busier. Lots of work. People knew what they were doing. Still, I got no complaints."

"Then it's a good place," she said.

"Where you from, Miss, if you don't mind *me* asking a personal question."

"I don't mind," she said, staring out the window. "And it's Safir, remember?"

"I remember," Jefferson said.

As the car accelerated the streetlamps became glowing silver dollars threaded like beads hanging in the evening air.

"A town called Hereke, near Istanbul, but apparently that's not where I was born. I used to live in Paris, then I lived in Brooklyn. Now I live in Manhattan." She looked down at her gloved hands. "I'm sorry, Thomas. I sound like a spoiled child."

"You're the furthest thing from that," Thomas said. "You've seen a lot of this world," he said.

"I suppose I have," Safir said, catching his glance.

She awoke with sunshine on her eyelids. It filled her room, and the pale blue walls reminded her of a robin's egg. With her toe she felt for the lump at the foot of the bed that was Mustafa. He slept in luxurious sprawl. She laughed, threw back the blanket and opened the curtains. The boulevard trees were in bloom, pillows of pink floating below her. Central Park was a thick, green ribbon before her eyes. She pulled on her robe and scratched the cat's head as she passed.

"Breakfast," she said, and Mustafa hopped off the bed to follow her.

Her toes tingled at the feel of thick carpet, so much warmer than old linoleum and no chance of getting a splinter from the scuffed hardwood of her hallway. She filled the kettle with water and set it on the stove to boil. While she waited, she fed Mustafa and opened every drawer. The contents of each lay obediently in place on a bed of floral paper that looked like it had been placed the day before. No crumbs, no stains, no smells. A kitchen to put even the fussiest housewife to shame.

"What do you think?" she asked Mustafa, but he was too intent on his food to look up.

She found the teapot. It was Georgian. She imagined Lord and Lady in their English castle, entertaining other lords and ladies. She was royalty, or at least a reimagined Pygmalion.

When the kettle boiled, she removed the lid. She was about to fill the pot when she noticed something inside. She thought Weldon had left an old tea bag to dry out, so out of keeping with everything else, but her hand emerged with an envelope, folded in three.

To celebrate your new beginning! was written across the front with a fountain pen. She tore open the envelope and counted one hundred and fifty dollars in various denominations. More than two month's wages. She spread them across the counter and her hands began to shake.

Weldon came to the apartment later in the morning. She greeted him at the door, and he sensed her agitation at once. "You found my gift," he said. "Have I offended you?"

"I was surprised," she said, pecking his cheek. "After all you have done for me."

Weldon removed his coat and hat and hung them in the hall closet. "Can't a father show his daughter his gratitude? You have come back to me. There isn't enough money in the world to measure how happy I am." He hugged her, then stepped back, his eyes sparkling. "I was hoping you would come with me to church this morning," he said. When she agreed, he hurried down the hall and disappeared into the spare room. He reappeared with a package tied in string.

"This is for you. Will you try it on? I hope everything fits."

The dress fit almost perfectly. Long in the sleeves, but she rolled them up and pinned them at the wrist. The green and pink floral print shouted Spring. She wore it with her best shoes. There was a pill box hat and matching belt. They walked out of the building, arm in arm, to the car. Jefferson tipped his hat when as she approached. He drove them to the Episcopalian church in midtown Manhattan. Safir sat next to her father on the polished pew and sang the hymns as they appeared on the Order of Service. The senator introduced her to many acquaintances after the service. She blushed beneath their enthusiastic hugs and smiling compliments on her fashion. She listened as they encouraged Weldon for victory in the coming election. She answered many questions politely, *where do you live? what do you do?* and *what do you think about events in China?* It was overwhelming and exciting and she was relieved to be back in the sedan, speeding to the apartment.

And her outfit was so pretty and she felt so beautiful for a little while.

It snowed through the night. The way into our cavern was completely blocked and we had to dig ourselves out. All signs of our presence had been erased. The clouds were thick and grey and close enough to touch. We were a somber lot, especially those of us who knew what lay ahead. Paul and the men from Yelatan struck out at once, and were waiting for the rest of us when we arrived at a narrow turning. Snow lay thick around us, covering all evidence of rock and turning the landscape into a child's rendering of a mountain in winter, bereft of sharp edges. Sounds were absorbed into whiteness. The trail hugged the mountain at our right hand, while on the left the mountains had separated, creating a deep chasm below our feet. There was enough width for three to pass abreast, but the clumsy skis we wore did not help. I thought we might discard them, but my pole vanished into the snow beneath my feet. It was deep enough to swallow a child.

Paul had dug through the snow to the rock beneath. He had already anchored one end of the rope. His plan was to take the other end of the rope forward and anchor it. Each person would then secure himself to the rope whether by hand, rope or looped through clothing, and make the traverse over the bridge in a secure fashion. It was Paul and the men from Yelatan who had to make the traverse without benefit of anchors. He relayed his instructions then forged ahead in the snow. His tightly wrapped leggings covered his legs from ankle to knee. The cold did not appear to affect him. His movements were quick, decisive, and confident as he swum through deep drifts, pushing aside snow as he progressed. He carried the coil of rope over his shoulder. An ice hammer and nails were visible beneath his belt.

It seemed like hours before the rope that I held onto began to shiver. Like a fish on a hook, Paul was sending a signal that it was safe to join him on the far side. I led the first group across. A wind raced down the canyon. It carried snow that stung my face. As I inched away from the shelter of the rock wall I peered over the edge, into a grey, fog-shrouded abyss. Somewhere down there was the river that had made this valley over thousands of years.

"Don't look down," I said, to myself as much as to the Armenians. The way was somewhat level, but barely two metres wide. On a summer day I may not have crossed it without a rope. Today we needed children and elderly women, men carrying packs and dragging sleds, on skis for the first time in their lives, to cross. I used extra leather straps for bindings to secure each skier to the rope, and showed each how to hold on with one hand while using their pole with their left to help keep the skis facing forward. The first to make the crossing were Piruz and Toomas. He let out one whimper as he shuffled forward, but a sharp word from his mother silenced him. I held onto Piruz as tightly as was decent, and only let go when we reached the place where the face of the next mountain met the path. Then I knew she was safely with Paul and the guides. I crossed back to assist the rest in similar fashion. In this way the entire caravan made the traverse. Nurse Doebli struggled mightily, her maimed foot nearly useless. Solvein had to support her weight, and the two of them pulling on the rope gave me fear that it would pull away from the rock. But it held.

It took nearly two hours for our people, horses, goats, and sleds to cross the perilous throat. Our passage made the way compact and icier so the last groups encountered a different challenge than the first to cross. I fell twice, once nearly going over the edge. I waited for Sabik and Koehlrasch, the last save me to cross. I then removed the nail and coiled the rope around my shoulder, relying on the forward anchor near Paul to protect us.

He greeted me with a scolding. "You were supposed to stay at the front," he said.

"They needed an escort, it was faster this way," I said.

He grunted, but said no more. "The way ahead is still narrow and steep. It will be slower, but we must use the rope."

Paul set the anchor for the next traverse and in this way, we continued our descent, always fighting deep snow. Paul was right, the wait between traverses was the worst part, for the cold penetrated our clothes into our bones. When the last of our caravan had made the next traverse, Koelrasch released the rope from the anchor and skied without support, so that Paul could ski ahead and set a new anchor into the mountain. Many of us shivered uncontrollably. I longed for a cask of brandy to share.

Then it began to snow.

Paul pushed us to go faster. We could no longer wait for one group to reach the farther end before sending the next. We trusted Paul's nails, but it meant leaving the length of rope behind. He was loath to abandon rope, but it was that or freeze to death.

Daylight, or what was left of it, was fading when we reached our final traverse. It continued to snow. I remained to the last with Sabik and Koehlrasch, shivering and stamping the blocks of ice that were my feet. We shared snippets of conversation. The Austrian was from Salzburg, a city I longed to visit. He told me of the shops along the *Getreide Gasse* and summer nights swimming in the river Salzach. We conjured memories full of heat to counter the biting cold.

The avalanche struck Sabik squarely on the head, engulfing him instantly in a rumble of snow, ice and rock. He pinwheeled over the edge. Koehlrasch was caught in the rock fall and swept into the abyss with Sabik. Two men of Sabik's crew also fell, sucked backwards into the maelstrom, their screams echoing across the valley. The silence that followed was worse than the roar of the avalanche. I shook uncontrollably. Where Koelrasch and Sabik had stood there was now a tower of snow, blocking my way. I was alone, cut off from the rest of the party. I fell to my knees and peered into the valley, expecting to see Sabik and Koelrasch sprawled on the ground, but I saw only snow and the exposed rock of the mountain, the valley bottom a thousand feet or more beyond the limits of my vision. They could not have survived. I looked up, expecting to see another avalanche falling like a hand to swat me from my perch, but there was only grey sky thick with snow.

Without thinking I rushed the ice wall, tearing at it with my hands. The ice peeled the skin off my fingers and remained solid in my path. But it was a narrow plug, for I could hear voices on the other side. Then a spray of snow flew into my face. An ice pick broke through. The hole grew, until it was large enough for Paul to push a loose jumble of rock over the brink.

"Are you alone? Are you hurt?" he asked, reaching out his arm.

I pointed over the cliff. "They are gone."

"Take my hand," he said, "we must hurry before there is another slide."

I took off my skis and fed them through the breach. My knees were knocking as I climbed through the ice. When I was through, I sagged to the ground and began to weep. Paul rested his gloved hand on my shoulder. "No time for that." He skied past the huddled, sobbing refugees and unfastened the forward anchor and disappeared into the storm. I supposed he would tell Piruz that her husband was dead.

It was dusk when we halted, but we saw no sunset that day. The snow had stopped, only a few flakes floated onto our heads. It took all our collected efforts to start three fires, not enough to warm our whole party. I worked with Solvein and Doebli to comfort the families of those who had fallen. The Austrians formed a tight circle, remembering Koelrasch. When and how Paul told Piruz I do not know, but when I came to the camp she worked in grim silence while her son lay curled in a heap, sobbing without end. His cries, and those of the others, filled the cold air and echoed off the lifeless heights. I lay near one of the fires and closed my eyes, but all I saw was the avalanche, a hammer blow of snow that used Sabik and Koelrasch for its anvil.

The next day we continued our trek. Nobody spoke. By afternoon we had descended below the tree line. Squat evergreens and stunted shrubs with waxy leaves, some with clusters of forlorn berries still clinging to brown stems, grew around us. Patches of bare ground appeared, and the snow thinned. Paul ordered that our skis be removed and stowed. "They are firewood, now," Paul said.

Bare birch trees lined the banks of a noisy stream leading to Yelatan. The hills gave way to rocky meadows tufted with dead grass. Hazelnut trees, still dormant, dotted the land. Smoke from distant chimneys rose into a grey smudge of sky. Paul marched in front with the soldiers and the men who called this place home. The rest of us followed as closely as we could, but the travails of the descent, multiplied by hunger and grief, meant that our caravan stretched longer than a mile. Behind me came Solvein and Doebli, whose progress was measured by the sick and infirm. I stationed myself with Piruz and Toomas. Piruz did not waver. She marched on, Toomas's little hand in her tight grip, her eyes fixed on the path ahead. When

I offered to take some of her burden, she shook her head. It was an agonizing day. Though his bones lay buried in the deep snows behind us, Sabik's ghost walked with us.

The occasional wild goat, dully chewing the grass, watched us as we passed. Huebner shot a beast with a long, grizzled beard. Paul scolded him mightily, but that night the tough, nearly unchewable meat was added to a broth and shared as far as it would go. When we halted late that afternoon, we were in a landscape almost free of snow and ice. We passed a cold night on stony ground, doing our best to shelter from the wind blowing out of the mountains. I camped near the Austrians, but close enough to Piruz and Toomas to provide help if needed. I lay with my head propped against one of the sleds and kept watch, but if Piruz stirred in the night, I did not see it.

Early the next morning we were on our feet, our bodies stiff and sore. Piruz and Toomas kept to themselves, silent and grim. Before noon low, stone and sod buildings appeared, spaced far apart, as if good neighbours were distant neighbours. We followed a beaten path next to the river. Nearer Yelatan frozen drifts of dirty snow lay piled by the same stiff wind that flung dust in our faces. As the afternoon sun disappeared behind the jagged peaks we had put behind us, Makiymowicz waited patiently for us to catch up. He told us that Paul had found the Red Cross encampment near the centre of the village, and that we should make haste. I asked if there were Americans there, but he did not know, and hurried away as fast as he could.

"We are nearly there," I told Piruz as she walked. I had convinced her to let me help with her burden, and now dragged a sled of her possessions behind me. All she owned lay bundled in a blanket secured to the sled. Her feet were heavily wrapped in rags. I was afraid she suffered frostbite, but when I gestured to let Solvein attend her feet she shook her head. Her hair stuck beyond the fringe of her headscarf. Long, ebony plaits shiny with sweat lay plastered against her face. In the failing light she looked exhausted, defeated.

Her eyes shone with suppressed tears. It was the fourth day since leaving Belemedik Dagh.

"Piruz," I said as I walked at her side, "I want to help you. Please."

She suddenly stopped, nearly pushed over by a woman walking behind her. She let her arms fall limp at her sides. I was terrified that by stopping she meant to give up the ghost, on this very spot. Toomas began to cry and tugged on his mother's arm.

"Kill every Turk," she said, her jaw set like stone. Gripping Toomas by the arm, and shaking him to silence, she resumed her trek, saying no more.

After church the senator took her for a ride in a carriage through Central Park. He continued with his tale, talking energetically, ignoring the comings and goings of the people around them. The sun was shining and the cherry trees were finally in bloom. Safir breathed deeply, enjoying the fresh air. She saw how happy Weldon was and guilt gnawed at her heart. When she was very young, she had taken Theo's money and moved into an apartment he had found for them. She had made plans around his promise that he would leave his wife. It was a day like this one, in the Luxembourg Gardens, that she'd agreed to all of it. Eighteen months later and still Theo had not left his wife, and she stood, in a daze, on the deck of a steamer as it pulled out of Le Havre. Somehow, she'd been approved for a visa, only days before the German invasion.

As their carriage rolled through the park, she watched cherry blossoms floating on the breeze. They landed softly, only to be whisked aloft in the spokes of the passing wheels. Where they came to permanent rest was at the mercy of the breeze. She clenched her jaw. She was no cherry blossom, exquisite, delicate, soon to be mashed underfoot. She was a dandelion, or a thistle; able to grow between the cracks in a sidewalk if needs must. Her mood lifted, lightened by the rhythm of the carriage and the clop of horse's hooves. She settled herself against the backrest, enjoying the sun's warmth on her upturned face.

The news of shelter quickened our pace, but it was still dark by the time we reached Yelatan's centre. Brick and mortar buildings stood shoulder to shoulder, lining a road that had improved only marginally. The locals leaned out of second floor windows to gape at us. Many more stood in the doorways. None offered us assistance. They stood in dumb watchfulness, a mix of fear and mistrust in the flickering lantern light. Though we needed their help to survive, as I looked upon their blank, curious faces an anger woke in me. It was villagers such as these who looted deserted Armenian homes. I was overcome with the urge to shout obscenities, but I kept my mouth shut. It was more important that we find shelter.

At the far end of the town we passed through a low, stone wall into a flat courtyard, crowded with those who marched ahead. They were unpacking what little they had in the corners, some improvising their skis into makeshift shelters. Many lay on the hard ground, too exhausted to move. The courtyard was well lit by lanterns strung from the beams. As we entered, two men dressed like porters swung the iron gates shut behind us. I led Piruz and her son toward Solvein and Doebli. I wanted them to check Piruz's feet. We collapsed in a sliver of space. I pulled Doebli to Piruz. The nurse at once began to tend to her. Piruz slapped her hands away.

Nurse Doebli stuck her finger under Piruz's nose. "You saved my life," Doebli scolded. "Now it is my turn."

I moved Toomas out of the way. "Your mother needs to sleep," I said, but he did not understand. He did not want to be separated from his mother, but I gave him no choice. He began to wail, rousing Piruz. Finally, Nurse Doebli's reassurances calmed the boy and I was able to lead him off. I had gone only a few paces when I met Makiymowicz.

"Where is Paul?" I asked.

Makiymowicz waved at me. "He's inside. I believe you and the doctor are to set

up inside also."

"I will tell the doctor myself," I said. I did not want to cause a delay in Piruz's treatment. Once distracted by other needs, she might have to wait hours before the doctor would have time to check her.

Toomas and I followed him between groups of tired, hungry Armenians. A narrow entrance opened into a wide room that had been cleared for straw pallets, laid out across the floor. The smell of cooking cabbage wafted into the room, and as much as I have always disliked it, at that moment it was heaven sent. Beyond this room lay a kitchen, but instead we were led to a stairway. The Austrian pointed to the top. "You go there," he said. He nodded toward the front of the building. "That space is for the doctor," he said.

Toomas and I climbed the stairs and ducked under a low lintel, into a good-sized room. Its windows overlooked the road. There were tables, upon each a lantern had been placed. Blankets had been shared among a row of straw pallets, side by each, along the furthest wall. I grabbed Toomas by the hand and pulled him after me. "This is where you can rest," I said, but when I looked into his eyes, I found no sign he'd understood. I left him lying on a pallet and retraced my steps to Piruz. The doctor and nurse were applying dressings to her feet. She appeared to be sleeping through it.

"Poor thing, "Doebli said as she worked. "She has frostbite, but that is a minor part of her suffering."

I shot Doebli a questioning look.

"She needs to bury Sabik, and she cannot."

"Will she heal?"

The nurse held my glance. I noticed, in the failing light, how much Doebli had aged since our mission's beginning. She blinked, shrugged, and resumed her bandaging.

When Doebli was finished I bundled Piruz into my arms. She did not wake. I lay Piruz on the pallet next to Toomas. She did not move as I covered her with one of the blankets. Toomas curled up next to his mother.

I left Piruz and Toomas and passed through two low arches into a large room lit by candles, made brighter by freshly whitewashed walls. Paul and the Austrians sat around a long table. The aroma of whiskey filled my nose. Paul waved for me to sit near him.

"Here is *our* American," he said, in English. I thought I detected a note of pride in his voice.

Three men stood to greet me. Before any of them spoke I knew from their appearance they were American. I was overjoyed.

"Mr. Scott, we have been expecting you." A tall fellow with a shock of red, curly hair reached across the table to shake my hand. "Patterson, Jack. Ambassador Morgenthau dispatched us. The Red Cross were able to secure this property a week ago. It's a little tight for this many of you." He tilted his head toward Paul. "Quite a feat, eh? One hundred and thirty-four souls escaping like mountain goats in deepest winter."

"One hundred twenty-nine," Paul said.

"We lost five in an avalanche," I said.

"So we heard, that's tough," Patterson said. He turned to the two men beside him. "Mr. Harry Clancy and Mr. Donald Fortune. They're from the State Department, most recently Rome station. They will travel with us to our consulate in Aksaray, where the Armenians will be safe. We—that includes you, Mr. Scott—will then travel to Constantinople and report to the Ambassador."

I shook their hands gratefully, overwhelmed by the news.

Clancy's was a narrow frame draped in a loose-fitting suit. His ears and nose were still red from the cold. "As a neutral party the

United States cannot pursue military options. But the Ambassador has secured assurances from the Turkish government for the Armenians' safe passage."

"This is the best birthday present I've ever received," I said.

Fortune laughed, twirling the end of his prominent mustache, but Patterson remained serious. "Your lot is the only bunch to receive such consideration," he said. "We're not really certain why, we think it's because they badly need their railway and because your direct intervention is a potential world-wide embarrassment. Even so, the Ambassador pulled on a lot of strings."

"Understood," I said.

Paul slammed the table with his fist. "Whatever the reason, we are safe, thanks to the United States of America." He turned to face me, his glass of whiskey in hand. "This victory is yours, Weldon Scott," he said, making a toast. "Greater than that of an entire army." He cocked his head to the side. "Now what day is it?" he asked.

"January ninth," Patterson said.

Paul grinned, his blue eyes sparkling. "Then we must toast us both, for it is my birthday also!"

Patterson stood, his chair scraping the floor, and raised his glass. Everyone around the table stood, glasses raised. "Here's mud in your eye," he said, emptying his glass.

She was weary after their ride through Central Park, but Weldon insisted Safir accompany him to dinner.

"I will be gone soon. I don't want to squander any of our time together."

When they arrived at *Bemelmans* the Maître d' greeted her as *Miss Scott* and led them to their usual table. As she glanced over the menu she said, "A month ago I had never heard of Armenians. Of the atrocities. It was never spoken of in my home, nor in the houses of my friends. And yet it happened. To my own mother."

"I'm sorry, Safir," Weldon said. "But you deserve to know the truth."

She looked up from the menu. "I deserved to know years ago," she said.

The waiter cleared his throat. Safir ordered a New York steak, rare, with garlic mashed potatoes. "Growing up we never ate steak. Or potatoes," she said.

"Potatoes came from Ireland, I believe," Weldon smiled. "Or was it the other way around? I can't remember."

"We always ate rice. Sometimes my mother would put in raisins and nuts."

"That sounds delicious," Weldon said. "We didn't eat a lot of rice in my family."

They ate their meals in silence and did not linger over dessert. Weldon paid the bill and the waiter retrieved their coats. As the car neared the apartment Weldon said, "You don't need to work."

Safir stared out the window. "I have to fill the days," she said.

"Why not tutor students on the piano? I have many friends who would pay good money for you to teach their children. Or them."

She raised an eyebrow. "I do not play, anymore."

"But you're wasting your talents," Weldon said. When he saw the look on Safir's face he raised a finger to his lips. "I'm sorry, I shouldn't have said that. But maybe one day?"

Safir looked at her hands.

"I am planning a pre-election tour, at the end of summer," Weldon said after a long silence. "It would be wonderful if you could come with me."

"Where?"

"Pennsylvania," he said.

"Philadelphia?"

"Yes, and every other city, town and hamlet in the state," Weldon chuckled.

She thought a moment. "I would like that," she said.

"Do you mean it?" Weldon said, eagerly.

"I do," she said.

Jefferson stopped the car on Central Park West. Safir said goodbye, giving Weldon an affectionate kiss on the cheek. She waited for the car to disappear then hurried inside. She nodded to the doorman who pushed the button for the elevator. Inside her apartment she hurried to her bedroom. She undressed, hanging her new clothes carefully in the closet. Her dress looked lonely in the yawning spaciousness. She washed her face and brushed her teeth and put on her nightgown. She stared at the ceiling, making patterns out of the shadows. An Autumn tour with Weldon would be another chance to get to know her father. Then she thought of Celik and Piruz and an ache squeezed her chest.

Monday morning a strange sensation enfolded her the moment she hung up her coat. It followed her to her desk. It clung to her as she worked. When she raised her head, her coworkers looked away. She wanted to scream. At ten o'clock a secretary approached her desk and stood at attention in front of her. She wore a tight, woolen skirt with matching high heels and regarded Safir over the rim of her pearl-studded eyeglasses. She held a clipboard protectively in her arms, like a mother holding a baby.

"Come with me, please. The Director will see you in his office." The woman turned abruptly and walked away, her heels clicking smartly across the floor.

Safir glanced at her colleagues, now openly gawking at her.

"Hurry," the secretary scolded her, "he doesn't have all day."

Safir stood, scraping her chair across the parquet tiles. She buttoned her sweater and caught up to the secretary near the elevator doors. "Am I in trouble?"

"It is not for me to say," the secretary said.

In the elevator the secretary stared at the doors, admiring the golden hue of her reflection in the polished brass. They ascended to the highest floor, where senior managers had their offices. The secretary led her through a heavy wooden door, past an empty desk and tapped her knuckles upon another polished door. *Dr. J. Hooper, Director* was stenciled across a frosted glass pane in bold, black type. A gravelly voice within commanded them to enter.

Doctor Hooper was a large, balding man in a tight-fitting, dark suit. His high-collared white shirt buried itself in his neck like a cookie cutter in too much dough. There was enough of him to spill over the sides of his high-backed leather chair. He made the massive oak desk before him appear inadequate.

"Be seated, Miss Turan," Doctor Hooper said. Sunlight pouring through the narrow windows behind him made it difficult to make out his expression. He used a white handkerchief to polish the lenses of wire rimmed glasses with great vigour. "Thank you, Miss Parker." The secretary closed the door with a well practiced sweep that ended with a soft, but terminal, click.

Safir sat in the lone chair facing the Director. She straightened her shoulders, laced her fingers together on her lap; the soles of her shoes pressed flat against the floor.

Doctor Hooper replaced his glasses and leaned forward to rest his elbows on the desk blotter. His chair creaked mightily at every movement. He cocked his head. His thick, grey eyebrows arched expectantly. The smile that appeared frightened her. "Mr. D'Angelo will not bother you anymore, Miss Turan. He is no longer an employee of this institution."

Safir flinched.

"I am apologizing, Miss Turan, for the misconduct of your supervisor. I had no idea. I am sorry it took as long as it did to sort out this matter."

Fireworks went off in her head. She felt as weightless as a sleeping baby's breath.

"I will personally oversee the hiring of the next supervisor. Do you have any questions?" Doctor Hooper pushed back his chair and extended his right hand. "Good. All settled. Let's get back to work, shall we?"

As Safir opened the office door, Doctor Hooper cleared his throat. She paused.

"Would you please give my best regards to Senator Scott?"

"Of course," Safir said, and fled back to her desk in the basement.

A strange thing happened. A colleague approached her to say hello. Then another. By Tuesday her desk was a popular place for Archives staff to gather. She learned more than their names, and she told them a little of herself. She began eating lunch in the cafeteria, sitting elbow to elbow at a circular table near the vending machines. It was a feeling she had never experienced, and she liked it, even as she worried that it wasn't her so much as the senator they wanted to know. At the end of the work day her colleagues said good bye and waved and said *see you tomorrow* like they meant it.

After work on Wednesday, as she stepped into the apartment elevator, the doorman handed her a large envelope.

"From Senator Scott," he said, and tipped his hat like he always did.

She laid the envelope on the hall table and took of her coat and sweater and bent down to scratch Mustafa's back. "I had another pleasant day," Safir said, scooping the cat into her arms and retrieving the envelope.

She carried Mustafa to the sofa and sat down with a contented sigh. The cat watched from her lap as she opened the envelope.

Several sheets of paper slid onto the coffee table, behind a single sheet of personal stationery.

Dearest Safir. By the time you receive this I will be back in Washington. I took the time to scribble the rest of our story onto paper, so that you don't have to wait to learn how it all works out. I won't be back until mid June, based on prior years' sessions. I hope you are comfortable in the apartment; it does my soul good to know you are safe in Manhattan. I will call when I can. By the way, don't be angry with me, but I hope things are better for you at the museum.

With Love,

Your Father.

She kicked off her shoes and stretched across the sofa to read, Mustafa's low purr a soothing vibration in her bones.

The first week in Yelatan we regained some of our strength. We lived and worked in the farmhouse-now-Red Cross-compound, tending the sick, setting broken bones, and restoring supplies. The weather was fine, for January. Days were dry, the sun appeared every day to chase away clouds, though nights remained bitterly cold. Even our skinny horses put on weight. Clancy and Fortune brought a second doctor and two nurses, who worked with Solvein and Doebli in the surgery. They were Italian, and hard workers, though Solvein quarreled with the doctor more than he did with the Austrians. There was always some minor thing that set off the Belgian. More than once Patterson had to remind Solvein the pair were allies, in order to restore a disgruntled truce to proceedings.

For Doebli and Solvein, they had never been happier. They worked ceaselessly from first light to late in the evening. They were joined at the hip. Thanks to their hard work, our company showed signs of recovery from the ordeal of Belemedik Dagh. To be of assistance I went often into the village with the Austrians to negotiate with the villagers for clothes and blankets for the women and children. Not much better than rags, they were, but I found the villagers grudgingly generous, despite their own poverty. Once I took Clancy and Fortune with us. As much for their safety as mine, for there was still a *fatwa* against any Christian who was not Austrian or German, and though most we met were friendly, even shy, one could never be sure. I wanted the townspeople to see the Austrians, in uniform, and connect them favorably to America.

We gathered enough clothes to burn the flea-infested rags the Armenians had worn since being driven from their homes. There was enough food so that the children did not cry from hunger. It appeared, as we worked, that the veil of horror had been lifted, if only a little. I heard laughter and children's shouts as they ran about the compound, chasing each other or playing with a stray mutt they'd coaxed through the bars of the gate. After sunset the sound of the *duduk* wafted through the compound. Piruz was not the only Armenian in our caravan to possess this instrument. Its notes were accompanied by the sounds of a lute—an *Ud* as Paul told me—and together the instruments made mournful but beautiful melodies.

I did not see Paul much those days, for he often left the compound alone, or with Clancy and Patterson, for purposes other than mine. He wore his fez and coat and once more resembled an Ottoman *vilayet*, and took the men who had been our guides and sat with the local headman and Imam to commend the guides for their heroism. Though initially suspicious of us, and amazed at our numbers, the headman had heard little news beyond Yelatan. Through the Imam Paul learned a little of the outside world, to supplement the news Patterson had brought from Constantinople. War had come to Turkish shores, but the British *Infidels* had been bested by the soldiers of the Faithful. Paul took this to mean the war would not soon be over, and that beyond Yelatan the fate of the Armenians was still in doubt, regardless of American assurances. The Imam knew that to the east many Armenians had been sent into the Syrian deserts, but to his mind they were criminals and prisoners from the fighting, not women and babies. The scale of suffering was unknown to him, and he was shocked when Paul told him otherwise.

I kept myself busy preparing for the trek to Aksaray, over one hundred and thirty miles away. A trek like that could take ten days, considering the weather, the age and condition of the Armenians, and the fact that not all could travel by cart or horse. I had secured three broken wagons and two ramshackle carts for the elderly, the pregnant women, and the smallest children. They were dragged into the compound, and the Armenians worked on them as best as they could, repairing them for the trek. We poured over maps, determining the route to take. I hoped we could connect with the railway and travel the entire distance to Constantinople. Once there I was confident Ambassador Morgenthau would shelter all the Armenians under the American flag. And it would be quicker to travel a thousand miles by rail than one hundred on foot. But Patterson would not stand for it.

"The Turks are using the railways to transport Armenians. We would not make it as far as Konia."

"This has become a holy war for the Turkish government," Clancy said. "They are using all means at their disposal."

"It is the scale of it I cannot comprehend," I said.

I tempered my despair with the knowledge that traveling on foot meant more time with Piruz. When I was not with the Americans, I was with her. I brought her food, found better clothes for her and for Toomas. Since Sabik's death he clung to his mother, or remained in a corner of the room above the surgery, wrapped in a blanket, inconsolable. Piruz rarely spoke, but as the days passed the wariness in her eyes began to recede. She smiled when I came near, and once—as we ate supper (the Americans had found a store of tinned mushrooms and red wine on their travels)—she reached across the table to brush the crumbs from my beard. She said *Thank you* in English. My heart swelled to bursting.

We were resigned to traveling by road, and reaching Aksaray was all we could hope for, until hostilities ceased or the Turks ended their campaign against the Armenians. We needed to gather food and fuel, water for us and our horses, for the road we planned to take was across the plateau, high, dry, and desolate this time of year. While we bartered for extra supplies in the village, accompanied by one of the men from Belemedik Dagh, Paul and the Austrians gathered weapons. Pietschmann's brigade had three rifles among them—the reliable Mausers they cared for better than they cared for themselves—and Paul's pistol. But ammunition was limited. And while my efforts went largely unrewarded, Paul found a way.

None of us had coin or notes, and Ottoman scrip was worthless. The promise of American money some time in the future meant even less to the locals. But Paul had not wasted the mining tools at his disposal and his foresight most certainly saved us all. The Taurus Mountains were rich in minerals, and during drilling in the tunnel Paul had set up a sifting table to separate gemstones and valuable minerals. He had filled several pouches with silver ore and gemstones. (Paul told me, many years after, that the pouches Sabik carried were worth twice what his were, but they were lost with him.) Just a small portion of Paul's treasure was more than enough to make the locals part with their guns and ammunition, additional horses and extra food.

After six weeks it was evident we must soon leave Yelatan. We did not want to overstay our welcome. Though it was still winter, the weather had changed for the better. Small clusters of wildflowers bloomed around the compound, even the fruit and hazelnut trees were in bud and the swallows nested in cracks under the eaves. An early Spring was in store. The Americans, too, were keen to leave. Patterson, especially, worried that the Turks would go back on their promise to Ambassador Morgenthau. When he was not scribbling reports or poring over the map, Patterson would stare out the second-floor window, gazing north, as if seeing the road clear to Constantinople.

It was during this time Piruz made her decision. While I slept, she came to my room and lay beside me on my pallet of clean straw. She said nothing, we did nothing immoral. She simply put her arm around my shoulders and slept. Sometimes I felt her sobs, muffled against my spine. Then she let me hold her, and though I should have been thrilled, I was filled with guilt for Sabik's death. My joy came at great cost, a cost paid by others. Three nights later, in the darkest hours of night, we were like husband and wife and I promised her I would look after her and Toomas. I didn't know if she understood my words, spoken into her hair as she dozed in my arms, but I am sure she knew their meaning.

During the day we made no mention of our nights. If Solvein or Doebli noticed, they said nothing. Solvein would have been sympathetic, considering how his own relationship with Doebli had begun despite having a wife in Belgium waiting for his return. War and deprivation have a way of scraping away societal and religious conventions, and with them, guilt. In the meantime, I longed for the days to be done and for the nights never to end.

The courtyard was crammed with supplies for our journey, bundles wrapped in blankets and tied to sleds or stashed in the carts. The mood among the Armenians was jubilant, and they worked without complaint preparing for the exodus to Aksaray near the great salt lake of Tun Golz. Patterson had sent word of our coming through the Red Cross, but in truth we were on our own until we arrived. We planned to camp, avoiding the few towns along the route we had chosen. We hoped we had gathered enough supplies, and Patterson was convinced that this way our travel would be less conspicuous. In private Clancy and Fortune confessed that their main worry was not the Turks, but bandits who operated beyond the reach of local governors. Raids were commonplace among the helpless caravans of dispossessed. Even the townspeople of Yelatan spoke with fear of Kurdish tribesmen who took advantage of the diaspora to loot, kill, and rape those they had hated for generations. Tales of their depravity made the Turks seem like amateurs in cruelty. But we were confident that our road was so isolated bandits had no reason or profit in lingering, and the presence of Habsburg soldiers and four Americans, with Paul in the van dressed in his Ottoman fez and jacket, would be enough to deter all robbers and thugs.

This was the fashion of our days, preparing as best as we could, in secret many among us content to stay one more day. I more so than anyone. Piruz had done away with any pretense of hiding her feelings for me. I didn't care. I was madly in love. And I was sure that Piruz felt the same.

Then, early one morning, as if sensing we were about to leave Yelatan, the Turks came. Soldiers, a dozen or more on horseback, flanked the *Vilayet,* who wore an ornate jacket heavy with medals of all sizes and shapes. A braided, golden tassel dangled from his red fez. His thick black mustache was waxed into dagger points beneath his eyes. He was a fatter version of the governor Sabik had thrown off Belemedik Dagh. The squad halted at the closed gate. A crowd of locals hung back to watch. Two soldiers dismounted and tried to fling open the iron fence, but the chain held, and the clamour of the Armenian women roused the rest of us. As the women fled to the far wall of the compound, children in tow, Paul, Patterson, Clancy, Fortune, and I met the delegation at the gate, but we did not open it. The chill air sharpened the sounds of bridles clinking and horses stamping the compact earth of the road.

Patterson shoved Morgenthau's signed orders through the gate, and a Turk soldier carried them to the governor, who remained on his horse. He glanced at the paper and handed them back to the soldier. I doubted he could read, let alone understand what was on the page. The Turk passed them back to Patterson with a sneer on his face.

"Hand over the Armenians," he said, gesturing for us to open the gate.

Patterson leaned close to the gate. He spoke in English, jabbing his finger at the words on the document. "These orders are signed by Talaat Pasha. *Talaat*. Your great *Effendi*. These people," he waved at the huddled Armenians, "stay here." He pointed at the ground. "Here."

The soldier wagged his finger in front of Patterson's face. "Lies. We take all the people."

"Bloody hell you won't," Clancy muttered.

If Piruz fired the first shot she neither admitted nor denied it. I doubt it was Solvein, and certainly not Doebli. Makiymowicz, Bildstein and Huebner were in the command room, and said the shot came from above the surgery. Maybe one of Sabik's miners took matters into his own hands. Someone on the second floor took one of the bartered rifles and pulled the trigger. The shot was excellent. The bullet knocked the governor off his horse. The *Vilayet* lay on the ground, unmoving, blood quickly pooling beneath him.

Some of the Turks rushed to surround their fallen governor. As the Turkish soldier at the gate raised his weapon, a volley of Mauser fire exploded from the second floor. Two Turks fell, including the soldier who had spoken to Patterson. The remaining Turks fired at us. Clancy pushed me to the ground. Fortune collapsed, holding his leg. Another volley from the second floor was all it took. Three more Turks went down and the remaining soldiers fled, leaving their fallen comrades behind.

"We are in for it now," Patterson said, stooping over Fortune. "Doctor Solvein!" he shouted at the windows behind him. He gave me a worried glance. "Time to be gone from here, Mr. Scott. Pray that Aksaray is still an option."

Paul gathered the Austrians to drag away the dead. "We leave today," he said as we half carried, half dragged the lifeless governor into the compound.

We left without burying the Turks. Villagers lined the road, pointing at us and waving goodbye. Apparently, the governor was not well-liked in his district. News of the skirmish raced through the village. Everyone, it seemed, wanted to see for himself the ones responsible for killing their governor. Our status had been elevated from curiosities to heroes. Some gave us loaves of bread, others presented us with scarves and caps. To much applause our train wound its way through the village and into the rocky bench lands. We had escaped Yelatan and the Turks with little hurt, for Fortune's wound was not serious, though he could not put weight on his leg. Solvein had removed the bullet and stitched him up. The Italian doctors had done the same for three wounded Turks. We had locked the soldiers in the compound, trusting the villagers to release them after we left. We kept their rifles and ammunition, and now I, too, had a weapon. The villagers ran off with the horses, perhaps in repayment for their extended generosity. How they intended to keep them from the Turks was not our worry. Maybe they planned to eat them.

We made camp beneath a row of birch trees, in a sheltered vale where the river took a lazy bend. Our campfire that night was a happy one. There was music and song and enough food for everyone. We were under the invisible wing of the American government, vulnerable no longer. Having Patterson, Clancy, and Fortune in our midst was proof.

Makiymowicz and I shared the first watch. We sat opposite each other around a small fire a short distance away from the camp. Alexander was the youngest of Paul's company, though by the lines around his eyes he appeared older than I by a few years. He told me about his village in the Tyrol, and another Christmas away from his family. I asked him what he missed the most.

"The food!" Alex said, rubbing his stomach. "*Gröstl und Schnapps.*"

He explained how the potatoes are cooked in bacon fat and onions and topped with a pair of fried eggs. We had eaten well, but his description sent pangs through my digestive system. "Where did you meet Paul?"

"I was on several climbs with him, before the war. He was a student of Zdarsky's; he can ski like the wind. Pietschmann would not leave Austria without him."

"He is a good leader," I said.

Alexander nodded, glanced over his shoulder into the darkness. "We wanted him instead of Pietschmann," he said, "all of us."

"Why?"

Alex resettled himself. He reached for a stick to poke at the embers. "Viktor Pietschmann is most happy behind a desk. Did you know he is a biologist? He dissects fish." Alexander sniffed. "We think Pietschmann has gone back to Vienna."

"Without you?"

"Truth be told, we would have stayed with *Effendi* just the same. You saw how he got us out of the mountains." He fell silent, like me, remembering Koelrasch and Sabik. "If not for him more of us would have died many times over."

When Patterson and Clancy relieved us, I bid Makiymowicz good night. I walked beneath a moonless sky brimming with stars. I collapsed next to Piruz and Toomas and listened to the river. A shooting star fell out of the west. Piruz, still asleep, draped an arm across my chest. I had never been more content.

It took a week to travel halfway. There had been no pursuit. Nevertheless, we traveled by shepherd's paths and unmarked trails, avoiding the main road north. It was slower, but safer, and a feeling that we might make it to Aksaray unmolested grew in our minds, if not our speech. We made good progress, all things considered, but Paul was never satisfied. It was Patterson who insisted the day's trek was done, though Paul would have gone farther. Every minute not traveling, it seemed, rankled him. He did not share Patterson's confidence in Turkish assurances of safety, and the incident at the compound had confirmed his suspicions, but in a show of good faith, each afternoon he relented when Patterson made the suggestion to halt. After camp was made, I often found him a short distance away, sketching. He had reassembled his easel from his skis, little the worse for wear. He, too, seemed content, not that he ever said as much to me.

I spent my days walking beside Piruz and Toomas. Only once Piruz rode one of the horses, but she complained the motion made her dizzy, and thereafter she walked, despite the pain in her feet. I tried to support her by shouldering her belongings. Solvein and Doebli were left to organize our supplies and make arrangements for their transport. If they were angry with me about this, they hid it well. Their words and actions acknowledged Piruz's decision. Though no words were spoken, we were now together. We had cemented this fact those last nights in Yelatan. As we walked my mind raced into the future, far beyond Aksaray, to the day we returned to Pennsylvania. I imagined introducing Piruz and Toomas to my mother and father and brothers. What would they think? How would they react? I admit, I had my doubts. I had been thinking, long before ever laying eyes on Piruz, that Europe was the place for me. Now, with Piruz as my wife, it seemed more likely I would remain. If Bethlehem, Pennsylvania was not possible, we would live in Geneva, or Lucerne. We could be a family there, safe from war and judgement. These were the dreams that filled my head on the road to Aksaray.

It was exactly two weeks since we'd left Yelatan. A cold rain, whipped by wind, fell from the darkened sky. Our caravan still needed to cover fifteen miles, when a convoy of vehicles appeared from the west. We heard the growl of engines before they came into view. We were strung in a long line, on low ground, with little cover. A general panic ensued. A few broke from the line and ran away. The Austrians formed a defensive line across the road. We had time to angle two of the carts to use as a shield. Patterson protested loudly when Paul directed the Americans behind the carts, out of sight of the approaching vehicles.

"If the Turks mean to take the Armenians, neutral America will carry less sway than allied Austria. If we fail to negotiate safe passage, you can decide the next action."

Patterson was somewhat appeased, and led Fortune and Clancy behind one of the carts. He gestured for me to join them, but I refused, staying instead with Piruz and Toomas in the knot of refugees that had formed well behind the carts. Piruz gripped my hand tightly, her face grim with fear.

Three trucks, each flying the Ottoman crescent, drove at us with speed. In all my days in Turkey, I had never seen their soldiers on anything but horseback, or on foot. The trucks stopped in a line, two strides from the Austrians spread across the stony road. For a long minute nothing happened. The only sound was the sputtering of the engines as they idled. Their windscreens were masked with mud. Three men jumped from the lead truck. They wore the uniforms of Imperial Germany. The senior officer, his shoulder epaulets shimmering, approached Paul and saluted. Paul returned the salute, then motioned to his men to lower their rifles. He approached the Germans. They shook hands. Several among our caravan cheered. The tension vanished. Patterson, Fortune, and Clancy appeared from behind their cart.

Paul motioned for the Americans to stay where they were. He walked with the German officer some paces away from the rest of us, too distant to hear what was said. From my vantage point the conversation appeared to be between a German and a Turk, for Paul's fez and jacket gave him an authentic Ottoman silhouette. As the pair conversed, the Austrians joined the Germans. They shared cigarettes and jokes as the rest of us guessed at the proceedings.

The secret discussion did not take long. Paul turned and walked toward us. The German officer returned to his truck, motioning to his men to join him. But the trucks did not move. I squeezed Piruz's hand and joined the Austrians, Patterson, Clancy, and Fortune. I arrived in the middle of Paul's explanation. He spoke calmly, but it was clear none were happy.

"What of the Armenians?" Patterson asked.

"They will be safe," Paul said. "The German High Command is aware of the Turkish assurances given to Ambassador Morgenthau."

"Safe passage to Aksaray?" Clancy asked. Suspicion knitted his brow.

Paul nodded. "Two trucks will escort you the rest of the way."

"*Rest of the way"* I interrupted. "You're not coming with us?"

Paul stared at me, as if seeing me for the first time. In the grey, cold morning he appeared much older than thirty-two.

"That is correct, Mr. Scott. It seems the rumours we heard are true. Pietschmann has returned to Vienna. We," Paul gestured at his troop, "are to return also. Our work in Turkey is done."

A shocked silence fell over us. The Austrians were clearly conflicted with news of their deportation. I took it as a sign of their love for the Armenians that a return to Vienna, away from the hostilities, was seen as second best.

"I can file a protest," Patterson said. "Your presence is required to see us safely to Aksaray."

Paul shook his head. For a brief moment I saw anguish in his face as his glance swept over the convoy. "The Germans, as usual, have seen to every detail. They have trucks and soldiers to protect you. They have secured shelter for the Armenians. We are," he shot me a wry smile, "superfluous to the situation."

Paul removed his glove and shook Patterson's hand, then Clancy's and Fortune's. The Austrians followed suit. They were saying good bye and nothing I could do or say would change that. Tears formed in my eyes as Paul stepped in front of me.

"A privilege, Mr. Scott," he said. "Remember. Always climb higher."

Paul turned on his heel. He swung himself into the front passenger seat of the truck. Makiymowicz, Bildstein, and Huebner climbed into the back with the German soldiers. Alexander waved to me. He looked as unhappy as I. The truck reversed with a grinding of gears, then sped away in the direction whence it had come. The remaining trucks waited for us.

"Right then," Patterson said, the first to snap out our collective trance. He clapped his hands. "Let's get as many into the trucks as we can. The rest will ride the carts and horses. We can make Aksaray by dusk."

"This is a good thing?" I said, wiping tears out of my eyes.

Patterson shrugged. "Tough loss, Scott, but yes, for us it's a damn good thing. If the Germans know our lot is protected, we can drive all the way to Constantinople if we want."

"What happens to them?" Fortune asked, staring at the empty horizon.

"Once they get back to Vienna?" Patterson said. "Probably reassigned to one front or another. They are in a dogfight in the Alps. My guess is with their skills that's where they'll end up. Now let's get these people onto the trucks, as many as we can."

I rode in the back of a truck with Piruz and Toomas. We were jolted and shaken by ruts in the road that the driver was expert at finding. Piruz did not speak. She sat in glassy-eyed silence with her back pressed against the side of the truck, her arms around Toomas.

I did not see Paul again for six years.

Chapter 4

Safir found satisfaction in her work now that D'Angelo was gone. She got to know her fellow archivists, their histories, their likes and dislikes. She was amazed to learn that they held D'Angelo in the same low regard, and, like her, had endured his taunts and demeaning behaviour. Some praised her courage for facing down the bully and advising management of his transgressions. She let their misconceptions lie, refusing to admit what of course they had to know, but were too polite to say to her face. She was cautious in her interactions with all except Brian, the archivist across the hall, who shrugged off Safir's confession like old news.

"If my father was a senator, I'd be asking for favors everyday!" he said as they shared lunch on a bench in the green space between the museum and the library. Brian's specialty was ancient metalworking; she envied how much he loved his vocation. He regaled her with tidbits of information from the objects assigned to his care, whether they were ornamental or utilitarian, brooches or padlocks. Brian was tall and slender, his pale features hidden beneath a tangle of thick, black hair. His tuna and onion sandwich almost disappeared in his long fingers. "In fact, my new-found purpose is to convince you to ask him for an original set of keys to Fort Knox. For my collection," he added, "not because I want to break in."

"I'll see what I can do," Safir said, laughing into the back of her hand.

In the first week after Weldon's departure to the Capitol, Safir established a new routine. She made her lunch, a sandwich on white bread, neatly sliced in half on the diagonal. She filled it with egg salad, or tuna fish or liverwurst, and it was better than its damp, luncheonette counterpart. One of her coworkers would be willing to trade up for a half; a slice of pie or a wedge of chocolate cake was the best. She took the subway from Manhattan, traveling from Central Park West in an uncrowded car headed to Brooklyn. She got off in front of the museum on Eastern Parkway. At six o'clock she reversed her route into Manhattan. She strolled the last block to her apartment building and greeted the doorman with a smile and a nod, like she'd seen some of the other tenants do. She changed out of her work clothes, unpinned her hair, made herself a modest meal—usually fish or vegetables with rice—saving a bit for Mustafa. He, too, seemed to enjoy his new digs. He prowled through every room asserting ownership, returning always to the sofa in the living room. He perched on the backrest with a view to Central Park, but quickly curled into a ball to nap. Safir smoked a last cigarette and readied for bed. She slept in the master bedroom. The mattress was firm and ushered her to sleep without the familiar, dull ache in her hips and shoulder, a regular gift of her old mattress.

One Friday evening Weldon phoned from Washington. It was complete luxury to sit in her living room smoking and drinking coffee while speaking on the phone.

"Did you finish my story?" Weldon asked.

"I did. At Bemelmans you told me Toomas died. Did he make it to Aksaray?"

"We all did, under German escort," Weldon said. "Sadly, Toomas died in the camp a few months later. It was summer. Typhus spread through the town. It took half the children, Turks and Armenians alike. Not to sound cruel, but there's nothing like an epidemic to prove we are all the same, in the end."

"There are other ways," Safir said. "That must have been hard for my mother."

"When Toomas died, she refused to eat. Doebli and Solvein resorted to force feeding her to keep her alive."

"If death was what she wanted, I don't know why they'd force her to eat. I don't blame her, how awful."

"Because of you, Safir," Weldon said. "She was carrying you."

Safir promised herself she wouldn't cry anymore at the mention of her mother. Her body shook with the effort. She wiped her nose with the back of her hand.

"You were born in Aksaray. Nurse Doebli delivered you. The sixth of October, 1916. Such a shock of hair you had! So much like your mother's."

The silence on her end of the phone prompted the senator to keep talking.

"The first eight months of your life were spent in Aksaray. The Turks kept their word, after Paul was taken. But official orders from Constantinople were for the Armenians to remain there, it would have been a risk to leave. The men found work, some moved into abandoned homes and resumed a regular life. The townspeople accepted your people without hesitation. Some became teachers, others farmers. As the end of the war approached the situation changed. The United States came into the war on the side of the Allies. The Turks responsible for the genocide fled. By then most of the families who had been at Belemedik Dagh were living normal lives."

"So, you stayed too?"

"No. I was forced to leave when America entered the war. But before that Piruz and I lived as husband and wife. We shared a small house with Solvein and Doebli. Those were my happiest months on this earth. You were on the way. We were a family. Then the Typhus struck. Toomas died. Your mother became a ghost. She refused to speak. She no longer attended the barn repurposed as a church.

Someone had been carrying a small painting of St. Gregory in his possessions, and it became the new altar piece. I tried to heal her mind, but I could not reach her. All Summer and into Fall she kept to herself. I didn't blame her, she had been through so much, but I missed her. Nothing changed, after your birth. Doebli took you away and found another woman to nurse you. A woman from the town whose own infant had died. I was terrified that if Piruz remained as she was, you would be adopted by the wet nurse and disappear. It was all we could do to convince Piruz to bring you both to Constantinople. I said goodbye to Solvein and Doebli, with whom I had spent the better part of three years. Our American troop found a truck, and after, traveled by train. It took us nearly a month to reach Constantinople, that's how chaotic things were. When we reached the American Embassy you and your mother were given shelter there, within the compound. But my pleas, even to the Ambassador himself, were denied. I was ordered to return to the United States alone, without you."

"Why?"

"To fight. I joined the army as an interpreter. They made me a Lieutenant and assigned me to France, of all places. I never saw fighting, however. Lucky, I guess. I was attached to the French command staff in Paris."

"And after the war?"

"I petitioned the Red Cross to resume my work in what had been Ottoman lands, but the closest I got to Piruz was Lebanon. We wrote to each other. I sent her money. After the peace treaty was signed and the League of Nations created, I went to work with the Committee for Refugee Settlement. I believed it would take me to Turkey, and I was right, but the soonest I was able to return was 1922. Five years had passed since I'd last seen you."

"You came back?" Safir lit another cigarette with trembling hands, the phone tucked between her shoulder and jaw.

"I did. But when I arrived in Istanbul, I learned that Piruz had remarried. A Turk. I was shocked. I had no idea. Celik Turan was a widower, he had come from Hereke with the owner of the rug company that supplied sought-after carpets to the Embassy. Celik was a master dyer and the owner wanted to show off his most skilled artisans. On one of these visits Piruz was in the Embassy. She had abandoned her Armenian faith and customs. Celik fell in love with her, just as I had done, and Sabik before me."

"You gave us up to Celik."

"Safir. That's unfair," Weldon said, his voice tinged with hurt. "I spent a long time believing that Piruz had abandoned me. At first, I could not accept it. I wrote even more often, I begged her to come to Geneva. But as the years passed, I grew to understand your mother's motives. She converted to Celik's faith. She hid every trace of her Armenian heritage."

"Why would she do that?"

"Think, Safir. She'd lost everyone she'd cared for."

"Except me."

"She needed to protect you. Disappearing into Turkish life was the only way."

"You didn't want her anymore?"

"You're not listening. Of course, I wanted her. She did not want me. You know how stubborn your mother was. Alone, far from the only home she'd known, no husband, no son, a young daughter. The Americans wouldn't let her stay forever. There were so many refugees displaced and dispossessed. She was smart, and figured Celik was her best chance."

"By turning us into Muslims."

"By turning you into Turks," Weldon said. "By hiding her Armenian identity Piruz was building a wall around you. In case past evils returned."

"But they didn't," Safir said. She could hear the complaint in her tone and it made her angry. "My mother buried the truth for nothing."

"She didn't think so," Weldon said, "but I confess it hurt that she turned her back on me. In Geneva she would have been safe to dress in her clothes, go to her church, raise you as the daughter of an Armenian. By the time I made it back to Istanbul too much time had passed. She was committed to the life Celik could give her. It took many years, but I have finally forgiven her."

"And now you want me to forgive you."

There was a long silence on the other end of the phone. Weldon cleared his throat. "I do," he said.

"Good night," Safir said, hanging up the phone. She smoked two more cigarettes and drowned her turmoil in the repeating patterns of the carpet beneath her feet.

Though days were warmer and her mood improved after Weldon's phone call, she woke to a bad cold that kept her in bed. Her muscles ached, as if somebody had beat her with a stick while she slept. She took her first sick day. She remained in her apartment, wrapped in a blanket, rarely stirring from her nest on the sofa. Even Mustafa knew something was wrong, but he was unable to rouse his mistress. The weekend came and went. Monday she was too sick to work. She existed on chicken broth and cigarettes. It took her an hour of hard work to reposition the heavy sofa so that she could look out the window. Better than lying in bed staring at the ceiling. A cough settled in her chest, so thick and wet it hurt her ribs with each spasm. Mustafa kept his distance, annoyed that the sofa had been commandeered by his mistress. He took to wandering the apartment, jumping on furniture, looking for a satisfactory perch away from the strange sounds his mistress was making.

Safir tried to read, but was too weak to hold a book for long. Three more days passed in this fashion until her cough began to clear and strength returned. She slept in long, dreamless stretches, waking with the morning sun streaming through her windows. And while she slept the senator's revelations carried away the truths she had known, like moths feasting in a darkened closet of clothes.

During her convalescence a small package came from Istanbul. Ernie Linklater had forwarded it, along with a few pieces of mail. In the packages was a letter from Bey.

I love you, Sister, and miss you terribly. With Father gone, I, too, feel abandoned. We are orphans now. What are these secrets you cannot tell me? I beg you to share them with me! Are you married? Are you pregnant? I cannot bear not knowing! When I think of our mother, I remember only kindness. I see her smile. Though when she was angry, how her eyes flashed! She was never as affectionate as our father, but I never doubted her love. It was a good home to grow up in. But Safir, if you are unhappy, you must find a way to come home. I know Hereke has not been home for many years, but I still think of you as on an extended holiday. I look for you at my front door, bearing flowers for me and chocolates for the children. In my mind's eye you are still nineteen, tall and beautiful as ever. Then I see myself in a mirror and know that is not possible. I am a fat, old woman now. There must be grey in your hair, like mine. I am being silly, so will end my complaining. Memet is doing well in his university classes. Osig still loves his football more than anything else. Husband sends you fondest wishes.

All my love, Bey.

Bey's memories were not like her own; Celik had never been affectionate. Bey's life, within the same four walls, was not her life. She set down the letter and reached for the squashed package of Turkish cigarettes Bey had slipped into the envelope. She whispered a prayer of thanks, lit a cigarette and coughed deeply. She closed her eyes, trying to conjure the childhood Bey remembered. Meals shared in silence, eyes lowered. Walks to mosque, in silence, her mother grim and distant. Relief came at school, or sitting at the piano in the owner's office. If Bey's memories were genuine, they occurred beyond her orbit.

Safir woke early Thursday morning, determined to shrug off the lingering effects of her cold and go to work. She missed the museum more than she had thought possible. She made a sandwich and put on her coat as Mustafa mewled.

"So now I am better you can't get enough of me?" She picked up the cat and nuzzled his cheek with her nose. "Now you have the run of the place." She set him down and locked the apartment door against his plaintive calls.

The doorman greeted her like a long-lost sister. "Good morning, Miss Scott," he said, opening the heavy door for her. "How are you?"

"Better, finally," she said. She did not correct him; she liked the sound of her new name.

"It has been going around, for sure," he said, tipping his cap as she passed.

The work day passed quickly. Her colleagues came by one by one to ask after her health. They had missed her. Brian stopped by her desk to scold her. He made her promise to meet him for lunch the next day in their regular spot. "I don't like eating lunch by myself," he said. "Everybody knows all my stories."

After her shift she walked to the library and found her desk, the *reserved* sign still guarding a shrunken stack of books. She took off her jacket and pulled the top book from the pile. She had not been at it long when she felt someone at her shoulder.

"Haven't seen you in awhile," Harriet Dickinson said.

"Good evening, Miss Dickinson," Safir said. "I know, I'm sorry."

"We were about to reshelve the books." The librarian stood with arms crossed and wore an expression of gentle reprimand.

"I was unwell, but I'm better now."

"Oh, I'm sorry to hear," Harriet said, her body unfolding to reach out to Safir. "Is there any other subject you are interested in? I can search for you if you like."

"Thank you," Safir said, "I am fine." She paused and thought for a moment. "Are there many Armenians in New York?"

Harriet glanced at the ceiling, a finger tapping her chin. "Yes, I believe so. Give me a minute." She hurried away with a swish of her woolen skirt. When she returned, she carried a directory of New York churches. "There's an Armenian church on East Twenty-seventh Street, in Manhattan. *Saint Illuminator's Armenian Apostolic Cathedral.* Quite a mouthful. They have been there since the war."

"I'd like to go," Safir said.

"That would be a nice way to round out your research," the librarian said. "I will show you on the subway map."

On Sunday Safir wore the dress Weldon bought her and rode the southbound subway to the morning service. The church was brick building surrounded by a black, wrought-iron fence. She slipped past the intricately carved double doors. The room was already three quarters full. She slid into a creaking pew near the back. The walls were clean and bright, hung with paintings of Saint Gregory and the crucified Jesus. She listened to the priest in his purple robe and tried to sing the hymns but she could not understand the words. The alphabet, scrolled across the nave, was utterly foreign, impossible to decipher. When the service ended, she dashed out ahead of the crowd and hurried along East Twenty-seventh, her cheeks flushed with embarrassment, as if she had been an unwelcome interloper. She ran to the subway station that would take her back to the apartment, to Mustafa, to safety.

Monday evening, after work, Safir returned to the library. She was determined to learn, to study, to shed the guilt that had overcome her in the cathedral. And, if she was truthful, she loved the library's quiet, the smell of polished wood, the table Miss Dickinson kept just for her. She hung up her coat and sat in the straight-backed chair and opened a book with the title *The First World War in the Near East*, and settled on the chapter where the Turks defended the Dardenelles from the British Navy. Mustafa Kemal had commanded the army positions. This would have been at the time her mother and Weldon and Paul and Sabik and Toomas were trapped in the mountains. She did not hear Harriet approach.

"Sorry, I didn't mean to startle you," the librarian said. Her glasses perched on top of her head, its beaded string hanging in lazy loops below each ear. "I did some research of my own," Harriet said, smiling triumphantly. She set her glasses back on her nose as she scanned the cover of the small book in her hands. "This was in our Special Collections, too fragile to be in the stacks anymore." She smiled and handed it to Safir, who accepted it with both hands. The book looked as though it would fall apart in a gust of wind.

"We don't usually let patrons borrow these, but if you promise to be careful, you can take it with you for a day or two." The librarian handed Safir a small pair of white gloves. "I would appreciate if you wore these when you read the book. It prevents oil and perspiration transferring to the pages."

Safir nodded. She placed the pamphlet on the desk and put on the gloves.

"It won't take you long to read, but it seems exactly what you are looking for."

Harriet Dickinson smiled and pointed at the title page. "It was written by a nurse working with the Red Cross. She witnessed many of the horrors. It has been translated from French, so it must have been somewhat popular in its day."

Safir picked up the booklet. "*A Nurse's Journey to Hell and Back. By Angela Doebli.*" A shiver ran down her spine. "Thank you, Miss Dickinson, I will take good care of it." She rose from her chair and hugged the librarian, who blushed.

Safir hurried home, brewed a pot of coffee and stayed up late reading through a cloud of cigarette smoke. Near the middle of the nurse's account, Safir sat up straight, goosebumps rising on her arms.

We escaped the Taurus Mountains thanks to the genius of an Austrian engineer. He gathered Armenian men, women and children to work in the tunnels. They were protected as long as there was work advancing the railroad. The Turkish governor came to inspect the tunnel often, demanding the Austrian engineer hand over all surplus Armenians. The Austrian engineer refused. There was violence, after many weeks of refusal to allow the Turks to take Armenians away. The governor and his soldiers were killed in a rock slide. As the pressure from the Turkish government became too great, the Austrian engineer devised a way of escape that the Turks did not expect. He deviated the drill and excavated a small escape tunnel. He had us fashion crude skis and poles using boards and barrel staves. In this fashion we escaped the mountains unbeknownst to the Ottomans. Some refugees died along the way, but despite our travails we reached a small village where we were able to offer the poor souls food and warmth and a respite from the terror. This was in the town of Yelatan. The townspeople were kind, as a rule, and supplied us with food and firewood. I remember our weeks there as the happiest days of my entire service in Turkey. The Engineer and his fellow Austro-Hungarians were detained by the Germans, allies of the Turks. I do not know what became of them, but thanks to them, and to the Americans who secured us sanctuary, our caravan was saved. In my travels across Turkey I saw death on a daily basis, which I have described in other chapters. But in our little troop of refugees that escaped the mountains there was also evidence of life's persistence. God did not just take life, He gave it. In Aksaray, where refuge was granted, a baby girl was born to her still-grieving mother, widowed by an avalanche as we fled through the mountains.

Safir re-read the passage several times. She was able to put the booklet in a safe place as a wave of sobs coursed through her body. The gloves Miss Dickinson had given her were soaked through. Mustafa hopped onto her lap and rubbed his head against her arms.

The next day, her eyes still swollen, she wrote a letter to Angela Doebli, care of the orphanage in Lebanon where, according to the book's publisher, she lived. Or had lived in 1939. She had no idea if the nurse was still there, or if she was still alive.

My name is Safir Scott-Turan. I live in New York City. I work at the Brooklyn Museum. Until recently I thought I was born in Hereke, near Istanbul, but I have reason to believe that my mother was Armenian. I have been told, by Senator Weldon Scott, my father, that I was born in Aksaray on October 6, 1916. My mother was Piruz Oshagian. You delivered me. Have you information about my mother's life before the war? Is Weldon Scott my father? I had a brother, Toomas. Did you know him? My mother died in an accident last year and my stepfather, Celik Turan, died very recently.

Yours in gratitude,
Safir Scott-Turan.

She transcribed the telling paragraph from Doebli's book and included it with her letter. After work that evening, she posted the letter to Antelias, Lebanon, at a mailbox near the subway station. She retreated to her sofa, her cigarettes and her cat; her defences arrayed against the abyss.

The next days she moved as if her limbs were stuck in tar. One bright spot was an invitation from Brian to attend his son's Bar Mitzvah in June. He told her what a Bar Mitzvah was over lunch. She accepted. Friday afternoon, the first day she felt fully recovered from her cold and nagging cough, she got off the subway one stop early and shopped for vegetables and fruit and milk. The cashier gave change with a smile. The doorman opened the apartment door with a flourish. Everywhere people were friendly. Once in her apartment she put away her groceries and fed Mustafa. She chose one of Weldon's recordings of Strauss, set the record onto the phonograph and waltzed across the living room in the arms of an imaginary partner, leaving a trail of Turkish cigarette smoke in her wake.

She undressed for bed, turned off the stereo and set Strauss back in his cardboard sleeve. She turned off the lights and called to Mustafa. He was not on the sofa. "Mustafa," she called again. She cocked her head, listening for his reply. He was down the hall, in the spare room.

"Mustafa," she scolded as she entered the room. "Bedtime."

She switched on the ceiling light. The cat was not on the bed. His muffled reply came from the wardrobe. The doors were shut, but there was a key in the lock.

"How did you get in there, you nosy beast?" she said, peering between the row of dowels above the door. The space between each paling was too thin for a full-grown cat to squeeze past, but somehow Mustafa had done it. She turned the key and opened the door. Mustafa sat on a shelf a foot away from her.

"What are you doing in there?" Safir said, her voice tinged with annoyance. "Come on out of there."

Mustafa rose, stretched calmly, as if he was bored by the fuss, and jumped onto the bed.

Safir examined the door, and soon found one of the dowels was loose. When she touched it, it wiggled like a loose tooth. While Mustafa watched from the bed, Safir flung the door wide open. The wardrobe was empty. Its interior smelled of old, well-polished wood. At the bottom, below where clothes would have hung, was a small shelf. Tucked beneath this shelf were two drawers, barely visible even in the brightly lit room. Safir crouched and tugged on the drawers. They were locked. She rose, hands on her hips.

"Well that's a mystery," she crooned as she picked Mustafa up and took him to her bedroom.

The cat's only reply was a purr from deep in his throat.

Saturday morning at the museum she sought out Brian. "I need a key to open drawers in an old wardrobe," she said.

"What vintage?"

Safir shrugged. "'I don't know. Late Eighteenth Century. Swiss or German. Maybe Tyrolean. I'm just guessing." she said. "I didn't see any markings."

"You wouldn't," Brian said. "They would be on the back."

"It's too big to move," she said.

"Come on," Brian winked at her. "I have so many keys." He led her down a corridor stacked high on both sides with drawers and boxes. Each was coded. "Here," he said, opening a thin, wide drawer.

There may have been two hundred keys laid out by size, material, age. They ranged from spidery wisps fashioned out of wood, to delicate Scrimshaw ivory, to brass, bronze and iron keys.

"This is glorious, but I'm not trying every key," Safir said.

Brian laughed, pointed to a group of keys each around the size of her little finger, their polished shanks gleaming like well-kept machinist tools. "Here's a couple you can try. They're the right vintage. Central European. Furniture locks are pretty basic, I'd bet the key you need is here."

"Can I take one?"

Brian grinned. He grabbed four keys from their cushioned resting place. "Just don't tell anyone, Okay?"

She held the keys in her palm. "I'll bring them back Monday," she said.

"I know," Brian shrugged. He gave her an envelope and pointed at the largest key, the only one made from brass. Its bow was barely large enough for her thumb and index finger to grip. The bit was a small square, smooth and plain, neatly attached to the shank. "A chicken salad sandwich says it's this one."

"You're on," she said, slipping the keys into the envelope, folding the envelope into her purse.

The subway could not get her back to Manhattan fast enough. She rushed through the apartment, calling for Mustafa. Sure enough, the cat was again inside the wardrobe, sitting contentedly on the shelf. In the dim only the green of his eyes and the white fur of his paws was visible.

"I don't know what you like about this place, but I'm coming in," she said, swinging open the door. She tried the drawers again, but they were as locked as before. The first key rattled in the lock but would not turn. She tried the next, but it did not fit. The first three failed, leaving her with Brian's preferred choice. She slid the brass key into one of the locks. It turned easily. She tugged on the drawer and it slid open, revealing a small, cardboard box. It was plain, and clearly quite old. She lifted the box out of the drawer and opened the lid. Inside were bundles of envelopes, bound with string. She pulled one set out of the box. The script on the envelope was compact, small, hard to read. She did not think it was English. There were three more bundles. She set the box of letters on the bed and used the same key on the other drawer. It slid open easily. No cardboard box, but a carved, wooden box inlaid with silver burls at the corners and around the hasp. A tiny padlock hung from the hasp.

"Thought you could have this all to yourself, didn't you?" she said to Mustafa, who followed her into the living room, mewing loudly. "We'll see about that," she said.

Brian's keys were too large for the padlock. When she picked up the wooden box and shook it gently something inside rattled. She set the box on the dining room table and opened the cardboard box. She pulled one letter out from its string binding. It was written on onion skin, thin as a dragonfly's wings. A small, slanted script filled the pages. She could not make out any words. She refolded the pages and returned them to their original place.

One of the bundles of envelopes was smaller than the other three. She untied the string. The envelopes were unsealed. On thin onion skin, nearly transparent, was a sketch. She opened each envelope and unfolded a drawing from each. Pencil sketches, ten in all; scenes of tall mountains, impressive buildings, glaciers that loomed behind little farmhouses in a meadow of wildflowers. The last sketch was larger, on heavier paper. It was a drawing of a grey, stone building, four stories high. It occupied the left foreground, its prominent entrance straddled by Roman columns. Parallel to it lay a busy avenue dotted with clusters of ornamental street lights, and next to that a canal or river. At the edge of the painting a bridge arched over the water, vanishing off the paper before it reached the far side. Indistinct knots of pedestrians in long coats and hats dotted the sidewalk. Probably a winter street scene in Paris or Bruges, it had a dreariness to it that made her shiver. The word *Metropole* had been written in the lower corner, next to the initials *PB.* She immediately thought of Paul Bahr. She laid all of the drawings on the dining room table, careful not to tear them. They reminded her of the work done by amateur artists in Central Park, their easels set up in the shade to paint summer scenes in charcoal.

Safir opened every bundle. The rest of the envelopes were letters, all written in the same efficient, but impossible to decipher script. They were in German. She scanned several pages but did not see her mother's or Weldon's name anywhere. She slipped the letters back in their envelopes and returned them to the cardboard box. She stared at the two boxes at the edge of the table until her eyelids grew heavy with sleep.

She woke the next morning, made tea and toast and as she realized that she would not be at peace until she knew what the letters said. Her mother's life was sealed inside, she was certain of it.

She selected two letters from each bundle. She put them into an envelope and closed the box. She took both boxes back to the wardrobe. She locked the wardrobe drawers, but left the key in one of the locks. The other keys went in her purse, to return to Brian. She owed him a sandwich.

She spent Sunday doing errands, trying not to think about the letters. It was early afternoon when she finished ironing her work clothes. The pull of the boxes was strong. She grabbed her coat and scarf and went outside to keep herself from unpacking them again. The weather was fine. She caught a southbound bus. She hummed Verdi as she looked out the smudged window. She got off on Second Avenue and walked the half-block to the front doors of St Illuminator's Cathedral. Inside the cathedral the air was warmer, a little musty. She wondered if the regulars noticed. She walked around the perimeter, her heels clicking across the wooden floor. In a corner along the western wall she found the priest's offices. She saw movement through the frosted glass of the door. She knocked.

The man who opened the door was not the priest she'd seen on her previous visit. This one was much older, his silver hair long enough to graze his shoulders, his beard full and tapered to a point in the middle of his chest. His face was deeply creased, and the skin around his eyes had the appearance of melted wax. Thick hairs sprouted from his ears, enough for birds to nest in.

"Can I help you?" His accent was strong, Middle Eastern.

"No," she said, "Yes, I mean, I was looking for the priest."

"I am a priest, or at least I am also a priest. I am the Archbishop."

"My name is Safir Scott-Turan. I came last week. I am looking for the priest who gave the homily."

"Ah. You mean Father Michael. He is not here today. But he is presiding over next week's service, if that helps."

"Thank you, but I wanted to speak with him privately."

"Do you wish to confess?"

"You do that here?" She felt a blush rising on her cheeks.

The Archbishop laughed. "You are not a member of this congregation, are you? Forgive me, but I am not the resident here. I travel around the Prelacy, helping where I can. My name is Artibian. Hamig Artibian."

"Nice to meet you," Safir said. His hand, covering hers, was warm and soft and slightly moist, but not unpleasant.

"Turan is not an Armenian name," the Archbishop said. "Nor is Scott."

"No. Turan is Turk."

"Ah. You are one of our Muslim sisters?"

Safir shook her head. "I am not a good Muslim. I have never been as good as my father—Celik Turan—wanted."

"We are all in that same boat, at one time or another," the Archbishop said with a slight shrug of his rounded shoulders.

"I am here because my mother was Armenian."

"*Was*?"

"She died. I have only now learned a little of her past."

"What town was she from? What was her father's name?" The Archbishop moved closer to her, his eyes glistening.

"I don't know. Her married name was Oshagian. He died in 1916. There was a son, but he also died."

The Archbishop frowned. "1916. Every Armenian knows that time." He squinted at her. "Though I feel it is new to you," he said. He pointed to a chair in front of the desk. "Won't you sit down? It seems we have more than pleasantries to exchange."

Safir let herself be led to the chair. The Archbishop followed, after closing the door to the office. "I think you must be one of Armenia's orphans," he said, letting out a deep sigh.

"I have been reunited with my real father."

"I was speaking metaphorically," the Archbishop said, squeezing into the chair behind the desk. "Armenia suffers from an overabundance of orphans."

Safir glanced around the office. It was a small room with crowded bookshelves set against every wall. Magazines piled on chairs threatened to topple over at the slightest touch. A small icon of St. Gregory hung on the wall behind the Archbishop. The saint was surrounded by a golden halo. The mustiness was stronger in the closeness of the room, combined with a hint of perspiration and sour breath.

The Archbishop stretched his legs with a loud sigh. "These old bones get tired quickly," he said, "I am not young like Father Michael." He rested his hands across his stomach, his fingers interlaced. "Do you need money? Education? Our people are hard working, successful. But many of our orphans are not. They have led difficult lives."

"I don't need money," Safir said. "I have been reading about what happened."

The Archbishop nodded. "Good, good. You must learn the truth. Terrible things, I know. We have suffered much. But we have persevered, like the Jews have persevered, despite the genocide they, too, suffered. Your mother, she lived through this, didn't she? I, too, am a survivor," he said.

The Archbishop leaned over the desk, his elbows taking the weight of his head in his hands. He ran his fingers through his beard as he spoke. He told Safir of his childhood in Van. He described executions and starvation. He told her of fighting alongside the men of Van, resisting the Turkish army.

"I escaped with a handful of others, across the lake. We made our way to Russia. I was captured and spent three years in jail, until the Bolsheviks took over. They did not take kindly to religious men, of any denomination. I escaped from there and made my way across Europe and took a steamer to America. I have never returned to the city where my parents and sisters died. What of your mother's family?"

"My father is American. He told me about Van."

"There was an American mission in the city. They helped us in our resistance. Perhaps I met him."

"My mother was, I think, from Erzerum. But I was born in Aksaray, a town where the Armenians from my village were taken to escape the Turks."

"And you want to know why she hid this from you?"

"She married a Turk after the war. Perhaps he did not allow her to worship according to her faith."

The Archbishop shook his head, his beard a whisking the desktop. "Our persecution goes back many, many years. Centuries. The end of the First World War offered promises, but no guarantees." He smoothed his beard absently. "Thousands of Armenian children were raised by Turks. Many led good lives, but they grew to adulthood thinking they were Turk. Their children will never know the truth. You," he pointed at Safir, "are one of the lucky few."

"I am lucky," she repeated, slowly.

"And you wish to return to your people," the Archbishop said with a growing smile. "It is God's work that I was here when you came, I was going to leave yesterday and return to Boston. But here you are, in front of me. I take that as a sign."

Safir shifted in her chair. "I want to learn..."

"Do not be nervous, Safir," the Archbishop said. He opened a drawer and searched for a pen and paper. He began to write in the language she had seen on the pamphlets and around the nave. The pen made insect noises beneath his heavy strokes.

"We will announce you to the community. Your story will join the chorus of Armenian survivors who proudly say to the world that abandoned them: we are here!"

"That is not what I want," she said, "not yet."

The Archbishop kept writing, his script bold and black against the white page.

"Your story will be published in our journal, I promise you. Evidence of God's good works."

"Please, no," she said.

The pen stopped moving, hovering over the paper. "*No*?"

"Thank you, but no. I don't want my story published. It is all I can do to make sense of it myself."

"Then why did you come?" The Archbishop's eyebrows knit in puzzlement. "If not to reveal your story, your pain, to the church, to God?"

"God knows my pain," she said. "I have been asking him to end it for many years." She stood and retreated toward the door. "I came to learn about my mother's world, so I can make sense of mine."

"The church was your mother's world," the Archbishop said.

Safir shook her head, turned and fled the office, past the pews and through the cathedral doors onto the sidewalk and the noises of East Twenty-seventh Street.

The Archbishop's words haunted her for days after. Could there be thousands like her, born to Armenian parents but raised unaware in Turkish homes? Better, perhaps, than starving to death in the desert. She tossed in her sleep, waking more than once from nightmares of dust-filled roads lined with weeping mothers, bent over the bloated bodies of their babies.

The days were better. She found that her colleagues were a welcome respite from her tormented thoughts. She returned three keys to Brian, and one chicken salad sandwich wrapped in waxed paper. As he took the sandwich, he waved away her promise to return the fourth key in a week. At the end of her shift she stopped at the library to read. The stack of books at her table shrank.

Next Sunday afternoon she returned to St. Illuminator's Cathedral. Instead of finding a quiet place to think, the church was noisy and full. She sat at the back. A funeral was in progress. There was organ music. It began softly, reverential, then grew louder, defiant. After the last notes faded, the priest, Father Michael, rose from an ornate chair and strode to the plinth. His long, black robe, sweeping the floor, gave him the appearance of floating. The pews were jammed. Many in attendance wept; others dabbed their eyes with handkerchiefs.

Safir sat with her hands folded in her lap. She liked the music; she noticed how her mood climbed to the heavy timbered rafters with the highest notes, or dropped, like a stone, with the solemn ones. She stared at the frosted windows, set high in the walls. A soft, soothing light filled the hall. When Father Michael spoke, he began in Armenian, her mother's language. Then he switched to English, speaking directly to the family.

"Her pain has been washed away. She is in everlasting happiness at the feet of the Lord God. Never again will she know suffering or sadness. Rejoice, for she has life eternal, as is the reward for the good, the hardworking and the honest."

Safir was comforted. He was speaking to her, as much as to the family of the deceased.

"Karinn endured," Father Michael continued. "She survived, while her mother, father, husband and children did not. She was strong, and the Lord God was with her always. She made a new life in New York: she married Kaleg, raised his four magnificent children as her own. She put the horrors behind her and lived a good, decent, God-fearing life."

Safir stared at her hands. Piruz married Celik and began a new life. She lived as a Muslim wife and mother. Bey was born. Piruz buried her past, alongside Sabik, Toomas, and perhaps others from a family Safir never knew. Piruz had also forgotten Weldon. And her eldest daughter. Was that why Piruz stood silent, as cold as a marble statue, when Safir boarded the train for Paris? Organ music filled her head and Safir squeezed shut her eyes to hold back tears.

A hand on her shoulder roused her. Father Michael stood at her side. He was smiling. She did not know how long she had been sitting alone.

"Please," he said, "join us for the reception." He gestured toward the line of people filing through a side door.

"No," she said, clearing her throat. "I can't."

"The Archbishop told me a woman visited him last week. I believe that was you?"

She nodded, clutching her purse to her chest.

"Then I insist that you join us," he said. "We celebrate the life of one of our own. Karinn would want a lost daughter to be part of her farewell."

Safir bowed her head and sidestepped the priest, following the sweep of his arm.

Father Michael walked beside Safir with his hands clasped behind his back. He turned his head to look at her. "Your mother survived, as Karinn did?"

"She did," Safir said. Her heels clicked softly on the flagstones. "But she never told me."

The priest nodded. "Many Armenian children were raised, like you, in the faith of our persecutors." He stopped at the swinging doors leading to the kitchen. He waited for her to slip past him into the reception room. "They were good parents, they loved their children as their own, but the goal, of course, was to put an end to us." He opened his arms wide and smiled. "We are still here!"

She entered a large, bright room, filled to bursting with family and friends of the deceased. The men wore black, their faces smudged with stubble. A small army of women, wearing colorful aprons, carried plates of food to tables that lined the walls. Rice, bread, skewers of cooked meats, plates of steaming dumplings swimming in sauce, bowls of almonds and fruit. The aromas made Safir's stomach rumble.

"I should go," she said.

"Nonsense. Don't be shy. Give me your coat and hat, I will hang them up," Father Michael said, steering her into the room. "The family are honored you are here. There is food for everyone and then some; the Ladies' Guild don't know when to stop!" When he returned, he picked up a white teacup and tapped its side with a spoon. The low chatter instantly subsided.

"This is Safir Scott-Turan. She is a survivor, like Karinn, like many of you. She was raised, never knowing the truth of her ancestry. Please, welcome her back. When Karinn's soul reaches Heaven on the fortieth day, she will take this love for our new-found daughter with her, along with your love for her."

A crowd immediately formed around Safir. Women of all ages lined up to hug her. Someone put a plate overflowing with food into one hand, a fork in the other. She was escorted to a chair near the wall and surrounded by well wishers. One of the men, his mourning beard black and bristling, knelt beside her, clearing his throat as if to speak to her, but three stout women pushed him away, wagging their fingers at him.

"Away with you, Arpun! Ignore him, Dear. He thinks we don't know that he comes to funerals only for the food and to find a woman to marry!" They laughed and shooed him to the far end of the room and set a cordon around her, so that he could not return.

Safir was unable to leave, if she had wanted to, but she was content, in a dizzy, upside down way. Her only want was for a cigarette, but inside the noisy, chaotic chatter she felt safe. She listened to old men speaking a language her mother would have spoken. She watched Karinn's extended family eat, drink, and move about the room, making sure everyone ate more; that no one was without. There was purpose in the business, strange to her as the outsider, but embraced by all who belonged.

After the reception Father Michael drove her home in a rusty, sputtering Ford owned by the prelacy. She sat crammed into the back seat beside three other women, all older than her mother would have been today. She expected to be dropped first, as her place was so near, but the priest drove in the opposite direction, to Queens. It was dark and the Ford had only one working headlamp. One by one he dropped off his passengers, who smiled shyly and whispered to each other in Armenian.

When she was alone in the back seat Safir called, "This is very kind of you."

"It is a very good thing that you stayed. Karinn's family were greatly honored."

"They are very generous."

"The ladies think I might be sweet on you," Father Michael said. He smiled at her through the rear-view mirror.

"Is that what they were whispering about?" Safir said.

"Do not trouble yourself," he said, shaking his head, "you are safe."

"I am not worried, but you should have dropped me first. Now they will have something to gossip about."

"My plan exactly," Father Michael grinned. "At their age gossip is good. It keeps their minds occupied and their hearts pumping."

They arrived at her apartment building. Father Michael braked to a stop and shifted into neutral. "You live in a very nice place," he said as the Ford idled dyspeptically. He leaned out the open window. "I hope that, in time, you will come to think of us as family."

"I would like that," Safir said. "It is difficult, being a stranger."

"You are no stranger to us," Father Michael said. "You are our sister."

Safir smiled and waved as the Ford drove away.

Chapter 5

On Monday Safir asked Brian if he knew someone who spoke German. He said that a woman in Administration could; he thought she might have been born there.

"She works in Doctor Hooper's office," he said.

Safir was too nervous to approach the woman herself, and begged Brian to ask her. He said he would, but Brian was forgetful and on Wednesday had still not asked.

As she was packing up her desk Thursday evening, a woman's heels clicked across the floor. Safir recognized her from the time she'd been summoned to the Director's office, when D'Angelo had been fired. She worked in the secretarial pool. The woman was younger than Safir. Her hair was neatly coiffed and her red lipstick gleamed like a leading lady from a Hollywood movie poster. She wore a bright, yellow sweater pulled tightly over her low-cut dress, buttoned once, at the throat. A necklace of pearls lay against her creamy skin.

"You must be Safir," she said in a strong, Brooklyn accent. "Brian asked me to come see you. I'm Frances Siegel."

"Nice to meet you," Safir said, extending her hand.

"Same here," Frances said, shaking hands.

Safir offered Frances a chair next to her desk.

Frances sat down, smoothing her dress. "You want me to translate something? I gotta tell you, my German isn't as fresh as it once was."

"You sound so American."

Frances arched her penciled eyebrows. "I *am* American, aren't you? You look Arabian or something."

Safir nodded. "Since 1940."

Frances patted Safir's forearm. "I'm just ribbing you. I've lived here since I was a kid, but my mother, that's another story. She'll never change. She speaks German all day long. My father insists she speak Yiddish, but she prefers German. It drives us nuts."

Safir removed the letters from her desk drawer. "These are just a sample. There are a lot more like that."

Frances held one letter between her finger and thumb, as if she were holding a wet handkerchief. "Oooh, that's gonna be tough," she said. "Who writes so tiny?" She squinted and turned to hold the letter up to better light.

"I believe it was Lydia who turned me over to the Gestapo," Frances read, squinting and halting several times to decipher the script. "Wow, the guy didn't want to waste paper! Who's Lydia? She seems like a piece of work."

"I don't know," Safir said. Hearing the first spoken words gave her goosebumps. "These were in a drawer in my apartment. I need someone to translate them. I can pay you," she added.

Frances perked up. "I could use the cash. There's a cute dress at Macy's I really want. How much?" She handed the letter back to Safir.

Safir's pulse quickened. She had no idea of a fair price. She had meant to ask Brian, but had forgotten. "I don't know," she stammered. "Ten cents a letter?"

"*Ten cents*? Are you nuts? No way I'll do it for less than two dollars a page."

"There are more than fifty letters!" Safir protested.

"Suit yourself," Frances said. "I got a bus to catch."

"Wait," Safir said. "Twenty-five cents," she hastily thumbed through the envelope, "I can pay you half right now."

Frances hesitated. "Make it a buck."

Safir thought a moment. "Per letter. Some are very short. But you have to translate them here, at my desk."

"Why?"

"I'm not giving you the letters. I'll be transcribing as you read." Safir counted out ten dollars from her purse. "A down payment," she said, handing the bills to Frances, who recounted them and slipped them into her bra.

Frances sniffed. "What the hell. But you pay me every ten letters. And bring an extra sandwich, okay? I don't know if it's the change in the weather but I've been starving by lunch time."

Safir nodded. "All right. I will. See you tomorrow."

The next day Frances arrived at her desk five minutes into lunch break. Safir rolled a chair beside her own.

"Where's my sandwich?" Frances said. She wore a pale blue dress with matching shoes. Safir was uncomfortable with the girl's low neckline but said nothing. Frances' earrings were clusters of cut-glass beads, fashioned to look like bunches of grapes. She plunked herself into the chair and smiled expectantly.

Safir unwrapped the sandwiches, spreading the waxed paper across her desk.

Frances practically jumped on the food. "Got a napkin?" she asked, her mouth full.

Safir had forgotten napkins. She dashed to the bathroom and brought back a wad of tissues.

"Good," Frances said, still chewing. "What's in this?"

"American Cheddar," Safir said, leaning back in her own chair. She took small bites of her sandwich and chewed with her mouth closed.

"I get it's cheese," Frances said, "but it tastes different. What makes it different is what I'm asking."

Safir shrugged. "There's pepper, but..."

"That's it!" Frances said. "So good. I gotta remember pepper."

When they finished eating Safir cleared the desk and took out the letters. She moved her desk lamp closer, so that the bulb shone directly onto the pages. She offered Frances a magnifying glass.

"That'll help a lot," Frances said, wiping her hands on her dress and grabbing the handle. She stared at Safir through the lens. "Wow. You should pluck your eyebrows."

Safir made a face. "Can we start?"

Frances brought the letter close to her face, the magnifying glass hovering between. "This is still hard," she said. "What's with this guy, writing like this? It's like he was afraid he'd run out of paper."

"Maybe you can tell me," Safir said. She crossed her legs, her pen and notepad at the ready.

July 8, 1938. Hotel Metropole, Vienna.

I believe now it was Lydia who turned me over to the Gestapo. She will do anything to keep Peter and Hansi to herself. I have no one to confide this to, other than Finkbeiner, and our communication has been severely curtailed. I have not seen Weldon since before the Anschluss. He might be in Geneva still, or perhaps has returned to the United States. When I was brought here the Kommandant told me visits are not common, but in prison, it seems the rules work opposite to life outside: the lower one's position the more likely one is to receive visitors. Finkbeiner has been allowed to visit me once every two weeks. During Isaac's last visit I was overwhelmed with emotion. I am a youth in Leoben once more, standing at the foot of my mother's death bed, next to the priest who mumbled in Latin and watched her die, as helpless as anybody. I was able to control myself until I was taken back to my room, where I sat at my desk and pretended that my blurred vision was only rain on the window panes.

"God!" Frances said, leaning back in her chair. "I have a headache already."

"But we still have fifteen minutes."

"I'll see you tomorrow, Safir. Don't forget my sandwich."

Saturday Safir went out of her way to Katz's Deli and bought two tuna fish on rye and splurged on a dill pickle, sliced lengthwise. If Frances was going to eat well, so was she. Frances was even later to arrive. She did not look thrilled, but the dill pickle improved her mood. She wiped her hands when she finished her lunch, showing Safir her hands, like a child called to dinner, before she took the magnifying glass. Safir switched on the extra desk light she had lifted from an unused desk.

"This one comes from a different bundle," Safir said.

Frances rubbed her palms together, squinting at the script. "*Zufaellige Gedanken.* Random thoughts."

Safir wrote the words across the top of the blank piece of paper in front of her.

Mayrhofen, September 1946.

My Trip to the 1900 Paris Exposition.

The train pulled into the Gare de l'Est. It was evening and the city was busier than ten Leobens at high noon. Paris was so much larger, grander than anything I had seen in my sixteen years. There was a freshness about it, even in November. My uncle hailed a hansom cab outside the train station. Our apartment was located in the Second Arrondissement, on the rue de l'Université. A friend had loaned it to him, for he was in New York until December.

"A relief mission," Uncle Max said, describing the trip's purpose to my father. I did not realize that it was for MY relief. Throughout my life I have been slow to understand subtleties and too late to express gratitude. At the age of sixty-two that assessment is still true.

Only the most stubborn leaves clung to the chestnut trees that lined the boulevards. The days were cool and damp, but there were dry days as often as wet. Chestnut vendors were everywhere, and I could not resist. The paper cones warmed my hands, and the sweetness of the roasted chestnuts was luxury. The smell of coal smoke and gasoline filled my nose. There were few engines in Leoben, beyond the mine, but in Paris they were everywhere. We were brought to the Champs de Mars on double-decked cars that left us at the vast entrance portal in a rush of clanking gears. The crowds were thick, but the Exposition grounds were so large, stretching from the Eiffel Tower to the École Militaire, so as soon as we were inside it felt as if we had the Exposition to ourselves.

"It is good we came at the end of the fair; the crowds were worse in the summer. Let us meet here at seven, for supper," Max said, and with a tip of his cap he strolled away, leaving me at the entrance.

That was how every day began. Max would wander away with a smile. Where he went, and what he saw or did, I still do not know. I never asked. Today I have my suspicions, but then, a sixteen-year-old with the entire Paris Exposition at my disposal, I did not care. I spent hours in the pavilions. I watched mechanical demonstrations in the Agricultural Pavilion. Machines that could plant, thresh, harvest, do the work of twenty men. In the American Pavilion I watched Rudolf Diesel demonstrate his new engine. I returned many times to the Palace of Water and Electricity, fascinated with the turbines that generated power by turning huge, bladed wheels as water flowed freely between them.

It was then I decided to become an engineer. While medicine strove to cure the body, engineering strove to master the forces of Nature in order to make life better. While priests chanted about the heavenly realm, engineers worked to improve this one. It seemed, as the new century beckoned, that there would be no end to the progress of civilization, and I had to be part of it in some small way.

It was with the mining displays I was truly captivated. I had been through the salt mines of the Salzkammergut before: I crept through narrow tunnels first dug by the Celts a thousand years ago. These were newer drilling machines, mounted on rails, underground train lines, descending to the very guts of the earth. Iron, coal, silver, and gold could be drawn from the rock like never before, using water and air power to blast ore, sort the valuable from the waste, circulate higher volumes of clean air, pump water from the depths and power the cars back to the surface. I returned everyday to the pavilion, opposite the Rue des Nations, to hear engineers speak of the mines in the Allegheny Mountains, of the coal seams in the English Midlands, the diamond mines of Transvaal, and of the wealth that was now accessible thanks to modern methods. Wealth that would, in turn, build better roads and bridges to move goods cheaply, affording citizens a better life. Schools would result, and hospitals to cure disease. I sought out the exhaust fumes that made fine women cover their noses with perfumed handkerchiefs. To me they were the vapors that ignited my imagination.

Frances set down the paper and without waiting for Safir to catch up, picked up another.

March 10, 1948. Mayrhofen.

It is Peter's twentieth birthday. He is leaving to study at Temple University in Philadelphia. I am saddened by this news, even though he is overjoyed at the prospect of seeing the United States. I do not blame him, he is young, and Austria is broken. Peter's eagerness reminds me of my own, many years ago. As soon as I could walk, my uncle introduced me to skis. Thereafter I escaped the house and my responsibilities as often as I could. By ten I was on my second pair of refashioned skis and had mastered the new, Norwegian method of downhill skiing. I could keep up with Uncle Max and, because I was reckless, often beat him down the steeper slopes that circled Leoben. I had, therefore, no desire to remain close to home. I begged my father to follow Uncle Max to Mayrhofen, in the Zillertal, where he owned a modest cottage, and where we spent days guiding rich English and German tourists. I would have been content to spend all my life in those mountains, shedding my town skin and growing the mutton chops of our Emperor sported by every farmer. But then my sister Paulina died during a cholera outbreak. I blamed my father, for as a doctor, he could have saved her.

January 11, 1949. Mayrhofen.

I have been very ill of late, bedridden and weak. Frau Schmidt demands me to call the doctor but I am unwilling. Instead, while I idle away my time, I think about my childhood. Lately I think of my father. How he, a converted Jew, could be so full of hatred toward those professing other beliefs, be they Moslem, Protestant or Jew. For the latter my father showed no mercy. And for me he kept a special form of hatred, for I returned from Paris with an announcement at supper so profane there could be but one possible reply.

"If there is a god, why did he not foretell such machines, such inventions?"

The conversation at the table ceased. "This is blasphemy of the worst sort," my father said, lowering his knife and fork and placing each carefully beside his plate. The flickering candle before his face reflected an anger that marred his features, for his jaw tightened beneath his beard, and his eyebrows knit together over the sparks shooting from his eyes. I had never seen his surgeon's hands shake before. My brothers on either side of the table lowered their heads, trying to make themselves invisible. My stepmother disappeared into the master bedroom. There was nothing she could say or do to protect me.

"It is observable fact," I said. "I looked through a telescope at the stars. Ground glass lenses reveal the vastness of the universe. I saw no heaven, but saw beyond the heaven of the bible. There is no place left for god to hide."

As his fury grew, his voice softened, became quiet, so much so I had to strain to hear. "You are an impressionable boy full of excitement from his first trip to a modern city. Paris has filled you with absurd thoughts. It is like a fever, it will pass."

I shook my head, determined to send my father into a rage, though I truly believed what I was saying. "I saw a dead horse near the railway station. It was lying at the side of the road. A block away there was a drunk, unconscious. He looked like the horse. We are all animals. When we die, we rot, just the same."

"We have souls," my father said.

"We have opposable thumbs. That is biology, not grace."

"You are an arrogant fool, Paul. Do not sully my house with dangerous, boastful thoughts."

"It is you who is arrogant, Father. You wish to have it both ways. You say that God willed Paulina's death, but you claim to cure the sick."

My father sprung from his chair and tried to pull me out of mine. He struck me across the face, once, with the back of his hand. He tried to slap me again, but I grabbed his wrist and pulled his arm away. I was as surprised as he at how easily I forced his arm away from me. My days in the mountains had made me strong. He tried, but could not free himself. My brother Franz began to cry.

"Never touch me again," I said, with a coldness that pierced his anger.

"Leave my house," he said. "You are not my son."

"Finally," I said, meeting his gaze and holding it, "we agree on something."

I gathered my clothes, books, sketches, and, of course, my skis. I found my way to my uncle's home on the outskirts of town, the home my grandfather once owned.

"You may stay here, a little while," Max said. "But you must earn your board. Your father will no longer support you."

"I wish to become an engineer, like you," I said. "I will teach rich Americans to ski, to earn my tuition. And when I am graduated, I will join the Imperial Army, as an engineer, if I have no other way to make a living."

"I believe you will do that," Max said. "For you are as stubborn as you are dedicated. The blood of your ancestors flows in your veins." He carried my suitcase across the threshold and bolted shut the door. "Maybe you are too young to know this, Pauli, but there is a price to be paid for single-mindedness."

I turned sixty-five two days ago and I am just beginning to understand.

Frances set down the letter and sighed. "I should have charged more."

"You are doing so well, we have time for one more," Safir said, tapping the desk with her fingernail. "Here's one from the first bundle."

Frances groaned, shifted her weight in her chair and began to dictate.

January 9, 1939. Hotel Metropole. Vienna.

"Happy Birthday, Pauli." I sit at my small table and unwrap two small cubes of hard Appenzeller, rations I have set aside for this auspicious day. January ninth, 1939. My fifty-fifth birthday and my seventh month as a guest in the National Socialist's hotel. I remember previous birthdays, spent in the mountains near Leoben, or in the Tyrol with my uncle. When I turned thirty-two, I was in a mountain village called Yelatan, in the Taurus Mountains. That was a difficult time. My American friend, Weldon Scott, shares the same birthday. He is forty-five today. Wherever he is, I hope he is celebrating.

I pull my chair closer to the desk and blow on my fingers to warm them. The heat in my room comes and goes. It sometimes blasts through the gurgling register when there is no need, or else it is as cold as a bishop's heart. I use my sleeve to wipe a peephole in the fogged and sleet-blotted window. Even my wool sweater and Loden jacket cannot warm my bones. I bite into the first piece of cheese and chew slowly, carefully, savoring its sweetness as I protect the bad molar on the right side of my jaw. It aches incessantly. So far, I have avoided an outright abscess, but the pain makes eating uncomfortable. Luckily there isn't much to eat. Our rations are strictly controlled, and the kitchen is completely closed each Sunday, meaning if we fail to set aside a little food through the week, we do not eat from Saturday evening until Monday morning. In order to indulge myself this day I had to go without all of last weekend.

Near my hand sits a carved box, given to me years ago by my uncle. Cherry and apple wood, with ornate silver hinges securing the lid. I use it to hold the pencils Isaac brings me. Its inner surface is painted with one of my favorite scenes: the view of Ötz from the hills near Sollen. I painted it when I was twenty-eight, freshly graduated from university, before my first employment in the coal mines of the southern Steyr. It was our last time together before the Great War. Uncle Max and I spent two happy weeks climbing the highest peaks of the Ötztal and the Dolomites, painting scenes between strenuous climbs that tested our skills to the fullest.

I peer through the rain streaked window overlooking the Franz Josefs Kai. There is little traffic about for a Monday afternoon. A few bundled shapes hurry over the Donau Brücke. I watch as they vanish from view. I wonder where they are going and what awaits each at his destination.

I hear the guard's approach well before his head appears in the open doorway. The Gestapo have removed every door on this and the other floors, believing a machine pistol can provide better restraint than solid oak. They have also shut off the water to the sink in my room. Six months back Knauer started a flood in his room, one floor above mine, and I was transferred to my present room. I do not know what happened to Knauer, but he is no longer held in the Metropole.

"Dining Room now. You have a visitor."

They speak thusly to me everyday, careless of manners, tone or intent. I refold the remaining treasure of cheese and pocket the tiny bundle in my jacket. I am taken downstairs by the slow, clanking elevator, a black-uniformed guard at each elbow. I enjoy the extra walk, for my legs are weak from lack of exercise. On the ground floor the elevator opens to a brightly lit lobby and hallway. I know the velvet brocade wallpaper so well I no longer recoil at its garish tint. It will haunt my dreams the rest of my life, however many days await me…

Frances halted, put down the onion skin and glanced at Safir. "How long you worked here?"

"Nearly four months."

Frances' eyes widened. "No way!"

Safir nodded. "All of them at this very desk."

"Huh. I was sure you only started a couple of weeks ago." Frances turned back to the letter. "Weird that I never noticed you."

... The guards lead me through a nearly deserted main foyer. Four Austrian Gestapo are the only occupants. They lounge in leather chairs, watching me with open disdain. Two of them are very young. I recognize one from my time at the Ministry of Mines, but he pretends otherwise. He is my superior now. The dining room is reached through two heavy glass-plated doors. There are lingering smells of cigarette smoke and meals heavy with cream. Isaac Finkbeiner sits alone at a small table in the middle of the room. All nearby tables have been pushed to the walls. The white table cloths have long ago disappeared. But the plush chairs remain and I am directed to the one opposite Isaac. We are not permitted to shake hands. He rises, nods, and smiles widely, but I note the dark, sunken shadows beneath his eyes and a small nick in his chin where the razor has drawn blood. I sit, momentarily enjoying the comfort of the upholstery. I allow myself to settle in, conscious of the aches in my bones. I hope the guards will not rush us this time. Without a word my escort retreats. According to the rules a guard must remain at my back at all times, but lately protocols have become laxer and the guards can be found camped at a long banquet table at the end of the Speisesaal. They play cards or dice games and laugh boorishly, pretending to ignore us, hoping for an excuse to abuse their authority.

"How are you, Pauli? Your beard is coming in nicely."

"Is it as grey as I think?"

"Yes. Or more so."

Officially Isaac is my solicitor and agent, but in truth he is my friend. Only Weldon has known me longer but I have not seen him for nearly a year. That was in Geneva, before the Anschluss. We argued and since then he has not written. I am too proud to be the first to write. Despite our long friendship, and all we have been through together, we are different at the core. There is a truth to Weldon that grows from a life lived in America, land of the rebellious patriot. But Isaac, though first a business associate, is as Austrian as I, and shares a perspective that goes deeper than occupation, upbringing or politics. He fought in the Alps against the Italians and was lucky to survive. Now, as a Jew, he is suddenly unpatriotic. Still, Austria is in our blood.

"Forgive me," he says. "I left a small package with the guards. A birthday gift. There is a little jar of caviar inside. I pray they do not steal it."

"They will," I say, "but I will complain to the Kommandant. It will provide almost as much joy, for he does not like it when the guards keep the best loot for themselves. I will say it was Sturmbannführer Lueger who took it. He deserves a comeuppance."

Finkbeiner is also showing his age, though he is three years my junior. His hair is now fully silver, though I remember two summers ago, when he brought Ester and Jacob and Simon to Mayrhofen for a short holiday. His hair was black, blacker than anyone's I have known, save one. I took them into the Tuxer Alps and we hiked with nailed boots over the Hintertux glacier. The sun was so strong. Our goggles turned the sky green. Isaac's sons did well. They are older than my sons, but Peter and Hansi are experienced climbers. We roped together, Jacob behind me, then Peter, Simon, Hansi and Isaac. After three hours climb, we were on the glacier. We ate our lunch and drank cocoa from metal sleeves and let the summer sun warm our bones. There is no feeling like being at the top of the world. The air that fills one's lungs is clean, fresh, young, borne by winds unsullied by cities. Isaac laughed with joy. Today his features are grey and worn, even his bushy eyebrows are streaked with silver. His eyes, always quick, sharp, are red. There are deep shadows beneath them. Since the events of last November, he has not been the same. Steinmueller, his brother-in-law, has a tailor shop that was vandalized. Perhaps the guards here, or their friends, took part in the destruction, eager as they are to collude in the fury against Vienna's Jews.

"I have some news." He leans closer. "There is no publisher to be found for your book. None in Vienna, New York or Milan. I cannot get anyone to look at the manuscript."

I was not expecting this news. At our last visit Isaac was confident that a deal could be done. Folk tales are popular again, though the stories and legends I have collected are particular to the mountains and the miners who delve them.

"Unless you want it published in Berlin," he adds. "Didn't think so," he says, seeing the revulsion in my face. "Perhaps you need to find another agent? One who can move about more freely?"

I risk having my next ration withheld, but I reach for Finkbeiner's hands and cover them, briefly, with my own. His are warm and I feel instant relief. "It is Isaac Finkbeiner or no-one," I say, squeezing firmly. "Besides, as my agent you will work all the harder to keep my alimony payments low, and my advance high."

"Thank you, Pauli," he says, bowing his head in mock deference. "How are your supplies?"

"Good. But they are wasted. My sketches are terrible. Either my memory fails or my hand no longer follows my commands."

The guard suddenly appears at our table and our visit is done, my birthday over. I am taken back to my cold room, where I do not take off my jacket before retiring to my bed.

"You know," Frances said, setting down the magnifying glass to finish the remnants of her sandwich and pickle. "I know a family called Steinmueller. I wonder if they are related? Anyway, I'm pooped." Frances set the magnifying glass down and rose out of her chair, stretching like a cat. "I'm getting the hang of his handwriting, though."

"Thank you," Safir said, rubbing the goosebumps on her arms.

Safir went to church on Sunday, and stayed after the service to have coffee with Father Michael. They sat at a small table set against the wall in the kitchen. While the ladies of the Guild bustled around them, Michael told her stories of other Armenian survivors whose children were part of the church community.

"Many of our congregation came out of Lebanon, where the head of our order now presides. They did not want to leave Armenia, but there was nothing left for them, even after the war. They came to America out of hope for their children."

"I know what starting over is like," Safir said.

Father Michael stirred his coffee with a spoon. "We try to move on, but we have not forgotten Armenia. The bones of our ancestors lie there."

Safir refused his offer of a ride and walked the entire distance home in sunshine. Her steps were quick, light across the concrete sidewalk, for Father Michael's manner had a way of brightening her mood. She spent the rest of Sunday reading her library books, while Mustafa napped beside her on the sofa.

On Monday she bought Frances a pastrami sandwich, a dill pickle of her own, and took plenty of napkins. Frances appeared ten minutes into the lunch break, blowing her nose as she approached. She appeared at Safir's desk, her nose red, her eyes puffy.

"You look sick," Safir said.

Frances dabbed her eyes with a handkerchief. "I feel awful. My head hurts. My mother practically forced me out of bed."

"I brought pastrami," Safir said. When the woman shook her head, Safir felt a murmur of panic. "I'm sorry you're sick. Take the sandwich home, if you want."

"Sure," Frances said. She tucked her hanky up her sweater's sleeve. "Let's go," she said thickly.

August 7, 1938. Hotel Metropole. Vienna.

I should be grateful that it took them until June to arrest me. Schuschnigg was taken at once, of course, as were Schlechter, Fischer, Waldenegg, and those of the cabinet not National Socialist dupes or agents. Being Schuschnigg's secretary, I had calculated it would take the efficient Germans no more than a week to arrest me, but after three weeks of uncertainty, I went back to work. A sense of foreboding surrounded all bureaucrats, in every ministry, every department. My colleagues wagered I would be arrested any day: Minister Seyss-Inquart, now Hitler's Governor of Ostmark, a stump of land formerly Austria, had it in for me. When the Anschluss came Finkbeiner warned me to get out of Vienna, to return to Leoben, or to my cottage in Mayrhofen, or best of all, to Switzerland. But I told him, "My sons are here. If you and your family are staying, then so must I." Besides, I did not want to draw attention to my uncle by moving into the same village. He has been a stalwart instructor of engineering for nearly forty years, a loyal Austrian of the highest order, but now to be a Jew is to be foreign, unworthy of the rights of citizenship. Twenty-three years ago, I witnessed the same persecution of a people guilty of nothing beyond their race, with terrible consequence.

Austrian National Socialists are a cruel bunch. They sense the tables have turned and it is their time to shine. Ditch diggers and criminals, the older ones carrying wounds from the Great War, limping and sneering, fanatics all, infatuated by the rantings of their failed postcard sketcher. Hitler resonates with men such as these, men with nothing to lose and everything to gain at the end of a rifle. Men like Isaac Finkbeiner and his brother-in-law Steinmueller suffer for it.

Frances coughed so hard she crumpled the letter in her fist.

"Let's stop for today," Safir said, taking the letter away. "Why don't you come for Sunday dinner? I can make a nice stew, if you like."

Frances' eyes widened. "How 'bout steak?"

Safir shook her head. "Sorry, I can't afford that."

Frances picked up the wrapped sandwich as she pushed herself out of the chair. "I like stew. Especially if you have lots of white bread to sop up the sauce."

"Stew it is," Safir said. She wrote down her address on a piece of paper. "Come for five, we can work through as many letters as we can before supper."

"Manhattan? And you can't afford steak?"

"It's a long story," Safir said.

On Saturday Safir cleaned the apartment, even the windows. The apartment seemed brighter, despite the rain that tumbled out of dark clouds draped above Central Park. She went to the grocers for a loaf of bread and a stick of butter, then to the butcher for a half-pound of stewing beef and a bit of liver for Mustafa. On Sunday she went to St. Illuminator's Cathedral for the service, lingering long enough to share a cup of tea with Father Michael, then hurried home to make supper. She sliced onions, carrots, celery, and potatoes into the stew pot. She added spices brought from her Brooklyn cupboard. By mid afternoon the apartment was filled with the aromas of her childhood: cardamom, cumin, and turmeric. She changed into a dress, stockings, and put pins in her hair to keep it out of her face, but let its length fall loose down her back. She found a half-full bottle of sherry at the back of the cupboard and set it on the table, with two crystal glasses. Paul's letters lay in two neat stacks at one end, her notebook for translations and a pen at the other. She put on a recording of Beethoven's *Missa Solemnis* to remind her that this was a business meeting. She counted the money to pay Frances for what she had done, and did the arithmetic for the remaining letters.

Frances arrived at five on the dot, still sniffling, but on the mend.

"Nice place," Frances said. She twirled around, taking in the art on the walls, the furniture. "It smells good, too," she said, "not like any stew I've ever eaten. Is that sherry? I'd love some."

Safir poured Frances a glass. "Please, have a seat. Here's what I owe you."

"Thanks!" Frances said, and plunked herself in the middle of the sofa and kicked off her shoes. "Cool rug." She lit a cigarette. "So, this is your place?"

"My father's," Safir said. "He's letting me stay here awhile. How about we knock off a couple of letters before dinner?"

October 23, 1938 Hotel Metropole, Vienna

I have received two letters since my incarceration. More accurately: I have been allowed two letters. The first was from Lydia, soon after my arrest. It was short and direct, stating that being held by the Gestapo did not absolve me of financial responsibilities as laid out in our divorce settlement. The second letter came today. A package, dated April 20th, the beloved Führer's birthday. From La Queue-en-Brie, in France. I recognized the town, but could not remember why. How it came to the Metropole after so many months I do not know, Finkbeiner insists he had nothing to do with it. I could not decide whether to open it right away, or to save it for Sunday, to help keep my mind off my hunger. Ridiculous. I used my pencil to open the package along the seal the guards had re-glued to make it appear they had not gone through the contents first.

The letter is in French. My understanding of French is as good as my knowledge of English. But my tired eyes labour with the cobweb-thin ink strokes.

"Greetings. My name is Helene Rouart, grand-daughter of Monsieur Henri Rouart, who I believe you met, many years ago. I was going through a box of his belongings and found this envelope of sketches. I believe they are yours, done during a visit to my grandfather's estate. I return them to you, along with a small painting he intended you to have, with the high hopes and good wishes that they find you in good health and spirits, despite recent events. Adieu. Mlle. Helene Rouart. April 8, 1938."

There are sheets of stiff paper, folded in the envelope. All but one are sketches I drew when I was in Paris with Uncle Max. The smallest one, an oil, is of the mill and waterwheel and stream that runs through La

Queue-en-Brie, as was painted by Rouart himself. It is very good. Mine are paltry imitations of a style he had plainly mastered. The first of mine is of the Eiffel Tower, a typical tourist's view from the Champs de Mars. The tower, little more than ten years completed, stands behind rows of young trees with pale, almost white bark. I know little about flora or fauna beyond the Alpine region. The sketch is in pencil and suddenly I am transported back to that time.

"'We are meeting a colleague of mine, you will like him," Max said as we boarded the train. We have taken our suitcases for Uncle Max has arranged an overnight stay.

I stared out the window as the buildings of Paris gradually dissolved into countryside. Each village is surrounded by neat, furrowed fields and copses of chestnut, beech and elm trees that hug the banks of small, clear-flowing streams.

"Monsieur Rouart owns a successful engineering firm and is well respected in the field. But he is a fine painter in his own right. Some of Europe's best artists—the ones they call Impressionists—have been sponsored by him."

Monsieur Rouart met us at the station and took us by carriage on smooth, gravel roads overhung by giant weeping willows. The scent in the air was faintly sweet from recent rain on ploughed fields. We passed under a fine, wrought-iron arch set in high, stone walls. It was a small estate but huge by city standards. It was difficult to believe we were only two hours removed from Paris.

Rouart was a tall man with a trim, pointed beard starting to turn grey. Though well into his sixties, he was energetic, high spirited, and gregarious, obviously happy to see my uncle. It was clear the two men shared a mutual respect. He greeted me politely, German tripping easily from his lips, but his attentions remained with my uncle as he toured us around his estate. It was a pleasant day for November. Behind his stone walls it was easy to imagine a time before the Revolution, when the words of Rousseau and Voltaire were new.

We were sipping coffee and smoking cigarettes in the study when our conversation turned to art. At Max's urging I retrieved my sketches. Rouart spread them across his study table. He stood over each, pulling on his cigar, a brandy snifter in hand.

He picked up a sketch of the Tuxer Gletscher near Mayrhofen. "You did this from memory?" When I said yes, he nodded. "You have captured more than the landscape. See how the road curves into the background? It contrasts well with the natural elements. A strong sense of the modern colliding with the natural."

He turned to face me directly. "You must decide how you will represent the world. Take my friend Monet. His eyesight is no better than yours or mine, and no worse. Well perhaps a little, at his age. But see?" Rouart paced to the end of the salon where a small painting of a garden and stable hung above an ornately carved bureau.

"See how each brush stroke is but a dab of colour? A child does this. But step back, and look again. The colors coalesce. They form the image you see, the image the artist intended. And more crucially—the image that your senses invoke. True genius." Rouart returned to the sofa and dropped easily onto the upholstered cushions. "How will you translate the world? That is the artist's purpose."

After we boarded the train to Austria, I remembered I had left my sketches in Rouart's study.

"Do not worry," Max consoled me. "They are in good hands."

Uncle Max was right. Thirty-eight years later those sketches have come back to me.

"One more, then we can eat," Safir said, refilling Frances' sherry glass.

January 14, 1939. Hotel Metropole. Vienna.

The pain of my tooth is getting worse. I must ask the guard to summon the dentist.

Before the Anschluss the Hotel Metropole was a favorite haunt of Patriotic Front ministers who boasted that the Parisian cuisine here was the best in Vienna. (Not true, I still believe the Hotel Bristol and the Regina both exceeded the Metropole's.) Three hundred rooms and modern amenities made the Metropole a popular tourist destination. Its ballroom was known for Christmas and New Year's parties. Now it is Gestapo headquarters.

When I am not writing or sketching, I pace the length and breadth of my room. It is four metres by three and, I am told by the guards, one of the largest rooms on the second floor. There is space enough between the foot of the bed and my desk, if I push in the chair, to walk. A right turn takes me toward the south wall. Two purposeful strides bring me to the end of my road, where a small nightstand blocks my way. I reverse, turn left, pass the desk and window and, three strides later, find myself at the threshold, the open doorway to the hall. My room is at the far end of the corridor. If I take one more step the guards will shoot, at least this is what they say. To be confined in this manner is unbearable.

The one good thing about converting a hotel into a prison is that the prisoners are separated from each other, as its guests once were. That is a relief. Schuschnigg and his cabinet ministers are on the top floor. The lowly secretaries and deputy ministers such as myself occupy the lower levels and receive less attention from the guards. On with my walk. Another left turn and two paces bring me to a small porcelain sink beneath a narrow mirror of polished steel, bolted to the wall. It is where I see how frail and aged I have become. I have become used to my smell. It reminds me of when I took long climbs in the mountains, when the Alpenhütte were not open and the only hot water was what we boiled for cooking. I take my exercises twice daily, consisting of fifty circuits. I must try to keep strength in my legs, but I know when—if—I am released, I will be unable to make even the easiest of climbs. The expeditions I once led from Leoben or Mayrhofen would be difficult, while the peaks of the Zillertal or the Dolomites are out of the question. I walk with my hands behind my back, and imagine the clear, rushing streams above Ötz. If

I am able to concentrate, I can smell the hay on the alm and hear the comforting chorus of cowbells. This is my only hiking trail now.

A dentist is finally sent to tend to my infected tooth. His name is Hauptsturmführer Holzhacker. He is about my age and likes to talk. He fought in Galicia in 1914 and was wounded by artillery. His limp is obvious, but he is a good dentist. He asks me what service I was in during the war and I tell him I was in Turkey. That impresses him, though I tell him not to be, for as inept as the Russians were, the Turks were worse. He laughs. A guard stands in the doorway, clearly dismayed by the doctor's friendly banter. But Holzhacker is allowed to complete his mission of mercy without interference. He seems decent enough and I wonder about his political inclinations. Too many old soldiers support the National Socialists. As he gathers his paraphernalia to leave, he sets a quarter-full bottle of Scotch on my night stand and warns the guard with a scowl that I am to finish it by the end of the night to prevent infection. Perhaps he is not a National Socialist after all. I need no urging. I recline on my mattress, my head against the wooden headboard fastened to the wall and tip scotch from the bottle. It is from Banffshire in Scotland. My mouth is bathed in velvet. When I was young, I dreamed of making a trip to the British Isles, but work as mine manager kept me occupied. I finish the bottle, and despite what is said about whiskey and the quality of sleep, that night I suffer no bad dreams.

Frances polished off two helpings of stew. Safir had not seen a woman eat so much, so quickly.

"Feed a cold, starve a fever," Frances said.

Safir brewed extra strong coffee, lest Frances nod off.

"What's for dessert?" Frances called.

"Rice pudding," she called back.

"I hope you made extra," Frances said.

Safir emerged from the kitchen, wiping her hands on a dish towel. "While the coffee brews let's translate some more, then have dessert."

Frances rolled her eyes, but picked up another letter.

February 24, 1939. Hotel Metropole. Vienna.

I owe my sanity to Finkbeiner. The pencils and paper are indispensable. I have tried to talk him into emigrating, but he is stubborn. He waves away my concerns and tells me Ester loves Vienna too much. I do too, but Vienna is no longer our city. He admits that Ester's sister is considering going to America. Steinmueller would do well in the United States. I gave Isaac Weldon's home address, in Pennsylvania. He will help with the papers. He knows people in the State Department. Jack Patterson was in Yelatan with us. He might still work there. I can pull one or two strings if my reputation means anything. I tell Isaac not to waste time, and to secure visas for as many of his family as possible.

March 20, 1939. Hotel Metropole. Vienna.

I have not written for almost a month. I tried my hand at some sketches but their quality is poor and I am ashamed when I look at them. I have suffered from a severe lack of strength, so extreme I was unable to walk. The guards insist I make my visits to the toilet, but after collapsing once they decided to let me sleep. I did not rise from my bed for two days. I am much better now, and to accompany my recovery the weather has turned fine. An added cause for celebration is that Finkbeiner is permitted a visit. We speak of my legal affairs: Lydia's lawyer continues to make outlandish demands. I am happy to hear that Finkbeiner was able to thwart her request to hand over the Mayrhofen cottage in exchange for renouncing my bid for joint custody of our sons. I am still financially stable, but at a high cost.

"What did you do to her to make her vindictive? Did you beat her?"

I shake my head. "Never. She is demanding and precocious. She is a city dweller, and I prefer the mountains, alone if possible. I confess I never loved her, but I was lonely and she is twenty years my junior. We are from different generations."

"Well, you are alone now," Isaac says.

"For more than twenty years," I said.

"My eyes are sore," Frances said.

It was dark outside. The chandelier cast a warm, buttery light on the letters.

"I understand," Safir said, reaching for the next folded square of onion skin, "just a little longer. It will give us a head start on next week."

Frances groaned and rested her head in her hands. "I guess so," she said.

April 20, 1939. Hotel Metropole. Vienna.

Today is Hitler's fiftieth birthday. Vienna both officially and unofficially joins the celebrations throughout the Reich. Meaning there are thousands who would say, privately, that they opposed the Anschluss, but who nonetheless throng to the celebrations in Stefansplatz or in front of the Swastika-draped Rathaus. The Gestapo are like giddy school girls. The guards tell me—proudly—that our leader is enjoying the festivities in Berchtesgarden, his retreat west of Salzburg. I have climbed those mountains as a young man. They are beautiful, but I prefer the Zillertal and the Dolomites for breathtaking majesty. When it comes to the glorious alchemy of ice and light those peaks are sublime.

I am provided an extra ration in honor of the Führer. An extra Semmerl, fresh this day, a small pat of butter and a pinch of salt, to accompany a thin, meatless soup. As soon as I have eaten, I slip into bed and close my eyes to shut out the light from the hallway. I am used to living without a door. I can hear the guards coming and have time to hide my letters among my folk tale collection, though if they discover them, I may not be punished beyond confiscation of property. That is how little I matter.

I asked Finkbeiner if there has been progress with visas. He is reluctant to say much, but I learned that he received a letter from Jack Patterson, who remembered me and sent his regards. It concerns me that Isaac is not more determined to leave.

Frances stretched like a cat. "I am beat," she said. "I will turn cross-eyed if this goes on much longer."

"I will see you at lunch tomorrow," Safir said as she walked Frances to the door. "Thanks," Frances said. "Pastrami sandwiches tomorrow?"

"Sure thing," Safir said and closed the door. She tucked the letters into the box. She took her notebook to bed and re-read it until she dozed off. She scratched Mustafa's head.

"Every page," she whispered to the cat. "I'm going to translate every last page."

Chapter 6

Safir discovered that a well-fed Frances was a willing and cooperative translator, despite her complaints. She took the detour to Katz's Delicatessen on her way to work and bought a corned beef sandwich and dill pickle. She resisted the mouth-watering smells of smoked meats and warm bread while standing at the counter, remembering the sad cheese sandwich she had made for herself on leftover bread. When Frances came for their lunch date, she clapped her hands in delight.

"You're a doll!" She wouldn't begin to translate until she had licked every finger twice. Her recent cold had not long affected her appetite.

April 28, 1939. Hotel Metropole, Vienna.

What makes a man abandon the faith of his ancestors? My father never spoke of this to anyone, certainly not to me, but I believe that his desertion was the root cause of the anger that followed him like a whipped dog until his death. He thought that Catholicism would open doors otherwise closed to a Jew in the Emperor's Austria. And he shunned those, especially Uncle Max, who reminded him of his betrayal. Seeing the quiet certainty behind my uncle's every action drove my father insane.

I told this to Finkbeiner, during our last meeting before my incarceration. A beautiful May Day in Vienna and we shared coffee and cigars at Café Landtmann. With newspapers full of Hitler's triumphant procession through the city and the first decrees limiting the freedoms of Vienna's Jews, religion was where my thoughts coalesced.

"You are guilty of the same crime," Isaac said. "Except that you fled all religion to become a godless atheist."

It was hard to ignore the red, black and white banners hanging from the street lampposts. "I am firmly and irrevocably on the side of Science."

"So, you are still a man of faith," Isaac said.

"Science and Reason don't give a fig whether I accept them or not. They simply are."

"You are without a compass, then, in the storm-tossed seas of human affairs," Isaac said with a smile.

"Morality is not the exclusive preserve of the faithful."

Isaac set down his cup. "Good, we haven't forgotten our lines. Look out the window and tell me about morality." Finkbeiner lit a cigarette. He blew a smoke ring into the air, watching as it slowly lost its shape, deformed in the air currents of the coffee house. "Reason has deserted Austria," Isaac said. "God help us all, even the godless."

May 12, 1939. Hotel Metropole. Vienna.

Isaac's family is making plans to leave Austria. Their visas were approved. Jack Patterson personally intervened on their behalf. The Steinmuellers join a growing list of Viennese Jews who cannot tolerate what is happening to their country.

"They have sold everything, the shop, their furniture, most of their clothes and belongings. Their train to Geneva leaves next week," Isaac said.

"You should be on that train also. Papers can be forwarded."

"Soon," Finkbeiner replied. Scratching his newly grown beard has become an unconscious habit. "I must find you a publisher first."

It took me a moment to understand he was joking, but my bitter laugh drew the guards' attention. They frowned at us but are lazy and do not move.

"You are a cruel man, Isaac, to point out my futility even as you belittle your own situation. My scribbles are nothing against your family's welfare."

"Forgive me, Pauli," Isaac said. He sighed. "But in all seriousness, there is still business to be done, and other families need help."

"I hope you are not meaning mine," I said. "You have done all you can."

"Do not sell yourself short, you have opened the doors of the State Department."

"Then listen to me, Isaac. Send Ester, Simon, and Jacob with the Steinmuellers. You can follow later if you must stay."

"Do not get between Ester and me, it will cause you greater suffering than you have ever known." He glanced around the dining room. "You are stubborn, but you are an amateur next to Ester." He broke into a mischievous smile, one I have not seen in months, and the years and care suddenly vanished. "She promises to make me miserable each day we remain in Vienna past her sister's departure."

"She loves you deeply, then.".

His shoulders shook with suppressed laughter. "I cannot thank you enough for what you have done."

"Thank me when you are in America."

Isaac sighed, lowered his gaze to his hands. "Rachel's boy, Benjamin, is excited to see New York. The Empire State Building, Coney Island."

"He is older than Peter, no?"

Isaac nodded. "A little. He is seventeen. Too smart for his own good, but a good boy. He works with Julius in the haberdashery but there has been little work since the Anschluss."

"They will like New York, though I have only seen photographs. On the whole, I prefer Paris, but in these circumstances," my words trailed away. "Do not wait too long, Isaac," I said, lowering my voice.

"How can we be so stupid," Isaac said, rubbing the backs of his hands. They are a landscape of a much older man's, tattooed with liver spots and bisected with thick, blue veins, translucent beneath papery skin. "Is twenty years so long we forget everything?"

Safir stopped at Katz's again the next morning. Though she rued the time and expense, she loved the noise and bustle of the place. As busy as the counter staff were, as gruff as they sounded, there was a sense of community, of belonging. She left through the glass doors clutching her package, content and wistful at the same time.

June 6, 1939. Hotel Metropole. Vienna.

I have been locked up for a year. A most unhappy anniversary. I admit that I have been treated well, compared to the stories the guards tell me about the camps. They say I should be honored to be afforded such luxuries, since I am a criminal, betrayer of the National Socialist cause. Every morning one of them, Zeller I believe is his name, reminds me I should be shot for my involvement in the old government. It sickens me to believe the guards are right; that many Austrians are worse off than I for committing no other crime than being a Gypsy, homosexual, or Jew.

I have lost too much weight. My skin is so dry it bleeds where I scratch it. My heart pounds with any exertion. My eyes have grown weak; thin black worms float at the edges of my vision. I could not climb the lowest peaks of the Rot Spitze or Achenkogl, let alone reach the summit. A month in the Tyrol would cure me but that does not seem realistic and it is too painful to conjure those favorite places. Perhaps it is time to begin a chronicle of my time in Turkey. I will, reluctantly, if my situation worsens, for I may have no other opportunity to tell my sons about this chapter of my life. A most painful chapter, in so many ways.

"I'm going to need glasses if this keeps up," Frances said, as Safir counted six dollars into Frances' palm.

"Not much longer. Same time, same place?"

"See you tomorrow, Safir," Frances said, tucking the money away. "How 'bout liverwurst? I swear, I've gained five pounds since we started."

After work Brian walked with her to the subway station, complaining unconvincingly of having to traipse across Brooklyn to make arrangements for his son's Bar Mitzvah.

"You're still coming, aren't you?"

Safir glanced at Brian. "It's months away, and yes, I am still coming."

Brian shook his head. "Three weeks, Safir. You've been so absorbed with the letters. Do you even know what month it is?"

"September?" Safir said.

Brian rolled his eyes. "Fine," he said, "just don't forget."

Safir said goodbye two stops later, and rode the rest of the way alone. She thought about Paul and Isaac and Vienna, remembering her own life in Paris before the German invasion. How unfair it was to know the end was coming, to know resistance made no difference. How selfish it was to complain, when so many others suffered much worse fates. She dreamed of Rue Montorgueil, near Theo's apartment, but in her dream the doors of the shops were hidden behind blood red banners and the sidewalks were thick with broken glass. Safely in bed that night, she read what Frances had dictated at lunch.

June 8, 1939. Hotel Metropole. Vienna.

It is cold for June. A grey rain pelts the windows. Today I received a letter from Isaac that Uncle Max died. He was seventy-eight. Cancer of the blood. He has no children, no widow to mourn him. His will stipulated that I was to inherit his Mayrhofen cottage, not far from mine. But because he is a Jew the state has claimed his estate. I feel only anger at his passing: anger that I could not see him again; anger that I knew nothing of his illness. I am truly helpless. I will miss him. If there is anything good, it is that he died in the home he cherished.

I fear for my sons, should I die here. Will they be denied their inheritance? But fear is replaced with bitterness at the severity of relations between Father and Son. No son knows, or experiences, the early years of his father. There is no empathy. Peter and Hansi do not know what it was like for me. They cannot see the shame, the anger, the disappointment that consumed me, how much dislike I had for my own father. What they understand of those years is what I have told them, and that is little. It is not a father's place to complain about his own circumstance, but to ensure that his sons have opportunities that exceed his. Strictness is a shield that protects our sons from the cruelty of the world.

Opportunities may vanish as rumours of another war grow louder. If it comes, may it be swiftly done, for better or worse, before my sons are of fighting age. I cannot bear that they may witness what I have seen. I would warn them but am afraid if my letters are found it will be worse for them. I think if the National Socialists aim to remove all those who oppose them, they will need many more camps.

June 21, 1939. Hotel Metropole. Vienna.

In 1914 I was thirty, old for a regular soldier. But my role was a peculiar one. I never told Lydia about what I saw and did in what is now the Republic of Turkey. Finkbeiner does not know. Weldon comes closest to knowing the truth, for he was present for some of it. There is one day, among many, that stands out: at our camp on the flanks of Belemedik Dagh, where my crew were sent to blast a tunnel for the railroad that would eventually connect Berlin to Baghdad. It was clear, crisp, the winter snows lay deep on the track that led to the tunnel opening. At sunrise the first shafts of morning struck the snow-covered heights. Out of the corner of my eye I saw a smudge of color. Blue against the shale where the snow could not reach. I climbed a dozen feet above the path. At my feet was blue Enzian. Gentian, to Weldon, the same flower that greeted me on my climbs in the Hohe Tauern. Fearless against the ravages of winter, this brave flower appeared to warm my heart. I did not pick it. If this tiny flower could survive in this terrible place so could I. The Enzian confirmed the decision I had made to find the Armenians protection.

July 24, 1939. Hotel Metropole. Vienna.

I am not allowed a radio or newspapers, or any contact with other prisoners, but the boredom that afflicts the guards means I am treated to long-winded recitals of recent articles from the Volkischer Beobachter, the National Socialist sham of a newspaper. The Poles are corrupt and are torturing German nationals in Danzig; the Slovaks should be taught a lesson; Franco is not grateful enough for the destruction of the Republicans. Hitler is the only one to right all wrongs. And, always, the Jews are to blame for every ill that ever has or ever will befall the Reich.

I heard the guards speaking about the recent Independence Day parades that took place in the United States. I miss Weldon. I do not know if he is still in Geneva, perhaps he has returned to Pennsylvania. I would not blame him. I have no real experience living in a democratic country. The guards may brag that the Reich is the pinnacle of nationhood, but America must be better. I have come to believe, too late, that it is not the differences of opinion between people that are dangerous, but the wish to silence certain opinions at the end of a rifle.

August 12, 1939. Hotel Metropole. Vienna.

I broke a molar on a crust of stale bread. I believe infection has set in, for the pain is unbearable. My jaw aches, my head pounds, I can sip my tea only after it has cooled. I have trouble writing for my vision is impaired. My teeth are become like the rest of me: brittle and easily damaged.

They have sent for Hauptsturmführer Holzhacker but say he will not arrive today. I write to think of something other than the pain, but it is hard. In my current state pain affects me more, for I have endured greater injuries and do not remember such agony. The bullet wound at Sarakamis should have killed me, but for Sabik Oshagian. Perhaps it is the passage of time but I remember none of the pain of it.

The wait until lunchtime was excruciating. Safir kept looking up from her work, then to the bundle of letters on her desk. She jumped out of her chair when Frances appeared in front of her.

"We're so close," Safir said, guiding Frances into her usual seat.

"I'm so tired of this," Frances said as she picked up a letter.

August 20, 1939. Hotel Metropole. Vienna.

Holzhacker came. He pulled the stump of my tooth and drained the pus. He told me I was delirious and barely conscious. He administered morphine, I believe, for in an instant the pain vanished and I was suspended on cushions of warm air. Last night the fever broke. I awoke drenched in perspiration. I am as weak as a newborn, but can think clearly, even if I can barely hold this pencil. He left me the same Scottish malt as before. I wonder, how many bottles has he finished since his last visit?

September 5, 1939. Hotel Metropole. Vienna.

Austria, as part of the German Reich, is now at war. That I am alive to witness a repeat of 1914 is too much to bear. If I were a religious man I would pray. For my sons. For all sons. I have not seen Finkbeiner for many weeks. I can only hope…

Frances slapped the magnifying glass onto Safir's desk and leaned back in her chair. She scrubbed her face with her hands. "I can't do this anymore," she groaned. "I'm going to be cross-eyed for the rest of my life!"

"You're doing so well," Safir said, flexing her fingers to ease the ache in her right hand.

"Pay me now, Safir, for all of them. I need an advance."

"We have an agreement," Safir said, "and I bought you lunch."

Frances jumped out of her chair. "That's not fair," she said, stamping her foot. The skin on her throat turned as crimson as her lipstick and fingernail polish.

"Look, we're almost done," Safir said. She held four letters in her hand like playing cards.

"No. I quit!" Frances snatched a pair of letters out of Safir's hand and tore them into tiny pieces. She threw the fragments to the floor and ground them under her shoe. "*Now* we're finished," she said triumphantly.

In a single motion Safir picked up the magnifying glass and threw it, striking Frances on the shoulder. Frances howled and fell as if shot. People rushed to Frances, whose wails ricocheted off the walls.

Safir knelt to gather the remnants off the floor. The paper was torn and mangled; it could never be translated. Whatever Paul had written—about the coming war, the fate of the Finkbeiners and Steinmuellers—was gone. Hot tears fell onto the bird's nest in her hands. She slid the mess into her purse, straightened and wiped her eyes defiantly as her colleagues helped Frances to her feet. She turned off her desk lamp, slid the chair neatly against the desk, and walked into an overheated Brooklyn afternoon.

She spent an hour at the library, at her little desk, thumbing through a collection of photographs of the Austrian Alps. She tried to imagine Paul and his uncle climbing the jagged peaks in summer, or skiing the snow-covered mountains in winter, sleeping in the stone *Alpenhütte* on straw mattresses, eating cheese and dark bread and drinking brandy, before guiding wide-eyed foreigners onto trails they knew better than they knew the streets of Vienna. She closed the book, rubbed her eyes with the back of her hand and retraced her steps to the museum.

She ignored the sidelong glances of co workers. She resumed her work, head down, conscious of the heat rising off her scalp. She was expecting a summons to Director Hooper's office, but when the secretary suddenly appeared at her desk her stomach did backflips. Safir followed meekly and when she walked past the secretary into the dark paneled office, she knew she was crossing more than one threshold. This time the director did not offer her a chair.

Safir was escorted downstairs by a different secretary, who watched, arms folded, as Safir checked her desk drawers for personal items. There were none, no forgotten lipstick tubes or nail files, no photographs, nothing but her purse and scarf, which she gripped tightly as she walked to the exit. She spotted Brian near one of the stacks, a safe distance from the spectacle she had become. He gave her a hasty, *thumbs up* sign as she turned and pushed open the door.

Chapter 7

Safir refused to get out of bed, except to pee and to feed Mustafa. She tried to drown herself in sleep, and, when her mind started to turn over what had happened, she pulled the blanket over her head and curled up into a ball, her knees tucked under her chin. The mattress rocked with each series of sobs. Mustafa sat at the foot of the bed, or patrolled the perimeter. She ignored his attempts to console her; she struggled to block all thoughts as they formed. Fleeting images of her mother caused the keenest pain.

On Thursday she rose, bathed, dressed, and rode the subway to Brooklyn, to the museum. She did not pin up her hair. Her black locks hung down her spine, as free as a Gypsy woman's, lacking even a single pin or ribbon. As she stood on the sidewalk facing the museum her skin prickled and perspiration rose on her forehead. She did not remove her coat, though the day was warm and her heart was thumping in her chest. She took the stairs to Administration. Frances was at her desk.

"Are you even allowed in here?" The other secretaries raised their heads and stared at Safir, their penciled eyebrows arched in curiosity.

Safir reached into her purse. She pulled a ten-dollar bill and set it on the reception counter. "Here's what I owe you," she said.

"I didn't finish," Frances said, after a long silence. She rose out of her chair and approached the counter.

"I don't want you to," Safir said. It surprised her to hear the strictness in her voice.

Frances blushed. "I like your hair," she said.

"Thanks," Safir said. "I'm sorry I threw the magnifying glass."

"It really hurt."

"It was cruel."

"I told Doctor Hooper that I was partly to blame," Frances said.

"You didn't have to do that."

"I shouldn't have torn them up," Frances said. "I know how much they mean to you."

"I better go," Safir said, turning away from the counter.

"Will you talk to Doctor Hooper? I bet you can get your job back."

"Goodbye, Frances." Safir left without speaking to anyone else. She'd contemplated finding Brian, but quickly dismissed the idea.

She emerged into the morning sun and headed directly to the library. Harriet Dickinson waved brightly from behind her desk.

"Haven't seen you in a while." The librarian took off her glasses to get a better look at Safir. "Are you okay? You look a little peaked."

"I'm sorting a few things out," Safir said. Her confidence leaked away like rain in a gutter. She turned away, embarrassed, hiding tears.

Harriet came around the counter and put an arm around Safir's shoulders. Her Lily of the Valley perfume made it easier to give in, to unknot her muscles and melt into the librarian's hug. Miss Dickinson patted her on the back and took her hand. She led her to a large wooden table with heavy, ornately carved legs, a short distance from the main foyer. She pulled out a matching chair.

"Sit," she said.

"Sorry," Safir said, "I'm being stupid. I lost my job."

Harriet dragged out the next chair and dropped into it, resting her chin on her fist. She produced a handkerchief from her sleeve. "What happened?"

Safir told the librarian about the letters, about Frances and the magnifying glass.

"I can see why you lost your temper," Harriet said. "Tearing up those letters was a cruel thing. Though hitting people *is* wrong."

Safir wiped her eyes and blew her nose. "I don't know what came over me. I was just so angry."

"How many letters have you left?" Harriet asked.

"There's one bundle."

Harriet patted her arm. "I have to get back to my desk, Safir," she said, "but if you need anything, if you need someone to translate them, I can ask some of our regulars. I am sure there are a few who would be happy to help. For free."

"Thank you," Safir said, returning the wadded handkerchief.

"Keep it," Harriet said, "I've got a spare." She squeezed Safir's hand and walked back to the main desk, looking over her shoulder once to smile. Safir stared at the ceiling, slowing her breathing. She listened to the sounds of patrons coming and going; of chairs scraped and shoes chirping like crickets on the hard floor. She lost track of time, emerging from her reverie when the twinge in her back blossomed into outright pain. She rose, pressing a hand against her hip, and slid her chair under the table, careful not to make a sound.

As days passed the shock of unemployment began to recede. She wrote to the senator to tell him that yes, upon reflection she would love to accompany him on his Fall election circuit. She tried to create a routine, returning to the library each morning, willing herself to sit in the cubicle, reading until her stomach rumbled with hunger. In the late afternoon she took the subway home, cooked an egg and drank a cup of tea and re-read her notes from Frances' translations until late in the evening. The days formed a chain whose end she could not see.

She devoured the books Harriet had found for her about Armenia, its history, its religion, its destruction by its imperial neighbours. She read about Turkey, the League of Nations, Austria in the 1930s, and Nazi Germany. When history overwhelmed her, she leafed through picture books of the Austrian Alps and flower-strewn meadows and cows and whitewashed houses at the verge of glaciers.

Sunday evening, she sat on the sofa, smoking a cigarette. A recording of Abbey Simon playing Chopin on the phonograph. His interpretation of the Étude both transported and diminished her. Simon was six years her junior; a New York native, already renowned internationally. He occupied a space so nearly hers, up to her mother's death, and though it stung to think about the vast gulf between them, there was no denying his genius, the deftness of his right hand in making Chopin's composition come to life. She took a deep drag on her cigarette and stubbed it in the ashtray.

"We're doing all right for ourselves, aren't we?" She scratched Mustafa behind his ears. He sat against her shins, keeping her legs warm.

She returned to her notebook of hastily scribbled translations open on her lap. "*...Ester's sister and her family are considering going to America. Steinmueller is a tailor.*"

Safir glanced through the living room windows. The light gave the leaves on the distant chestnut trees a golden hue. Frances said she knew a family called Steinmueller. If they were still in New York couldn't she find them herself? They may want to know that the letters existed; that someone they knew from Austria, someone who claimed to have had a hand in securing their visas, had written about them. Maybe they would translate the rest.

She jumped off the sofa, knocking Mustafa to the floor, and hurried to the telephone table near the front door. She flipped through the phone directory. There were two Steinmuellers, both living in Williamsburg. She picked up the phone and began to dial, then hung up. Better to show up than to scare them off. She found a pen and piece of paper and wrote down their addresses. They might think she was crazy, calling them out of the blue. She would visit and ask if they knew Weldon Scott and Paul Bahr. Tomorrow.

It took a long time for her to fall asleep.

At nine o'clock Monday morning Safir rode the bus to Williamsburg. The sun warmed her through the scuffed window. She clutched her purse with the letters tightly; it would be just her foolish luck to be mugged today. She hopped off the bus near Hewes Street and double-checked the address; she was only a block away. She walked quickly, eager and afraid.

She stopped in front of a brick apartment building. The mortar was shrunken and loose between soot-stained bricks. Four steps up from the street an elderly woman sat, watching her. The woman wore a long frock of a housecoat, faded blue, with matching scruffy slippers. A knotted scarf, also blue, restrained a pile of silver hair. Safir smiled, but the woman gave no sign of acknowledgement. She climbed the steps and opened the glass-fronted door and looked for the Steinmueller name on the row of mailboxes. She found it quickly, apartment 3A. The apartment was on the first floor, she could make out the number above the threshold from where she stood. With a glance back to the old woman, who seemed to have forgotten she existed, Safir knocked on the apartment door. There was no answer. She tried again, louder, with the same result. Her shoulders sagged. She retraced her path. "Excuse me," Safir said to the old woman, "do you know the Steinmueller family?"

The woman turned slowly. She blinked, her pursed lips moved, but no words followed.

Safir asked again. She was about to ask in French, or even Turkish, when the woman nodded.

"You do? You know the Steinmuellers?"

Another nod, this time emphatic, but still no words.

"They don't seem to be home. Do you know where they are?"

The woman continued to nod, and a teasing smile appeared on her lips. Wisps of hair came loose and drifted over her skull like long grass in a breeze.

Safir descended to the lowest stair and sat down, tucking her skirts around her legs. She could wait. When anyone approached the apartment building, she stood, said *Excuse me?* in a shy voice and asked if they knew the Steinmuellers. The first three she met either ignored her or shook their heads, giving the old woman a sideways look as they passed.

Safir had waited nearly two hours when a woman appeared. She wore a scarf over her thick, greying hair and a long jacket that hung unbuttoned over her dress. She wore boxy shoes with thick, hard soles. She stopped when she reached the stoop, a wary eye on Safir. She carried a string bag of groceries in each hand, and set them down on the step to catch her breath.

"I'm looking for Julius and Rachel Steinmueller. From Vienna. Can you tell me where to find them? I need to speak with them."

"Why?" The woman took hold of the groceries and began to climb the steps.

"They might know my father. Weldon Scott."

The woman froze. "That's a name I haven't heard in a long time."

"Are you Rachel Steinmueller?"

The woman nodded and bustled past Safir. "And she," Rachel said with a noticeable German accent and sticking her chin in the direction of the old woman, "is my mother-in-law."

The elderly woman struggled to her feet, smoothed the front of her thin dress and shuffled her slippered feet inside. Safir was sure the old woman winked at her.

"She doesn't speak to strangers—or her family—unless she wants something," Rachel Steinmueller said. "What can I do for Weldon Scott's daughter?" She set down the bags on the middle step and flapped her arms in relief.

Safir pulled out the envelope. "My name is Safir Scott-Turan. Senator Scott found me. Then I found these letters. They were written long ago, in Austria."

Rachel Steinmueller moved close to Safir. "Who wrote them?"

"A man named Paul Bahr. He mentions you. Your family."

Rachel's eyes widened. "God in Heaven," she said, sinking onto the stone step.

Safir handed a letter to Rachel, who held it close to her face and began to read, her lips moving as her eyes devoured the text.

"I know Paul Bahr." Rachel said, returning the letter. She placed her hands on her knees and pushed herself into a standing position, wheezing with the effort. "These old legs of mine aren't as strong as they used to be." Rachel picked up her bags. "Herr Bahr is the reason we are alive. Come inside, Safir Scott-Turan," she said, "we must talk."

Safir followed Rachel through the foyer and into an apartment much larger than she expected. The living room was chock full of furniture: four sofas and three mohair chairs made it almost impossible to walk. Everything was covered in white, lace doilies. Rachel pointed at one of the mohair chairs as she passed through the room to the kitchen. "Sit," she ordered, "I will put on the tea."

Safir pulled the bundle of letters from her bag and set them on the low table that made a bridge between opposing sofas.

"Where do you live?" Rachel called from the kitchen.

"Brooklyn. I mean Manhattan. Right now, at least. Senator Scott has given me his apartment." Safir settled into the sofa. This apartment had a good, lived-in smell.

Rachel emerged from the kitchen, wiping her hands on a tea towel. "You have two apartments?" Her eyebrows formed an arch over each eye.

Safir shook her head. "No, my apartment is in Brooklyn, I've lived there since I came to New York. The senator has loaned me his for awhile. We are trying to get better acquainted."

Rachel nodded. "So, you are recently introduced? Your name is not American."

Over a pot of tea Safir told Rachel the story of coming to New York, of trying to make a living as a pianist, of working at the Brooklyn Museum, of meeting the senator. They drank from porcelain cups decorated with a band of red roses. The pattern matched the saucers. Rachel listened without interrupting, refilling her cup often, each time adding two lumps of sugar from a matching sugar bowl.

"We, too, left because of the Germans," Rachel said. "We lived in a quiet suburb of Vienna. After the Anschluss we were not welcome in our own country. When you have children all you can think of is keeping them safe. Benny was seventeen when we left. He's our only surviving child. His brother, David, died at two. Scarlet fever."

"I'm sorry," Safir said.

Rachel shrugged. "Leaving was the right thing to do. I'm sure you believed the same."

"It was, but I miss Paris terribly."

"How did you come to be in Paris?" Rachel asked.

Safir looked at her hands. "My mother thought I could be a concert pianist. She said Paris was the way to success. I was nineteen when I left home."

"And your mother is still there?"

Safir shook her head. "She died last year. Struck by a bus on a street in Istanbul."

"We have both known suffering," Rachel said, "I saw it in your eyes the moment we met."

"My sister is still in Turkey. I miss her very much."

"I tried to talk my sister into leaving Vienna, but Ester was so stubborn. They had their visas; everything was in order. But she refused to leave without her husband. We offered to take their boys with us, but Ester would have none of it. She didn't want to break up their family. She thought there was time enough." Rachel looked out the window.

"They stayed in Vienna?"

"The Germans took them away. They died in Mauthausen."

Safir felt ill.

Rachel exhaled loudly and rubbed her face with her hands. "It feels like yesterday," she said, smiling sadly. "So, Mr. Scott is now a senator?"

Safir nodded. "Did you know him well?"

"We never met, but Ester spoke of him several times. He was one of the Americans Isaac contacted for our visas. Julius might know more about him. All I know is I thank God for men like Weldon and Paul. I need to put the chicken in the pot. I'll only be a minute," Rachel said, retreating to the kitchen.

Safir ran her fingers across the sofa cushions. The fabric was stiff, scratchy against her skin compared to the soft, mohair furniture in Weldon's place. It tickled the backs of her legs through her stockings. A square clock, delicately carved, sat on the mantelpiece and chimed the noon hour. As if on cue Rachel appeared.

"My manners are terrible. Are you hungry? We normally don't bother with lunch here. Julius is at work, *Mutti* naps until three and I nibble as I cook."

"I'm fine," Safir said. "The tea was more than enough," she said.

"I have bread, if you want, some jam?"

"Really, I am not hungry. My meal habits seem to be changing, lately."

Rachel stared at her. "What does that mean, I wonder?"

Safir looked down at her hands. "I was fired from my job, last week."

Rachel frowned, taking a seat on the sofa opposite Safir. "Why? If I can ask such a question, we have only just met."

"Of course," Safir said. "I don't have many people to speak to about it." She sketched for Rachel the events leading to the incident of the magnifying glass.

"We know the Siegels, distantly, from Synagogue," Rachel said. She propelled herself out of her seat and picked a folded newspaper off the sideboard beside the dining room table. She opened it and thumbed to the back section. The articles were in Yiddish. "Not the best people, in my opinion, and their daughter, well, she's a brazen one. Never mind, there are always some situations in the Want Ads. We can look together." She moved to Safir's side and dropped onto the sofa. "Let's see. What can you do?"

"No, really, I'll be fine," Safir protested. She glanced at the newspaper. "I can't read any of this."

Rachel laughed. "I knew that," she said. "I can translate for you."

"I would like that," Safir said, "but please, translate the letters first."

Rachel let her arms fall, crushing the open newspaper. "They are that important to you? More important than a job?"

"Yes. Much more important."

"Well then," Rachel said, setting aside the newspaper, "I will read these and we will see. I confess I have been waiting for you to ask me." Rachel smiled, the confluence of lines deepening around her sparkling eyes. "This one is dated 1944," Rachel said, leaning over the letter.

November 11, 1944. Innsbruck.

Dear Weldon,

I hope, wherever you are, that you are in good health. They are sending my squad to France, to stop the American advance. There may not be mountains as there are here, but it is winter and our skis are needed. They have been threatening to return me to active service for two years, but until now they have resisted, finding me of more use managing gold mines in Tyrol since my release from the Metropole. The National Socialists need gold, no matter that the cost to extract it exceeds its value. The war has turned badly, if a man of sixty is needed in battle. My squad are young, Peter's age, not more. They are the only ones left to press into service. I have been ordered to train them for Alpine combat. It has brought back memories of Koelrasch and the others in Turkey. I think of him often; of the life he would have had but for that avalanche.

Rachel looked at Safir. "When Julius comes home, he can tell you more about this Paul Bahr. Do you know where he is now?"

Safir shook her head. "I will ask Weldon, when he is back." Her blush deepened. "He doesn't know that I found these letters. I am not sure he will be happy."

Rachel shot her a puzzled look. "Why not? You should know every detail of your life."

"Then why hide the letters?"

"Why do you think he was hiding them? He is a man of means, seemingly. If he really did not want you to discover them, he could have stored them anywhere. But he did not. I think he meant for you to find them. Or he meant to share them, in good time." She patted Safir's knee. "No need to torture yourself with guilt."

Rachel hurried into the kitchen to check the chicken on the stove. She reappeared, wiping her hands on a dish towel. She picked up another letter. "I feel terrible. If Ester told me anything about Paul, I've long forgotten. I should have memorized every detail about him."

November 23, 1944. Innsbruck.

Dear Weldon,

They have converted the government Tariffs and Trade Office near the river into a barracks. The view from my window is partly blocked by the next building, but I can still catch a glimpse of the Inn. The water is grey, though when the sun shines it runs as green as Chinese jade. I have climbed in the headwaters, some of the most beautiful countryside. The sun refuses to shine. Snow lies deep on the ground. I have just returned from reviewing the squad. Twelve boys, none older than fifteen. They should be in school, not preparing for battle. Most have fathers and brothers that are dead or missing. Another generation of Austrians lost.

When they conscripted me, they made me a Colonel. It was not out of loyalty. They had to, after five years of war, I am too old to be a Captain. Our squad will not last long. The armies bearing down on Germany and Austria are battle worn, experienced and determined to end things. I take consolation in the change they portend, even if they mean to murder us. Their hatred is well deserved.

Rachel was translating when Julius Steinmueller arrived. A short, stocky, man, his spine rounded beneath stooped shoulders, Julius removed a shapeless, battered hat and pushed it onto a wooden peg next to the door, placed his ring of keys on a rickety side table and walked directly to Rachel, who automatically offered him her cheek to kiss. Wisps of silver hair in need of a barber's scissors fell over his large ears. He kissed his wife and patted her shoulder. Their eyes lingered on each other just long enough for Safir to feel like an intruder.

"That Weintraub boy will be the death of me," Julius said, "never happy about anything, always complaining. I took out the waist of his trousers—again. He should stop eating so much, his pants wouldn't be so tight!"

"Julius," Rachel said, glancing at Safir, "you remember the American Weldon Scott? He's a senator now, in Washington DC. This is Safir. His long-lost daughter."

"Is that so?" Julius shuffled around the sofa to greet Safir. He squinted behind thick eyeglasses. His smile widened. "A pleasure," he said, his accent strong. He gripped both of Safir's hands in his own warm hands. "You are most welcome in our home."

"Imagine, Julius," Rachel said, "finding out that your parents are not who you thought they were. Think about that! Safir has discovered she is not Turkish. She is Armenian. And American."

"That would be difficult," Julius said, nodding. He chose a seat on the sofa opposite Safir and fell backwards with a sigh of relief. "I think everything must feel upside down to you? Tell me what you have been reading," he said, leaning back against the cushions.

"Tea, Julius?" Rachel asked, half out of her seat.

"No, I am fine, *Schatze,*" Julius waved her to sit down. "Do what you were doing."

November 24, 1944. Innsbruck.

Dear Weldon,

I was permitted two days of leave. I traveled by train to Mayrhofen. As you know, it is the one place I feel at peace. Frau Schmidt knew I was coming. She put on a fire, though our stock of firewood is low, but the house was warm and inviting. I slept better than I had in years. The snows are deep in the mountains, but not so deep in the village. I took my snowshoes and skis and climbed the Ahornspitze. When I was released from the Metropole, I could never have attempted it. I had the mountain to myself. I heard a chamois whistle, but did not see him. At once my thoughts returned to my youth; to summer climbs with my uncle. The sun emerged after my noon rest. The air in the Alps is better than in Vienna, or Berlin, or any city. When I returned to the house at dusk my supper was ready. I feasted on potato soup with a piece of rye bread and a glass of wine. I have not been so content in years. I dug from the shelf an old copy of Hofmannsthal's Green Cockatoo and read until I fell asleep. Do you know it? I think I asked you that before, when you were in Vienna, that would have been 1926, when I married Lydia. It still makes me yearn for a world that has utterly disappeared. I suppose every old man has the same complaint. The familiar is gone. It was my own generation that blew up the world we knew. Twice. What arrogance! What hubris! We engineers are no exception. We think we can make the world better, instead the engines and machines we designed are used to lay waste to the edifices our fathers built.

Have men always hated their fathers? I remember a discussion of our fathers, in Yelatan, I think, when we both struggled to understand them, or was it the other way around? In either case the results were alike: our fathers banished us from their lives, blaming our intransigence on the temptations of the modern world, and our ignorance in resisting them. I believe it was their inability to cope with change, like quicksand beneath their feet, that put them at odds with us. Perhaps by now you and your father have reconciled? I hope so. To lose one's father opens an abyss at one's feet, like a crevasse that splits a glacier. Narrow at the surface, easy to skirt or leap over given enough warning, but a deep, never-healing wound nonetheless.

Yours,

Paul.

Rachel set down the letter, smoothing the paper between her hand and the table. She hurried into the kitchen. An uncomfortable silence settled over the room.

Julius cleared his throat and glanced at Safir. "Those were terrible days," he said. "Where is your father now?"

"Washington DC," Safir said. "Until July, I believe."

"I never met the man," Julius said, shaking his head. "Strange, don't you think? I met Paul once or twice, before the Anschluss. I know they were friends. Isaac told me they met in Turkey during the first war. Did you know that Paul was arrested because his wife wanted custody of their sons?"

"That is in one of the letters," Safir said.

Julius nodded. He brought his hands together and made a tent with his fingertips. His knuckles were sharp ridges of bone beneath mottled skin. "Imagine turning your husband over to the Gestapo to keep your children for yourself." He pondered a moment. "I suppose people will do anything where their children are concerned."

"Was Paul that bad?" Rachel said, reappearing in the outline of the kitchen doorway.

Julius shrugged. "Isaac told me that he was very strict with his boys."

"He loved them, is the sense I have," Safir said.

Julius shrugged. "Goebbels loved his children also. So much he poisoned them ahead of the Russians."

"Julius! You insult the man who helped us escape monsters like Goebbels."

"Paul was not a Nazi," Safir said.

"I believe that," Julius said. "Isaac called him an Austrian patriot, but that is not the same thing as a lover of democracy, at least in those days."

"Ever the philosopher, my Julius," Rachel said.

"Paul worked for the government before the Anschluss," Julius said. "He came with Isaac to my shop and bought a suit. That was in 1934, after the civil war. I made him a wool suit in Styrian style, a stiff collar, antler buttons." He shook his head. "I never liked that look, it reminded me of Imperial aristocrats out on a hunt, but I admit on him it looked fine. Isaac always said Paul was only at home in the mountains."

The apartment door opened and closed with a bang. Rachel hurried out of the kitchen, her arms flung wide to welcome the man in the hall.

"You're here!" she cried happily. "Benny, come and meet our guest."

Benjamin Steinmueller hugged his mother, hung his hat on a hook and patted his father's shoulder. He was a taller, younger version of Julius, with dark, softly curled hair that swept low over his forehead. His chin was sharper, his cheek bones more prominent than his father's. He loosened a narrow blue tie worn over a white, short sleeved shirt. He held a paper bag in one hand. "Dessert," he said, extending his arm.

Rachel opened the bag and inhaled deeply. "*Rastkügeln!* You are so thoughtful," she said, rewrapping the bag. "Benjamin, this is Safir. She is Senator Weldon Scott's daughter."

"A senator? Whew! That's impressive. Call me Benny," he said, stepping around the sofa to shake Safir's hand. His limp was pronounced.

Safir stood and extended her hand. "Nice to meet you," Safir said. Benny's hand was warm, softer than she expected.

"Sit down, rest awhile," Julius said. "You must be tired."

"I'm fine," Benny said. "You're the one who should be tired. Still putting in too many hours. I don't know how your eyes have held out so long."

Julius chuckled and batted Benny's words out of the air.

Benny lowered himself into the chair next to the sofa. His left shoe was larger than the right, thick soled and square at the toe. He ran his hand through his hair and smiled politely at Safir.

"Benny was wounded in the last war," Rachel said, moving between the kitchen and dining room.

Safir averted her glance, she didn't think she'd been staring.

"Run over by a tank," Benny said, rolling his eyes. "One of ours, two weeks before the war ended."

"They were the first to reach Hitler's fortress," Julius said.

Benny shrugged. "Not much of a fortress, but a nice view." He grinned.

Julius made a clucking sound. "The top brass wanted the 101st Airborne to claim the prize, but the Cottonbalers beat them to it." He winked.

"*Cottonbalers?*" Safir asked.

"Our nickname," Benny said, "The Seventh Infantry Regiment goes back to the War of 1812."

"We were petrified with fear," Rachel said. "We didn't want him to enlist, but Benjamin is stubborn."

"I wonder where he gets that?" Julius said.

Rachel made a face at her husband. "We escape before the war, then he," she jabbed her finger towards her son, "volunteers to go back! I don't know how I survived, worrying about him." She clapped her hands together. "But that's over, praise be to God! Come to the table, everyone, supper is ready. Julius, call Mutti."

Safir sat across from Benny. She watched as he held his father's chair, patting Julius affectionately on the shoulder as he settled himself at the table. He repeated the act with his grandmother, who sat next to Safir. Benny tossed her a polite smile as he sat, drawing his chair close to the table and straightening the knife and fork on either side of his plate. "Smells great," he said, as Rachel carried a soup tureen to the table.

"Eat," Rachel clucked over the steaming chicken stew, "there'll be no leftovers tonight."

After supper Julius, Rachel and Mutti withdrew to the living room to listen to music on the stereophonic radio. Safir helped Benny clear the table and wash the dishes, over Rachel's vain protests. She donned Rachel's rubber gloves, for the woman had filled the sink with scalding water. Inside the gloves her hands felt like they were soaking in melted paraffin; the damp heat drew out the tension in her arms and shoulders. Benny took up a position at the far side of the sink, dish towel in hand. He plucked each plate from the rack the moment Safir set it to dry. When Benny leaned closer her skin tingled.

"Your mother said you're a teacher?" Safir said, keeping her gaze on the sink of soapy water.

"PS 17 Henry Woodworth," Benny said, "here in beautiful Williamsburg."

"What subjects do you teach?"

"Mathematics," Benny said. "I also coach the basketball team."

"Isn't that hard? I mean..."

Benny raised his leg. "What, this?" He turned his foot sidelong, revealing the shoe's bulky profile. "I can't run worth beans, but I still shoot the lights out," he said, stacking the dried plates on the counter. "You should come to a game, it's a lot of fun."

"I might," she said. "You didn't follow in your father's footsteps? Sorry, no pun intended."

"Nah," Benny said. "I worked in the shop when I was a kid. That was in Perchtoldsdorf, outside Vienna. It wasn't for me. Cramped, dark, the customers never happy, always complaining. Here it's the same thing all over again. I guess people are people wherever you go." He grinned. "Now it's the kids who complain, but that's okay, in my classroom they have to do what I tell them."

After the dishes were put away Rachel served Benny's Rastkügeln and strong coffee. She gathered Safir's letters, set her glasses at the end of her nose and began to read.

November 29, 1944. Innsbruck.

Dear Weldon,

They have sent word that we are to leave for France. We have been poorly equipped. Even the Turks managed better in 1914. But then, we have been at war for more than five years. When I look at these boys, I see Peter and Hansi, who have grown up during this war. They left Vienna to avoid the air raids, again fleeing Hungary to escape the advancing Russians. They have missed their childhood. I believe they are now near Salzburg, in a Wehrmacht base. Peter is to join the Luftwaffe. Hansi will be sent to fight the Russians. I would do anything to find them, but I am powerless. This is the end, of me, certainly, and perhaps of my family. My brother, Herman, lost his only son at Stalingrad. If I believed in a god—any god—I would pray for their safety.

Yours in despair,

Paul

Rachel removed her glasses and rubbed her eyes. Julius, sitting next to her, stroked her arm.

Benny looked at Safir. "Did he die?"

Safir startled. "No. There are letters and diary entries up to last year."

"Huh," Benny said, reaching for a piece of dessert. "Must have been tough, after the war."

"The Russians were not kind to Austrians and Germans," Julius said. "Cruel things were done to avenge the Nazi invasion. Not nice, but understandable and much deserved."

"You should read," Rachel said. "My eyes need a rest."

Julius shrugged. "Let me see," he said, squinting at the compact script.

He read aloud in German and when he paused, Rachel translated for Safir. She was too tired to transcribe the words into her notebook. She closed her eyes and listened to the rhythm of their voices, how Rachel's strong, alto voice picked up when Julius's baritone faltered. There was a symphonic quality to the duet, a call and response that filled the room with a music of its own. She did not want it to stop.

April 19, 1948. Mayrhofen.

Dear Weldon,

It is time to fill in the gaps, for you, perhaps for my sons, who are leaving Austria for America. Retirement and scarcity provide a surfeit of time in which to contemplate the past.

When the war was officially over Austria was divided. After three months in an American prison, l left Vienna for Mayrhofen. I believe that you are responsible for my early release? If ever you write me, I would like that question answered. I have no other friends. Isaac and Ester and their sons are dead. I have used my old connections to search for them, but with no luck. I should contact Julius Steinmueller, in New York, perhaps he has information more recent than mine.

Peter is at Temple University in Philadelphia. He has vowed he will not come home. He says I am too difficult to be around. Austria is big enough for both of us. Hansi is in Vienna, at law school. He barely speaks to me, but when he does, it is to remind me that once he has finished his studies, he will join Peter in the United States. I will not follow them, though I did consider it. Legally, I am still a married man. In a foolish act to convince the Nazis I would make a better guardian than Lydia, I married Maria—you met her once—she was my secretary at the Chancellery. She is even younger than Lydia, and, if rumors are true, prefers women. I rarely see her; she has an apartment in Simmering district. I am sixty-four years old and am more alone now than ever. I have become my father, despite all my efforts to the contrary. I sit in my study and edit my collection of folktales of the miners, or scribble notes in a diary no one will read. Not very much different from my year of confinement in the Metropole, except that I can walk in the mountains when I want.

Yours,

Paul

June 20, 1948. Mayrhofen.

Dear Weldon,

The weather in the Zillertal has improved, the snow is gone from the valley, but there is a heaviness in my chest I cannot explain. I think this must be what utter loneliness feels like. As bad as this is, it is preferable, however, to life with Maria. If Lydia was a mistake, Maria was a disaster, and all of my own making. Maria and I were incompatible from the beginning. Maria loves Vienna. She claims the Tyrol and its inhabitants are parochial, backward, stuck in the ways of a long-vanished Empire. She might be right. She came to Mayrhofen, once, for our honeymoon, also a humiliating disaster, but she refuses to return and I refuse to beg. We are married in name only, and when both Peter and Hansi refused to live with me I realized, too late, the flaw of my plan.

Did I tell you I had Koelrasch and Sabik properly buried? This was shortly after the war. The American government helped to bring Koelrasch back to Salzburg. His bones had been buried where he and Sabik fell. They tracked down Sabik's cousin, in Erzerum and transferred his remains to him. I think of them often, among others from that period of my life.

I trust you are in good health, and are making a well-earned living. I read somewhere you are a senator? I am not surprised. If you are in contact with Peter, please tell him I think of him fondly and miss our talks. I would be very happy to receive a letter from him.

Yours,

Paul

It was very late when Safir rose to leave. Her body hummed with contentment, a feeling that did not only come from Paul's words, but from Rachel and Julius and Benny. She hugged Rachel and Julius. "I'm afraid I have overstayed my welcome," she said.

"Ridiculous," Rachel said, waving her hand. "It was wonderful."

"You must come again," Julius said, "and bring more letters. They are a window to another world."

"I want to," Safir said. "There are only four left to translate."

"Benjamin will walk you to the subway," Rachel said, repacking the letters into Safir's envelope.

"I am fine," Safir said. "I know the way."

"But it's dark outside," Rachel protested. "He's going home now, too. Right, Benjamin?"

Benny shrugged. "Tomorrow's a school day, so I guess I am. I'll get my hat."

"Thank you," Safir said.

They did not speak much as they walked. They passed through the circles of light cast by street lamps. Safir watched Benny as he fixed his glance on the way ahead; the smooth skin of his face would take on a luster, as if, upon entering each funnel of light, his youthful features became marbled, like a Greek statue, smooth, pearlescent, ageless. She wondered how Benny would describe her appearance, as she walked beside him. Did he see anything like that, or was she merely a spinster with crow's feet and greying hair sharing the sidewalk, a friend of his parents' requiring the favour of an escort. They covered the distance to the subway station sooner than Safir expected. Benny stopped at the entrance.

"I thought you were taking a train?" Safir asked.

Benny shook his head. "I'm that-a-ways," he said, pointing back from where they'd come.

Safir laughed. "Now you have to walk all the way back, alone. What if I walk *you* to your door?"

"Then I'd have to walk you back here. We'd be doomed to walk these same crummy streets for eternity," Benny said with a grin.

"That wouldn't be the worst thing," Safir said and blushed as the silence lengthened.

"You're right," Benny said, staring at the sidewalk. "It wouldn't be the worst thing."

"Good night," Safir said, and hurried down the steps to the platform, her heart skipping in time with her feet.

"Good to meet you, Safir," Benny called after her.

Chapter 8

Safir received a postcard in the mail. A photograph taken with the Lincoln Memorial in the middle distance. On the back, Weldon had written: *Dearest Safir. Hope you are well, enjoying your new digs. Things here are winding down. Plan to be in NYC as early as next week. Love, Father.*

"*Father,*" Safir repeated aloud. "Faaa-*ther.*" *Her* father. A senator for Heaven's sake. He'd pushed Celik off the map of her world and she didn't much miss her Turkish stepfather. It was another thing to feel guilty about, but something that—so far—only nibbled around the edges of her being. She set the postcard, Lincoln Memorial side up, on her mantelpiece, and headed out the door.

Safir took the subway and bus from Manhattan to Williamsburg every day for a week. Every day but one. On that day she'd met Brian for lunch, outside the library. It was a fine day and they ate egg salad sandwiches Safir had made. He told her of the daily goings on in the archives, how much he and the others missed seeing her around the place, what collection they were working on, who was the latest person in trouble with the Director. He reminded her of his son's Bar Mitzvah.

"Crown Delicatessen is catering, Kosher of course," he said. "It makes me hungry, just thinking about it," he added.

"Is it all right if I bring someone?" she asked.

Brian leaned closer. "You're blushing!" He patted her sleeve. "I'm sorry, of course you can. Neither of you will need to eat for a week after! Tell me everything about him."

She described Benny and the Steinmueller family: their apartment in Williamsburg, the letters and their connection to Rachel's relatives lost during the war.

Brian nodded as she spoke. "My family's been here generations. But they can't even talk about the war. I had cousins that vanished. It changed everything."

She hugged Brian and promised to bring Benny with her. She rode the bus to Williamsburg.

"Every day I promise myself I won't cry. I am such an old fool," Rachel said.

Julius hugged his wife and gave her a peck on the cheek. "Your heart is made of stone if these letters do not touch you."

Rachel blew her nose on a handkerchief. "Quiet, now, I'm reading," she said.

August 7, 1948. Mayrhofen.

Dear Weldon,

I told you how Sabik Oshagian saved my life at Sarakamis. I was finished, unable to move from a bullet through my thigh. I was delirious with pain. Though wounded himself, Sabik used a leather binding to staunch the blood. He strapped one of my ski poles to my wounded leg. Sabik tied my legs together, I had one ski for both legs, and threw my arm over his shoulder. We were a monstrous, three-legged beast carving through the deep snow, a trail of blood behind us. It was extremely steep country. Sabik had a piece of shrapnel in his hip. To this day I don't know how he was able to move, let alone help me. We were half a kilometre from the Russian army. Sabik's cousin prepared a small fire under the trees. We burned pieces of my useless ski, and those belonging to the dead Turkish soldiers near us. I was given a strong tea and allowed to rest. Minutes later we resumed our trek. Pietschmann and Koelrasch took turns leading. The silence was immense. We were the only beings moving in that terrible place. Ottoman dead filled the valley. We emerged from the forest and joined a few others lucky to escape. A surgeon was found. In the rudest of shelters, he removed the bullet and bandaged my leg. He patched Sabik, and though he saved Oshagian's life, he was not the same man after. On Belemedik Dagh, when we were alone, he confessed to me that he was unable to be a true husband to Piruz, thanks to the surgery than the shrapnel itself. But if not for Sabik, I would be another forgotten name on the endless casualty scrolls of the first war. Would that we have fewer heroes because there are fewer wars!

Yours,

Paul

"Here's the last of the letters," Safir said. She handed Rachel the fragile onion skin. Rachel sighed and settled comfortably into her chair.

September 12, 1948. Mayrhofen.

Dear Weldon,

I never told you that I had feelings for someone long before Turkey, before Lydia. She is my own age, or would be if she is still alive. The apartment she lived in was destroyed in the air raids, I don't know if she survived, nor have I searched for her among the casualty lists. Her name was Petra Bathory, her family was Hungarian. She claimed to be a direct descendant from a Magyar king. She worked at the university, in the mechanical engineering wing, assisting the Department Head with cataloguing periodicals. I was amazed she agreed to meet me for coffee and pastry. After a month I asked her to marry me. Of course, she said no. I have never forgotten how crushed I was. I can still summon the shame and embarrassment. The look on her face was one of disbelief, as if I were a lost dog begging for scraps. When I was offered the position of mine engineer in Wollan. I accepted immediately. Petra was the woman I wanted to be with. Until I arrived in Erzerum.

Benny arrived after school. It was the end of the school year, summer vacation loomed and Benny's excitement was contagious. Rachel brewed a fresh pot of tea. Safir helped Rachel in the kitchen, putting out teacups and saucers and filling the cream jug. She asked Benny how he planned to spend his vacation.

"Listening to your letters," Benny said, taking the teacup from Safir's hands.

Safir laughed. "They'll be done by then. Besides, wouldn't you rather be at the beach?"

"Absolutely," Benny said, rubbing his hands together. "I'll bring the food, you bring the letters. We can translate under an umbrella."

Safir caught the look Rachel shot Julius as she retreated to the kitchen.

"Piruz is your mother's name," Julius said. "She must have made an impression on Paul," Julius said.

"I don't think I can hear anymore today," Rachel called from the kitchen.

"I should be going," Safir said, "thank you again for translating the letters."

As they had done before, Safir and Benny walked together to the subway station. They were walking slower, it seemed to Safir, then during their first walks together.

"What are you thinking about?" Benny asked. He reached out his arm, protectively, to steer her around a broken bottle lying on the sidewalk. He allowed his hand to linger on her shoulder.

"The last time I saw my mother," Safir said. She liked the weight of his arm on her. "We were at the train station in Istanbul. It was such a busy place, the noise of the trains, the crowds, peddlers calling. I was overwhelmed, it was so much busier than Hereke, where I lived. I don't remember what she said. If I had known I would never see her again, I would have paid more attention."

"But you didn't know," Benny said.

Safir stopped and turned to look Benny in the eye. "I hadn't wanted to go, but as soon as we arrived at the station, that changed. I wanted to go, to be far away. From her, from Celik. I was angry. I wanted to punish them for their coldness, for the way they treated me compared to my sister Bey. Now I see: I reminded my mother of a life stolen from her. Her son and husband died. Her family lost. Her home taken. I was the only connection to that life. Every time she looked at me, she saw ghosts." Safir started to cry. Her hands balled into fists. "Now I'm blubbering like a fool."

"No, you're not," Benny said.

"Why didn't she tell me?" Safir said.

"To protect you? Maybe she planned to, when you were older. Maybe when you had kids of your own."

Safir shook her head. "No, Benny. She planned for me to leave. She *wanted* me to leave."

"You really mean to punish yourself," Benny said. "None of this is *your* fault."

"Says you. Your parents would do anything for you."

Benny gripped Safir by the shoulders and turned her so that his face was directly in front of hers. "Listen to yourself," he said, "you're not making any sense. Sure, your mom went through a lot. As did you. But what you're going through now is because a rich American senator tells you he's your Pops and wants to give you everything. Boo-hoo. War does terrible things. It ruins everything."

Safir twisted out of Benny's grasp and dashed for the subway entrance, aware of the heat rising off her face.

"Wait!" Benny shouted.

Safir stopped next to a street lamp, gasping for breath. She tried to dig holes in the concrete sidewalk with the tip of her shoe.

Benny limped beside her, his face red. "Look, I'm sorry," he said, breathing hard.

She ignored him, turning to avoid his eyes.

"I had no right to say that," Benny said. "You're nothing like that. You're one smart egg. I know it's hard, but you'll figure it out."

"No, you're right. I sound like a spoiled child."

"I meant that lots of folks suffered, not that you didn't. It's terrific that you've found your father, that you are putting it all together."

Safir sniffed, brushed her cheeks with the back of her hand. She looked at Benny. "Do you really think I'm smart?"

Benny smiled and put his hand on her shoulder. "I really do," he said. "And pretty."

Safir covered Benny's hand with her own. "I'm not totally oblivious to what you and your family have gone through."

"Then stop knocking yourself. You think I didn't blame myself for my parents leaving Austria? I enlisted the first chance I got, I was so angry. I still am, though lately I'm feeling pretty happy." He shot Safir a shy look.

"Walk me the rest of the way?" Safir said, leaning into Benny to rest her cheek on his chest.

He put his arm around her shoulder and pulled her into him. They were near the subway station when Benny stopped. "Something else is bothering you," he said. He kissed her above the ear.

The night air was warm, possessing a weight of its own after another hot and humid day. "I think, Paul loved my mother," she said.

"Not a surprise," Benny said.

"Weldon has never said anything about that."

"Jealous, I guess," Benny said.

"But Paul wrote this recently. I need to find him, to talk to him."

"If he's even alive," Benny said.

Safir fell silent. "Why would you say something like that?"

Benny shrugged. "Why else would your father have Paul's papers?"

"I intend to ask him that when he's back later this week," Safir said.

When they arrived at the station entrance Benny pulled her close to him. "I'm sorry for our fight. Did I tell you how perfect you are? I'd like to walk you all the way home," he said. "To make sure you're safe."

Safir hugged him. "Thank you, but no," she said. "I am safe, now."

"When?" Benny asked.

She looked up into his eyes. They were shining. She kissed him. "See you tomorrow, Benjamin Steinmueller. Don't forget our date."

Benny raised his arms in surrender. "I haven't forgotten. Scouts honor."

She kissed him goodbye and left him at the top of the stairs. Safir smiled all the way back to Manhattan.

It was Safir's first Bar Mitzvah, and it was wonderful. It was her first time, not counting their walks, with Benny anywhere other than his parents' home. She wanted to impress him. She wore the dress Weldon had bought her. She pinned her hair beneath a new hat, and wore the gloves she'd bought with the last of Weldon's money. She spent more time in front of the mirror, checking her looks, then scolded herself for her school girl anxiety. Benny looked dapper in his suit, a little worn but perfectly tailored and nicely pressed. His hair was combed flat, stiff and shiny. Benny had ridden into Manhattan from Williamsburg. Safir took the bus to the Lower East Side, found Benny standing on the corner of East Tenth, leaning against a skinny tree planted in front of a Catholic Church. She waved at him through the bus window, skipped to him like a schoolgirl.

They held hands as they walked the last block to the Synagogue. They were a little late, but Brian and his wife, Hannah, welcomed them like long lost family, and led them into the crowded hall. Safir drank punch, danced with strangers, and watched proudly as Benny helped hoist the son, then the father, into the air on metal chairs that were stronger than they looked. They spoke briefly with the Rabbi and his wife. He and Benny exchanged histories of their military service, while Safir and the Rabbi's wife talked about music. They had a shared love of Chopin.

Brian found a moment alone with Safir. His face was shiny with perspiration and joy. "You found a good translator, I think," he said and winked.

She blushed. "Yes, I guess it looks that way."

Benny appeared beside them. Safir introduced him to Brian.

"Great you could come," Brian said.

"Thanks for the invitation," Benny said. "I see some folks I know. We belong to Beth Elohim in Williamsburg."

"I know it well," Brian said. He glanced at Safir. "Converting soon?"

"So many choices," she said.

It was late in the evening when they walked back to the subway. Their faces glistened, their clothes clung to them, as if they'd been caught in a summer rain. Safir's feet ached, but she couldn't keep from smiling. Benny hooked his finger through his jacket and swung it over his shoulder. He offered Safir his cigarette, which she took, gratefully. "Did I tell you how nice you look?" Benny said.

"Yes, you did," she said. "More than once. You also."

"Thanks," Benny said. He held out his arms. "No excuses when your dad's a tailor." He took back the cigarette and stuck it between his lips.

They resumed their slow walk, as if they had nowhere to go and nothing but time to get there. Benny draped an arm over Safir's shoulder. Safir threaded her index finger through one of Benny's belt loops. They turned north on Second Avenue, following a squat, wrought iron fence. The arrowhead palings were rusting where the black paint had come off. In the dark they more suited a haunted house on a hill, than a staid church in lower Manhattan. The fence ended at a stone pillar. A shape lurched at them from the shadow of the pillar. A stranger, a beggar, looking for spare change. The figure did not stop. It charged them, knocking them both to the ground.

Vincenzo D'Angelo stood over Safir.

"So, you got yourself a boyfriend," he said. "Well ain't that grand." He spat.

Benny jumped to his feet and pushed D'Angelo away from Safir.

D'Angelo took two strides back, then attacked, waving his arms wildly. "I hate you!" he screamed. One of his fists struck Benny on the side of the face, spinning him around. "Does your senator sugar daddy know you're two-timing him?" He lunged toward Safir.

"Get away from me!" Safir screamed, her hands, now fists hovering between them.

"So high and mighty, aren't you?" D'Angelo stopped short. "I bet you don't have a spare thought for your old boss." His hands were shaking as they brushed the lapels of his rumpled jacket.

"I'm glad you were fired!" Safir said. "Stay away from me."

"Get yourself a better bodyguard," D'Angelo said, glancing at Benny as he turned and ran away.

Benny started to chase D'Angelo, but Safir shouted at him to come back.

"It's okay," Benny whispered, his arms encircling her waist.

Safir began to shake.

Benny led her to a stone bench half a block behind them. A slight breeze shook the leaves of the elm trees whose branches stooped low over them. Safir watched the leaves shiver, feeling her breathing slow, willing the pangs of nausea to pass.

"My dress is ruined," she said, noticing a tear in the hem.

"My dad can fix that," Benny said. He gathered her hands in his. "Did he hurt you? That Son of a Bitch."

Safir shook her head. "He stopped, I guess he saw you coming," she said. "Thanks."

"I was pretty useless," Benny said. "He got in a lucky shot, right on the button."

"I wanted to kill him" she said. "I've never felt like that before."

"Shhh." Benny pressed his cheek against hers. "Let's get out of here."

"Take me home, Benny," Safir said.

She slept poorly, still unsettled by D'Angelo's ambush. She attacked the apartment with mop and duster, even cleaning the windows as Mustafa watched from the sofa. She was sweating, grimy and tired when the buzzer rang. Benny was at the front door. She rang him in reluctantly. He held a bunch of roses in front of his face as the door swung open.

"What are you doing here?" Safir said, "I wasn't expecting anyone. I'm a mess."

"Nice to see you, too. By the way, you look amazing," Benny said, kissing her on the cheek. "I got a surprise for you."

"Thank you for these," she said, taking the roses and hurrying to the kitchen. She arranged them in a vase and set them on the dining room table. "You didn't have to."

"I wanted to. Now get dressed, we're going on a trip."

"What? Where?"

"No more questions. Hurry up, we got a bus to catch."

"Benny, no, I'm not presentable."

Benny looked at his wristwatch. "We're in good time. Quit stalling and get ready."

She washed, pinned up her hair, put on her makeup and dressed for a weekday morning.

"Bring the letters," was all Benny said through the bathroom door.

They rode the bus south on Eighth Avenue to Penn Station. When Benny stood to hop off the bus, Safir was nearly left behind. "Where are we going?"

"C'mon," Benny said, grabbing her hand. "Our train leaves in ten minutes."

"Benjamin Steinmueller, where are you taking me?"

"I'll tell you when we get our seats," Benny said. "It's a surprise, remember?"

When they were seated on the train, Safir pulled Benny's face away from the window to hold his glance. "This train goes to Washington. Is that your plan, to meet my father?"

Benny shook his head. "No way. I'll meet him soon enough. Guess again."

"Benny, I haven't a clue."

"We're going to Philadelphia," Benny said with a flourish.

"Why?" Safir asked, glancing over his shoulder at the train started to move.

"Peter Bahr. He lives there."

"Paul's son?"

"The same. I called him."

"What are you talking about?"

"You brought the letters, like I asked?"

"Yes, but how did you find him?"

"He's taking his PhD at Temple. It wasn't hard. I told the secretary at the Graduate Faculty that I was an old friend from Vienna. Which is kind of true, when you think about it."

"You talked to him?"

"Sure thing. He invited us to his apartment."

Safir slid down in her seat, her shoes pressed into the seat back in front of them. "What did you tell him about me?"

"Just that you're Weldon Scott's daughter, and that you found a bunch of Paul's letters and tracked down my family to translate them. He remembers the name Steinmueller, but I don't think we ever met."

The journey was short, the train made good time, and they got off at Broad Street Station in North Philadelphia. The day was warm, the air thick and sticky. Benny flagged a taxi outside the station. Safir read out the address to the driver, who rolled his eyes.

"You could a walked," he said, shifting into drive with gears grinding.

"You want the fare or not?" Benny said. He slammed the door and banged on the side of the car.

The taxi rolled away from the curb. Safir leaned close to the open window, but movement offered little relief. The driver was right; the cab had gone only a few blocks when he pulled over. The taxi idled in front of an apartment building, a low, square Stalinesque building on the north fringe of the campus. Benny paid the driver. They hurried to the front door. The lock was broken. They hiked up two flights of stairs, the air hotter in the staircase. The sound of children's voices through the walls accompanied them down the linoleum-floored hallway. Safir wiped a bead of perspiration off her forehead with the back of her hand and knocked on the door in front of which Benny had stopped.

The man who answered gripped a pipe in one hand and a book in the other. He wore a white tee shirt, baggy trousers and corduroy slippers shiny with wear. His round, thick glasses gave his eyes a frog-like appearance. His hair, nearly as black as Safir's, had been cropped close to his skull.

"Yes?" He spoke with only a hint of an accent.

Benny held out his hand. "Benjamin Steinmueller. We talked on the phone last week."

Safir frowned at Benny. He'd been keeping this secret longer than she'd thought. She shook Peter's hand. "I'm Safir Scott-Turan. Weldon Scott's daughter."

"Come in," Peter said, pointing with his pipe. "I remember Mr. Scott."

The apartment was small and dark with every curtain drawn. A fan hummed noisily in the corner of a cramped living room, where books lay in jumbled stacks on every horizontal surface, including the threadbare sofa. Safir wondered how the place would look if they'd dropped in unannounced. Peter shuffled ahead and carefully lifted a stack of books from a chair, then stood, blinking, unsure where to place them. He took them into a tiny kitchen and set them on the stove.

"Here," he said, gesturing to the chair. "You'll have to fight over it. Or I could move the books off the chesterfield. I don't get much company," he grinned. He sat cross-legged on the floor opposite, tilting his head to see past three stacks of text books that rose off the floor like miniature sky scrapers.

"Don't bother," Benny said, and sat on the floor beside Safir.

"I can make tea, if you like," Peter said.

"You'll have to move the books again," Benny said.

Safir shook her head. "We're fine, really. Benny told you I have some of your father's letters."

"He did, yes. How?" Peter asked. He took a pen knife out of his pocket, opened the blade and began to clean his pipe.

"They were in a wardrobe, tucked inside a drawer," Safir said. She pulled the bundles out of her purse and handed them to Peter.

Peter lit his pipe, then slid a letter out of one of the bundles. He held up the paper to the lamp behind him and squinted.

"Is it all right if I smoke too?" Safir said. When Peter nodded, she lit a cigarette and exhaled gratefully. "You came here for school because of Weldon?"

Peter shook his head. "Coincidence, is all. Weldon Scott is a Yale man. No, Temple offered me a scholarship, through the American Embassy. That was right after the war. My father was furious. He said

I could stay for a year. But I liked it, and refused to return to Austria. Now I'm into my dissertation year and have applied for citizenship."

"You won't go home? What does your father say?" Benny asked.

Peter took a deep pull on his pipe and blew smoke rings toward the ceiling. "Doesn't matter. He's dead."

Safir's heart raced. "Paul Bahr died?"

Peter nodded. "Cancer. Last year."

"That's probably why your father has the wardrobe," Benny said.

"You have a brother?" Safir said.

Peter nodded. "He's still in Vienna, though he tells me he wants to emigrate. The country is still divided, and in the Russian zone life is pretty tough."

"Will he come here?" Safir asked.

"Doubt it," Peter said. "He's thinking of Canada. He wants to live near the ocean. Maybe Vancouver." Peter shrugged. "We aren't that close, which is strange when you think about it. We've been shot at by the Russians, chased by the French. The Americans were kind, I have to say." He cleared his throat. "So, I have some of Paul's notebooks," Peter said. "Do you want to hear some?"

Safir nodded. "When he was in Turkey. With my mother. Until a few weeks ago I never knew she was Armenian."

Peter pulled himself up with help from a stack of books. "Let me get them. They're around here somewhere." He began moving piles of books and file folders from one teetering pile to another.

Benny squeezed Safir's hand. She leaned over and kissed the top of his curly head.

When Peter had rearranged every stack in the cramped living room he straightened, relit his pipe and stood with his arms on his hips, surveying the clutter. "I know!" He shouted and dashed past Safir and Benny, into the bedroom. After several minutes he returned, his glasses askew, his pipe clenched between his teeth. It had gone out again. In his arms was a box, still covered with string and butcher paper and postmarks.

"I mailed all this stuff home after the funeral," Peter said, grinning with triumph.

"Looks like you never opened it," Benny said. "Need a hand?"

Peter's grin faded as he scanned the room for an empty place to set the box. "Not yet. And actually, yes. Could you take those books and put them over…?" He gave a vague wave.

"Sure," Benny and Safir answered together. They picked three piles of books off the coffee table and did the same country dance as Peter, looking for a spot to set them. They added to stacks against the wall, for stability's sake.

"Thanks," Peter said, dropping the box on the table. He settled onto his knees and cut the string with his pen knife. "I grabbed these from my father's library. Maria was going to throw them out."

"Maria's your stepmother?" Safir said.

Peter looked up and met Safir's glance. "You know quite a bit, if you know that."

"It was in one of the letters," she said.

"She only came to the house to make sure Hansi and I didn't steal anything. She trusted Weldon enough, though. They were always close, for some reason I could never fathom."

"How long were they married?" Benny asked.

"Before the Anschluss. My father thought he could win custody of us if there was a woman around. Didn't work. They were miserable together. After he died, she took everything, including the Mayrhofen house and all its possessions, though probably she was there twice, including after the funeral."

"My father was in Mayrhofen?"

"At the funeral, yes. He didn't mention you, but I see a little family resemblance."

Safir frowned at Benny while Peter unpacked several bound scrapbooks from the box. "When did Paul die?"

Peter stared at the ceiling. "Let me think. I had to get Carlson to cover my political theory class, it had just started, so that would have been September."

"My mother died in October."

Peter snapped his fingers. "That reminds me," he said, and set the scrapbook in his hand back in the box. "Give me a minute." He jumped to his feet and disappeared into the bedroom.

"Wonder what's in here?" Benny began to thumb through the scrapbook Peter had put down.

"Benny!" Safir scolded. "Wait."

"Why? He was just going to show us," he said. He spread the heavy, yellowed pages apart on a set of black and white photographs. In the dim light it was difficult to see.

"Those are your eyes, I'd know them anywhere," Benny said. He lifted the book so Safir could see.

"That's my brother, Hansi, "Peter said, leaning in between them. He'd appeared behind them without a sound. "Here's what I meant to show you." A small, framed portrait slid in front of Safir. Peter set it against the box on the coffee table.

Safir gazed at her mother, half smiling yet somehow remote, perhaps sad. She knew those eyes, the line of her jaw, the nostrils that so often flared with disappointment.

"When I first saw you, I knew you'd like it," Peter said.

"Safir, are you okay?" Benny draped an arm over her shoulders.

Safir shook her head, pressing her palms against her face.

Peter cleared his throat, retreating to the other side of the coffee table. "It says *Piruz. Yelatan, 1916.* On the back. It was one of his possessions Maria was going to toss, so I took it. My father was a pretty fair artist."

Safir wiped her eyes with the back of her hand. "Yes, he was. There were some sketches he did in the Metropole."

Peter crouched in front of the box and took the scrapbook from Benny. "There are some of my baby pictures in here. You think Safir looks like Hansi?"

Benny nodded, but kept his glance on Safir. "You going to be okay?"

"Just a shock, is all," Safir said.

"You can have it," Peter said.

Safir blinked. "You can't be serious?"

Peter cleared his throat. Safir thought she saw him blush.

"I'm a little overcrowded here. And it's your mother, right?"

Safir nodded. "Thank you, it's beautiful."

"Sure thing. Oh, here's something," Peter said, flipping past the photos of baby boys. "This guy," Peter pointed at a photograph of an officer in SS officer's uniform, "lived with my mother during the war. While my father was confined. In fact, I'm pretty sure he got him locked up."

Benny squinted at the mustachioed officer. "He's a *Sturmbannführer*."

Peter nodded. "Doctor Moro was his name. He's still alive, I think, though my mother's not with him anymore. Hansi doesn't believe me, but I am convinced she took up with him in order to punish our father. This guy meant business," Peter said, tapping the photograph with the end of his pipe.

"Is that your mother?" Safir's finger hovered over a photograph of a handsome woman in a dark suit and tie, with neatly coiffed hair and a prominent nose and chin.

"Lydia Muehldorfer," Peter said. "One smart lady. This was taken when she got her Doctorate in German Literature. She was only twenty. Puts all of us to shame. Her father was a mining engineer, like Paul. And only three years older. Classic father issues. You know, Freud was right about everything."

"They divorced before the war," Safir said.

"They did. I was ten, Hansi eight. We bounced around. Lydia tried to have sole custody, but until the Anschluss she wasn't successful. Then Doctor Moro came on the scene and Paul was arrested and we were with her."

"After Paul was released from the Metropole, what did he do?"

"He went back to the Mining Federation in Vienna, but that didn't last long. There's entries from that time in here somewhere." Peter rifled through the box, before lifting a fragile looking notebook and riffling the pages. "See, mostly blank pages. This would have been around May 1940, when the Germans invaded France."

"I was there," Safir said.

Peter chewed the end of his pipe. "Visas weren't easy to come by. Did Weldon help?"

Safir shook her head. "Theo had money."

"Theo was her professor," Benny offered.

"Huh," Peter said. "Lots of rich Frenchmen couldn't get visas. You sure Weldon didn't *'grease the wheels'* as they say?"

Safir stuck out her chin. "No, and I don't really care one way or the other. I want to hear what Paul said."

"Sure thing," Peter said. He pushed his glasses up the bridge of his nose and cleared his throat.

May 14, 1940. Hotel Metropole.

The guards whisper that I am soon to leave this place. I am glad of that. One month shy of two years is long enough. But it is the way they whisper that infuriates me. Am I to be released or transferred? Their hints are another form of torture, building false hope while insinuating worse to come. And if transferred, where? To one of the camps? To Germany, or worse, to Poland? Rumours of these camps, and the thousands who are sent there, grow. I haven't seen Isaac in months. When I ask, I am told to mind my own business; that the Reich is always right and what is right is securing the purity of its inhabitants. I am told this by men whose own families rubbed shoulders with Bohemians, Croats, Serbs, Galicians,

Hungarians, Italians on every street corner of Vienna. If I believed in prayer, I would pray that Isaac and his family have joined Steinmueller in New York City.

"But they didn't" Benny said. He stood and paced the room, circling between stacks of books.

"I met him, and your cousins, we climbed together once. Simon was about my age," Peter said.

"Do you know what happened to them?" Benny said.

Peter nodded. "Dachau, then eventually to Mauthausen. They were arrested while my father was in the Metropole. He was heartbroken when he found out." Peter exhaled, gesturing to Safir for the photograph album she held. She handed it to him. Peter flipped backwards, stopped and turned the book so that Benny and Safir could see what he was looking for.

"Him," Peter said, stabbing the picture of Doctor Moro.

Benny frowned. "He ordered my uncle's arrest?"

Peter nodded. "It's not the only possibility, but the simplest answer is often the correct one."

"I don't understand," Benny said.

"To make my mother happy," Peter said. "I love her, but I know her and she was obsessed with hurting Paul. Isaac was his best friend. Doctor Moro did whatever Lydia wanted. Another reason I couldn't stay in Austria. Too much hate between them."

After a long silence Benny tapped the photograph of the SS officer. "Can I have a copy of this?"

Peter set the scrapbook on top of the box. After a lengthy search, he returned with a pair of scissors. He neatly cut around the photograph and handed it to Benny. "Glad to never see it again," he said.

Benny tucked the photograph in his shirt pocket.

Safir squeezed his hand. "They did release Paul, eventually?"

"On the second anniversary of his arrest," Peter said. "The Nazis knew the exact day. I shouldn't say it, but when I read the entry, it struck me as funny."

"Funny that he was released?" Safir asked.

"Did they throw him a party?" Benny asked.

"You tell me."

June 7, 1940. Weimarer Strasse 4. Vienna.

I am home, two years and a day since my arrest. I count myself fortunate, there was no transfer to one of the camps. I am to report to the Mining Federation offices in Innsbruck, next week. There is a push to raise the extraction rate of gold from the Tyrolean mines. It seems I am the one who can accomplish this.

I can find nobody to tell me about Isaac. His disappearance is a grave concern. I half expected him to meet me at the Metropole. Instead I walked alone, with a small bag of letters and sketches and only the clothes on my back, to the street car. My legs and lungs were burning, worse than the heaviest day on skis. The building superintendent let me into my apartment. Maria was out with her friends playing cards. She was both surprised and disappointed to see me, but she perked up at the news I will be leaving for Innsbruck, for an indefinite span of time.

I am at my old desk in my study, taking in the smells, the sight of my books on the shelves. I have put on a phonograph of Beethoven's Sixth Symphony; the First Movement fills me with joy and hope long extinguished. Now that I am released, my thoughts turn to my sons, both of who are with their mother. Lydia has taken up with a medical doctor, he tended her father on his last days and seems to find excuses to be at the apartment in Grinzing. Worse, he is SS. I will ask him about Isaac before I go to Innsbruck.

"His wife didn't care that he was free," Safir said.

"It was never a real marriage," Peter said. He lit a match and set it to the bowl of his pipe. "She's homosexual, you know," he said.

"Then why marry?" Benny asked.

"Like I said, custody," Peter said, looking for a place to set the extinguished match. He set it on the plate he had filled with cold pipe tobacco.

"They stayed together, that's something." Benny said.

"They lived different lives," Peter said. "Paul should have divorced her. But he was too proud. He figured if he stayed in Mayrhofen, Maria could live happily in Vienna. Which is what they did."

"She was at the funeral," Safir said.

Peter laughed. "To remind us she owned it all," he said. "She took everything, except the few knick-knacks I was allowed to bring home."

"That's tough," Benny said.

Peter shrugged. "I didn't want his money, what there was, but Hansi took it badly. He shouted about entitlement and inheritance and banged his fists and made a scene. It wasn't personal for Maria. She's greedy, is all. If Hansi offered to buy the house she'd have sold it in a heartbeat."

"Where did Paul meet Maria?"

"She was his secretary before the Anschluss. Paul made a business decision to improve the odds of getting custody and it didn't work. His solution, afterwards, was to keep as much distance between them as he could."

"So, he spent the rest of the war in Innsbruck."

Peter nodded.

"Did he see action?" Benny asked.

"Yes, Paul fought in the Ardennes. You Americans call it the Battle of the Bulge. Then his unit retreated, all the way to Berchtesgarden."

"I was at Berchtesgarden!" Benny said.

"You must have been one of the youngest."

"I joined up as soon as they would take me."

"That's where your leg, you know…"

Benny nodded. "One of our tanks ran over my foot."

Peter laughed. "Sorry, not what I was expecting."

"Me neither," Benny said.

"When did Paul return to Mayrhofen?" Safir asked.

"After the war ended, he was arrested by the Americans. But they only held him three months. Weldon denies he was responsible for the shorter term, but he must have had a hand in it. The Allies weren't fond of enemy officers, even ones who helped Jews."

September 17, 1945. Mayrhofen.

I am free, thanks to the mercy of the Americans. They have ever been decent, fair, and true to their word, in my experiences from Anatolia to Austria. I will write to Weldon, wherever he is, and tell him so. I have locked away my notes and sketches from the Metropole—I never want to see them again—but I will ask if he can search for Isaac's family, I can find nothing definite. Otherwise, I have much to be thankful for. My sons are alive in Vienna, in the American Zone, with Lydia. They have returned to their studies. Maria is happy on her own. I will try to find a routine, to occupy my days. Climbing, sketching, and perhaps, I will play the piano again. As much as I relish the silence of the mountains, there is a need for more music in my life. Perhaps I will own a dog, a hound of some breed. I am told they are fine companions.

They worked into the evening, going through the scrapbooks and diaries. At one point, Benny mentioned that they needed to catch the train, but Safir ignored him, hanging on Peter's every word. After it got dark, Peter took them to a grocer's around the corner and they bought chicken salad sandwiches and bottles of cola and hurried back to the apartment.

"Weldon told you about the last time they met?" Peter took small bites from his sandwich and chewed thoroughly.

Safir shook her head. "He's said nothing."

"It was a month before Paul died," Peter said. "His cancer was aggressive. He insisted on going to Istanbul one last time. I know Weldon was there. And, I think he met your mother."

To Safir it felt like another body blow. "I didn't know," she said in a small voice.

"Here," Peter said. He brushed the crumbs from his hands and picked up a notebook. "I've actually not read these."

August 24, 1949. Mayrhofen.

I am riding the train to Istanbul. It is difficult to sit for very long, I am never without pain, but I can manage for short periods. As I get closer to Piruz I remember when we first met. After Sarakamis, as our convalescence progressed, Sabik invited Pietschmann and me to his home for a meal. I should have refused, for—I can say now—that was the day my life changed forever. Sabik and his cousin led us through a twisting maze of low, stone buildings. Pietschmann and I were dressed in our Ottoman uniforms and I was uncomfortably warm in my fez. I still needed crutches, so the walk was slow and painful. Cooking smells surrounded us, and my stomach protested its empty condition. I told this to Sabik, making gestures that I liked the smells and rubbed my stomach and the Armenians laughed and nodded and slapped me on the back.

Sabik made two quick turns, and we found ourselves on a narrow street, nearly deserted. He stopped at a heavy wooden door set deep into a stone arch. His cousin pounded on the door. "Iron locks and hinges protect our families when we cannot be home," he said as the door swung inward.

The most beautiful woman I have ever seen stood in the exact centre of the doorway. Her hair was black, blacker than the darkest vein of coal. A series of crescent moon curls formed a fringe around the embroidered red scarf she wore. They fell to her shoulders. Her eyes glowed the smoking green of uncut emeralds. I could not look away. It was Piruz Oshagian.

Sabik kissed her on the cheek and limped inside, gesturing eagerly for us to enter. His cousin followed us in and set two heavy bolts. Piruz helped Sabik and me take off our boots. Slippers were provided. I removed my fez, grateful to lose the weight of it. I was dizzy, but it was neither pain, nor hunger. We sat at a heavy, plank table worn smooth by time and many shared meals. We drank warm beer brought to us by Sabik's young son, Toomas. He was a thin, undernourished, stick of a boy, and Sabik was gentle with him. I could tell he loved Toomas and the boy worshipped his father. Looking back, I am sorry I discounted what a feat that was, for in my experience, being a father is not easy. It is painful, too, looking back, knowing it is too late to do things differently.

Peter paused, pulled on his pipe, then resumed reading.

Piruz made dumplings—khinkali—Sabik called them. Pouches formed from wheat flour and shaped like fat garlic bulbs, stuffed with meat. Sabik grabbed one by the stem and bit off the entire dumpling, sucking in his breath at the heat inside. He grinned and took a deep swallow of beer to wash it down. Before I ate, I watched Sabik's cousins. They chewed a hole in the side of their dumplings, then sucked noisily until the juices were drawn out, before tearing into the remainder. Pietschmann did neither. He bit one in half and the juices ran down his chin and onto his uniform. Sabik roared with laughter.

"That is not the way to do it," he shouted. "Try," he said to me.

I bit into the side of mine, and sucked out the hot broth from the cooked lamb. It was delicious. When I had drained the dumpling, I bit the pouch off its doughy stem, and chewed with delight while Sabik and his cousins applauded. Piruz remained at the stove, stirring more of the dumplings, but she was smiling.

When I thought I could eat no more—six stems lined my place at the table—Piruz removed a large earthenware pot from the stove. She carried it to the table, setting it down on a tin plate. She took off the lid. Such aromas attacking my nose!

"Kchooch," Sabik said. He took the spoon from Piruz and served us two heaping plates. Chicken, lamb, eggplant, onions, chickpeas; each spiced in a manner I had never before experienced. I ate until I thought

I would burst, and drank beer until my vision began to blur. The beer made me bolder, and I watched Piruz as she worked in the kitchen. Her sun-browned skin glistened with perspiration. Silver earrings hung from her ears, reflecting the subtle light from the candles. (The medallion around her neck was the very same one I found in the dirt of the compound at Yelatan, after Sabik died. I believe she tossed it away out of grief. It sits on the table next to my notebook, for I intend to return it to her when I see her.) There were no false colors on her lips or cheeks like a European woman. Her smile, shy, and rare, revealed straight white teeth that made her entire body radiate strength.

After the meal Piruz cooked us strong, bitter coffee sweetened with honey, then joined us at the table. The coffee cleared my head, preventing me from saying or doing anything to dishonor myself or her in front of her husband.

Piruz brought out a swatch of felt and unwrapped it, revealing a reed instrument, similar to a clarinet. She called it a duduk. She was very good. (I hope she will play for me one last time, but I doubt it.) Sabik sang along to her tune. The melody was warmer than the fire flickering behind them. It filled the room, even Sabik's cousin, who doubtless had heard it many times, bowed his head and closed his eyes. I was lifted out of the room, on currents both mournful and inspiring. I, too, shut my eyes.

When the music stopped, I was reluctant to open my eyes. When I did, Piruz was looking straight at me. I nodded, smiling in gratitude. She returned my smile and I was unable to speak.

"I was right," Safir said, "Paul was in love with my mother."

Peter set the notebook in his lap and fumbled for his pipe. "It would explain the portrait. But I am not sure she felt the same way." He reached for one of the other notebooks. "This one I did read, here's an entry from before I was born."

"We better go if we are going to catch the train," Benny said.

"Stay," Peter said, "I insist."

"We didn't bring anything," Safir protested.

Peter jumped to his feet. "I can move this stuff around," he said, waving at the stacks of books on the sofa. "You can sleep in my room, Safir. Benny and I can camp out in here."

Safir glanced at Benny, who stared back at her, his hands raised in surrender. "I'm good if you are, we can catch a train back tomorrow."

"But Mustafa," Safir said.

"He'll be fine," Benny said, "he can afford to miss a meal."

Safir pursed her lips. "He's going to be so angry with me," she said.

April 15, 1922. Vienna.

Dear Piruz,

I have been invited by Atatürk to Istanbul. The Republic of Turkey wants to give me a medal for what I did during the war. Pietschmann has also been honored, but I am told he will not attend. I will go, in hopes of seeing you. The medal is nothing compared to that. It has been more than six years. I wonder what you look like, how your life of everyday is. Are you happy? I wish that you are, though your happiness means you have forgotten me. Should I live to be 100 I will not forget you. How would you like Vienna, I wonder? How would you like the Alps? In my dreams I take you with me on walks above Mayrhofen, show you Salzburg and Innsbruck. Feed you Leberknödelsuppe and beer. I play the piano, you the duduk. There is always music in the house. We raise our children in the high mountains, with the chamois and ibex. Our daughter picks Edelweiss and Alpen rose and weaves them into a circlet for you. Our son is a better climber than I. The Alpine women are so jealous of your hair, your eyes, your smile. I am the envy of all the men, and to prove my happiness I bring you gems from the deepest veins beneath the mountains. That is be our life, at least in my imagination.

Paul.

"I can't find anything from Piruz suggesting she met him," Peter said.

Safir looked at her hands. "Paul played the piano?"

Peter nodded. "He was very good. He liked to play when he was in Mayrhofen."

"My father never mentioned it."

Peter took a pull from his pipe. "He probably never saw him play. There was a long stretch when he did not."

"When did your parents meet?"

Peter blew smoke rings that shone blue in the anemic light thrown by the lamp. "In 1925. My grandfather brought my mother to an engineering conference where Paul was speaking."

"So, the correspondence ended then?"

"I don't think so. My parents' relationship was not an easy one. I remember the arguments. Broken china, smashed bottles. I was relieved when my father moved out." Peter flipped pages to the end of the notebook. "Here, he wrote this just after I was born."

February 17, 1926.

Dear Piruz,

It must be you returning my letters. I believe this one will suffer a similar fate. So, it will be the last I write to you. My son, Peter, was born a week ago. He is beautiful. His mother, Lydia, is well. She is an intellectual, from a good Austrian family. Her father does not like me much. But he is a grandfather now, so he shows me respect. I tell you this as a way of saying goodbye, Piruz. I have waited 10 years for any evidence of your existence. I have asked Weldon, as part of his work with the League, to seek you out, to pass on my words, to give you money, but he tells me he has had no luck. I do not believe him. I am jealous of his work, that takes him to your piece of the world. I believe he found you and won you over. That is enough to drive me to despair, but I tell no one of them. Now I am a father. I will try to be a better father to Peter than Franz Joseph was to me. It is a father's job, after all, to teach his son how to be a man. I remember Sabik, with Toomas. He was so good with the boy. I think maybe Toomas is a father perhaps?

Goodbye, Piruz.
Paul.

"He never knew Toomas died," Benny said.

Peter frowned. "Sabik's son?"

Safir nodded. "The boy died of Typhus. A few months after Paul was sent back to Austria."

"What did Paul do after his time in Turkey?" Benny asked. He stretched his legs in front of him, leaning against the chair Safir sat in.

"Worked. With the Mining Federation and the Austrian government. Until the Anschluss. He was angry, after that."

"With reason," Benny said.

"He was always difficult to talk to. Bitter, cool to the world. All he wanted to do was climb and sit in his study, staring at the mountains."

"Is that why you left?"

Another shrug. "I guess. It was a good scholarship and frankly, my parents were exhausting."

"Do you think your mother knows Paul had feelings for Piruz?" Benny asked.

"If she knew, she never said so," Peter said. "But she has always complained that my father was distant, unfeeling. After reading these letters, I don't agree. He just didn't have feelings for her."

"So unfair," Safir said.

"I wonder what the senator would say," Benny said.

"I'll ask him," Safir said. She plucked a small book out of the box. "What's this?"

Peter yawned. "It's a collection of stories my father wrote. About the miners in the Alps."

"Paul wrote stories?" Benny glanced at Safir.

"Not stories," Peter said, thumbing the pages. "he wrote down some of their superstitions and folk tales."

"Isaac was trying to find a publisher, while Paul was incarcerated," Safir said. "Can you read one?"

"Sure." Peter took the book from Safir and thumbed through the pages. "Here's one, it's called *Divine Grace*. Though Paul was an atheist, he liked the stories where God rewards the virtuous, and punishes the bad. Maybe deep down he wanted the world to be equal."

"Or he just kept score, like most of us," Benny said.

Peter laughed, almost disappearing in a plume of smoke.

Many centuries ago a man came from foreign lands into the region now known as Vienna. He loved the land he found, with its rolling hills covered in lush, green forests, and the rushing streams flowing with cold, fresh water and full of fat trout. He loved it so greatly he decided to settle there. He was a miner who, over the years, had worked successfully in various mines throughout the land. He had been as thrifty as he was industrious, and as a result, he was in possession of some money. So, he built a house on the very slope of the mountains, surrounded by forest and near one of the clear streams. He lived there with his young wife. He was very happy and satisfied.

But soon the inactivity of days wore at his soul. The miner's blood in his veins made him restless. When he looked up to the mountains around his house, he imagined digging long tunnels and deep shafts, searching out the precious ores he was sure were locked inside.

"Only the courageous earn God's Grace," he said to himself. "Nothing ventured, nothing gained."

He set his sights on commissioning a mine on the Kahlenberg. But where to start? He gazed onto the heights, day after day, looking for inspiration. One fine day he noticed a small bird that flew over and over to the same small hideaway in the rocks. Curious, he hiked to the place and found only an empty nest in the thorny bushes.

"I will take this as a sign that God wants me to begin here," the man said.

So, he began to dig. He worked day after day, sweating heavily, breaking the rocks where the empty bird's nest had been. Weeks passed, and the shaft he made went deep and wide into the Kahlenberg itself. But only waste rock came to the surface. His wife worried that her husband would kill himself from his labours, but the man did not despair. He was confident he was earning God's Grace.

When it became known around the district that the man was mining for gold, others came and offered their services. The man was grateful for their assistance. They dug with renewed energy. The work progressed faster now, but still no veins of gold revealed themselves. Eventually his helpers stopped coming, their own hopes fading into despair. At last he was alone again, digging with the certitude of a man in God's good keeping.

Many months passed, and still the miner worked on. One day it seemed the rock was brighter than before. He brought his lamp closer to the bare rock and could not believe what he saw: a vein of pure gold the color of warm butter. With his heart pounding with joy, he brought the rock into the full sun and saw what he had first hoped in the dimness of the tunnel: precious gold, purest of all metals, burning like a sun in his calloused hand. With a sigh of relief, he sank to his knees and gave thanks to God.

And so, the miner became rich, and workers came from all over to work and earn good money in the mine he owned. Soon there arose homes and shops around the mine owner's house, and a thriving village grew. But the richness of the ore did not change the mine owner. He remained as simple and hard working as before, and he treated the poor and weak with respect and was appreciated by all who knew him, right up to his death at a ripe old age.

After his death, the mine passed into the hands of another. He increased the production of the mine, earning greater profits. But the mood of the village changed. Though there was more wealth, the shares were reduced, and the poor suffered more for the owner did not care for them. The faces of the villagers grew hard despite the richness of the mine beneath their feet.

One evening, at the dinner table, the new mine owner shared wine with the senior men of the mine. Among the guests was an elderly man who had been the first to join the previous owner in his quest for the gold of the Kahlenberg. "He was a hard worker, unafraid of want or discomfort," the elder said. "He always relied on God's Grace to see him through."

"Nonsense," the new mine owner scoffed. "All the grace of God would have been worthless if there was no gold in that mountain. He was lucky, is all."

The elder and the other guests crossed themselves and muttered prayers under their breath. The owner drank late into the night, alone.

But the next day, when the ore carts rolled out of the mountain, the miners were amazed—every cart was full of waste rock. Not a single nugget of gold came out. The same happened the next day and the day after that. It was as if the precious gold vein had dried up like shallow waters on a hot afternoon. The terrified miners ran to the mine owner to tell him the news. He hurried into the mine, to the deep shaft where the rich gold had been but three days before. "By the Grace of God!" he cried, and fell, stricken, grasping his heart. He was dead on the spot.

No more gold was found in that mountain. The tunnels were abandoned, and one by one collapsed, and the few families who remained in the valley had no choice but to begin life as farmers.

"There's lots more," Peter said.

"I can't keep my eyes open," Safir said.

Peter closed the book and stretched. "Right," he said, suppressing a yawn, "Your palace awaits," he gestured toward the bedroom. "Benny and I will bunk out here. Just like boot camp, right Benny?"

Safir waved at Benny as she closed the door on his less than happy expression. He didn't think he was coming with her, did he? The bedroom was as dim as the living room, illuminated by a battered table lamp next to the twin bed. She opened the yellowing drapes to see a fenced, paved courtyard immersed in shadow. A single street light, its cover missing, let fall a harsh cone of electric light as yellow as the curtains. No movement, no sign of life, though the apartment building surrounded the courtyard on all sides. Light leaked through a half-dozen windows. She imagined insomniac graduate students or assistant professors reading philosophy or chemistry textbooks until dawn. She slid shut the drapes and turned to the bed. Peter had left a white undershirt on top of the blanket. For her, she presumed. She undressed, slipped on the shirt and took one of the pillows out of its case and arranged it over her unpinned hair. The knots she would have to brush out tomorrow were enough to make her regret staying over. She snapped back the blanket, expecting to see bedbugs running for cover, but there were none. Despite the clutter, the place was clean enough, and did not smell. She crawled onto the mattress, which groaned and sagged mightily under her. She shut off the lamp and stared at the ceiling, straining to hear the men on the other side of the door. If she were honest, she did want Benny beside her. The weighted silence pushed her deeper into the mattress. She laced her fingers together on her chest and closed her eyes, imagining a small Alpine house with red geraniums on the balcony and smoke curling out of the chimney, serene beneath the relentless gaze of jagged mountains.

Safir woke with a stiff neck and a sore back. She dressed, left the shirt on the bed, and peeked through the door. Peter sat in the only chair, smoking his pipe. A cloud of blue-grey smoke gave him the appearance of a much older man. Benny was still unconscious on the floor, half-covered by a blanket.

Peter saw her and waved her over. "There's tea, sorry, I don't have coffee. How did you sleep?"

She stood over Benny. "He's out cold. I slept fine, thanks."

"He talks in his sleep," Peter said.

"Does he?" she said. She nudged him with her toe. "Rise and shine, Mr. Steinmueller. We have a train to catch."

"I think he was dreaming about the army. You have to go so soon?" Peter's face showed disappointment.

She felt sorry for the younger man, suddenly. Like her, he'd left home, alone, far from family. With no prospect that things would improve any time soon. "I should get home. I'm expecting my father any day."

"Sure, I understand," Peter said. "Give Weldon my regards."

"I will." She poked Benny once more, a little harder this time.

Benny groaned, opened his eyes. It took him a moment. "Safir! Man, I was out cold."

"Ship shape, Steinmueller," she said. "We don't want to overstay our welcome."

Peter walked with them to the train station. "Running low on tobacco, anyway," he said, locking the apartment door behind him. He set a fast pace, and though he didn't complain, it was all Benny could do to keep up. They cut through the apartment courtyard Safir had looked over last night. Several children played with a basketball at one end. Safir carried the portrait of Piruz under her arm.

"You're sure you want to give me this," she said.

"You gave me the letters. Fair trade," Peter said. "Besides, she's your mother."

They walked in silence along empty sidewalks until they were off campus. As if a switch had been pulled, cars, buses and bicycles choked the streets.

"Strange that my father and your mother died so close in time," Peter said.

"My mother was hit by a bus."

Peter chewed the end of his pipe. He said goodbye with a firm handshake on the steps of Broad Street Station.

They watched him walk away, his hands in his pockets, pipe smoke in his wake. They bought tickets and ate fried egg sandwiches while they waited. Safir liked looking at the people coming and going, the soles of their shoes echoing off the stone floors, rattling into the rafters high above. She couldn't put her finger on what exactly had changed, but she felt different.

"Don't choke on it," she said, as Benny ate his sandwich in three bites.

He grinned at her, his mouth so full he could not chew. She laughed, he laughed, spitting out bits of fried egg.

On the train they didn't speak much. Benny dozed off with his head on her shoulder as the train tripped the tracks toward New York. She kept looking up, to the portrait stowed on the luggage rack over her seat. She leaned into Benny and closed her eyes to catch the rhythm of his breathing.

They walked from the bus stop to the apartment hand in hand. Safir was tired, but her mind raced. The streets around Central Park were quiet, the breeze carried hints of stale cooking oil, cigarettes and over-ripe garbage. The doorman held the elevator and tipped his hat and avoided eye contact. That it meant Weldon had returned from the Capitol did not occur to Safir until she opened the apartment door.

The senator did not rise to welcome her. He remained on the sofa, the locked, wooden box on the coffee table in front of him, next to a full glass of red wine. Safir stood in front of Benny like he needed a shield. Mustafa ran to Safir mewling loudly. She picked him up and nuzzled the fur on his neck. "Wel-Father!" she said.

"You look like you've slept in your clothes." He glared at Benny, but did not rise to shake his hand.

"I didn't know when you were coming back. It's good to see you."

"And you," Weldon said. He stood and made a dramatic bow. His white hair fell thick across his eyes. They were red and swollen.

His speech was clumsy, off balance. Safir guessed it wasn't his first glass of wine. "Who is your silent friend?"

"Benjamin Steinmueller. Benny, this is my father, Weldon Scott."

Weldon cocked his head. "Steinmueller? I know that name."

Benny moved closer to shake the senator's hand.

Weldon sat down, ignoring Benny's hand. He raised the wine glass and took a deep swallow. "See what you have driven me to? I never drink this early in the day." He tilted his chin toward Benny. "So, you're Julius' son." "Bit of a limp you have," he added.

Safir flushed. "He's a veteran."

"I know that," Weldon said. "I know more than you think. Where did you get this box? Where were you?"

"We went to Philadelphia, Sir. It was my idea." Benny said.

"Philadelphia? What for?"

"To see Peter Bahr," Safir said. She picked up the portrait that she'd leaned against the wall in the hallway.

Weldon took two steps back, as if struck.

"The box was locked in the wardrobe. There were letters, I gave them to Peter," Safir said, talking quickly. "They were from Paul. I had them translated. That's how I found the Steinmuellers. They live in Williamsburg."

"I know exactly where they live."

"And you know where Peter lives," Benny said.

"Why didn't you tell me you knew him, that you were at Paul's funeral. That you were in Istanbul, before my mother died," Safir said.

Weldon collapsed on the sofa, his hand trembling as he lifted the glass to his lips. "You could have sent me the letters. I would have translated them."

"You were already gone, I didn't want to bother you, you've done so much."

"So much, eh? You didn't stop to think that a new apartment, new clothes, a new life was enough?"

Safir blinked. "That's not fair."

"Here I am, setting you up, leaving you money, preparing to take you with me across Pennsylvania. How do you repay me? Rummaging around in my personal possessions, consorting with men, traipsing all over Hell's Half Acre?"

"Excuse me, Sir. Why are you so angry?" Benny rested his hands on Safir's shoulders. "You should be proud, Safir is doing exactly what she needs to do."

"Proud? Proud?" Weldon jumped to his feet, swaying, holding the back of the sofa to steady himself. "I'm so *Goddamned* proud." He staggered the length of the hall, stumbling as he pulled open the door. Without a backward glance he slammed the door behind him.

Safir's fists were frozen at her sides. "I need to get out of here," she said.

Benny frowned. "What are you talking about? This is your place, too."

Safir shook her head. "I can't stay here, not like this. Help me," she said. "Put Mustafa's food in a bag." She ran to the bedroom.

She threw some clothes, a hair brush, comb and toothbrush into her suitcase. She picked up Paul's box, still locked, weighing it in her hands. "We're taking this, too," she said. "We're going to Brooklyn." She scooped up Mustafa and headed to the door.

They rode the subway, ignoring the inquiring looks from other passengers. Safir stroked Mustafa's head, listening to the wheels passing over the track, thinking about an unfinished railroad high in the Taurus Mountains. Benny sat beside her, tapping his shoe against her suitcase, as if making sure it was still there. They switched trains at Central, then rode the short distance to Montague Street. They walked past St. Ann's church and Mustafa hissed at the stray cats on the stoop.

"He's telling them he's back, they better watch out," Safir said, and started to cry.

Benny put his arm around her. "Hey, it's not so bad," he said.

Safir stopped at the front steps and wiped her eyes. "This is it," she said.

Benny carried her suitcase up the stairs to her front door, and waited while Safir fumbled with the key. A rush of dry, heated air welcomed them. As she crossed the threshold, Safir wondered how she would make next month's rent. Mustafa jumped out of her arms and made for the kitchen, to where his supper dish used to sit. Everything was just as she had left it.

"Where do you want this?" Benny asked, still holding the suitcase.

"Anywhere is fine," Safir said, without looking.

Benny set the suitcase on the floor in the hallway. "For what it's worth, I like this place better," he said. He turned for the door, still open to the landing. "More like you."

"*More like me,*" Safir repeated. "That's hilarious. I don't even know who I am and you're making comparisons."

"I believe I'm allowed, it's in the Constitution."

Safir began to laugh. She reached behind Benny to bolt the door. "You most certainly are, Mr. Steinmueller. Is it my right to keep you off the streets this fine day?"

Benny smiled and pulled her into his arms. "Yes, I believe the right of peaceful assembly is in there somewhere," he said and kissed her.

Chapter 9

Safir and Benny rode the bus to Williamsburg late in the afternoon. The wooden box nested in Safir's lap. Rachel said that Julius knew a locksmith who could open it. They held hands, each leaning into the other's body. Safir could not conceal her smile. She inhaled the aroma off Benny's skin, their shared perfume lingering beneath his shirt. She squeezed his hand, convincing herself he was real. Her muscles quivered; an electric current connected them, amplified by the memory of his hands, his bare skin against hers.

"I like the ribbon," Benny said, glancing at the embroidered blue band that tied Safir's hair.

"Your mother gave it to me," she said. "She brought it from Vienna."

"I recognize it," Benny said. "I think my Aunt Ester gave it to her. She likes you a lot," he added.

"I like your family a lot," Safir said. "Especially you, Mr. Steinmueller."

The day was stifling hot when they emerged from the subway station.

"Let me carry it," Benny offered, reaching for the wooden box.

Safir pulled it out of reach. "I'm not letting this out of my hands."

"Weldon didn't like that you found Paul's letters," Benny said, jamming his hands into his pockets.

"I'm a snoop," Safir said. "Not his idea of a grateful daughter."

"I guess," Benny shrugged. "But how could you *not* be curious, with all the things he told you?"

Safir did not answer. They walked in silence, the heat like a weight on their shoulders.

"He never told me that Paul was in love with my mother," Safir said as they neared Rachel and Julius' apartment.

"Because he loved her, too. Us guys are jealous," Benny said as they climbed the staircase.

Rachel greeted them both with kisses. "I'll fetch lemonade," she said. "We were beginning to worry; we hadn't heard from you both. How was the party?"

"Good," Benny said, glancing at Safir. "They did it up real nice. Moshe Zilberman and his wife were there."

Safir had made Benny promise not to say anything about the confrontation with D'Angelo, their trip to Philadelphia or Weldon's return.

"It went late?" Rachel said from the kitchen. "I called but you didn't answer."

"I must have just missed you," Benny said, "Safir and I went to the natural history museum."

"It's so near to Weldon's apartment, I'm ashamed I'd never been. Benny was a terrific docent." Safir patted his hand.

"We worry, is all," Rachel said, drying her hands on a dish towel decorated with the Empire State Building. "Your hair looks beautiful, Safir."

"Thank you," Safir said, touching the ribbon gently. She set down the wooden box. "I was hoping Julius could open it. I think there may be more letters inside."

Rachel examined the box without picking it up. "It's lovely. My father had a box like that. He kept his watch and ring inside."

"Where is Pops?" Benny said.

"At the shop, of course," Rachel said. "When you see him tell him to come home, he doesn't need to put in so many hours."

When Safir and Benny had finished their lemonade and were ready to leave, Rachel asked Benny to go ahead. "Ladies only, Benjamin. Don't look so worried, I'm not going to bite her," Rachel said, closing the front door after him. "Come," she said to Safir, "let him wait. Let's sit for a minute."

Safir followed Rachel to the sofa.

"I am so grateful you asked us to translate the letters," Rachel said.

"It's me who is grateful," Safir said, her eyes riveted to the jewelry box.

"But Safir," Rachel said. She tucked a stray length of silver hair behind one ear, "I am worried."

"There's no need," Safir said, "I'm okay, much better now. We're in love," she whispered.

Rachel startled. "Of course you are! We knew that *weeks* ago. I'm sure Benny was the last to know," she chuckled, patting Safir's hand.

"I don't understand," Safir said.

Rachel gently lifted the box out of Safir's hands. "Be careful," she said, stroking the lid. "Most of us don't have our lives uncovered by voices from the past."

"You think I shouldn't open it?"

"No, Julius can do this. But these letters, the stories Weldon has told you, they may change your idea of yourself, but not who you are."

Safir frowned. "I don't know who I am."

Rachel sighed and stroked Safir's cheek. "Yes, you do." She walked to the apartment door. Benny stood in the hall, leaning against the wall, his hands in his pockets. Rachel offered her cheek to her son, who bent forward to kiss it. "Promise me, Safir, you don't forget to live your life." She embraced Safir tightly. "It's the best way to honor those we lost along the way."

Blum's Fine Apparel was a narrow slice of East Williamsburg real estate wedged between an Italian grocer's and *Steindl's Sheet Music.* A suited mannequin kept solitary watch in a window overdue for cleaning. *Men's Suits & Women's Dresses* had been stenciled onto the glass many years before; the third *S* in *Dresses* was smudged and looked like an *r.*

Safir pointed at the sign. "In French, that could mean *Women's uprising.*"

"I don't get it," Benny said.

"As in: *come inside, Women, we'll raise you high.*" She shrugged. "Or it could mean *we've set a trap—dresser un piege pour les femmes.*"

"There's no trap in here," Benny said. "Unless you think opening that box is one."

"I want it unlocked," Safir said as they passed under a faded awning and pushed open the door.

A bell rang in the depths of the dimly lit shop. Julius Steinmueller hurried from the back, adjusting his suspenders as he squeezed by shelves filled to overflowing with bolts of cloth.

"I'm all alone today, forgive me," he said, pushing his thick glasses up his nose. "Safir! Benny!" A wide smile erased two decades of care from his face. "I didn't recognize you! Saul doesn't want to pay for more lights, says it is bad for the cloth. Hot enough today, isn't it?"

"Too hot," Benny said, embracing his father. "How do you put up with this stuffy place?"

"It's not so bad," Julius said, waving off Benny's concern. "The fan in the back works fine, and I keep the door to the alley propped open. To what do I owe this fine visitation?"

"You said you could open this box," Benny said. Safir held up the wooden chest for Julius to see.

"Come into the back," Julius said with a wave. "I have something that will do the trick."

He led them down the narrow aisle, over creaking, wooden floors shiny from years of traffic.

"Saul's the owner," Benny said over his shoulder, "Pops has been with him since we came."

"That's right," Julius called. "For twelve and some years. Saul's son is a jeweler. Nathan keeps his spare tools here. He doesn't trust his landlord."

The back room was larger and cooler than the front of the shop, though just as dark. Paneled wood, black as ebony, framed the walls, lightened only by sheets of yellowed paper—suit patterns, dress outlines—that had been pinned to the panels for decades. Julius patted the workbench. "Set it there," he said, "I'll be right back."

Benny offered Safir the only chair. She refused. "Sit," she said. Benny shrugged and sat down.

"You worked here?"

"Not so much. Saul owns a garment factory on the Lower East Side. That's where most of the work is done. Saul keeps this place for sentimental reasons. He lets Pops and one or two others work here. It's stuffy but quiet. And close to home. Some of their older customers prefer this store to the other place. Reminds them of the Old Country."

"I worked in the basement of a museum," Safir said. "Not as stuffy, but I'm fond of the quiet."

"What did my mother say when she sat you down? You okay?"

Safir smiled. "You heard her as we were leaving. I was terrified, I thought she was going to warn me off you, that I am too old to be seeing as young a gentleman as yourself."

Benny laughed. "Are you kidding? My mother adores you!"

Safir smiled and reached for Benny's hand. "It's mutual."

Julius returned carrying a cloth-wrapped bundle. He set it on the bench and untied the ribbon, unfolded the felted cloth to reveal a set of picks and screwdrivers of Lilliputian size.

"This should do it," he said, glancing at Benny's arm around Safir's waist. When he turned to face the wooden box, he was smiling. He adjusted his glasses and chose one of the smaller picks. His hands were steady. The pick turned; the lock released.

"There you go," he said, still grinning triumphantly.

"Open it," Benny said.

Safir placed her hands on either side of the box. The lid opened smoothly, silently on its silver hinges. The inside surface of the lid had been painted—an Alpine landscape of snow-capped mountains and distant forest. A lone *Alpenhütte* stood in a meadow of wild flowers. At the lowest right-hand corner was an inscription. *Zillertal. Meine Heimat. PB.*

"Your homeland," Julius read. "You carry it with you, everywhere."

Across the bottom of the box lay an envelope, wrapped with an ornate blue and green ribbon. A medal hung off the ribbon, a golden crescent moon inlaid with a diamond star. Safir untied the ribbon. On the envelope a few words had been written in Turkish cursive. The script was large, lavish, bold, in faded blue ink. She translated.

To Dr. Paul Bahr, Engineer and Alpinist. For deeds of heroism and bravery during wartime. With Gratitude, Kemal Atatürk, President of the Republic of Turkey, Ankara, September 2, 1923.

"I thought the Turks were on the other side," Benny said.

"During the war, yes," Safir said. "But after, when Atatürk became President, the government denounced those who led the persecution."

"That must have been weird, getting a medal from the bad guys," Benny said.

"Maybe why he kept it locked away and hidden," Safir said.

She tipped out the envelope. A single sheet of onion skin appeared. As she pulled on the paper, a small, silver pendant fell into her palm. Safir plucked it between her finger and thumb, turning it over several times. An engraved Madonna and Child with faded gold halos etched on the front, plain silver on the back. A loop for a chain had been soldered into the top, but it had been broken a long time ago, judging by the smoothness of the silver.

"What is it?" Julius asked.

Safir could not speak.

"Was this your mother's?" Benny asked, his hand stroking Safir's arm.

"Remember what Peter read to us?" Safir said, her voice near a whisper. "He wanted to return it to her, before he died."

"You think he changed his mind?" Benny asked.

"She refused it," Safir said, shaking her head. "That's what I think."

"This was important, I assume?" Julius said. He held out his hand, and Safir placed the pendant gently in his palm. He held it close to his face, lifted his glasses and squinted, his thumb running across the engraved figures. "It needs a good polish," he said.

"Weldon told me it was the first thing he noticed, when they met in the mountains," Safir said.

"What does that paper say?" Benny said.

Safir pulled the sheet from the envelope and unfolded it. She recognized the script, identical to Paul's compact handwriting from his days of confinement. She handed the paper to Julius. "Do you mind? Benny, let your father sit."

Benny guided his father by the shoulders onto the stool. He turned on a desk lamp. "You want a magnifying glass or something?"

Julius waved Benny away. "I can make this out just fine," he said, clearing his throat.

August 30, 1949. AKH.

I am in the general hospital of Vienna; the doctor says I should have been dead a month ago. The nurse is kindly transcribing for me, as I cannot get out of bed to write anymore. I am on a strict regimen of pain killers. I have warned Ulrike, that is my nurse, that she must write whatever I dictate, no matter how crazy it seems.

Maria is making arrangements for my return to Mayrhofen. I refuse to die in the city. Though after Istanbul, Vienna seems pastoral. My visit with Piruz transpired as I feared. When I arrived at the house she lives in, she would not answer the door. Her daughter, Beyheim, relayed the message and refused me entry. I then went to the rug factory, with the intention of begging Celik Turan for the chance to see his wife again. He also, unsurprisingly, refused to speak with me. I tried to give him the pendant Piruz discarded in Yelatan. That was on the day I had convinced her to sit for a sketch. I blame myself, for in those minutes in the weak sun, a cold breeze in her hair, the weight of consequence was more than she could bear, and I have ever felt the burden of responsibility even as I covet her face as it appeared that day. Celik threw the pendant back at me and I was ordered off the property. I was still hopeful that he would change his mind, so I took a room at a hostel in the north end of Hereke, but I contracted a fever and was bedridden for two days. The hostel owner sent for a doctor, whose only cure was to recommend I purchase my return ticket immediately. I hired a driver and was assisted onto the train. Now I am here, unable to walk, unable to eat, unable to do much more than sleep, which, in truth, is a blessing. The cancer lies upon me like a mountain, but it weighs less than a feather next to the consequences of decisions and actions I have taken. Looking back, my journey into loneliness began the day I stormed from my father's house a half-century ago. Two wives, two sons did nothing to correct that path. I add Piruz, Isaac, Weldon to that resumé. Now, at the end, I would ask them all: is there one thing of mine that redeems this unhappy existence?

"That is all," Julius said. They sat with the silence for several slow, excruciating moments.

"He must have made it back to Mayrhofen," Benny said, "otherwise the wardrobe would've been empty."

"She never saw him," Safir said.

"She made her decision many years before that," Julius said. He returned the letter to Safir.

Safir folded the page and slid it into the envelope, with the pendant.

"There's more in the box," Benny said, nudging Safir.

Beneath the envelope was a small, felt bag, its drawstring wrapped several times around its mouth. Safir unwound the cord and shook the bag gently. A half-dozen rough stones spilled onto the cloth on the workbench.

"What are they?" Benny said.

Julius leaned close, still squinting. "They are gemstones. See how the light catches this one. I think it might be a sapphire." He exhaled loudly and picked up the stone, rolling it between thumb and forefinger, before carefully placing it in Safir's palm. "I can't imagine what they are worth. You are named for the jewel, no?" Julius asked.

It was cool against her skin. "I don't know," she said. "Paul found many gems in the tunnel of Belemedik Dagh. These could be from there, but he worked in mines all his life."

"You should get them appraised," Julius said. "Saul's son will tell you their worth."

"They aren't mine," Safir said. "They are Weldon's. Or Peter's." She returned the stones and the envelope to the box and closed the lid. Julius tied the box shut with a cord. Safir kissed him on the cheek.

"One more thing, before we go, Pops," Benny said. "Don't get up." He pulled the photograph of Doctor Moro from his shirt pocket. "Peter Bahr gave me this," he said. "He thinks this guy's responsible for Aunt Ester and Uncle Isaac."

Julius held the photo and his hands began to shake.

"Sorry, Pops, but I thought you should have it."

Julius fished a handkerchief from his pocket and wiped his eyes. "Thank you, Benjamin. You're a fine son."

Benny clapped Julius on the arm. "You closing up soon? Safir and I gotta go."

Julius nodded. He pointed at the SS officer. "I know someone who can find you and your kind." He glanced at Benny. "I don't think I'll tell your mother, yet."

"See you later, Pops," Benny hugged his father.

"Thank you, Julius," Safir said. "You've been so generous." She picked up the wooden box and followed Benny into the alley. "Your father's going to be okay?"

"He's one tough customer. Now he's got a purpose. He's like a bulldog when he gets his mind set on something. Where to?"

"I need to think," Safir said. A weariness pressed on her from all sides.

"I'm starving," Benny said. "That's what I'm thinking about. Mostly."

"Then come home with me. I'll cook for you," she said, "but there's no food in the apartment."

"There's the grocer's," Benny said, pointing with his thumb to the store next to Blum's.

Benny lay stretched out on Safir's bed, half covered with a sheet. The faint smell of cooked onions wafted through the bedroom door. "You're too good of a cook."

Safir slid next to Benny, wrapping her arms around his neck. "You inspire me," she said, nuzzling his cheek, "but it's just potatoes and onions."

"I'm not talking about the food," Benny said, kissing Safir on the neck.

They dozed in each other's arms. Safir let her toes explore Benny's hairy shins. When she caressed his foot, she felt him tense and move away.

Safir opened her eyes. "You don't have to be shy," she said.

Benny sighed, rolled onto his back. "Sorry," he said. "Nobody wants to see that."

"I do," Safir said. She pulled back the sheet and twisted in the bed, bringing her face close to his damaged foot. "Tell me what happened," she said, tracing the edges of his big toe. Where the other toes should have been was a livid scar, crescent-shaped, the scalloped ridges reminding her of a disfigured clamshell.

Benny clasped his arms behind his head and closed his eyes. When Safir touched the flattened stub of a lost toe, his leg twitched reflexively.

"We were sent to Berchtesgarden to mop up. A symbolic gesture, the Germans were gone. If Paul was there, he bugged out ahead of us. Just a few servants and administrative staff hanging around. They knew we were coming. The French were supposed to be the first. Ike wanted the 101 Airborne to go, and our guys, we just went for it. We were only a mile down the road anyway. When we got there the guys went through every room, every building, starting to loot the place. Some of them got drunk on the brandy they found. When the French arrived, were they ever P-O'd. We were called back, forming up in the field right in front of Hitler's villa. Our CO ripped us a new one and sent us packing. We jumped on whatever equipment we could find to scoot. I was the sixth guy on a jeep, got tossed off the hood just as one of our armoured carriers went by. My foot got stuck between the idler wheel and the track and that was that. Lucky to have kept my toe."

"It's a beautiful toe," Safir said, and kissed it. She slid over Benny's body, feeling his skin warm under her touch. "I think you've said enough for now."

Safir woke after sunrise to a rumbling in her stomach. Benny was awake, looking at her. She kissed him. "Hungry?"

He nodded.

"I'll make us something." Safir climbed out of bed.

They were eating supper in Safir's kitchen when a loud rap at the door froze them in their seats. "My father," Safir said.

They ran to the bedroom to finish dressing, stumbling over each other for their shoes. Safir opened the front door in the middle of another insistent burst. She was still arranging her hair as the door swung open. "You're not Weldon," she said, exhaling with relief.

"No, I most certainly am not." An indignant Ernie Linklater stood at the door in his bathrobe and slippers. Cigar smoke hung in the air over his head. He looked like a theatre understudy of Augustus Caesar, his attempted comb-overs a crown of laurel through the smoke. "This came for you," he said, not bothering to take the cigar out of his mouth. "Don't know why the postman brought it to me. Guess he didn't want to interrupt you," He said, glancing past Safir toward Benny. He handed her an envelope, covered with stamps Safir did not recognize.

"Thank you, Mr. Linklater," Safir said and closed the door in his face.

"Who was that?" Benny asked.

"My downstairs neighbour. I guess he looks out for me more than I thought." She showed Benny the letter and read the handwriting on the back. "Antelias?"

"Where's that?" Benny asked. He followed Safir to the living room.

"Lebanon," Safir said, sinking into the sofa cushion. Mustafa jumped onto her lap and she pushed him away. "The priests told me the Armenian Prelacy is there."

"Why are they writing you? Are they selling life-time memberships?"

Safir slapped Benny's arm. "Behave yourself, Mr. Steinmueller. I don't know what this… Nurse Doebli," she shouted. "I wrote her a letter."

"Who?" Benny asked.

"She was there," Safir said. "With my mother and Weldon and Paul. The whole time, in the mountains, in Aksaray. Where I was born!" Safir's fingers trembled as she opened the envelope. Inside was a thin sheet of stationery, its margins decorated with the design of entwined roses, repeating on all four sides.

May 23, 1950

Dearest Safir,

I was so thrilled to receive your note! I confess to weeping like a child, something I haven't done for many years. Thank you for writing and for the knowledge you are alive and well, though you are so very far away. I remember your birth as if it were yesterday, it was a happy moment for us in a sea of sadness. Your arrival, days before Christmas, was proof that God had not utterly abandoned us.

"My birthday is October 6th," Safir said.

"Don't complain, now you're two months younger," Benny said. "I'm kidding," he said as Safir's brow furrowed.

Safir, your father loved your mother from the moment he set eyes on her. She was a married woman and he respected her husband. But after Sabik Oshagian's death in the mountains, they came together, although it was clear to me that your mother still grieved for her husband. She confessed to me, in Aksaray, that since Sabik's wound at Sarakamis two years past, they had not been intimate, but they were close notwithstanding. She was alone, a widow with a young son. She needed protection, and your father proved, at the time, best able to provide it. She seemed to brighten, for a while. When Toomas died, I and the other nurses had to force your mother to eat, otherwise she, too, would have died. Despite all that happened, you were born. We were afraid those first weeks, whether you would make it, but you were fiercely strong. You survived and thrived. God bless the Americans and their supplies.

But your mother needed to be convinced to stay among the living. She stopped eating, refused to rise from her bed. Weldon and Clancy and others helped to feed her, to keep her going. A weaker woman would not have lived. By February, Piruz was out of danger. I believe that was when the photograph with you was taken. Her struggles were made harder as your father was gone, before you were born. He was taken by the Germans before we reached the sanctuary in Aksaray.

Safir handed Benny the letter and ran to her bedroom, slamming the door behind her.

Benny read to the end, rose from the sofa and knocked on Safir's door. "Can I come in?" There was no answer. Benny turned the knob and opened the door. The bedroom was dark behind drawn curtains. "Safir?"

Safir lay face down on the bed. Mustafa pushed past Benny and hopped onto the bed next to Safir's head. He curled up in the nest of her uncombed plaits. Safir moaned.

"Do you want to hear the rest?" Benny said. He sat at the foot of the bed, turning the letter to catch the muted light that leaked between the curtains.

Safir lay motionless on the bed.

Safir, Weldon Scott is not your father. I do not know why he would tell you this. I remember Weldon as an amiable, competent sort. He was certainly young and good looking, and your mother was attracted to him, as was I. But, if I might put this delicately, he was not romantic toward women. I would sit and flirt with him on the deck of the ship during our voyage from Trieste to Constantinople, but he would have nothing to do with me—or any woman. Twice, I caught him below decks in the company of men. I was old enough to be jealous, but too young to know what was going on.

With the benefit of more than thirty years I can say if Weldon loved anyone, it was Paul. As much as Paul loved your mother. It was a hopeless triangle and all three were miserable as a result. I have heard nothing from any of them, but can only hope they sorted matters out and found some degree of solace.

I found, in my belongings, two photographs from that time. I believe it was Clancy, the American, who took the one of your mother and father, in Yelatan, a place we first stopped on our trek out of the mountains. The other picture was taken later, in Aksaray. The Americans had left, because their country had joined the war. Dr. Solvein took this one. Your mother is carrying you. That is me standing beside her. Your letter has made me as proud as I was that day.

Many blessings upon you, Dearest Safir. Your name is a beautiful reminder of the jewels the men found inside Belemedik Dagh. Paul gave some to your mother, perhaps he foresaw that they would not be together long. I suppose he is still in Austria. Whatever his life was like, I do not doubt his genuine love for your mother. They have been through so much, as have all of us who witnessed those terrible times.

With heartfelt love and wishes,

Angela.

"These are the pictures," Benny said.

Safir rolled over and sat up, wiping her eyes. She crawled to the end of the bed and collapsed again, her cheek resting on Benny's lap. Benny gave her the photographs. Safir squinted through puffy eyes. An Armenian woman carrying a small child wrapped in blankets. Only its forehead and swirl of black hair were visible. Another woman, dressed in nurse's uniform and cape, held one hand under the child, as if sharing the weight of it with the first woman. They stood in front of a crumbling, stone building. Remnants of snow lay in shallow drifts near the wall. Piruz wore a headscarf, a long, loose dress, apron, and shawl that hung to the ground. The second snapshot revealed a man and woman, standing a little apart and stiff, formal: perhaps it was the graininess of the photograph that masked all signs of emotion. They stood in front of a high fence of iron stakes. The man was dressed like a Turkish soldier, in a dark coat with many buttons. He wore a fez. A thick, compact mustache adorned his upper lip.

"Is this them?" Benny asked.

"My parents," she said, "Piruz and Paul."

"Weren't you half expecting it?" Benny said. "I mean, after Peter's."

Safir swung herself into a sitting position her arms wrapped around his waist. "Don't talk," she whispered.

She hummed *Nessun Dorma* under her breath as she readied herself. The day promised heat and humidity, but it was early hours and she wanted to be at the library when it opened. She rode the subway with the Saturday morning office and retail crowd and was one of the first patrons through the heavy doors of Central Branch when they were unbolted for the day. Safir carried a handful of pansies to the reception desk. Harriet Dickinson saw her before she reached the counter and waited for her with a smile.

"Been awhile," Harriet said, coming around to give Safir a hug.

"These are for you," Safir said, presenting the flowers.

"How kind," Harriet said. "I've done nothing to deserve these."

"On the contrary," Safir said. "I want thank you for your help. I want to show you something, if you've got a moment?"

"Certainly," Harriet said, "come over to my desk. We can talk there."

Safir followed the librarian behind the reception desk and sat in a heavy, wheeled chair Harriet rolled next to her own. "Make yourself comfortable, I'll put these in water," Harriet said.

The librarian returned with a short, Chinese-style vase full of pansies and placed them on the desk between them. "Thank you so much."

Safir sat on the edge of the chair, her feet not touching the floor. "Remember the special collections book you loaned me? I wrote to the author. She knew my fa—Senator Scott. She wrote back, I'd like you to read it, but you have to promise not to tell anyone what it says."

Harriet cocked her head. "Do I need to read it?"

Safir looked at the letter in her lap. "I'm going a little crazy, is all."

Harriet leaned close and patted Safir's arm. "I promise," she said.

Safir handed the librarian the letter.

Harriet Dickinson read quickly, her expression never changing. She folded the paper and returned it to Safir. "I think you've come to the end of your search."

"I don't think so," Safir said.

Harriet smiled. "I didn't say the end of your journey. You know your real father; you know your mother's story. You're caught up to most of us."

"I never met my father," Safir protested.

"But your stepfather raised you as his daughter. You told me he was a good man."

"It's the sadness of it," Safir said. "The finality."

"Indeed." Harriet laced her fingers together, in her lap. "But you couldn't have changed anything."

"I might have met my father, before he died."

"Perhaps. But you didn't."

Safir's eyes welled with tears.

"My grandfather used to tell me not to cry over spilled milk. The past is past. The test of a good life is how you'll face today."

"That's what Benny tells me."

"Benny?"

"A friend," Safir said.

Harriet smiled. "A good friend, if he says that to your face. You might listen to him."

"I haven't seen Weldon in nearly three weeks. I don't know what to say."

"I look at you, Safir, and see that a veil has been pulled away. There's bedrock beneath your feet, now." She stood, opening her arms for a hug. Safir hugged the librarian and hurried to the doors.

Safir chose to walk the full distance home in the growing heat of late morning. She passed St. Ann's with a quickness to her stride. She reached the apartment and a car door opened. Jefferson jumped out of the senator's car and intercepted her.

"Miss Scott," he said, removing his hat.

"He's here?" Safir said. She peered into the back of the car.

"He's gone upstairs," Jefferson said. "He really needs to talk to you."

"Thank you, Thomas," Safir said. "I've missed you."

"As have I," the chauffeur said. "He's very sorry, if that makes any difference. He talks about you all the time."

"We'll see," she said as she started up the steps.

Weldon was seated on the sofa. Mustafa eyed him from the top of the piano. Weldon's clothes were rumpled, his hair mussed.

"You spoke with Thomas?" Weldon said. When he straightened his tie, his hands shook.

"I did," Safir said. She sat across from Weldon, the knuckles on her hands white.

"This is difficult for me, coming here," Weldon said. "I want to apologize for my behavior, and ask you to come back."

"Wait here," she said, and she hurried to the bedroom. She returned with the photographs from Nurse Doebli. "Is that Paul?" Safir said. She dropped the photos on the coffee table.

A wretched cry escaped Weldon's throat. His shoulders sagged. "That is Paul." He used the tip of his finger to slide the photographs closer. He tapped the grainy bundle in Piruz's arms. "And that is you."

"My parents," Safir said.

"Yes," Weldon said. He shuddered and met Safir's gaze with an anguished expression. "Where did you get these? Did Peter give them to you?"

"Angela Doebli. She wrote a book."

Weldon groaned. "That self-righteous prig?"

"One of the librarians at Central found it and loaned it to me," Safir said. "I wrote to her. She wrote me back and included the photographs."

"What did she tell you?"

"That you lied to me. You are a terrible man." Safir fell into a chair.

Tears rolled down Weldon's cheeks. He swatted at them with the back of his hand. After a long silence he blew his nose and cleared his throat. "When I learned that Paul was dying, I was heartbroken all over again. I thought if I claimed you, kept you close, part of him would be with me."

"Why?"

"You're too old to adopt, legally. Years ago, Piruz made me promise not to tell anyone, not Paul, and especially not you. She used money from the gemstones Paul sent her to pay for your passage out of France. I pushed Patterson to get your visa approved. Your mother wanted you here, far away from war."

"And her," Safir said.

Weldon nodded. "Yes." He covered his face with his hands. "I'm so sorry, Safir."

"But why?" Safir slammed her fist on the coffee table. Mustafa jumped off the piano and scurried down the hall.

"When Celik died there was nobody left who knew the truth about you," Weldon said. "Or me."

"Except for Nurse Doebli," Safir said. "I'm not a rug or a vase in Macy's Lost and Found."

Weldon stood, smoothing his jacket. "I am a fifty-six-year-old homosexual. I will be shunned if that gets out. My career will be over."

"*That's* what you're thinking about? You've lied to me since our first meeting."

Weldon ran his fingers through his hair. "Will you tell the newspapers about me?"

Safir looked out the window. "I will not," she said after a long pause, "but I'm not the only one who knows."

"Steinmueller," Weldon said. "I don't like him very much."

Safir leapt out of her chair. "Benny is a good man. He won't say anything, but there are others who might," she shouted.

Weldon rose from his chair. "Maybe I'll go back to Geneva," he said, "I still have friends there."

"Like Doctor Young?"

Weldon's mouth fell. "You knew?"

"At the moment, no," Safir said. "But in hindsight, it seems obvious."

"He's not important, not compared to you, Safir."

"I think you should leave."

Weldon hesitated, and when Safir made no movement he made a slow, uncertain progress toward the door. He stopped on the threshold, his hands gripping the lapels of his jacket.

"You are despicable," Safir said.

He took out his handkerchief and dabbed it across his chin. "If you say so. One last fact, since you're consumed with knowing the truth. Your mother killed herself."

"You're lying," Safir said as her knees buckled. She grabbed the back of the chair to steady herself.

"I was with her, in Hereke. She threw herself in front of that bus. We'd just received the telegram from Maria that Paul had died. Celik and I were beside her on the sidewalk. The bus flew by, I turned, seeing a blur. People around us were screaming. Celik began to wail. She was gone, in an instant. She couldn't live with the pain any longer."

Safir jammed her knuckles into her eyes. She bolted for the door, knocking Weldon over in her haste.

She ran down Montague Street, barely able to see, unable to breathe. Weldon's words burned in her chest, set her skin on fire. She stumbled down the steps of Borough Hall Subway Station and boarded the Manhattan-bound train. She collapsed onto the nearest seat, hugging herself, crying into her breast.

She got off the train on Twenty-Eighth Street, and hurried toward Second Avenue. Five minutes later she stood, perspiring in the heat, in front of Saint Illuminator's Cathedral. She pushed through the doors. The church was deserted but cool, and a few candles burned on the altar. She sat in the front pew and wept.

Footsteps approached from behind; she had no idea how long she'd been immersed in grief. Benny slid next to her, his arms enfolding her. His warmth, the scent of his perspiration, started a fresh stream of tears.

"I thought you might be here," Benny said.

"How did you get here so quickly?" She lay her head on his chest and wept onto his shirt.

"Jefferson came by," Benny said, stroking Safir's hair. "He told me what happened. He said he called to you as you ran by."

Safir pulled away, afraid. "Is Weldon outside?"

Benny shook his head. "No. But he told Jefferson and me to keep looking 'til we found you." Benny squeezed Safir tight. "I know what he said. Pretty rough."

"I don't know what to do," Safir said, hiding her face.

Benny kissed her on her forehead. "Come home."

"She killed herself, Benny. She thought that was better than seeing me again."

"You're wrong," Benny said. He gently tilted her chin until Safir had no choice but to look at him. "She loved you. Everything she did was to protect you, no matter the cost. So did Paul, without ever meeting you. Remember his last words? He wished for one thing to redeem his life. *You* are that one thing, Safir."

"I don't know how to forgive them," she said.

"Forgive yourself," Benny said. "Play the piano again. For them."

"I can't," she said, dropping her gaze. "Not yet."

"Marry me, then."

Safir stared at Benny, saw the sincerity in his eyes and felt heat like the sun radiating from his body. "I'll think about it," she said, and pulled him closer.

Epilogue

Harriet Dickinson's sister owned a newly-opened travel agency on Flatbush Avenue in Brooklyn. She made all the arrangements. Benny said it was going to be their second honeymoon. Safir reminded him that they never took a honeymoon. Benny protested and said that going to Philadelphia by train *was* a honeymoon, of sorts. Safir told Benny that meeting both her half-brothers twelve years ago—albeit a good and noble thing—did not qualify. She tucked a strand of grey hair behind her ear as she leaned over and kissed him on the top of his thinning scalp.

When school in Williamsburg paused for summer vacation, the Steinmuellers boarded an ocean liner bound for Le Havre, France. Not just an ocean liner, *the* ocean liner, the *SS France*, longest liner in the world, with its signature red and black funnels towering above its immaculate decks. Safir paid for their passage with money from Weldon's substantial estate. News of his death came to Williamsburg as the Steinmueller family rang in 1962. Peter told Safir that Weldon had fallen through one of the glaciers near Mayrhofen; a foot set wrong in a world where every step mattered. Lawyers from Austria and Bethlehem, Pennsylvania contacted her—the sole beneficiary of Weldon's possessions, including the Mayrhofen property that Weldon had purchased from Maria Bahr when he resigned his seat in the senate and moved back to Europe. Finally, Safir would see her father's house.

Isaac and Ester, when not in the swimming pool, spent their days carousing with millionaires' children in the playroom deep inside the First-Class Passenger area, while Safir and Benny lounged on the outside promenade deck in Tourist Class or, more often, sat in leather upholstered chairs reading newspapers and magazines, telling each other how silly it felt pretending to be rich.

"But we are, sort of, thanks to Weldon," Benny said over dinner.

"Just for today," Safir reminded him.

They drank champagne with the ship's captain, comparing their stiff, newly-bought clothes to the comfortable silks and tuxedos of their very rich table companions. After the children were asleep, Safir and Benny danced in the cocktail lounge. Safir sang in French into Benny's ear when the orchestra played *La Mer.* Benny told her she had a terrific voice and should have been a lounge singer. Safir laughed, held Benny tight, inhaling the familiar scent of him as they swayed across the parquet dance floor.

From Le Havre they took a train to Paris. They stayed three nights in a hotel near the Louvre. Safir took her family on long treks through the city, along the Seine, into the Marais, stopping once to point out the apartment where she had lived twenty-two years ago. She thought of Theo, but it was a brief, unheated thought, like remembering a book read years before: enjoyable, indelible perhaps, but oh, so long since it mattered.

They left Paris from the Gare du Lyon and traveled through France to Switzerland. They stayed in quaint pensions with over-stuffed quilts on narrow beds, window boxes filled to overflowing with geranium and pelargonium. In Interlaken they took the cable car into the thin air of the Jungfrau. Surrounded by jagged peaks and steep valleys, Safir thought often of Paul and Piruz and Weldon trapped in the Taurus Mountains. She imagined their makeshift skis, their precarious caravan, the icy wind whipping their inadequate clothes as they escaped the Ottomans.

After a week they arrived in Mayrhofen and stayed at a *pension* replete with red geraniums and Tyrolean façade. It was evening and the *Gasthaus* owner knew Frau Schmidt, the woman who had looked after Paul's house, up until Weldon's death. She stopped by early the next morning with keys and a list of instructions for the new owner.

It had been a wet spring in the Zillertal, but when Safir and her family arrived at the house the sun appeared through white, rolling clouds that slid past the mountain peaks, sometimes tearing in two as they brushed against their granite faces. Paul's house stood apart, and a mere stone's throw above the main road at the south end of the village. A narrow tributary of the *Ziller* flowed noisily behind the house. Its banks were submerged beneath churning glacier melt, milky green in the morning light. There was a barn of dark timbers set beside the house, and a green meadow beyond a wooden bridge where a solitary, caramel cow wearing a leather collar and tarnished bell stood and chewed hay and watched their approach. It was as Tyrolean as their accommodation the evening before: a stone and timbered home with a steep, shingle roof and black-painted shutters that looked back toward the village centre. Clusters of cheerful, red geraniums spilled from flower boxes that spanned the length of both balconies. A heavy door of blackened planks, hung on black iron hinges, faced the street. The noisy, orange, Opel taxi dropped them at the curb. A black cat appeared from behind the corner of the house and brushed its tail against their shins as they unloaded their suitcases.

"Mustafa!" Ester said. She crouched to stroke its back.

Safir glanced between her feet. The cat did remind her of dear Mustafa. "I'm afraid not, Honey."

"Can I keep him?" Ester pleaded.

"Leave him be," Benny said. "He's needed to keep the mice under control."

"The mountains are so close," Safir said. "I never imagined it like this," she said.

"Come on," Benny said, "Let's go inside." He took out the key Frau Schmidt had given him and unlocked the door. He ushered Isaac and Ester over the flagstone threshold. The house was cool and the air smelled fresh. Safir hurried from one room to the next, opening the curtains and windows.

"It's so beautiful," she said.

"Where do you want the suitcases?" Benny called.

"The bedrooms are upstairs," Safir said. "Isaac, help your father with the cases."

That evening, after unpacking and a walk into town for groceries, Safir and Benny sat in wooden chairs on the topmost balcony attached to their bedroom. The sun had deserted the valley bottom, but bathed the mountain faces in a dusty pink light. Safir smoked a *Gitane* while Benny nursed a glass of white wine. She could not stop grinning. "I wonder if Bey will like it."

"What's not to like? Besides, we'll know tomorrow."

Safir rose from her chair and leaned over the balcony rail, her elbows brushing the trailing tips of geraniums. The rush of water from the river calmed her spirit. The village church spire was just visible in the deepening shade. The Ahornspitze rose from the valley like a battlement. Its snow-covered peak pierced the sky.

"No wonder Paul wanted to be here," Safir said.

"And Weldon," Benny said.

They did not speak for several minutes. Safir watched her cigarette smoke dissolve on the breeze. "He must have hiked and skied every inch of these mountains."

"Well it's yours, now," Benny said as he wrapped his arm around her waist.

"Paul, I mean," Safir said.

"I know," Benny said. He rose and stood behind his wife, his hands on her hip. He nuzzled her neck. "Berchtesgarden is only a hundred miles away. Bet we could find some of my toes if we looked hard enough."

Safir laughed, turned and poked her husband in the ribs. "I know what you're doing, Mr. Steinmueller." She kissed him. "But I do want to visit my father's cairn." She nodded toward the mountain on the far side of the valley. "Up there is where Peter and Hansi scattered the ashes."

"He survives two genocides, two wars, and dies of cancer."

"Meaning what?"

Benny shrugged. "Meaning I'm hungry again. Must be the mountain air," he said, and kissed Safir on the cheek.

"I'll be right there," Safir said, but she remained on the balcony long after the electric lights of the village switched on and mirrored the spray of stars in the Milky Way.

They met Bey at the train station the next day. Safir recognized her younger sister the moment she stepped from the train, her red and gold headscarf a beacon in the middle of a parade of tourists who jostled each other as they rushed to a pair of buses parked in front of the station. Safir pushed through the crowd to embrace her sister, who screamed with delight as Safir's arms encircled her. Safir inhaled the scent of patchouli and pulled her sister away, the better to look her over, head to toe.

"Are you really here?" Safir said.

"Sister, you are as young and pretty as the day you left," Bey said. "Your hair, I like it."

Benny and the children joined the sisters as the crowd on the platform dispersed. Safir stepped back to introduce her family. The bracelets on Bey's wrists chimed like tiny bells as she hugged Benny, then Isaac and Ester. "I have presents for you, in my suitcase, when we get to your house," Bey said. She waved at a young man standing quietly behind her. He was about Benny's height, very dark complexioned, with short, black, wavy hair. "This is your cousin, Osip," Bey said to Isaac and Ester. "He is my youngest." Turning to Safir she said, "He's come along to see that I don't take a wrong turn and end up in New York City."

Osip slid into the space his mother created and shook Benny's hand. His wrists nearly disappeared in the sleeves of his suit jacket.

Safir kissed him on the cheek. "You look so much like your father. Very handsome." Osip blushed and shrank next to his mother.

"I hope you are up for a walk," Safir said to Bey. "Benny has a taxi to take the children and Osip to the house. They will make us a grand dinner. We will walk back."

"I will change my shoes," Bey said, gesturing to Osip to bring her suitcase. "It will be good for me to get a little exercise."

"The mountain air promises a sound sleep," Safir said.

The sisters strolled, arm in arm on clean, toothpaste-white sidewalks, from the train station to the house. "You are the rich American I read about in magazines," Bey said, patting Safir's arm.

"Hardly," Safir said. "We are still the same. We live in a small apartment across from Benny's parents."

"But your inheritance!" Bey said.

"Weldon was good to me, though I did nothing to deserve it."

"Very good, I'd say."

Safir raised an eyebrow to her sister. "I read his will. He called me *his beloved daughter of circumstance.* As if our meeting was by luck or chance."

"So, he loved you, for all his deceitfulness," Bey said. "Time away made him realize that."

"We only exchanged cards at Christmas, the past few years. We shared the most superficial news. I guess part of me liked the continued connection with my father's life. I wasn't surprised to find out he'd bought Paul's house. Maria never wanted it and was only too happy to be done with it. Peter and Hansi couldn't afford it."

"Will you keep it?"

"I don't know," Safir said. "Let's enjoy our holiday."

They stopped in front of a hair salon to admire glossy photos of Audrey Hepburn in *Breakfast at Tiffany's.*

"You should get this done," Safir said.

"What would Husband say if I put my hair up? I will tell him that you are a naughty influence." Bey said, and pushed through the door of the shop.

Safir watched her gesturing at the appointment book and pointing to the photographs in the window. She emerged three minutes later with a broad smile. "I have a one o'clock appointment," she said proudly, adjusting her scarf.

Safir clapped her hands.

"As do you," Bey said.

Safir's eyes widened. "Sister, what have you done?"

"We deserve it. You are much prettier than Audrey Hepburn. Even if you don't cut it, just color away the grey."

Safir stared at the photos in the window. "I'll think about it."

At three o'clock the next day they left the *Friseur* hand in hand, giggling. Safir lit a cigarette.

"You *are* Audrey Hepburn!" Bey said. "You only need a gold cigarette holder."

They walked past a restaurant with tables and chairs spread across the sidewalk. "Let's stop here," Bey said. "I'm famished."

"You just want to show off," Safir said. The breeze felt wonderful on her exposed neck.

"As should you," Bey said. "Though I would have colored in your streak."

Safir touched the vein of white above her forehead. She had forbidden the stylist from tinting it. "It reminds me of what my mother-in-law told me," she said.

"And that was?"

"That we all grow old, eventually, so don't waste time dwelling on the past."

"Well, it makes you look exotic. The men will be all over you, Sister."

They drank espresso and *Kirsch* and ate pastries and watched the cars and bicycles and pedestrians pass. Safir smoked another cigarette, one of many that Bey had brought. "I am so glad you came," she said.

"Twenty-six years is a long time," Bey said, reaching across the table to squeeze Safir's hand. "I have something for you, at the house," she said.

Safir frowned. "No more gifts. I will need another suitcase!"

Bey shook her head. "It's not a gift," she said. "Come along, I have been dying to show you."

Bey closed the door to the bedroom and hefted her suitcase onto the bed. Safir sat on the edge of the mattress.

"Memet found this last Spring. He was knocking out the wall of our father's—my father's—bedroom to make room for the newest grandchild." She lifted a bundle of cloth and set it on the bed. Bey unfolded the corners. A musical instrument, like a clarinet, only longer, lay on the cloth.

Safir recognized it immediately. "A duduk," she said.

"You know what it is? I had to ask all over to find out," Bey said.

"It's Armenian," Safir said. She ran her fingers over the wood. The reed was dried and split.

"It must have been our mother's," Bey said, "but I can't imagine she would have walled it up."

"Celik?"

"I think so," Bey nodded. "Perhaps he could not bring himself to throw it away, even after she died."

Safir trailed her fingers along the polished wood. She had never told Bey what Weldon had told her so long ago. "You should keep this at the house," Safir said.

Bey shook her head. "It is yours."

"Thank you, Sister. I will keep it in a place of honor." She wrapped the instrument in its cloth. "I have something to show you. Also our mother's," Safir said. She hurried to her bedroom and returned moments later with a small, silk bag. She upended the bag. A silver pendant of the Madonna and Christ, their golden halos faint but still discernable in the silver. A thin, silver chain had been soldered onto the pendant. Safir handed it to Bey. "My father kept it, always hoping to return it to Mother."

"I remember when he came to the house, looking for her. He was very ill. Will you wear it?" Bey asked.

"No," Safir said. "I've another idea."

The next morning Frau Schmidt's grandson arrived at the house. Safir and Bey were waiting. Safir led her sister to the room off the kitchen. The coat room was neat and lined with Weldon's sweaters, jackets and hats. In an earthenware pot were several carved and iron-shod sticks, two covered with tiny shields collected from the adjacent valleys and villages. Canvas packs and thick woollen socks and stiff leather boots waited for someone to take them into the mountains. Safir and Bey met Dieter in the driveway and loaded their borrowed rucksacks and walking sticks in the back of the Fiat. Benny and the children waved as the car backed down the drive, belching smoke.

Dieter drove in the expanding light to a graveled space high on the valley's southern flank. He nosed the car into a space between other cars left by their owners while they climbed.

The walk was not as steep as Safir expected, though the sisters were puffing and sweating within minutes. The breeze was cool against their faces, even as the sun rose above them and flooded the Zillertal with heat. The valley became a patchwork of green, light green, dark green, demarcated by thin, brown fences, arrow straight, meeting always at right angles. In some fields early haying had begun, pale stacks appeared in the meadows, and the tiny shapes of farmers moved like ants across the land. The river carved its way between the meadows and houses, a turquoise ribbon that caught the sunlight and threw diamonds into the air.

The trio stopped to rest on a bench near an altar of black wrought iron, where the crucified Christ hung beneath a narrow, tin roof to keep the rain and snow off his head.

"I don't think rain is his main discomfort," Safir said, gently rubbing the nails that pierced the figure's wrists and feet.

"Don't be mean." Bey said.

"Paul would have said it," Safir said.

They walked in silence for another hour. Safir enjoyed the rhythmic crunch their feet made on the stony ground. The breeze disappeared, and the sun was hot on their heads. They halted at the first *Alpenhütte* and ate some cheese and bread.

"Not much longer," Dieter said. He pointed west, shielding his eyes from the sun. "Over there is the Hintertux Glacier," he said. Safir and Bey moved to his side. "The glacier is behind those mountains."

Safir squinted, scanning the horizon. "It's so beautiful," she said.

Dieter nodded. "It is," he said, "but dangerous. That is where Mr. Scott fell."

Safir glanced at Dieter. "Were you with him?"

Dieter shook his head. "No, I'm sorry to say. It was the day before the New Year, I was with my friends. He went alone, I don't know why."

"Did he know the way?" Bey asked.

"O yes," Dieter said, nodding. "He was very familiar. He told me that a long time ago he had hiked the glacier with Paul Bahr, more than once. I guess he put a foot wrong. There are so many crevasses to watch for."

"I believe that," Safir said.

A half hour's hike from the *Alpenhütte* Dieter turned off the trail. He stopped and pointed to a rough pile of stones on which, without knowing its purpose, none would have wasted a second look. It was set on flat ground, surrounded by tufts of grass and clusters of pink *alpenrose*.

"Here is where they built," Dieter said, pointing at the stones with the end of his walking stick. "*Ich warte*," he said, pointing to a boulder up the trail.

"*Danke*," Safir said. She crouched in front of the cairn. It reached no higher than her shin. A dozen smooth stones, none larger than a dinner plate, had been stacked in an uneven heap. In time, grass would sprout between them, maybe a mouse would build a nest in the deepest cranny. Not an engineer's shrine; it lacked any semblance of precision.

Safir turned to take in the view. Mayrhofen lay hidden below the mountain's shoulder. Across the valley a wall of peaks disappeared into cloud. Their stony flanks were draped with sun-dappled forest and alpine meadow. The occasional note of a distant cow bell carried through the air. She pulled her mother's pendant from her pocket. It took both of them to raise the topmost stone. Safir set the pendant on the cairn and they lowered the stone, concealing Piruz's necklace. From her pack Bey pulled a spray of alpine flowers and split it into two bunches. They propped each against the stones.

"Not so far apart, after all," Safir said, staring at the western peaks.

"They can almost see each other across the valley," Bey said.

When they arrived back at the house, Safir kissed her husband and children, who were in the main room with their noses in books, quietly reading, their feet tucked into the sofa cushions. She kicked off her shoes, rubbed her hands together. Bey poured two glasses of wine. Safir turned to the piano and opened the cover. Ester and Isaac raised their heads, as if hearing something in the distance. Benny looked up, watching his wife.

Safir sat at the piano, exhaled, and began to play.

Map of Ottoman Empire

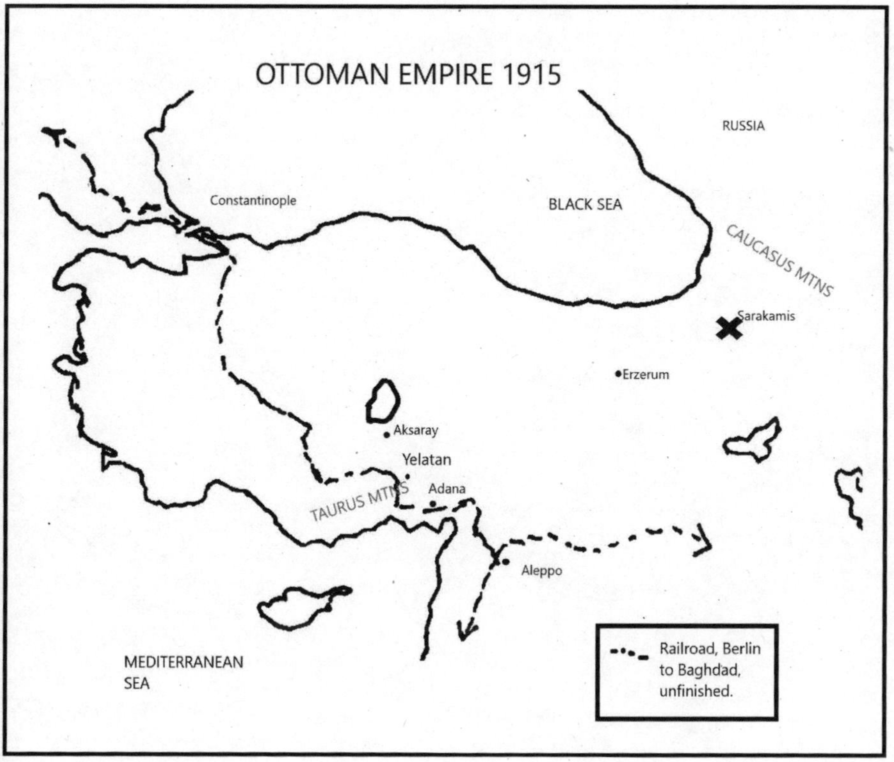

List of Characters by Place

UNITED STATES

Safir Turan- Born in Turkey, 1916. Lives in Brooklyn Heights with her cat Mustafa. Employed at the Brooklyn Museum as an archivist.

Mustafa- Safir's cat. Named after Mustafa Kemal Ataturk, president of Turkey, 1920-1938.

Weldon Theodore Henry Scott- Born 1894 in Bethlehem, Pennsylvania. American senator.

Vincenzo D'Angelo- Senior Archivist at the Brooklyn Museum. Safir's boss.

Ambrose Henry Scott- Weldon's father. Engineer for Bethlehem Steel (later Carnegie Steel).

Edith Lauterne Scott- Weldon's mother. Born in Geneva, Switzerland. Her family members are directors of the International Committee of the Red Cross.

Benjamin Julius Steinmueller- Born Vienna, Austria in 1923. Emigrated to the United States in 1939. WWII War veteran. A teacher in Williamsburg, New York.

Rachel Vogels Steinmueller- Lives in Williamsburg, NY. Ester Finkbeiner's sister and Benny Steinmueller's mother.

Julius Simon Steinmueller- Tailor in Williamsburg. Benny's father.

Hamig Artibian- Archbishop of the Armenian Prelacy in New York. Born in Van, Turkey.

Father Michael Gemashig- Armenian priest at St. Illuminator's Cathedral, Manhattan.

Harriet Emily Dickinson- Senior Librarian at the Central Branch of the New York Library in Brooklyn.

Frances Siegel- Secretary at the Brooklyn Museum.

Ernie Linklater- Safir's neighbour on Montague Street.

Thomas Edwin Jefferson- Weldon Scott's chauffeur.

Brian Escher- Archivist at the Brooklyn Museum.

Doctor Joseph Hooper- Director of the Brooklyn Museum.

Peter Bahr- Paul Bahr's eldest son, living in Philadelphia

TURKEY (OTTOMAN EMPIRE & REPUBLIC)

Piruz Turan- Safir's mother. Born near Erzerum, Turkey 1890.

Celik Turan- Safir's father. Born in Constantinople, Turkey 1889. A shopkeeper in Istanbul.

Beyhem Ossgyp- Safir's married sister in Istanbul.

Memet Ossgyp- Bey's eldest son.

Osip Ossgyp- Bey's youngest son.

Henry Morgenthau- American Ambassador to Ottoman Turkey in 1914.

Angela Doebli- Swiss nurse working with the Red Cross in Ottoman Turkey in 1915.

Doctor Henri Solvein- Belgian doctor working for the Red Cross in Ottoman Turkey in 1915.

Paul Viktor Bahr- Born 1884 in Steyrmark, Austria-Hungary. Mining engineer by profession, expert alpinist. A member of Pietschmann's brigade.

Sabik Oshagian- Armenian. Born in Erzerum, Turkey 1885. First husband of Piruz Turan.

Toomas Oshagian- Sabik and Piruz's son. Born in 1908.

Viktor Pietschmann- Austrian biologist and alpine expert. Commander of Austro-Hungarian Alpine specialists sent to Ottoman Turkey.

Otto Huebner- Austro-Hungarian ski expert, one of Pietschmann's brigade.

Albert Bildstein- Austro-Hungarian ski expert, one of Pietschmann's brigade.

Alexander Makiymowicz- Austro-Hungarian soldier and one of Pietschmann's brigade.

Helmut Koelrasch- Austro-Hungarian soldier and one of Pietschmann's brigade.

Harry Clancy- American special agent on assignment in Ottoman Turkey.

Jack Patterson- American State Department on Henry Morgenthau's staff.

Donald Fortune- American special agent in Ottoman Turkey.

Enver Pasha- Minister of War, senior Committee of Union & Progress (CUP) official in Ottoman Turkey up to and during WWI. Tried and convicted in absentia of war crimes.

Mustafa Kemal Atatürk- Turkish general and a member of the Committee of Union & Progress (CUP) and President of Turkey 1920-1938.

AUSTRIA (HABSBURG EMPIRE TO POST WORLD WAR II)

Franz Josef Bahr- Born in Judendorf, Austria-Hungary 1853. Medical doctor in Leoben and Vienna. Paul's father.

Max David Jacob Bahr- Born in Leoben, Austria-Hungary 1861. Younger brother of Franz Josef Bahr and Paul's uncle. Engineer. Instructor at the Leoben Mining University.

Isaac Finkbeiner- Lawyer and publisher. Paul's friend.

Ester Vogels Finkbeiner- Isaac's wife, sister to Rachel Steinmueller.

Paulina Bahr. Born 1884. Died 1900. Paul's twin sister.

Maria Strobl- Paul's stepmother. Franz Josef's second wife.

Lydia Rosalie Muehldorfer- Paul's wife. Born 1902. Married 1928. Divorced 1936. Mother of Peter and Hansi Bahr.

Maria Bettina Kolsch Bahr- Paul's second wife.

Viktor Mario Muehldorfer- Lydia's father. Engineer in Austro-Hungarian Army.

Hansi Bahr- Paul and Lydia's second son.

Simon Finkbeiner- Isaac and Ester's oldest son.

Julius Finkbeiner- Simon Finkbeiner's brother.

Doctor Hermann Moro. SS Sturmbannführer. Common law husband of Lydia Muehldorfer-Bahr.

Petra Bathory- Paul Bahr's first love.

Engelbert Dolfuss- leader of Patriotic Front. Chancellor of Austria until his assassination in 1934 by Austrian Nazis.

Kurt von Schuschnigg- Chancellor of Austria, 1934-1938. Arrested by Nazis after the Anschluss, March 9, 1938.

Sturmbahnfuehrer Karl-Heinz Holzhacker- Gestapo dentist.

Hauptsturmfuehrer Gunter Lueger- Kommandant of Metropole Hotel Gestapo Prison in Vienna.

FRANCE

Henri Rouart- Engineer, artist, patron of Impressionist artists.

Chloe Rouart- grand-daughter of Henri Rouart.

Theo Sauvé- Pianist, professor at Sorbonne, Paris.

Selected Bibliography

Akcam, Taner. *From Empire to Republic: Turkish Nationalism and the Armenian Genocide.* Zoran Institute, 2004.

Balakian, Peter. *The Burning Tigris: The Armenian Genocide and America's Response.* New York: Harper Collins, 2003.

Berben, Paul. *Dachau- The Official History 1933-45.* Norfolk Press, 1975.

Hovannisian, Richard G., ed. *Remembrance and Denial: The Case of the Armenian Genocide.* Wayne State University Press, 1998.

Ippen, Paul. *Denk- und Merkwurding in Oesterreiches Bergbau.* Vienna: Montan-Verlag, 1965.

Kain, Conrad. *Where the Clouds Can Go.* Rocky Mountain Books, 2011.

Kaiser, Hilmar & Paul Leverkeuhn. *A German officer during the Armenian genocide: a biography of Max von Scheubner-Richter.* Ann Arbour: Gomidas Institute, 2008.

Maass, Walter. *Assassination in Vienna.* New York: Charles Scribner's Sons, 1972.

McMeekin, Sean. *The Berlin-Baghdad Express.* London: Penguin Books, 2010.

Pietschmann, Viktor. *Durch Kürdisches Berge und Armenian Städte.* Vienna: Adolf Luser Verlag,1940.

Von Schuschnigg, Kurt. *Austrian Requiem.* London: Victor Gallancz, 1947.

Printed in Canada